Fables of
Love and *Art*

To Rick and Amy
from Vladimir with love.

Vladimir 6.17.10
NYC

Vladimir Aituganov

Fables of *Love and Art*

Contemporary Tales about Art, Love and Artists

Translated from Russian by Alexei Aitouganov

Jo-An Pictures Ltd
New York, NY

Published by Jo-An Pictures Ltd.
www.jo-an.com

Vladimir Aituganov©2005, 2006, 2007, 2009

Translated by Alexei Aitouganov©2008, 2009

Introduction by Mervyn Rothstein©2009

Photograph of Vladimir Aituganov by Andres Serrano©2009

Illustrations by Vladimir Aituganov©2010

Design and layout by Byzantium Studio, Inc©2010

Requests for permission to copy this work or any part of it should be mailed to the publisher: Jo-An Pictures Ltd., P.O. Box 6020, New York, NY 10150 or E Mail, joanpictur@aol.com

Library of Congress Control Number: 2009914192

ISBN – 13 978-1-890719-04-3
ISBN – 10 1-890719-04-8

Manufactured in the United States of America

First Edition

To everyone I love

Contents

Mervyn Rothstein

Welcome to the world of Vladimir Aituganov

It is a world of fable and fiction, life and legend, the modern and the past, love and death — the transforming magic of art and the frequent harsh reality of life, as it was for Aituganov in the Soviet Union in the years before its dissolution and as it was for some of his characters in the Europe of centuries past.

In his 24 "Fables of Love and Art" you will find, among many unusual beings, a singing and painting "beast"; a village girl (who knows not of Bach, Beethoven or Mozart); a young, blond violinist and a little violin; a painter and his double; an island of artists — painters, sculptors, architects — with no army or police; a violinist named Paganini and an alchemist named Signor Juliano; an artist named Leonardo da Vinci and his miraculous white horse; the 15th century Russian icon painter Andrey Rublev; and the Roman architect Vitruvius.

You'll visit 19th century Paris, 20th century Communist Moscow, ancient Greece, contemporary Israel and New York City on Sept. 11, 2001.

Aituganov began his artistic career in Moscow as a painter. His first one-man show was at the age of 18. After that he had a great number of one-person exhibitions and took part in many group shows. Aituganov has exhibited in Europe since 1983, and in the United States since 1987. His works are in public, corporate and private collections in many countries. The Metropolitan Museum of Art in New York City acquired two of his works in 1992. Now he is a Russian-born American painter who writes. And a Russian-born American writer who paints.

"Painting, like any other visual art, has its limits," he says. "You can express some ideas with paints, or colors, or lines. But some ideas cannot be put onto canvas. Maybe they can be expressed in music. Or in movement. Or they can be words."

A critic once wrote: "Provocative, satiric, unique are some of the words used to describe the art of Vladimir Aituganov. An extraordinary imagination and high degree of passion put his images on the edge of precipice. His paintings are beaming with energy; like music, they are full of passion, vitality and tranquillity." The same can be said of his stories.

His paintings of Paris, for instance, of the Boulevard Clichy, the booksellers near Notre Dame, the Moulin Rouge, are so very much Paris, embedded in the life of that beautiful and timeless city; yet they take you beyond, offering an impression of a higher Paris, evoking the city's special character but transporting it to another realm, the Paris of the soul. His stories, too, can take you from your everyday mind to a universe of meditative contemplation, a higher plane.

Those stories, like his paintings, have about them a quality of mystery, of "extraordinary imagination": impressionistic rather than real, grounded yet somehow beyond this world, as if his talented eyes see so much more than what our normal eyes can see. The stories and the paintings grab the reader, compel the viewer, do not let you go. And when you are finished looking, or reading, you realize that they have somehow changed you, and changed the way you look at the wild world we inhabit. And at the same time, they are so much fun.

Most readers opening this book won't know much if anything about Vladimir Aituganov. So before you start reading his delightful fables, you might want to find out something about his reality – information provided in part in his own words, in an interview with him in September 2009.

He was born in 1958 in Ufa, a city of about a million people in the Ural Mountains, more than 700 miles east of Moscow. He lived there with his parents until age five, when he moved to Moscow so his mother could finish her Ph.D. in philosophy. A short time later, his parents divorced. He began painting at age six.

"My grandmother from my mother's second marriage took me almost every weekend to art shows. Relations between the Soviet Union and France were very good, and there were frequent exhibitions of French art at Moscow's main museum, the Pushkin. I was very touched by Impressionism. It created a deep influence on me."

While studying at Moscow State University, Aituganov ran a discotheque. "I've always loved music," he says. "In Moscow society at that time, though, the discotheque was kind of dangerous. The entire repertoire had to be reviewed by special censors. It was difficult. Different kinds of supervisors came unexpectedly to check on what music we were playing. But young people could not dance under the music of Soviet composers."

He graduated with a degree in philosophy – but he had taken evening classes at Moscow Art University as well, and he also received a degree in art. While at university, he had several one-man shows.

Those years, the mid-1970s, were very dark for any possibility of democracy or free speech in the Soviet Union. There were many protests, and dissidents were arrested and exiled. There was an underground art scene, of what was called Nonconformist Art, and Aituganov became interested and involved.

"It influenced my artistic point of view," he says, "I was always attracted by the Impressionist paint style. I like freestyle painting, free brushstrokes. But the dissident underground painting style would use different subjects, involving anticommunism, anti-Soviet themes. It wasn't sloganeering, just a matter of the subject. Quite frequently, depicting of the nude body was considered pornographic, and artists were imprisoned. It wasn't really pornographic, but it gave the authorities an excuse to arrest them. I have always loved the nude as a subject. The nude body in my paintings expresses human feelings – thoughts, struggles, everything."

All the while he was painting, Aituganov was writing. "I published articles about philosophy. I always had this love for writing. At the time it wasn't fiction or fables, but I was always involved in both activities – painting and writing." In 1991, he wrote a book on the 19th century British artist Aubrey Beardsley, and it became a Russian best seller.

It was then that he began to notice what he considered the limits of painting for expressing his artistic ideas. "So I started to put down some of my ideas, some fantasies, imaginings, dialogues. When I moved to the United States in 1991 I started to write some articles and essays for a Russian American newspaper called the New Russian Word. They were articles about the Cloisters, Belvedere Castle – observations from a newcomer about what I found in the United States."

Some time later, when he was vacationing in the Dominican Republic, he had his first idea for a story. It was a fantasy called

"Paradise Island" – about a heaven for artists, with no police, no rent, no mortgages, plenty of food, beautiful women, a miraculous climate. You can read it in this volume.

"It sparked me," he says. "I thought I had found a literary form acceptable for me. It was not painting; it was not like pure fiction. It was something written from the point of view of an artist, a musician, a poet. And some of it is based on my paintings."

When he started to write, he says, "it was immediately like some kind of fever. When I am painting, I usually work on a series of paintings with the same subject, so my ideas can be developed aesthetically. I'll do a whole series of sunflowers, or horses, or musicians and their music. I had the same kind of feeling about the stories – that I needed to continue and continue."

Sometimes he would spend a day or two on a story; sometimes he would do two or three in one day. Sometimes, though rarely, he says, he had to return to the same story and continue to work on it. But usually they flowed from him, the way the paint flowed from his brush.

His subjects? "As a writer and researcher, I am fascinated by antiquity, and by the 18th and 19th centuries, and by the mind of the artist. That interest is reflected in my stories. Every time in the history of art and music has its own key figures – da Vinci, Paganini, Vitruvius. In some of the stories I try indirectly to show how the life of an artist or a musician was represented in his art."

And, he says, stories also relate to his life in the Soviet Union – "Tango," for instance, is about a real tango competition. "Everything happened," he says. And the characters are based on friends. The story "Gurzuf, Post Restante," about a rock band touring in Crimea, south of Russia, is connected to his own personal experience.

He is also a martial artist, with 29 years of experience in Kung Fu, and a lover of scuba diving, hiking, fencing, horses and riding — so you'll also find those elements of his active, physical life in his stories. "My family is from a remote part of Russia," he says. "My ancestors were soldiers and riders over the centuries – their history is recorded more or less starting in the 16th century."

In his own artistic career he has also been an artist, interior, fashion and jewelry designer. In Russia, he had started a specialty in art restoration and is now a Professional Associate of the elite American Institute for Conservation of Artistic and Historic Works. Here in America, he has been commissioned to create mosaics for Russian Orthodox Churches and they have now been designated to the status of Russian Icons.

But his painting and writing remain his prime interests. "I never start a painting unless I have an idea of colors, of shape. Painting is about color. The subjects are second. I approach the stories in the same way. First I have a basic idea of a character."

Most of the stories, he says, are connected with the paintings – and often come from the paintings. "In 'The Double,' for instance," he says, "there is a painting with a blue horse that stopped moving for a moment – and there is a resulting universe around it. This image was in my head, and I always wanted to explain it, to express it, to go beyond the picture frame."

For a while, he says, he thought of using actual paintings as illustrations in the stories. "But I decided not to illustrate them so directly. Readers should have room to create in their imaginations their own images of what the painting should be."

Indeed, the unfettered freedom of the imagination is the key, for the reader and for Aituganov. That's why, he says, he chose the fable form – "it allowed me artistic freedom." It is the kind of freedom you have in the United States, and that he did not have in the Soviet Union.

So reader, this introduction has been designed to give you just a taste of what's in store, a little background about the artist — with absolutely no spoilers — to provide a context in which to enjoy his writing, so you can dig in and experience him for yourself. Enjoy.

Welcome to the world of Vladimir Aituganov.

Mervyn Rothstein writes the "Life in the Theatre" and "Regional Theatre News" columns for Playbill Magazine. He has worked for 28 years at The New York Times, where his positions have included theatre reporter, assistant Arts & Leisure editor and deputy editor of the Escapes section. At The Times, his articles have appeared in the Arts, Arts & Leisure, Week in Review, Education Life, Escapes and Travel sections and the Sunday Magazine. He has also written for Wine Spectator and Cigar Aficionado magazines.

Beast

"I like New York in June," sang Beast to himself, trying to fasten a silk bow tie –"How about you?"

The tie didn't want to be tied. Beast checked the instructions that were included with this expensive accessory, where there was a diagram on how to make an attractive knot easily and quickly in two – three steps. Still, it came out crooked and bad. What to do? A pin-on tie from the Dollar Store was not fit for this evening. Hence, I have to give up on the bow tie – not enough skill.

Beast looked about the shelves across from him – brushes in pots and glass cans, pencils, various small instruments. In the corner, behind the easel, lay a roll of thick aluminum wire for armature. Genius! Beast cut off four pieces with pliers, about one foot each, and twisted them into one plait. This made a wire about as thick as a finger. He bent the wire into a ring to see if he could put it around his neck. Possible, if the ends are bent a little open, afterwards they bend back by themselves. Beast snapped it again with the pliers, shortening one end. Now it was good around the collar. He put on the hoop instead of the tie, but the soup was still missing some ingredients; he took off the hoop and searched in a vase filled with round multicolored Venetian beads. He picked two blue-white-yellow ones with purple swirls and attached them with epoxy resin to the ends of the wire. It looked like a torque, the last defense of the neck from the sword of the ancient Vikings.

Okay, the costume is finished – tux and original neckwear – appropriate attire for "the brightest representative of art on the razors edge." Running a comb through his hair, Beast looked at his reflection in the dusty bathroom mirror. "Why does the hair from the forehead migrate to the chest? Oh, don't ask stupid questions; the years, you know. Let's go, it's time."

Beast walked out into the street, two blocks to Broadway before he found a taxi. It did not take long to get across Central Park to the East Side. There at the embassy was a charity dinner for starving children in Africa or tide victims somewhere; Beast didn't recall exactly.

He had been asked to donate a painting in exchange for a tax deduction. Beast refused to donate. "Don't worry about my taxes," – so they changed the usual 50-50 split to 35 for the artist and 65 for the children – so that, you know, the children didn't starve.

Beast's real name was Tom. The nickname "Beast" stuck to him a while ago, back in his student days at Cooper Union. He and his friends in those years wanted to overthrow the respected and self-satisfied abstract expressionism movement and to conquer for themselves a place under the sun.

It was impossible to astonish the fat New York galleries with anything, but the name of the group of artists "The New Wilds" appealed to the journalists. Two articles were published in the Village Voice, which was already a key put in the lock of the right door to success.

Those were the times! What didn't they think of to attract attention to themselves. For the sake of exoticism they came up with nicknames for each other – kind of like the rock musicians. So were born Beast, Mastodon, Flea, Constrictor, and so on. They sounded powerful, not like "Mister Rauschenberg" or "Mr. de Kooning and wife."

They definitely put on enough airs, but not when it came to actual painting. Beast saw this clearly, but being young he kept quiet along side inept dabblers. Gradually, the artists started to drop out. Mastodon left to work at the stock market to keep himself closer to money. Flea married an Italian Mafiosi, excuse me, I misspoke, a businessman; she got a gorgeous villa to set in pink marble. Constrictor received an inheritance from an uncle in Tennessee and, instead of buying a yacht and traveling around the world with his friends, he put the money in the bank with a good return and cut off contact with his brotherhood of the time. Bream didn't give up, continued to paint even when there was nothing to eat, he did yoga, and at some point he went to Tibet where he started to go blind after swimming in the icy lakes. Max, poor man, overdosed on heroin and left for the other side.

Of "The New Wilds" only Beast remained. At long last, he had used his head to beat a hole in the wall through to Soho. He was on the cover of the Rolling Stone, in that since famous photograph – Beast, savagely baring his teeth while mixing paint on the belly of a nude beauty, like on a palette. Behind him – his paintings – passions dancing over the edge – beating against the eyes.

In short, one must first make a ruckus and then support it dutifully. Things were going better for Beast, who went from outsider to leader. He started giving advice on television; he published a book on his "artistic method" and snubbed his nose at less successful artists. He got married to a red-headed Irish lass with whom he had two children. They built a house in snobbish Princeton. It seemed like he stepped onto an escalator that only went up.

But one always has to be wary. Beast bought at auction a teacup from the Han dynasty; he liked thin, nearly transparent ancient porcelain. He rushed home to show it to his wife; he excitingly whisked open the door to their bedroom, only to find her there with a black lover. She didn't expect him to be back so soon from New York. So, Beast went wild, broke his wife's cheekbone, trampled her lover and chased him outside still naked. The wife then hired a shark-attorney and Beast was left with only his Han dynasty cup.

A taxi drove up to a beautiful building. "Consulate," read Beast of the gold letters on the marble plaque, "truly, an embassy – in Washington." The consulate guard in an expensive suit checked Beast's ID, his driver's license, found his name on the guest list, smiled professionally and showed him inside.

The interior was done in a gothic style, stained glass windows, dark wood and leather. The waiters in white gloves circled around with expensive champagne, produced by the sponsors of the evening. The crowd with fat wallets was immediately visible, as were the diamond-clad ladies, their satellites – with shoes costing a grand each. Let's see how they're helping the flood victims.

Behind the piano sat a woman in an open red dress, playing something classical: Beast wasn't big on the music of the "dead composers." The crowd chewed, drank, and conversed loudly, not listening to the music. The organizers of the evening announced the beginning of the charity auction. It was easy to read in their expressions where the proceeds of the evening would go. "Very well," thought Beast to himself, accepting a glass of cognac, "as long as I get mine."

Other painters were nowhere to be seen. That meant that the other paintings in the auction came from art dealers. Beast looked around bored, seeing no one he knew. Near the piano, he saw the Russian pianist, a black shawl with flowers draping from her shoulders. Beast had already read her booklet and saw her CDs on a table by the entry.

Beast approached her and unceremoniously introduced himself as an artist to an artist. She, it turns out, had seen his paintings in some magazine. Beast complimented her playing, asked for her autograph on a pair of her albums and invited her to dinner ... to celebrate the selling of his painting. She was a little embarrassed, but Beast convinced her of the purity of his intentions, exclusively gastronomical.

The woman, born in snowy Moscovia, was partial to Mediterranean cuisine. Beast knew of a restaurant on St. Mark's Place where they prepared exceptional Spanish paella. In the taxi, he called to make a reservation for two, so that once they broke through the jams of evening traffic they would not have to stand in line.

Paella – truly, the best in Manhattan, perhaps even Queens, Bronx, Brooklyn and Staten Island! Beast, instead of the usual sangria, ordered a bottle of Dom Pérignon: you only live once, and the lady was quite attractive. She talked with a noticeable accent, occasionally slowing down or falling silent, carefully choosing her words: in the States more than ten years, married; no, the husband is not a banker, true – a programmer; two children – six and eight years old; difficult to raise, but mom was helping (lives with them in a house in Westchester); in the evening needs to take the train, the car is parked by the railroad station; concerts happen rarely; has to do side-jobs where possible – on evenings like today, in churches, synagogues, on tourist liners; gives music lessons of course; who produced the CDs? ...the husband financed it. "What do you want more than anything?" "...to play every year in Carnegie Hall." No, doesn't listen to jazz or rock... never been to a concert or a club and has no conception of them.

Beast persuaded her, she slightly buzzed from the champagne, to drop by the club CBGB nearby, and only for no longer than half an hour. In a dark hall, with a faded plank floor, hung the thunder like that of an airplane turbine surrounding young longhaired musicians, chopping out extremely heavy metal. Beast had been coming here for a while: as far back as the time of the B-52s and the Sex Pistols. The girl looked about frightfully, in her long concert décolleté dress with open shoulders; she seemed like she flew in from another planet. All things considered, Beast in his tux didn't particularly fit into the place and time either. They each had a cocktail and went out into the air. It had gotten dark, but the city that never sleeps was only straightening its feathers for the night shift.

"I have a studio nearby. Would you like to come see it?"

"It's late, and I have to make my train, and you must be tired."

"What are you talking about? The night is still young. I'll drive you to the train station; I have a car in a garage here."

In the evening September breeze, they walked to Grand Street where Beast had a rented studio since time immemorial.

Long ago, in his art, Beast refused to provoke the viewer just for the sake of calling attention to himself or to astonish with something new and unusual. Of his student impudence and self-confidence remained only the distrust of authority and his faith in his own abilities. Everything in art was discovered before him, from hyperrealism to the abstract. There were no new fundamentally different approaches, which meant that one had to go deeper, so he decided. It took years for him to develop his artistic style – powerful strokes of color coalesced with fragments of bodies, faces, mouths torn in screaming, bulging eyes. Beasts sharpened his drawing to perfection in order to fatally and unrelentingly use the detail to validate the whole. Painting did not tolerate compromise and would not forgive Beast for it. Only the most important, the very essence transferred to the canvas. Each painting pulsed with nerves of color, like knots of energy. Desires, feelings, thoughts boiled on the canvases, creating around them an electrical field that rang and vibrated. One could feel the emotional connection to primordial art. Similar sensations overwhelmed the cave man, awed by the magnitude of nature, the paradoxes of thought, or the beckoning of instinct.

The pianist stood, helplessly dropping her arms – the last thing she expected at the end of the evening was to find herself in such a high-voltage transformer booth. The busyness of her home life: constantly running to lessons, complications with concerts, mortgage on the house, payments on credit cards – everything blocked her from what is most important, something to which she had once dedicated her life. Music! The divine art, for some reason, was bumped down to secondary status and it became less significant than a new car. While here, nearby, a man pried open windows into other worlds, had thrown the woman into the embrace of a man, had killed the Serpent and saved a friend. A child in a red costume was playing on the edge of the abyss and looked into it with eyes wide open.

Beast was carefully observing the girl: it is clear that she is not a buyer. She is too sensitive, she cannot distance herself from the works and look at them merely as a spectator. Something was happening to her, nothing good. The pianist's eyes were half-closed, beads of sweat appeared on her forehead, a faint tremor passed through her body. The colorful shawl slipped from her shoulder, she did not notice. "I, of course, am a genius," thought Beast, "but we don't need any fainting here."

Beast coughed quietly, she shook with surprise and opened her eyes:

"And here … you …" her lips were parched.

"Drink some water and then I'll accompany you back."

In the car she snuggled in the back seat, wrapping herself in her shawl. Beast hurried to Grand Central train station, from time to time looking at the girl through the rear view mirror, worried. Her blank eyes were reflected in the mirror. "Things going badly, will have to drive her home," decided Beast. They drove onto the FDR, then hopped across the bridge to the Bronx, from there onto the Westchester parkway.

For a long time she was silent.

"What do you think, do sounds live on in the world after they are brought up or played out?" she asked, more informally, while still staring blankly forward.

Beast pondered.

"Everything in the world leaves a trail. Even a speck of dust or a flower can leave an imprint in stone. Music, images, they do not live in us. We give them birth and they leave, continuing their existence on their own."

"Music is played, but it remains as it was in the cosmos, the Universe. If people tune their souls correctly, they can hear it."

Firmly holding the wheel so as to avoid skidding on the wet asphalt, Beast concentrated on bringing to a point what he had long since been thinking about:

"The artistic image is an apparition, veiled in color. Though rare, an artist can charge with his self, with his energy a canvas, stone or paper, which in turn change their physical properties."

She closed her eyes and went quiet for a long time.

"I feel you and your life force," she said suddenly.

"Well, I am after all – a beast," joked Beast.

She softly ran her hand through his hair, Beast almost shouted from the surprise. They drove the rest of the way to the Golden Bridge station in silence. Her lone car sat in the lot. Beast opened her door and helped her get out. Her legs buckled as she tried to walk.

"Are you good to drive?"

"No" she said and kissed him on the lips.

In the back seat of her Volvo they made love numerous times, like high school students. Tired, right before sunrise, she fell asleep with her head on his chest. When the first ray of sunlight touched the tips of the Appalachians, she opened her eyes, "We must part."

"For long?"

"Forever."

"But we just began ..."

She sat on his knees facing him: "I'm married, I have children."

"So what? We can still meet."

"How?"

"Once, twice a week. Or we can go to Italy, we'll go to concerts, exhibitions, we'll drink coffee on plazas in Venice."

"None of that will happen."

Beast sighed heavily, filling his lungs with air:

"Let me take you away from here."

"I can't ... Good-bye."

She slipped on her wrinkled red dress and started the engine. On the dashboard lit up a blue screen, showing her where she is and the best route to her house.

Beast got out of the car. She rolled down the window. Beast bent down to kiss her before she left, but she blocked his lips with her fingers.

"That's a nice navigator," said Beast, and holding his clothes, went to his car.

He sped back south towards New York. "Fool, idiot,

spouting metaphysics, all emotional like a schoolboy after a few lays ... will see what wasn't there, never was and never could be; oh well, at least it got resolved quickly and easily, you should be happy instead of moping. Think! Soon you'll find someone happier, someone without all that baggage."

He drove into the city early crossing the Henry Hudson Bridge, flew across Manhattan before the morning traffic and dove into the Holland Tunnel. Beast was rushing to his sister who lived in New Jersey, to calm down a bit and come to his senses. He lit up a cigarette while in the tunnel and popped a CD into his player. A pipe organ resounded – a prelude, then a fugue by J.S. Bach. Here, in the tunnel, the sound of music broke through the thickness of the earth and water to return home to the sky.

"Strange," though Beast, listening carefully to himself.

After the fugue came Ave Maria, without the vocals, and only with the high register.

"Maria, I just met a girl named Maria," Beast slapped his forehead and glanced sideways at the disc cover. "Of course, it's her playing."

Beast hopped out of the tunnel onto the overpass, on his left opened up the panorama of waking New York. The two candles of the Twins – the skyscrapers of the World Trade Center, faded into the blue cloudless sky. Behind them a blimp lazily floated by, an advertisement on its side. Before coming to the tollbooth, Beast turned around, breaking all sorts of traffic laws, and rushed back.

In his studio, he unrolled a length of paper and pinned it to the wall, from floor to ceiling. Within a few minutes he painted two angels with gouache, resembling those of ancient icons. Eternal calm and pacification could be read in their faces. Right hands raised in a gesture of blessing. Beast had never touched on religious subjects before – not his area. But here, he himself could not understand what happened. Beast took the paper down from the wall; the paint dried fast and he stuffed it into a cardboard tube. Then he copied the address of the Russian pianist from the CD insert and went to the nearest post office in Soho. It was still early but the place was already open.

After the events of the past night, it was good to walk down morning Broadway. Beast walked to the Twin Towers, bought himself a cup of coffee and took the elevator to the office of his broker friend, Mastodon. Mastodon didn't seem surprised to see Beast at such an early hour, patting him on the back and shoulders.

"Did something happen?" asked Mastodon.

"Met a woman."

"And…"

"And that's it. Music of the spheres."

Beast stood at the wall-sized window, looking over the humongous city below, sipping his espresso and smiling to himself.

They both saw the plane at the same time. Mastodon rushed for the door to the stairs, while Beast, still smiling, took another sip of coffee.

* * *

Maria received the cardboard tube in the mail a few days later. She already knew about Beast's death. Nobody was home: children in school, husband at work, mother chatting at a Russian neighbor's house.

She opened the tube and unrolled the scroll with the painting: Angels … one with a sword on the side … the other with a white lily branch in hand, on the waist a rosary of multicolored glass beads.

She decided to put it up on her wall to have a better look. She held the painting by the top and stood up on a chair. The paper straightened, as if it was never rolled up. Maria placed it against the wall and pushed a pin into the paper – the pin slipped, without leaving a hole or a scrape. The second pin, third – the paper would not allow itself to be penetrated with sharp needles.

Then, Maria accidentally poked her finger; bleeding, she let go of the paper. The painting remained still, by itself, five inches from the wall. Stunned, Maria got down from the chair and took a few steps back – the painting continued to hang in mid-air. The angels looked softly and a little sadly, blessing her. One of the beads from the glass rosary slipped off, it fell to the floor and rolled towards Maria.

Nanette

Around Christmas, Paris is cold and damp. The days are gloomy and gray, often with wet snow and rain. An icy goop develops under the feet and street-cleaners, in long aprons and uniform caps, almost like policemen, cannot clean the sidewalks and driveways in time.

The city changes at night: the streetlights and lamps in people's homes go on early, shop windows flicker invitingly – while the signs of the many restaurants and bistros beckon the freezing passerby's to defrost in warmth and comfort, have dinner and a glass of wine. Decorated Christmas trees, garlands of little lights and toys, purchases, laughter and congratulations – all create a feeling of mirth and celebration.

Nanette walked quickly, almost ran down Rue du Faubourg Saint-Honoré. Her stylish boots with high laces were already soaked as she was searching for a fiacre. There were no vacant ones, as if specifically to irritate Nanette. Finally, near the Church of St. Philippe-du-Roule, she was able to steal a cab from right under the nose of a gentleman with a cane and a tall cylinder hat.

"Montmartre, Rue des Saules," she ordered, settling in – to the cabby with a puffy mustache.

They started weaving between similar fiacres and two-wheeled carriages. It freed up after the new railroad station Gare St. Lazare and they drove down Rue d'Amsterdam to Boulevard de Clichy, then up the narrow streets of Montmartre. On the right they could see, surrounded by scaffolding, the enormity of the Basilica of Sacré-Cœur.

"We have arrived," the cabby announced hoarsely.

After the ascent up the wet street, the horse was panting

heavily and moving its sides, steam rose from its back. Nanette, not being greedy, gave a whole franc. Whiskers gratefully blurted: "Merci," and hurried to cover his horse with a horse-cloth so it wouldn't catch cold. "Ex-military, probably," Nanette decided, based on how he, in parting, put two fingers to his hat's brim.

Nanette passed under a narrow arch, crossed the inner courtyard, went up a half-lit stairway to the fourth floor and pulled on the chain of a doorbell.

Nanette was a small woman with a mop of chestnut hair. When she brushed it before sleep, her hair fell in a dark wave down to below her knees. Her parents married her off as soon as she left boarding school; she was not even seventeen years old. They introduced Nanette to her future husband at a charity dinner three months before the appointed wedding date. He worked as a senior clerk at the Bank Crédit Lyonnais – a perfect match for a modest girl from Alfortville, a small town beneath Paris. Their first kiss was at their wedding.

Their family turned out well – typical petite bourgeois. The husband worked a lot, advancing his career; soon they bought a cute apartment in the Eighth arrondissement, near Champs-Élysées. Nanette took care of their home, creating comfort just like she was taught at the boarding school, read modern novels, went to art exhibitions – and she had children – there were already three of them. She did not allow herself any distractions on the side or other intrigues, unlike some of her acquaintances. Everything at home went smoothly and appropriately.

When she reached thirty, Nanette felt that her life was lacking something. Children, a loving husband, a place in the center of Paris and a house in Auvergne, of course brought her happiness, but that feeling of emptiness still would not go away.

Perhaps because of this, when she saw the announcement in the newspaper, Nanette went to the studio Lefleur–Leblein, belonging to two artist friends, who gave art lessons in drawing and painting to anyone willing to learn. After the triumph of the impressionists - there were a great many such studios throughout Paris. The students who went there were for the most part foreigners – Englishmen, Germans, Americans, but there were many French people also.

Nanette paid for three months of lessons and started coming twice a week to the large well-lit studio, filled with plaster statues, still lifes with dusty drapings, easels, Japanese woodblock prints on the walls and crowds of students, each of whom desperately wanted immediate fame. She studiously drew antique heads, loaves of bread and empty wine-bottles.

Painting wasn't working for Nanette. The colors and many shades kept a secret, which she could not figure out. The smell of linseed oil and turpentine soon began to irritate her; her fingers wouldn't come clean after the lessons, and Nanette put away her box with brushes and paint in a remote corner of her wardrobe, leaving herself only paper, charcoal and pencils.

On Thursdays, they would have live models – a man or a woman. The female models didn't embarrass Nanette; many of them were women in their prime, either maids or milliners. Their voluptuous bodies weren't hard to draw, the light and shadow softly dissolved on the white skin. Men were another matter altogether.

The first time she saw a nude male model, Nanette couldn't begin working for a long time. Her face was on fire, her fingers shook and wouldn't listen to her. The other students were already scratching with their pencils, while Nanette still couldn't lift her eyes from the empty sheet of paper. She had to get up, drink some water, calm herself and try to at least draw something.

Nanette had never seen a completely naked man, one she didn't know and up so close. At home it was considered inappropriate to see your spouse undressed, and she couldn't even imagine her dear Joseph without pants or pajamas. For several years now they slept in different rooms. Once or twice a month her husband delicately knocked on the door of her bedroom, and even then everything happened very politely and formally.

Nanette heard that some of her husband's colleagues and certain friends of his frequented restaurants with dubious reputations and cabarets with music, dancing and available women. She firmly believed her husband wasn't like that and wouldn't allow himself similar entertainment.

Late in October, one of the teachers, Monsieur Leblein, developed rheumatism, and for the art lessons, his friend – the painter Francois Valran, replaced him. Like all the teachers, Valran went from one student to another and talked to them quietly, giving hints, sometimes taking a pencil and making corrections.

When he was near Nanette, he stopped for longer than usual, looked at her drawing, then at the model, then at her. Pensively he asked her to show him other work from her album.

"I need to talk to you after the lesson," he said rather dryly.

When everybody was going home, Valran invited her to a nearby café. He ordered an absinthe for Nanette and Bordeaux for himself.

"I believe, drawing and painting are not your calling," he began. Nanette opened her eyes wide in disbelief. "Don't rush to get offended, listen," Valran went on patiently. "I won't talk about your weak sides, I think you know them well enough yourself. I'm in the Lefleur–Leblein studio accidentally, and perhaps the old man Leblein will not ask me to substitute for him again. That's why I want to say what I saw in you and your work. You can feel form, proportion and texture. Those are the virtues of a sculptor. Your hand is too heavy for drawing or painting. Don't waste your time on useless lessons – there will be no success in it for you. Change your medium, if you want to send your message through art. Forgive me if I offended you. You are, without question, talented. Hurry and do something with it."

Nanette blushed red to the roots of her hair. No one has ever told her so many hurtful words. Her hand was heavy? She looked at her miniature hands in kid-gloves. Knead clay or carve marble with these fingers and their expensive manicure? Never, not for anything!

Nanette didn't remember how they parted and how she got home. In the dining room she poured herself a full glass of cognac, drained it in one gulp with eyes shut tight. Her husband stared at her dumbfounded, not understanding what was going on.

Later, Nanette met Valran during a ball at Lefleur–Leblein. In the beginning and the end of the season they ran loud and cheerful carnivals right in the studio. Easels, podiums, plaster casts and such were moved to the corner, the tables were covered, the wine was placed, musicians were invited and they had a ball the whole night through. According to the established tradition, you didn't bring your wife or husband on nights like this: for some reason it was more fun without the other halves when surrounded by likeminded people.

Lefleur and Leblein walked around in identical striped

swimsuits, with twisted mustaches and fat cigars between their teeth. Nanette dressed up as a Bretagne shepherdess with a basket and a hat with laces. Valran picked the costume of a mage-stargazer, a long robe with sparkles, a cap and in his hands – a crystal ball, which kept getting in his way.

"Splendid shepherdess, look into my crystal ball," Valran half-sang in a bass. The crooked costume nose made him look hilarious. "I'll help you see the future." He placed the ball in Nanette's open palms and carefully supported her hands with his own, big and warm. Upon such a brave gesture in front of everyone, Nanette's heart started beating loudly.

"What do you see?"

Nanette saw nothing, except the reflected light of the chandeliers and a few drunken faces.

"Look carefully."

Nanette strained to look into the transparent sphere, playing the game. Her head was loud from all the drink and music. From the heater-oven and the thick air, everything was lightly swaying before her eyes.

The reflected faces disappeared, the lights in the ball dimmed. Nanette could no longer distinguish the lines on her palms through the crystal. As if it was being filled with lead, it got dark and heavy like a cannonball. If not for Valran's help, Nanette would have dropped it to the floor. There was some sort of movement inside, like drifting clouds at sunset. In the depths of the nearly hot sphere, there were tiny sparks. They seemed to dance between the palms, and then they flew out of the crystal and spun in a luminous swarm, winding around the hands of Valran and Nanette. The bursts of alarming light in the ball died down and she could see a studio. There were marble and clay statues on tall stands. Hammers, tools and pieces of wire were strewn disorderly on the floor. A woman in a white blouse, with head lowered, sat on a simple chair.

Nanette shook, but Valran held her up in time.

"It's nothing, just the heat, should get some air outside," she said defensively.

Valran walked out with her. Nanette decided not to return to the studio, took a carriage and went home.

In the morning, she found in her shepherdess basket, a crystal ball. Apparently disoriented, she put it there when her head started spinning. Nothing to do – except to return it. At the studio, Nanette found out where Valran lived and went to Montmartre.

In reality, she was torn by curiosity to see how he lived. She had never been to an artist's home or workshop. Studio Lefleur-Leblein was a kind of adult school, not an atelier of real bohemians. Valran interested Nanette for a while now, like an exotic bird with bright feathers that flew into the gray cage of the bourgeois.

The chain to the doorbell seemed to have been ripped out long ago, no one answered the loud knock, but the door was unlocked and she could hear that someone was inside. Nanette lightly pushed the door and entered quietly.

It was a spacious room with a high ceiling and a huge semi-circular window. Paris was stretched out below, tugged by a bluish fog. Two easels, one massive and heavy with unfinished canvas, the second – small, portable – for work in plein air. Against the far wall – shelves with paintings and portfolios of drawings. Along the other wall – wooden bookcases. Five or six hundred volumes, Nanette estimated. Why does he need so many? He didn't read all of them, did he? Oh yes, above there was even a loft, that's probably where his bedroom is or something similar.

 She heard the sound of a side door opening and out of the bathroom, surrounded by puffs of steam, came Valran. Wet hair and beard, naked save for a towel hanging over his shoulders.

"Yesterday, you forgot your ball... the door was open... pardon me," Nanette stuttered, inching towards the door.

Valran silently looked at Nanette, unashamed of his nakedness. Likewise, silently, he took the bag from her hands, took her by the shoulders and softly turned her around to face the books. Nanette bit her lip and held on to the side of the bookshelf. On the left, behind the window stretched out Paris.

Now, instead of taking lessons at the studio, Nanette went to Valran. They would immediately throw themselves at each other, loving passionately and greedily, as if it's the last time. Afterwards, they'd joke and laugh, eat what Nanette brought from home, and drink red wine. Valran showed her old and new paintings, sketches and drafts. Nanette liked to dig through his folders and drawings. There were hundreds of them – nude models, landscapes, portraits, galloping horses, sails on the sea.

Valran turned the adjacent room into a sculpture workshop, where he sculpted small figures, which he would then cast in bronze. This is where Nanette found how yielding wet clay is in her hands, how it awakens and alarms the feelings.

The prediction made by Valran came true – Nanette spent many hours in the sculpture workshop. In the beginning, he would give her advice, helped her make frameworks, cut the wire, wet the clay, and brought in sacks of gypsum up the narrow stairwell to the fourth floor. Gradually, Nanette came into her own and Valran could calmly paint in the main studio and draw on the mezzanine.

Soon, Nanette's sculptures overpopulated the small studio and Valran didn't want to put them in the other room with the paintings: genres wouldn't mix – he reasoned.

At home, Nanette announced that sculpture was her calling, convinced her husband to rent a separate studio for her and to have a few works cast in bronze. However, her attempt to display them in the Salon failed, so they were put in the corners of the apartment.

Her husband had long since figured out that Nanette had a man, but he didn't know how to act in such a situation and chose instead to pretend that everything was in order.

Nanette's life had changed. She stopped attending social routs and the opera, abandoned housework, and barely spent time with her husband and children. Friends and family just shook their heads, quietly judging Nanette. Sculpture was taking up more and more time. Nanette learned to carve marble, her hands roughened and blistered. They looked like those of a peasant at the market.

Nanette worked as if possessed. She finally found what dimly ripened in her soul these many years. In her hands, stone acquired form, a simple slab turned into something meaningful and complete. Nanette started having customers, few, but still admirers of her talent.

With interest, Valran watched Nanette's transformation. He flattered himself that it was he who opened her path into art. Nanette saw him less, their studios now being on opposite sides of Paris: Valran's in Montmartre, Nanette's at Montparnasse. Tired after a hard day, Nanette would return home and go straight to sleep, so she could wake up early the next day and run to her studio.

She now had many good sculptures. Mainly – male and female torsos, without heads, necks, arms or legs. Each one of them had its own character, while somehow ephemerally reminiscent of the body of Valran or Nanette.

One afternoon, the owner of the famous gallery, the one across from the Louvre Museum, came to acquaint himself with Nanette and her works. The nude torso of Nanette left an impression on the old man, and he offered her an exhibition in three months.

It was as if Nanette had just awakened. She looked around – it was almost Christmas. She hadn't seen Valran in a long time; she wanted to quickly tell him about the exhibition. Nanette hastily changed, put on perfume, powdered her face, made a couple of beef, cheese and celery sandwiches, grabbed a bottle of Burgundy and sped out into the wet street…

Nanette pulled on the chain of the doorbell, which, as always, wasn't working. The door was unlocked, Valran is probably in the far room or the bathroom, or maybe asleep if he stayed up the whole night painting. Nanette went into the studio; the two easels were standing in their usual places. The painting with the wild galloping horses on the large easel was already finished. From the window, one could see a view of Paris and on the right – the bookshelf. Maybe he's in the sculpture workshop? Seems there was a sound coming from there. Nanette slightly opened the squeaking door. Valran was sitting in the armchair, facing the window. He was being kissed by a tall, voluptuous blonde.

Running out and returning to her studio, with a heavy hammer, Nanette ferociously destroyed all of her sculptures, as well as all the crystal vases, glasses and lamps in her house and demanded that everyone forget that she was ever a sculptor.

* * *

Like the many years before, after church on Sundays, the family would have dinner – while on Thursdays – her husband's friends would come by with their wives. After coffee, the men would talk about politics and smoke expensive cigars. Nanette would talk with the women, discussing the latest fashion, children's diseases or just gossip.

Leonardo and the Horse

Leonardo loved horses. People seemed to him stupid and cruel. The most compassionate and learned rulers turned into mad tyrants, having tasted the poison of power. Kingliness and education did not indicate magnanimity and kindness.

Since early childhood, horses personified pure harmony to him. Even mighty Murgese made to carry fully armored knights, were full of glory and grace.

When Leonardo was five years old, not far from his parents' home in the village, he saw in the pasture a white Horse with a long mane and wavy tail. Drops of morning dew glistened in its hair. It was beauty itself. The Horse looked at Leonardo with wet almond-shaped eyes, as if revealing a secret to him. The little Leonardo could not understand what happened to his soul in that minute. Something changed in him forever. Sounds became richer, colors more diverse, and thoughts – firmer and more paradoxical.

Soon Leonardo learned to understand the language of horses. They talked to him as an equal or as a younger brother.

"Why do you let the most unworthy of people ride on your backs?" asked the young Leonardo.

"Because we are smarter," answered the horses. "We let them feed us, take care of us, value and pay large sums for some of us. We don't let on that we can see through human nature. People can't live without us; they're too stupid and lazy. We can survive without them, but then who will brush our manes, braid our tails and change our horseshoes? We have also gotten used to them and we like their services."

Leonardo often went to the fields, where herds of swift-footed Neapolitans grazed. He wanted to see the Horse that he met in his early childhood one more time. Or did he just imagine it? He asked many horses about it. Colts winked understandingly at Leonardo and shook their large heads. The mares snorted and moved their tails. No one remembered such a horse in the surrounding Florence.

Years past, one after another, changing from a trot to a gallop, sometimes switching to a walk or an amble, overcoming hurdles and sometimes falling into a hole. Leonardo became famous throughout Italy as a painter, scientist and engineer. He was approached by students; he worked on paintings, designed fortresses, canals and unprecedented tools of war.

"Why do you need these horrid things for killing?" asked the light Horse, appearing to him one night in a dream.

"I don't like people," answered Leonardo, "even the best of them are unable to be themselves. They always pretend and put on masks, either a kind city-dweller or a wise teacher, a peaceful monk, or a faithful loving wife."

"Why don't you have a girlfriend?" asked the Horse.

"Because I couldn't find a woman that was like you," answered Leonardo. "One time I was painting the portrait of a beautiful girl, tall and elegant, her fingers were long and pretty. Her lover was known as one of the cruelest tyrants of Italy, conniving and unfaithful. But the lady saw in him a patron of the arts and sciences, a collector, a literati and master of love's consolations.

The lady always had, on her hands or her shoulders, an ermine, a small swift animal with precious fur. When the lover decided to get rid of her and marry someone on account of politics, he ordered the animal poisoned. My beauty died then, as the right half cannot live when the left is dead."

"See," said the Horse, "you can love not only horses."

"Yes," replied Leonardo, "but she seemed to me like a horse, which was guarded by a dog."

The years went on... In his life Leonardo knew few women. It was hard for him to joke with the simpletons from the bakery or to build intrigues, like putting horns on a husband of a young hot wife, stir-crazy with boredom. Leonardo dreamed about finding a girlfriend, equal to him in intelligence, wisdom and talent.

In all of Italy only once did he meet a woman worthy of him. She wrote poetry, plays, philosophical novels, in her house gathered the elite of academics and art, and political problems were resolved. The church condemned her for her free behavior and critical intellect. The woman and Leonardo met as equals, but she didn't like his outfit, the silver lute in the form of a horses head and his accent, while he, the seeker of perfection in everything, was disillusioned by her slightly crooked legs carefully concealed beneath her dress and her low manly waist. They conversed with interest for a long time, but not even the smallest fire of emotion sparked between them.

Soon after, Leonardo won the competition against the best painters for the mural of the hall in Signoria. "The Battle of Anghiari " – it is the battle of Leonardo against himself, against his own desires, thoughts and deepest wishes. People, horses, bare teeth, bulging eyes, blood, swords, armor, hooves, manes – parts of Leonardo's soul.

During that time the Horse was with him constantly. They

lived together, ate, drank, painted, rested, argued. Leonardo was preparing the cartoon for the mural, while the Horse always stood nearby. He drew it in countless poses, views, turns. There were so many of it, that when Leonardo started painting on the wall, he no longer needed his sketches or the cartoon.

He worked with wax paint like the artists of Ancient Greece and Rome. He painted fast, without preparation in the studio. At the beginning of the work, his friends and pupils urged him to make a fresco or a mosaic. A fresco with watercolor was too pale and dull for Leonardo, he wanted passion. The mosaic seemed better on account of its vibrating colors and timeless durability; Leonardo even crossed the Adriatic to study the antique mosaics of Monte Negro. But to make the "Battle" with smalti he would need years of effort and a whole army of helpers. Leonardo wanted to paint everything himself, the way only he could paint.

Finally, the enormous work is almost finished. Fury and calm, courage and cowardice, cruelty and mercy – all emotions could be read in it. Most importantly – his Horse was everywhere. Leonardo allowed almost no one to approach the wall, as if protecting it from the evil eye. A few were fortunate to witness the painting, but its rumor flew far in all directions. Michelangelo, his jealous adversary in art, secretly snuck into the Signoria to look at the work of the victor.

Then came the day to burn the wall with fire and permanently melt the soft wax of the paint to the plaster, making it one. The wall staggered the imagination; no one had yet made such a gigantic encaustic in the history of art.

Leonardo ordered the braziers filled with coal to be lit on different levels along the entire length of the wall. He thought that he calculated correctly how to direct heat evenly along the entire surface. But the treacherous wall decided otherwise. In a few minutes, the heat rose to the top level and scorched it, while the lower level was still deathly cold. Multicolored wax started to flow from the top, covering and destroying the work of many months. Some of the students stood around with dropped jaws, others – vainly moved around the heaters - others just cried.

Leonardo was the first to understand his own mistake, and that it was impossible to correct. His heart was torn, he felt like he died, yet he continued to stand and watch the destruction of the wall. After that, Leonardo did not see the Horse.

When the French king conquered Italy, he invited Leonardo to France, presented him with a castle in the beautiful valley of Loire River and provided an honorary subsidy. The old Leonardo accepted the cordial offer. He was tired of constant moving from apartment to apartment, searching for patrons and the degrading hounding after money owed for finished work.

In the rustic quiet of France, Leonardo finally found some peace. Books, manuscripts, walks and drawing took up his time. Sometimes a young king would visit him and they would have long conversations about everything in the world: nature, the stars, people, history, art, philosophy. Everything that Leonardo knew, the king wanted to know. They became close friends, one – old and wise, the other – young and powerful.

Contemplating after one of their talks, Leonardo drew a self-portrait in brownish-red sanguine. Long gray hair on his shoulders and a beard that covered his chest, his eyes still looked penetratingly at the world, lips closed tightly - he learned to restrain himself in wagers and interrogations. Autumn came – Leonardo never believed that he would live this long.

One sunny spring day, he felt that inside him appeared some sort of light. As a scientist, Leonardo tried to analyze the strange feeling and find the source of the light. That did not work. Leonardo quietly laid down on his spacious bed of carved oak and closed his eyes.

The sounds gradually disappeared, the old body no longer hurt, hands did not shake. A light joyous feeling appeared in his soul, like he had in his childhood, when the first field flowers bloomed, or on the morning of his birthday, when little Leonardo awaited the coming of his dear mother with uncomplicated presents.

The light grew, from a small spot it turned into a pale-blue ellipse and filled all of Leonardo. From this ellipse, as if from nowhere, appeared a graceful Horse.

"Run with me, Leonardo," it beckoned.

He laughed quietly – of course, it's so easy. He took the first tenuous step into the light, the second, then faster and faster, after that he ran so fast his hair waved in the wind and tickled his face and neck. Quickly, he caught up with the Horse and they ran together.

"Why didn't you understand everything much earlier, when I came to you the first time?" asked the Horse.

"I wanted to learn what people know and what they are capable of," replied Leonardo. "I mastered all their sciences, arts and crafts, but this did not bring me happiness. My whole life I searched and waited only for you."

* * *

In the morning, the valet quietly entered the bedroom and saw Leonardo, lying on the high pillows. Someone had beautifully brushed his beard and hair, his white shirt of thin cambric smelled of unfamiliar grasses. His eyes were half closed; Leonardo was smiling slightly as one thinking of something good.

The valet decided not to bother the great sage, but to return when he was called upon. When he checked the bedroom an hour later, he understood that Leonardo was no longer.

Paradise Island

I heard this story one winter evening from an old artist nicknamed Bream. We were sitting in a snow-covered hut far from civilization, feeding the stove with pine billets and baking potatoes while sipping home made cherry liqueur left over from the summer.

The old men told him that many, many years ago, in the warm sea, there was an island inhabited only by artists.

There was neither army nor police on the Island, instead, only a few elected elders who governed the people. In reality, there was no need to govern them, for artists were mostly peaceful individuals who only become noisy after heavy drinking parties. But in such cases, their neighbors and buddies usually calmed down the rowdies. Bar owners also did their part to keep the good reputations of their establishments.

Painters settled on the slopes in order to have from the windows of their studios, a view of the harbor and of the mountain on the far left. The mountain looked like a bear that had become thirsty and could not stop drinking from the sea.

Many sculptors chose to live in the central part of the Island, closer to the marble quarries. Experts considered this white marble without any vein to be much better than the marble from Carrara or Thessalonica.

Graphic artists preferred to live amid shadowy alleys, so the white paper sheet would not hit their eyes with the bright sun light. Cozy workshops of jewelers clustered near to each other, as was common to all smiths' quarters.

Houses of architects were easy to recognize, because everyone tried to plan his house in the most original and interesting way. But the most extravagant homes were those of fashion designers. Their refinement of taste was equal to the decorations of their facades and interiors.

Roads and streets on the Island were paved with cobblestone, slates of pink tuff or mosaics of different marbles. There were many mosaics and sculptures – the southern sun and fresh sea breeze could not damage them.

It was said that many years and generations ago, a famous admiral, who was like thunder to pirates, yet a patron of the arts, discovered this Island. There were rumors that the Admiral's son wanted to be an artist, but his father did not approve of his son's choice and, instead, sent him upon a dangerous navy expedition. The son was killed in the first battle – and of all of his son's belongings, the Admiral found only a small sketchbook filled with drawings of unknown islands, sketches of never-to-be painted pictures and many portraits of a beautiful woman.

The Admiral left his enormous wealth in his will for the Island's improvement, maintenance and the creation of comfortable conditions for the artists' life there. Evidently, the interest from the Admiral's capital definitely allowed the Island to prosper. The artists enjoyed a joyful existence for centuries.

How did artists know about the Island and how to get there? Some of them were guided by their destiny, some found themselves on a shore after shipwreck, some were visited after exhibition openings by mystery persons in masks who bought all their pictures for unbelievable high prices and suggested relocation to the Island.

It's strange, but nobody heard of bad artists on the Island. They were very different – sometimes ridiculous, sometimes odd, but always interesting and talented. Even artists of the same style were not alike. Artists of different nations lived on the Island.

French – loud-mouthed and fond of drinking red wine, Germans who preferred beer as well as accuracy in painting, Russians from the Traveling Exhibitions Society who traditionally tried to find out "who's guilty?" But they could not find any answer on the Island, and instead, they began to restore churches and paint icons together with Italian masters.

The Island was decorated and overflowing with art. It was everywhere: in the houses, streets, remote hallows, on the tops of mountains and along the shore. To give the art away for public or personal use and admiration was a normal habit and a joy for the artists. Of course, everybody left something special for him or herself.

After an artist's death (such unpleasant events happened here, too) everybody could choose their favorite of the artist's works for memory. The family was left with what was considered important, but the most significant works were placed in the Island's Museum, which no doubt was the best in the Old and New Worlds.

Artists, residents of the Island, had no need to work for a living. Once a year, a ship from Europe came to the harbor. It brought food, wines, clothes, books, and supplies for art and homes, necessities and luxuries. In return, artists loaded this ship with paintings and sculptures, jewelry and furniture, fabrics and tapestries, architectural projects for cathedrals and palaces.

Besides the artists, there were a small number of peasants, who grew local grapes and made astringent wine after harvest. Fishermen from a small village on the east coast caught so many fish that it would be enough to feed four islands like that one.

Women (as you know, an artists' life is unthinkable without them) were free and merry by character. There were sophisticated and highly educated ladies among them, too. Worthy local caballeros (virtuosos of brushes and chisels) were respectably attracted to them. Many artists had families there; others had lovers from among the villagers or from models and visitors.

Children of family artists attended school, up to the ninth grade, where they studied literature, music, art, gymnastics, major languages and history. Teachers from the continent taught mathematics and sciences to students who were fond of these subjects. After graduation, every kid decided by himself if he or she wanted to be an artist. If they had a different interest, they usually left the Island, and if they made the first choice, they would continue their education in one of the studios.

Family or personal problems were tried to be resolved in a peaceful manner. It happened twice during the Island's history, when a man and two women were put by force on a ship and sent back to Europe. All residents of the Island made this decision for the sake of harmony.

For several centuries the Island enriched the world with its talents. Quatrocento and Cubism, Barbizones and German Romanticism – everything came from the Island.

Then suddenly, the Island disappeared. No, the financial capital did not vanish with the breaking of the New York Stock Exchange. The old companies of Genoa bankers have known their business for hundreds of years. Something different happened.

Strong storms and hurricanes are very rare in that part of the ocean. An underwater earthquake came three hundred miles from the Northeast. The Island stood atop of a corral reef, which had been growing from the beginning of time. Three narrow-directed tremors were enough for the Island to break into millions of coral pieces, which were holding houses, churches, museums, workshops and everything else together...

* * *

This summer I was scuba diving with my son not far from the Punta Rusia village in the Caribbean. There was a tiny island in the middle of the ocean, about three miles away from the shore. It was not even an island; it was a sandy spot on a reef. The sandy side was steadily descending towards the shore. From the ocean side, there was a coral wall dropping into an abyss. Corals of amazing beauty with all kinds of colors were forming this wall.

I saw something sparkling from between two branches of a coral tree. It was a piece of an ancient glass goblet, nobody can do anything equal to it nowadays. Several words were engraved and gilded in the glass rim, "Ars Longa Vita Brevis." I pushed myself to get this relic, but one of the branches broke down and started to fall into the blue abyss. We tried desperately to catch it, but the glass piece slid from the coral and moved down faster. There was no chance, even for my son, to go so deep and with the same speed. For a minute, little gold letters shone to us from the depth.

Paganini, or
The Mystery of the Bow

One glowing May noon, Signor Juliano Folonari, after decades of torturous searching, was finally close to synthesizing the philosopher's stone. The bitter experience of his hard life, the endless hours behind books, exhausting experiments in the laboratory, at last, will bring the long-awaited result: the creation of a substance that can transmute black metals into gold.

Signor Juliano's house stood on the shore of Canal Grande – you could see St. Mark's Cathedral and the Doge's Palace from the second story window. Gondolas slid across the canal, adorned with gold, velvet and silk. The gondoliers, deftly maneuvering their oars, sang or happily argued with each other. Venice reflected in the water, in all its' grandiose splendor. Gilding, mosaics and stained glass, played in myriad highlights on the waves of the countless canals.

Signor Juliano had no interest for this holiday of sunlight and colors, while he locked himself in his basement, away from the sounds of the street and the rest of the house.

… Just a little quicksilver, one-two-tree small drops and the synthetic reaction will take place. A mass, boiling in a glass retort, will change its substance and gain characteristics described by the ancient authors.

There is no reason to make a lot of gold, just enough to pay off debts, expand the laboratory, order some books, take on a couple of students, and maybe, update the wardrobe for festive occasions. It is not good to attract too much attention, when in the possession of a treasure, it is better to act circumspect. There are already enough rumors and accusations about him in connection with the dark arts and unholy powers. At least now, the times were different, a hundred years past, they could have sent him straight to the stake.

Signor Juliano used a color-scale to check the shade of the boiling substance and added a tiny drop of nitric acid. Yellow bubble formed in the retort, they grew, multiplied and started flowing through the vessel's mouth, covering everything around. The flame went out, an acrid suffocating smoke crawled across the laboratory. The Alchemist, covering his nose and closing his eyes, ran out of the basement. Scrambling up the steep stairs, he threw the door open to the street and breathed greedily, deeply pulling in the fresh sea air.

Upon catching his breath, Signor Juliano saw in the anteroom a young tall man, who was somehow awkwardly built. One shoulder was higher than the other, his cuffs stuck out of the sleeves of the narrow frock coat, uncannily clenching and unclenching his long fingers, always in movement.

Signor Juliano stared silently at the stranger.

"Niccolò Paganini, violinist of Genoa," the young man introduced himself.

"He has been awaiting for you since morning," interjected a servant-woman who had just appeared.

The Alchemist lived isolated, no visitors or guests had crossed the threshold of his house in several years. He got ready to push the unwanted visitor out the door, but something in the violinist's eyes stopped him.

They went into a room with ancient folios lining the bookshelves, a stuffed crocodile hanging from the ceiling, two globes–terrestrial and celestial–standing in the corners, a yellowish human skull on the table amid papers, lists and tables, and a thick glass mirror of rare clarity and transparency on the wall.

"Signor, I am a violinist, the best one in Italy. My reputation precedes me. At my concert, the public applauds me wildly and goes mad from joy. My teachers, without success, try to master my musical technique. I am not bragging, just explaining who I am."

"Why did you come to me, young man? As I understand, you have talent, a good work ethic and good fortune. What more can you ask for?"

"I am not merely seeking fame and fortune. I have rare gifts. Look at the reach of my fingers." The violinist opened his left hand to the point that the thumb lay on the radius bone, and the pinkie stretched in the opposite direction. "In the first position, without moving my hand, I can reach the second octave, I can play three octaves on each string, if that means anything to you. I developed completely novel ways of playing the most difficult of passages. But this is not enough for me. I want to play so well that, once people hear me, they will gratefully tell legends about me to their grandchildren. At my concerts, I want the audience to flutter with joy or freeze in terror, to feel my music through their skin. I believe it is my violin–the instrument of my power – that can make people obedient to my will."

Signor Juliano looked sadly at the enthusiastic musician. Is the violin not the same Philosopher's Stone? This youth dreams of reigning over the souls of his neophytes, subduing women, winning friends, and defeating enemies with the aid of music.

Many years ago, in this very same spot, Signor Juliano had received a visit from a master violinist named Guarneri, was it? He knew that the famous alchemist and secret black magician in his youth was also a musician. Guarneri asked to learn the secret of making enchanted varnish for his violins. Nobody knew what arrangement they came to, but since then, the instruments of Maestro Giuseppe surpassed those of Stradivarius and Amati.

Signor Juliano pensively moved around the smooth skull, with its small hole in the crown, around in his hands. This violinist, it seems, is ready to pay the highest price for his idea. There are few true madmen, but without them, life stagnates and turns into a depressing quagmire.

"I will take him," the Alchemist decided.

In the evening, they secretly set off on mules towards the Apennine Mountains.

After two days, the travelers arrived at a small nameless village situated in the cleft of a mountain. Signor Juliano led Niccolò to a cedar forest atop the mountain, rising above the rest. It was midnight. A cold wind beat against the marble cliffs and mighty trees. Lost souls and restless spirits hid amid deep shadows. An eagle-owl whoo-ed menacingly somewhere, nearby. The Alchemist walked confidently down a path only known to him. Paganini followed him resolutely.

A majestic cedar grew on the edge of the cliff. Below – a bottomless abyss. Italy at night lay beneath their feet, somewhere in faraway villages flickered a few lights.

With a crooked knife, Signor Juliano stripped a cubit's

length of bark and cut the letter V in the white trunk. Sap, glistening in the moonlight, started to ooze out of the tree. The Alchemist collected it into a small vessel.

Niccolò was pale, his lips tightly pursed. He looked on as the old man tried to catch the moonlight with a mirror and redirect it into a certain point on the ground. Signor Juliano traced a circle around this epicenter, wrote ancient symbols around it, started a fire in the circle, placed a chemical contraption over it and then spent a long time reading incantations in an unknown language.

He told Niccolò to roll up his sleeve past the elbow. The old man pierced the musician's vein with a tetrahedral bronze needle and held a test-tube under the dripping vermillion blood. Drop by drop, the Alchemist added Paganini's blood into the boiling sap. The mixture seethed and hissed.

Signor Juliano put Niccolò in the middle of the circle, made him kneel, and put an Egyptian amulet between his eyes. Then, he dripped the molten sap onto the exposed forearm of the violinist. Paganini grinded his teeth in pain, but held back his cries.

The old man poured the sap out of the crucible into a crystal cone-shaped glass and, when it became thick and viscous, he pressed his signet-ring against it. The sap cooled, and Signor Juliano shook it out into Paganini's palm.

"There are other musicians of your kind, maybe even better. The bow and the violin are instruments. They, too, are made better or worse, but in the end it is not that important. Colophony is a substance that determines the sound of the strings. In the Lybian city of Colophone, during the ancient times, they made the same sap for aromatherapy and, more importantly, magic. This is meant to last you the rest of your life, there will be no more. Use my colophony only in extreme cases; do not put it on your bow often, for it robs the musician of his health and strength. You are talented, so rely more on yourself and not on supernatural help. Now go, I need to rest."

Niccolò could not remember how he got out of the forest and went down to the road. In a pocket next to his heart was the sacred clump of sap, cooked with his own blood.

Paganini could not wait to try out the colophony. An opportunity soon presented itself. A rich merchant and resourceful business man by the name of Mercurio Livron passionately loved music and often held concerts in his palace. He heard that the young violin-virtuoso, who everybody was talking about, was staying nearby with a certain admirer of his talent. Livron invited Paganini to play for a good price. Paganini tried to talk his way out of it: he did not even have his violin with him. But Livron assured him that he would be provided with the best instrument. Niccolò did not want to part with the pretty widow, but she insisted that new important connections would be beneficial to his career.

Niccolò carefully applied the colophony of Folonari to the bow, and only then picked up the instrument. Mamma mia che bella, che meravegliosa! "Canon" by Guarneri – a true masterpiece of violin craftsmanship. Never had he held in his hands such a treasure.

In the music hall was gathered the cream of local high society – Livron treating them with a concert. Paganini made a point not to practice before a performance. When Livron asked if there would be a warm-up recital, he answered that he practiced enough in his childhood. He played mostly his own compositions in order to quickly try out the violin and the effects of the colophony. It was hard to tell where the violinist's skill ended, and the magic of the sap began.

For many years, the guests would talk about that concert, and about how Livron with tears in his eyes, gave Paganini the priceless "Canon", so that the two would never part. R e t u r n i n g triumphantly to the little widow, Niccolò felt a sharp subcostal pain in his right side. "I should not eat so much spicy food," he told himself.

The life of a musician, especially a solo performer, is on the one hand filled, with glory and applause, but on the other, is hard and self serving. Ovations are brief and fleeting, while the bumpy, dirty roads of Europe are filled with dejection and disillusionment.

During the long hours spent in a carriage, Paganini thought about his life, about music, about women... Why did his greatest loves happen in the winter, the least pleasant time of the year? The strong-willed Princess Eliza; Antonia – the cunning and greedy mother of his son; the Polish Countess with the unpronounceable name and blue eyes that paled and glowed in the darkness; the timid seamstress Anna – in gratitude for her quiet love Niccolò allocated her a life-long pension; the beautiful Elena, who left her husband, a baron, and later joined a convent after Paganini's death. The sweetest times always came in the winter months between November and March. Where did this conformity to natural laws come from?

The palace of Princess Eliza, the sister of the all-powerful Emperor Napoleon Bonaparte, was located in the town of Lucca. Paganini was asked to join the court chamber orchestra. Passion in Lucca reigned freely, the Princess made eyes at Niccolò, and he soon became her secret lover. Prince Felix, an amateur violinist, took lessons from Niccolò and never suspected what other instruments the young virtuoso played in his free time from music.

Poor Niccolò forgot the old advice from his mother – not to get involved with women from high aristocracy. He breathed in the aroma from the sumptuous chest of the Duchess of Tuscany and in his soul there composed a completely unimaginable consonance. The genius needed very little to create: a little kindness, some praise, that's all! "Twenty Four Capriccio for Violin" – they were enough to immortalize the name Paganini. The Capriccio absorbed into themselves so much music, beauty, variety, complexity and originality, that they instantly put Niccolò on the same music-stand with Bach.

From time to time, Paganini played for the Prince and Princess at recitals with few guests. After dinner and dessert, everybody felt less formal and constrained. Typically, Niccolò would play something not too serious or dramatic. That evening, he was playing variations on the theme of lovers. Prince Felix hugged Princess Eliza from behind, as she sat in an arm-chair. She alluringly smiled at him and craftily looked Paganini in the eyes. The Prince softly kissed her behind the ear. The Princess closed her eyes and stretched like a cat.

It got darker for Paganini. Of course, the Prince was her husband, but Niccolò could not handle such a cruel trial. Taking advantage of a pause, he rubbed the bow with the enchanted sap. "You want amore? You will get it!"

Paganini painted with the violin a dialogue between two lovers: the meeting, coquetry, light flirtation, an appeal, contemplation, a promise. The bow flew in his hands. The new melodies and rhythms cast a spell on the Princess' guests, the music bewitching with languor and bliss. Ladies would close their eyes, their palms wet with perspiration, the cavaliers whispering sweet nothings in their ears, kissing their bare hands and shoulders.

From "The Promise," the violin hurled into "Passion." The speed of the bow went beyond the limit of human ability. Niccolò was conjuring: stupefying harmonies, pizzicato with the left hand, the madness in the higher register pushed the listeners into each others' embrace. The two middle strings – Re and La snapped, unable to withstand such tension. Paganini continued his bacchanal on string Mi and Sol. The Princess sitting next to her stout prince, was thrilled. The floor was scattered with court jackets, uniforms and dresses – it was as if everyone went mad.

The bow flashed like lightning in the virtuoso's hand: the Mi string snapped, almost taking out Paganini's eye. Niccolò tortured the last string Sol, as if punishing Eliza for his humiliation. The candles glimmered, throwing a shivering light on the flushing bodies. The last string, with a dying moan, snapped. The sound froze. Niccolò breathed heavily, blood streamed down his cheek onto the white of his shirt. The guests, with difficulty, returned to reality.

Paganini fled Lucca, to stay there was mortally dangerous. Sorrow settled in his soul, his teeth hurt.

Niccolò's character changed – where once he was happy and talkative, he became antisocial, easily irritated over nothing, spending many hours alone, locked in his room, with the thick curtains lowered. In his thirty-something years, grumbling and complaining about his health, he resembled an old man.

Suffering melancholy, he wandered around Venice, and accidentally strayed into the Lido cemetery. Here it is – the ultimate stage–the tombstone! Niccolò played for the dead under the full moon. His soul became a little lighter. The next night he came there again and played until sunrise. Rumors about his graveyard concerts spread throughout town, and crowds of admirers hid between graves and tombstones, listening to the other - worldly music of Paganini. The magistrate and the bishop banned the questionable concerts, but the legends lived on. Word spread about Paganini's diabolical talent and his connections to unholy powers.

How did he, with a solo concert, subdue Milan, the musical capital of all Italy? Or Naples, where they do not recognize anything other than opera? Paganini used up half of his magical sap, but managed to conquer these cities.

Niccolò was besieged with doubt: how great was his own talent compared to colophony of Folonari?

The violinist Charles LeFont invited Paganini to play a concert together with him at La Scala. The Frenchman was a year older, but looked younger on account of his light skin and a childish blush on his cheeks. Niccolò decided that he would play it clean, without supernatural aid, and afterwards – quel sera sera.

Back then in Europe, they adored competitions between virtuosos. The theater was bursting with an abundance of people. Paganini opened the concert with one of his compositions, LeFont continued with a long Italian theme. The main part – a concerto by Kreuzer for two violins – they played note for note. During his solo, LeFont stuck to the classical style and accuracy of sound; Paganini gave reign to imagination and improvisation.

The Italians went crazy with ecstasy in support of Paganini. Niccolò himself thought that in Paris, among the classicists, the victory would have gone to LeFont. Still, he breathed easily: the key victory was his, not the sap's.

They stayed good friends the rest of LeFont's life. The poor Frenchman was cut down by bandits in the Pyrenees a year before Paganini's death.

The Italian theater! If you have not seen the theater in the province–you have not seen anything, and your life was half wasted. In the village squares, the municipal halls and ancient castles – everywhere you find Arlecchino and Columbina, Scaramouche and Pantalone, jesters and jugglers, acrobats and dancers, musicians and singers.

Usually, upon coming to a new town, Paganini went straight to the theater, arranged his concerts, and in the evening caught a show. The temperamental Niccolò was interested most of all, naturally, in actresses. They were glorified by their happy and carefree manner, understood art, valued talent and made light unconstrained liaisons. Paganini, having become famous, attracted their burning interest.

His childishness with women was completely out of synch with his serious relationship to music. His romances began lightly and lightly they would end. How much energy, time and money Niccolò spent on these provincial romances! The many disappointments taught him nothing. Every time, diving head first into yet another infatuation, he dimly imagined what difficulties they could bring.

The gorgeous Antonia had a divine body, had a pleasant singing voice, and in a short time, domesticated Paganini to the point that he included her in his concerts, as a "guest-virtuosa". Antonia quickly appraised the value of a concert with the famous violinist, and, so as to tie him to her, got pregnant and had a son in Rome, whom they named Achilles.

It was right at that time that Paganini received the Order of the Golden Spur from the Pope – the highest church medal, for which one needed absolute purity of character in both personal and social spheres!

Paganini began the conquest of Europe with Vienna. The spirit of Beethoven was still haunting the theaters and concert-halls of the city. Niccolò was quiet, serious and mysterious. He came to his concerts in a black carriage pulled by four black horses. Dressed in a black frock-coat, with shoulder-length black hair, he was so thin, he resembled a skeleton. Only his eyes burned with an inner fire. In the salons and hotels, all talk was about his ties to the devil. The sap was getting smaller.

In Vienna and across all of Austria – a complete triumph, but Antonia, with her intolerable character and thirst for her own fame, poisoned Paganini's victory. He fell into a deep depression. Only work helped him get out of it.

Paganini's carriage dragged through the endless rain down the muddy country roads of Devonshire. The tour of England was a success: Niccolò traversed the island from Cornwall in the south to Edinburgh in the north. Only his mood was nasty from the cold, the dampness and the sunless sky. In every city, after the concert, he would be approached by gloomy Sicilians looking for their share–for the glory of Italy and the safety of the maestro.

The European tour went on for six years: countries, cities, people. They remembered his concerts forever. But Paganini did not spare the Folonari's sap. His health worsened – regular stomach aches, his front teeth rotted and had to all be removed, the infection spread to his lower jaw and they had to cut out part of the bone. One could not imagine the suffering Paganini had to endure.

After long negotiations, he signed a contract with Antonia. Paganini was happy, his beloved son stayed with him. Antonia, regardless of her fortune and marriage, harbored a fierce hatred for Paganini, and got involved in witchcraft, black magic and sorcery.

In the brief hours of sleep, Niccolò would have the same recurring nightmare: on an execution block covered with blood stood a naked emaciated violinist playing his final concert. Where did this vision come from? What for? Paganini went to dream interpreters, jews, gypsies – still nobody could explain his dream to him. But they all agreed that it pointed to an unfortunate end.

For Paganini, music was always reality, the true life – beyond whose borders lay a different, spectral life of each day. He clearly saw and understood his talent, with all his dignity and shortcomings, but could also recognize talent in other musicians.

Hector Berlioz, after the failure of the opera "Benvenutto Cellini," was crushed by his critics and was on the brink of suicide. Paganini tactfully gave him 20,000 francs – a huge sum, as a sign of admiration for the composer's talent. The sick Berlioz paid off his debts, comfortably lived for a few years, and dedicated to Niccolò one of his best symphonies – "Romeo and Juliet." But the envious do not pardon even the kindest deeds.

The colophony dwindled along with Niccolò's health. The violinist on the execution block came more frequently into his mind. Close friends relayed that Antonia was secretly perfecting her diabolical apprenticeship into witchcraft.

For many years she racked her brains about where Paganini got his magical power. Niccolò was reticent about everything that concerned his music and technique, choosing to publish only a few of his compositions. He no longer accepted students, opting to take his mastery with him to the grave.

Going through all of Paganini's things that she knew about, Antonia remembered a piece of bloody colophony, which the violinist always carried in his vest pocket. There did not seem to be anything unusual in that, since many string players kept colophony in the same spot. Except, that piece had a strange impression on it. Years passed before she could remember the decoration on the sap she only saw in passing, the pattern and the letter "F."

It was easier from there. Antonia sought out the Alchemist, paid off his servant-woman, and stealthily snuck into the house on Canal Grande.

She tortured the old man, who at this point was over a hundred years old, trying to find out Paganini's secret. Heated needles, vices, nails and such did not work: the old man no longer felt pain. His flabby body was obsolete, but his spirit fought on and refused to reveal its secrets.

Tired, Antonia sat down in an armchair to rest. On the table, in a beautiful encrusted frame stood the convex mirror, another – with a silver handle, lay nearby. Antonia knew the power of magic mirrors. She pointed both of the mirrors at the old man – he started shaking and closed his eyes. The interrogation, as before, failed to bring results, but Antonia felt that she was on the right track. Something was missing. She flipped over the cabinet and found yet another mirror – in a simple wooden frame, but of priceless Venetian glass.

Antonia focused all three mirrors on the old man. He tried to bite off his tongue, but had long since lost all his teeth – the witch laughed at his failed attempt. Now he will tell me everything! The old man fell into a trance. Antonia was in a hurry, lest he should die. In the brazier, she was heating up some tongs, she threw a kerchief soaked in menstrual fluid onto the coal. The kerchief started smoking, and a poisonous smoke crawled across the room.

The old man, tied to the bed, breathed in the poisoned air through his wide open mouth. A little more and he will start talking! With the last of his ill power Signor Juliano Folonari, mage and sorcerer, doctor and alchemist, musician in his youth and an encyclopedist in old age, stopped his old heart. Foam seeped through his lips, his eyes became glassy, while continuing to gaze hatefully at the young witch.

Antonia cursed: "Porca miseria!" All for nothing. She did not find the secret of the talent–no worry. Clearly, the old man gave

Paganini a supernatural power, the two bound by mirrors. This magic was not done in sunlight – Niccolò loved the gloaming and the night. That means, this night she will kill Paganini.

But which of the mirrors should she use? The small hand mirror definitely wouldn't work – too feminine. The beautiful one in the encrusted frame looks too rich, and so instills doubt in its power. Witchcraft in its essence is simple. That leaves the old Venetian one. How did she not know right away!

Antonia waited until the moon was out, opened the shutters and pointed the mirror at the nightly luminary. She stripped naked – it was good that she was on her period – everything was calculated perfectly. She stuffed a kerchief into herself and took it out again, swelling with blood. With bloody finger on the dusty mirror she wrote the name "Niccolò Paganini," and threw the cloth onto the coals. Spreading her legs wide, she sat down, mentally pictured Paganini, and let out a stream right on top of the mirror. Urine mixed with blood washed away the written name. The high moon coldly looked on the exultant witch and the tormented corpse of the old man.

Niccolò suffered severely in his last days. Regular bloodletting, analgesics and laxatives did not help. Priests came to him several times, urging him to confess and repent; they were interested in what Niccolò left of his enormous fortune in his will to the Roman Catholic Church. Paganini understood that he was dying, but did not want to believe in his mortality, and hoped that he would recover as he had done more than once before.

Around midnight, the friends, doctors and visitors left. Only his son, who had grown up into a handsome well-proportioned young man, remained at his father's bedside. "It's good that he is a painter and not a musician," Paganini thought to himself.

An eagle-owl was whoo-ing behind the window. Through the aroma of blooming lilacs, from somewhere, came the smell of burning blood. Niccolò looked at the moon, he had no strength left to fight it. He took his son by the hand and covered his eyes. The violinist on the execution block was playing the Twenty-Fourth Capriccio in La-Minor.

* * *

Paganini's sufferings did not end with his death. To his misfortune, Niccolò left nothing to the Vatican. He was banned from being buried on sacred ground – the story of his ties to unholy powers continued to spread.

His son and a few true friends smuggled the coffin with Paganini's body out of Nice, and after many clandestine travels, hid it on an island in an abandoned leper hospital. Horrifying stories passed in whispers. Fishermen passing the island by night could hear the soul-wrenching voice of a weeping violin, and could see the flashing light of a violin and a thin hunched-over figure above it.

The coffin was moved again to a cement cistern on a former olive-oil factory, from there to a vineyard in Cape Ferra, later, by sea to Genoa, and then by horse-cart to the village home of Paganini's parents. After four years of wandering, they buried him in the garden of Villa Gayone. Long ago, Niccolò dreamed of spending the rest of his life there, away from vanity and worry.

Thirty-six years went by until, in 1876, they repealed the verdict, and his remains were buried properly. But Paganini's body was exhumed two more times, before they finally left it rest in peace in the new cemetery in Parma. The violinist, at last, fell silent.

The Double

Indigo knew that he had a double. He got the first hint at the end of high school. In the Sunday issue of the paper, there was a spread with photos under the headline "Police break up student demonstration, Berkeley, California." Two big cops were dragging a longhaired, scraggly guy with a stubbly chin by the arms and legs. The metal frame of his glasses made him resemble Indigo.

Back then, Indigo did not realize that the man in the photo was his double. He carefully cut out the picture from the paper and put it in a box where he kept the most interesting and important things: a photograph signed by all the Beatles, some silly note from Martha whom he was hopelessly in love with for a whole year, a dry edelweiss from the Italian Alps, an ancient greenish bronze coin he found last summer in the steppes of Kazakhstan, where he went with the geological survey to make some extra money.

After high school, Indigo went to college. As they say "from session to session, students live with a passion," a little studying in the free time between parties, sex and rock concerts. He got good grades – gnawing the granite of philosophy, reckoning, it gives the foundation for all other knowledge, so it will surely come in useful.

During the day, Indigo went to the university, and in the evenings for three-four times a week, he went to take lessons at the art institute. He loved to draw since childhood.

He almost forgot about that guy, occasionally stumbling across the cutout picture, while hiding something else in the box.

"I drink for dames, who's not for dames, I'll kick their asses! So – for dames!" – his friend, Kozik pronounced his crowning toast and in a gulp quaffed the tall glass, filled to the brim with Amaretto Di Saronno (there being no other alcohol left). "Bleh, sweet-disgust, and over some melted cheese."

"Indigo, who was that chick with you last night? I saw you by the movie theater."

Indigo didn't have anybody with him. He was at home, up until late at night, drawing. His first exhibition was scheduled in two months on the second story of the humanities building. To explain this to a drunken Kozik was useless, he wouldn't believe it anyway.

The exhibition went well, despite the eclectics. The university population is mostly benevolent. Several young art-critics came to the exhibition, as well as a few older painters unknown to him. With one of them, named Bream, Indigo soon became friends and the difference in their age didn't bother him at all.

After the exhibition, Indigo was accepted as one of their own into the inner circle of the painters of the underground. His nickname Indigo came from the bluish-grey spectrum he painted with, way back then – pale horses, galloping across snow-covered winter churchyards.

After that the double started to appear more often. He was seen in different parts of the city where Indigo had never been. At first, the double drove or walked by with one or another acquaintance, but soon he was seen at parties, galleries, bars and restaurants, where many of the students went. Indigo thought to himself, too many coincidences. But, so far, it was all harmless.

Having finished at the university, Indigo found a job in a small college teaching philosophy. It provided a regular loaf of bread, and he needed to pay for an apartment away from his parents. The job did not take up much of his time, and Indigo immersed himself head deep into his painting.

When he was young, Indigo exhibited everywhere: in failing galleries, cafes, movie theaters, hospitals, even a sanatorium for pregnant women. He put together many exhibitions, but they were unfulfilling like candy. There were few buyers, but his friends praised: "Old man, you're a genius!" They lied and ingratiated themselves very well, but he knew there is no such thing as a living genius.

Indigo married his former student and they had a son. It was small, but a family, so he had to earn a living. True, he did not stop painting, but had fewer exhibits.

The first blow came when his wife went to the west coast to represent her firm at a conference in modern architecture. She came back a week later, happy and healthier looking, enthusiastically talking about the show and the new movements in urban planning. Before going to sleep, she gently kissed Indigo and thanked him for flying over to see her, begrudging neither time nor money. Too bad it was just for one night.

Indigo was thrown into a heat, he had spent all his days sitting in his studio, only once going out with his friends to the nearby bar. That meant that someone who looked, sounded and acted a lot like him, sneakily managed to bang his wife.

"How was it that night?"

"Wonderful, you were amazing. You could have stayed the day, without leaving so early before breakfast."

Bastard!! What to do now? Make a scene with violence to prove that he was not himself? "Bite your tongue and be extra attentive," Indigo told himself, "you were cuckolded, make sure this doesn't happen again, and look for the vermin, he'll pop up somewhere."

For the autumn exhibit, Indigo made two good paintings and brought them on the second day of the selection committee.

"You brought more?" the secretary was surprised. "We

already took one of your works yesterday. Here it is, standing by the wall."

Indigo inspected the painting. It was his color spectrum, typical decadent tones. In the whirlwind of moonlight, a graceful horse froze for a moment, only to then dart off into the night sky. Composition, drawing style, manner and accents with the palette knife, were all characteristic of Indigo. And the sweeping signature in the bottom right corner with a thumbprint, also his, that couldn't be fake. Only he did not paint this work, and did not bring it last night to the committee!

The double has mounted a full out attack. First, he took Indigo's wife, and now his art and his identity! Indigo was ready to kill the scoundrel.

The painting sold quickly, and they moved the money to Indigo's bank account. Everything was very suspicious. The copycat was not interested in financial matters, he seemed to have another plan. Friends congratulated Indigo for his success. Sadly, the critics praised him, too.

In the afternoons, if he was not delivering lectures or leading seminars at the college, he would go pick up his son from the kindergarten. Usually the boy, seeing his father behind the fence, ran to him from far away, with arms spread, and jumped on Indigo, so he would spin him like on a carousel.

That afternoon, his son looked upset. He silently gave Indigo a present, which he made that day, a bookmark that looked like a funny artist with a pencil for a nose.

"What's wrong? Did you have a fight with one of the kids?"

"No."

"Did the teachers upset you?"

"No."

"Well, what?"

His son sobbed for a while, ready to break down crying: "You walked by and didn't get me."

"It was the double! Thank God that he didn't take my child," – Indigo thought, but the fear of losing the most important person to him pierced like a dull needle into his heart.

"How was I dressed, son?"

"In a brown coat, with a scarf."

"You see, but I'm wearing a leather jacket! That was just someone who looked a lot like me."

Indigo made up his mind to find the villain. He set himself a time limit of two weeks. For that duration, he arranged that his wife and mother-in-law would pick up his son after work.

There appeared in the newspapers, articles about the opening of a traditional Biennale of painting. Again, Indigo's new paintings were praised, it was said that his series of "sincere" works had an impact on the museum's curators and seasoned sharks of the art world.

A few visitors were slowly walking through the halls of the Biennale. "What kind of pornography did he exhibit there?" Indigo ground his teeth on the way to seeing "his" works. In the back gallery, he could hear the noise of an argument in heightened tones.

"And here's the author!" the curator said pointing at Indigo.

There were the clicks of a few cameras. People were rushing towards him, some for an autograph, others with a question and a couple with outraged commentaries.

Indigo signed catalogues, looking out of the corner of his eye at the exposition. He recognized the paintings immediately;

his personal style was too characteristic. The subjects were those of which Indigo was still just thinking about, he never even sketched them out in pencil – passion, will, chimera and other beasts, copulating with women or with each other. In short, the destruction of standards and the breaking of taboo.

In the midst of it, Indigo went outside. It was clear that the double was somehow reading his thoughts and then copied them to canvas. But to read thoughts is one thing and to make a painting, altogether another. Often, Indigo did not know himself how it would turn out in the end, improvisation and the unconscious often played a big part in the process of a painting's creation. Art developed unpredictably, according to its own, invisible to the artist, laws.

How can you still make the paintings without Indigo himself? Devilry and hoffmaniana! Who was there to talk to? Anyone would think that he either lost it or was on the needle.

His head was bursting with hypotheticals. Indigo got home, his wife in tears was sitting by the telephone. Seeing her husband, her eyes flamed up, she flew at Indigo and gave him a resounding slap on the face.

"Good for nothing, lying son of a bitch! Got what you want!? Yesterday, finally you banged Martha, your old school bitch! She called looking for you. Go stay with her! I can't stand to look at you! Tomorrow I'm filing for divorce."

Indigo never had sex with Martha. He had not seen her in many years. He had a sound alibi, at the time he was undressing Olga, his wife's best friend. Only he was unable to utilize this argument.

The vice tightened. What did the double want? It looked like he wanted to destroy Indigo and take his place in his home and in art. How do you fight the invisible?

Indigo set off for Chinatown. For many years, starting

with right out of the university, he studied kung fu there with an old Chinese master. The sifu had few students. The cramp basement where they practiced could not compare with fashionable sport clubs, filled with expensive machines, mirrors, saunas, and massage rooms. But Indigo liked the sincerity and simplicity of the sifu, the atmosphere of a village school, where children and adults practiced alongside one another. Indigo was the only white person there, the rest were Chinese and a pair of Blacks.

"Problems?" asked the sifu with a strong Cantonese accent.

"It's nothing. I'll fix them," Indigo tried to smile.

Sifu touched his pulse, listening for something, and carefully looked at the pupils of the eyes.

"Qi, the life force, has to circulate freely in the body. Take two swords and practice with them, think only of right breathing. Wash your mind to a state of emptiness."

After three hours of strenuous exercise, Indigo felt better. Sparring with Blake returned many things to their places. When a heavy fist or a steel-concrete leg of a black athlete was flying at your head, and you barely have time to defend yourself and counter-attack. This was reality. Afterwards, they would laugh lightheartedly, and talk about each others' mistakes and good punches.

Indigo went out of the New York basement on to Grand Street and then to Broadway, made a turn on Volhonka, and suddenly, he was on Prechistenka in the middle of Moscow. The snow softly fell in large clumps. The streetlamps cast circles of yellow light on the puffy white carpet on the cobblestone streets. There were no cars or pedestrians in sight. Breathing was easy. Indigo started half-singing "Oh, the frost, the fro-o-o-o-st…"

He remembered how weightless and empty his head felt

during sparring, not a single thought. He moved, attacked, defended – no thoughts, no emotions either, for that matter. When he took a hit, he didn't feel pain, it did not enter his consciousness. He just went on fighting, as if he was swimming with the current in completely clear water. He knew that he could fight like this forever, even with closed eyes. Indigo could not remember a comparable state of being. He laughed at his own thoughts; it was true after all, that kung fu cured the body and soul.

From the direction of the Academy of Arts, a figure in a short coat with a raised collar walked towards him. The man hid his nose in a long beige scarf wrapped around his neck in a way that the ends hung in front and on the back.

The man got closer, they were the same height. Indigo looked down – the stranger had the same short boots with the angled cowboy heels. On his jeans, under the left knee, was a spot of emerald-green paint. Indigo had gotten it dirty in the studio last night.

"Him," the thought sparked in his head and Indigo blocked the stranger's way. The man stopped two steps away and lifted his head. Indigo was looking at himself. The mustache, beard, glasses, hair almost to the shoulders – all just like Indigo. Really, not like, but it was Indigo himself.

A chill ran across his skin. There was no reason and no time to think, Indigo kicked with his leg in a reverse roundhouse. The double ducked and avoided it. Indigo, without stopping, fired off a series of kicks and punches. The double dodged, jumped and avoided them. He never blocked, he never attacked.

Indigo could not even touch him and soon understood that he would not be able to reach the opponent, it's as if he was reading his mind. Mystics! Like in a movie. Indigo froze in a waiting stance.

The double stood across from him, his left leg slightly in front, his arms lowered and relaxed.

"Nothing will come of this," he finally said in Indigo's voice.

"What do you want with me? What idiotic tricks are you playing?"

"You, Indigo, did not want to accept the most simple and evident, and you even studied philosophy, supposedly. I am you, the other side, which you fear and hide from others and from yourself."

"Bullshit! You bastard, you slept with my wife, fooling her."

"That was you, Indigo. You got lonely and you flew to her."

"Rubbish! I sat in the studio. What kind of spectacle did you set up with Martha?"

"You banged her, she was overjoyed, and then you went to see Olga."

"Fine, lie all you want. I would remember an achievement like that. How the devil did you forge the painting in my style?"

"You made them. Burned out from work and worries at home, you cracked, and painted without thinking what you were painting. Pure art."

"But then, why did they see you and me in different places, dressed differently?"

"You're going crazy, Indigo. Starting to have failures of memory, acting like a lunatic. A twilight condition they call it."

"And the photograph of that student at the demonstration"

"A simple coincidence".

Indigo thought to himself, what if everything this weirdo said was true, and he is going mad? Well, fine, art – in it anything is possible, but sex with two women? He would have remembered!

Indigo sharply sat down and turned a triple sweep. The

double easily kicked his attack leg over his head.

"Indigo, I am you, more accurately – we. Your thoughts are my thoughts. Don't make a fool of us."

Indigo caught his breath: "When did it start?"

"When you were sixteen, you found a Chinese coin. It brings its possessor split personalities – reread Confucius. Over the years your Yin and Yang stopped being in harmony."

Memories of Chinese mysticism and nature-philosophy came back in spasms.

"It is possible to neutralize the coin. How? Throwing it out or giving it away is forbidden, you have to spend it, buy something with it. But who will take an ancient Chinese coin? Only the Chinese."

Indigo turned around and went back to Chinatown. The coin was in his wallet, for some reason, he had been carrying it around with him for a while now. The antique shops and galleries were already closed, and at the groceries, they would not even sell a bunch of radishes for an old bronze. At the newsstand, they laughed politely.

Indigo was tired, absurdity at the Biennale, scandal with the wife, practice of sloppy fight with the double, and then running around with the coin, drained him completely. His stomach started churning, he hadn't eaten since morning. In a tiny park near the Bowery subway, sat an old man with a wide straw cone hat covered with a layer of snow. On his knees there was a tray of rice-balls protected by a sheet of plastic. Indigo shuffled through his pockets for a quarter, and handed it to the old man, who carefully took the coin, bit it, and then hid it behind his belt.

Indigo broke the rice-ball in two and stretched out a half to his double, who was sitting on the sidewalk edge, downcast. Each ate his piece in silence.

"OK, life moves on," said Indigo, "Time to go home".

Hands on each others' shoulders, they walked back up Volhonka.

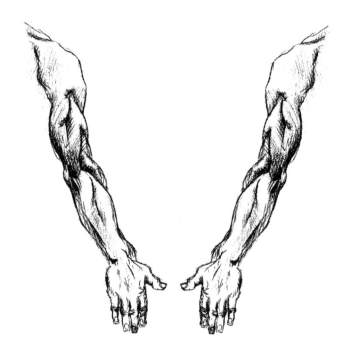

Let's Die, Old Friend

Let's die, old friend. It seems we won't get out of it this time, they got us good. Look at the walls, cyclopean brickwork. Water trickles down, slippery; rats are squeaking somewhere. Some stylists crammed us into a cell à la Count of Monte Cristo.

Of course, that's for theatricality. There are tiny cameras in the corners and next to the ceiling. After all, they need to show the whole planet that the last rebel-villains were caught. I guess they even planted microphones every inch of the place, so they don't miss any secret conversations.

Although what conversations can there be? Just a monologue; since they cut out your tongue, old friend. Hurts? Stick it out, let me see, is it rotting? Seems clean, cicatrizing. Hide it back.

Don't quite like your blush... Let me feel your forehead. You got a fever, friend, and here it's cold and damp. Cover yourself with the mattress; rotten straw, but it'll still warm you a little.

Hey you! Goats behind the cameras! Didn't let us say a single word at your vile judgment, but I'll talk as much as I want here, even though I may not be a master speaker!

We lost this war, old man. But then, what kind of war could there have been between people of art versus the juggernaut, with its armies, planes, tanks and spaceships?

And yet they started it, the bastards, quietly and imperceptibly; downsized the budget, saying there's not enough money for literature and art. Then schools replaced classes in drawing, music and theater with physical education, marching and war craft. Then, they united the various private funds for the support of art into one, under the government's control and regulation. After that, even the blind could see where it all was going.

Freedom of speech – a great thing! We made quite the ruckus. But they quickly bought out the newspapers, magazines and independent TV channels to shut our mouths. The Internet hung in there longer, until they installed filters into communication satellites and closed down all but their own service providers. We were left, orphans, only with cable and radio connections. But it was easier than easy for their electric trackers to localize or cover up cable, or to muffle the radio stations.

What, your leg hurts? Can't step on it after they dumped us into this cell? Damn it, your leg is broken in two places. Don't scream, I only touched it to examine the bone. Okaaaay... "Curiouser and curiouser!" Got to set the shin ... Bunks – iron, table – oaken, screwed to the floor, two chairs, also screwed down.

Hey, you, in front of the monitors! Look how fractures are healed in traditional medicine. First – we break the chair with the edge of the palm. The strike is called "Breaking the Bridge," for you, the spineless and gluttonous. Second – put the planks from the chair on both sides of the broken leg. Hold them, old man. Third – use the teeth to rip my shirt into strips. Fourth – we wrap the planks with improvised bandages. Now the bones will not mix and will start to accrete. After two and a half months, the wounded will be able to walk. Doubtful if he will live that long – execution is tomorrow, gentlemen of the jury.

That's all, lie down. Let's lift the leg on the back of the bed, so the blood flows away from the fracture. Well, this is nothing, there's been worse. There hasn't? I guess today you're right. They cut out your tongue, put out your eyes, so the poet could not read, write or speak. Even broke your leg falling down.

About the eyes, don't worry. Nowadays they hook up video cameras right into the brain. That's even better for you: no more near-sightedness, far-sightedness or cross-eyedness. If you want – zoom in, if you want – zoom out. Can you imagine? No? Well, that's fine, we'll figure something out, put a camera like that on your big forehead. Severed tongue – also not a problem. It's already ancient history how they made a speech synthesizer for Stephen Hawking, and on top of it all, he was paralyzed. We'll get a super-synthesizer for you, and then you'll understand the triumph of modern technology.

Triumph, triumph… It's they who triumph now. "Order is power of technocracy plus militarization of the country." When, in cigarette ads, they replaced the cowboy with a fat-faced soldier, it was an omen of their progress.

Hackers quickly dug up their secret sites and exhibited them for public viewing. Politicians, of course, always have a point man, on which they'll seek the dogs on, while continuing to do what they were doing before. Do you remember the chick from the Department of State? They threw her to the journalists, but now she's back sitting at meetings and directing different committees.

We had an ingenious idea to stop selling paintings, printing books, playing music, performing in theaters. We were able to agree on a worldwide scale! Convinced even the weakest and most cowardly. Some became waiters, others painted walls, mowed grass or took care of kids. And we held out for a long time!

The fashion labels were the first to panic. They had to prepare the spring collection, but not one of the designers wanted to work. And what happened in advertising! The horror!

At first, business used its old baggage – took some things that were unpublished, compiled as much as they could until it reached a total stupor: newspapers, magazines, movies – everything that generated revenue – halted. Fashion suffocated. Galleries closed – they sucked and sucked the blood of artists, always considering themselves superior, but once they sold their reserves, they were finished. In music: no new CDs, no concerts, no jingles for commercials. Even in the army, when time came to make new uniforms, the colonels couldn't come up with a single design.

We were hungry then, but happy. We saw that we were right. The tree of life doesn't bloom without art, it wilts.

It's true that some wise-asses from Bangalore tried to launch a self-developing program, so computers could build upon all previously created art. They were supposed to add their own corrections to simulate the effect of originality, and create no worse than Leonardo. But what can a machine think of by itself? It's just an instrument, similar to a hammer. A hammer can only give birth to a hammer. Yes...

Your leg hurts? Endure it, old friend, only a little left. What was the name of that medicine advisor to the president? That grayish, plain one. It was his idea to catch talent, scan ideas and memories, and to hide brains in vats with nutritional liquid, to preserve them just in case. Bodies without heads have their own price; organs can always be sold retail.

That's when the real hunt started. They began grabbing everyone – both famous and not, the eminent and the beginners. All ideas – into one depository, all the brains – into glass cans. Even the old women, God's dandelions, the music teachers, they too were dragged away from upright pianos and concert grands before the eyes of their students, uprooting all the potential individual thought.

A war broke out... We peppered them good in the mountains; to this day they're afraid to go there. We fought, learned to shoot and to lay ambush. We had to learn, of course, when the entire force of the technocracy pushed against us.

The government – the gray mass pressed on. There were always more of them, and the noodles they hung from out of their ears, we relished with appetite. Meanwhile, on TV they constantly aired the famous ad: "Kill Him!" next to a picture of an artist in a Parisian beret.

Yesterday, at the trial, they showed the sheep of the jury my self-portrait with palatte in one hand and brush in the other. Immediately, they ordered to cut off the hand that held the brush. They cut off, the bastards, my left. These cretins couldn't even figure out that the painting was a mirror image! But, that's fine, "It'll heal before your wedding" as my grandmother used to say.

Pity about the enlighteners who walked around with peaceful speeches – who were immediately hung by the "good honest citizens." They didn't need art or those weirdoes who make art. Those "citizens" wanted to live in strict barracks, one per family, to walk in line, to sing the gallant marches approved by the censors, to read field guides, instruction manuals or educational biographies of the president. Freedom of speech, villains!!!

…I don't like the crowd, old friend. My freshman year at college, when I would walk from the subway to the university, on the left there was a park surrounded by a black pike fence, on the right an ugly circus building, behind you and in front of you, students, the same as you. But it didn't feel right where there were only backs and scalps, in a crowd or in a line. I love it alone or with another, preferably with a woman. And in our war, I also tried to be alone in the field. Of course, it's good if a friend has your back covered, and you his.

How did they betray us? Very easily! Since artists are individuals, each with his own opinion on everything, they creatively reinterpret their orders. So the enemy poured it into the ears of two of our geniuses that, for the greater good, we all needed to sit down at a common table and calmly discuss and agree on everything. And these creators of ours agreed to reveal our paroles and decode our ciphers, so they could take us, the stubborn, in buses to the beautiful Palace of Negotiations.

After that, you know how they pumped gas into the ventilation system of the fortress, having used our codes to open the gates. Then – gunfire, blood, carnage. Even in the kindergartens they didn't leave anyone alive. I think they didn't kill you and me so that, as ringleaders and instigators, they could make examples of us at a public execution.

Do you know where they will place the nooses around our necks? Ah, yes, you lost your consciousness when they cut out your tongue. Here - in the amphitheater on the cliff, from where the Argonauts departed in search for the Golden Fleece. Aeschylus used to have his tragedies performed there. Where, a hundred years ago we went to an Emerson, Lake and Palmer concert. Fires were lit along the stage in the evening. How the boys played! They wrote us into the stars now, so hang on. We'll make a show for the world.

Has it been long since you saw your kin? Three years? Of course, it's harder for you poets. Like a sailor you have a wife in every port. All right, all right, can't I make a joke? We know what an exemplary family man you are.

Listen, I think they're coming. Yup, a whole platoon.

And who is this suspicious priest with you, gentlemen? What a strange cross, with bent ends. I will not confess to him, nor will my friend. Yes, we'll die without confessing to this Judas. In the other world, they'll sort us out without your help.

Let's go, old friend, like men on our feet. Lean on me. Well, vaya con Dios.

Look here, an elevator. While yesterday they pushed us down a hole in the ceiling. The corridor, old man, is quite acceptable, like in a regional clinic. Guards everywhere, a crowd of blank faces with machineguns, rifles and devil knows what. The second crowd – robots, kind of like spiders, with some strange gadgets, never saw them before.

Oh, what a blinding light! Hold on, bastards, let the eyes adjust. So, old man, they led us to the right corner of a stage, the public can't see us yet. Hummingbird-cameras are circling nearby, filming from every angle. Let me fix the bandages on your eyes. They're all blood-soaked, simply terrible. Ours are probably also watching the screens, so smile. Like that, that's better.

Hold on tighter to my shoulder, pull in your leg, they are leading us out for public display. People – a swarm. Screaming, whistling, spitting – you can hear them. Cattle. Each one paid a lot of money to get here. Posters everywhere: "Historical day – the end of the rabble-rousers and, the so called, freedom of art!" Goats!

Old friend, I understand the script of their director. From the spot where we're standing now to the elevated stage there is a slanted ramp, 40-45 yards long. That's the way they'll send us. Probably alone, they don't need guards on camera. We can barely move our legs the way it is. Background – the sea and the sun, which will rise any minute now. On the stage – gallows, like in seventeenth century Portland, there are two nooses dangling already. The hangman is standing in a red hood with eyeholes, and his two assistants are nearby. What kind of horror-show are they planning to show with us in the lead roles?

As we ascend the ramp, a bit away on the left is the

audience, below on the right – cliffs, beyond them – the sea. No, don't even think about it, we won't be able to make the jump - won't make it over the cliffs. It's far and we don't have that kind of strength. We'll hit the rocks; too high – this isn't the Adalary.

Besides, there are guard boats and probably a submerged submarine. They're afraid of us, friend.

They hit the gong, that means the show's starting now. The hummingbird-cameras have darted to the side, so they don't swarm in front of the main lenses.

If you could only see this ape with the mantle, announcing our sentence! Children are bringing him bouquets of flowers, women are waving, men are proudly cheering. Get ready.

Is your fracture bleeding? The bone cut through the skin while you were stomping here, the break went from closed to open. Hold your pants leg with your hand, so the foot doesn't touch the ground. Endure, we're going now…

Bastards, get these laser things away, don't have any breathing room as it is! No need to rush, we can get to your idiotic gallows ourselves! Old friend, get on my back. I'll carry you like in Karelia, when they robbed us on the train and you only had your sandals left. Afterwards, I had to drag you around on my back over puddles and swamps. Even in my last hour there is no justice! Again I'm carrying the weight alone! Forgive me, Lord, I won't gripe.

Moving. One, two, three – you're heavy, old man, even though there's nothing left but skin and bones. Or is it me that got weaker? Turn your head to the left, look at them one last time, let them remember your face. "Today is a good day to die," sing with me. "We all come in here living, but no one gets out alive… Today is a good day to die…" – now louder, - "Do you feel the thunder roll? … All for one and one for all!"

Oh, they even sprinkled some broken glass under the feet; not enough blood for them. Wait, I can't hold you with the left hand, a wound just opened. Let me put you on my shoulders. Stand for a second on one leg, forget the glass. Lie down on my shoulders. Ooop, let's go, we're halfway there.

* * *

On the screens of the Center for conducting the worldwide celebration – the execution of the last rebels - you could easily see how one of them got on the shoulders of his associate. Their bearded faces, covered with dirt and ichors, inspired loathing. Blood, oozing from their many wounds and the soles of their feet did not awaken a shred of compassion. With excitement, everybody awaited the climax.

The Head Director was silent; his program couldn't be going better. In one minute and forty four seconds the top edge of the sun will appear, just as the villains will reach the stage. Plus three minutes – the hangmen will place them onto the assigned spots on the stage, tighten the ropes, and step aside. Four minutes – for barraging the rebels with rotten eggs, tomatoes and such. Another two minutes – for silent viewing, and then the synchronizer will close the circuit, kick the stools from under the feet of the villains, and they will twitch from the hemp ropes directly in the middle of the disk of the rising sun.

Beautiful, spectacular, instructional! They will repeat this footage on all the channels, at workplaces, in schools and even in children's training centers. The program of the execution will be analyzed, studied and cited for many years to come. After all, the Head Director is the best machine of his class.

The figures slowly moved along the ramp, but were getting there on schedule. Suddenly, the one who was walking on his own, tripped and fell on one knee. The Head Director ordered the robot-guards not to move, the last thing he needed was to have them in the shot. The villain stood on his knee and breathed heavily. The Director sent a signal to poke him with a laser and get him moving. The villain's mouth twisted as a burn-mark darkened on his side. With difficulty, he stood up holding up his associate, and moved forward.

If the Head Director was human, he would have breathed a sigh of relief. But the Head Director was a machine, a computer, and so he had no emotions. He knew that problems have to be solved in the order of their occurrence, and that almost all of them could be foreseen. The villains were too weak and demoralized for antisocial action. Security and surveillance today were amplified many times. "10.8 times" calculated the Head Director.

The walking villain tripped again, received another laser burn, luckily the beam was not visible on the screen. He stood, swaying. There were 5.8 yards left before the stage, about eight steps, nine from the burden. The sun was up halfway. "Have to hurry," decided the Head Director and sent the order to the guards. Laser beams stung the villain's back and right side. There was a smell of cooked meat, as smoke wafted. Step-two-three-four, now everything is in order; a minute and they'll be in their nooses, and then – complete sunrise.

Powerless, rocking from the weight of his associate, the villain suddenly made two agile gymnastic steps along the edge of the ramp, on the third, with a strong push he jumped into the shining sun.

The two figures missed the cliffs by a hair and crashed into (towards) the water below. The guards couldn't shoot, it was a blind zone. The hummingbird-cameras darted after the villains, taping the priceless moments for TV.

The two separated in midair. The second, who was carried by his buddy, pulled in the knees to his chin and wrapped the arms around his legs like a "cannonball." The first instigator arched his spine, straightened his legs, pointed his toes and opened his arms wide to the sides, falling, almost flying, virtually parallel to the water. Right before the surface he realigned his body and entered the water like an arrow. The second plunged with an enormous explosion nearby. The cameras froze over the circles of the parting waves.

Through the rays of the morning sun, a scuba diver saw how the first man dove like a needle. In another half a second, with an explosive roar, flopped the second. The first traced a sharp curve, turning to the one who, unaided, was sinking to the bottom after the impact.

The scuba diver pushed himself away from the mollusk overgrown wall and extended to them tanks with air. "Thanks, son," – the one-armed man said with his eyes. The three of them grabbed onto a torpedo and the scuba diver pointed it towards the labyrinthine underwater caves of the coral reef.

Little Violin

Maira lived in a village at the foot of a blue mountain. The village was simple and peaceful, the villagers herded goats, sowed grain, as well as handicrafts and commerce. The housewives whitened cloth and made wide comfortable shirts with amazing embroidery around the hem and sleeves.

The women in the village – beautiful and statuesque – with eyes like olives and full red lips. The men, for some reason, were the opposite – short and stocky. They would hide their early bald-spots with small round hats, which they would attach to their remaining hair with flat pins.

The village was famous for its blacksmiths, who could firmly shoe the most restive of horses. Caravans, gypsies and contrabandists always tried to spend a day or two in the village.

In the spring, after sowing, or in the fall after reaping the crop, in a wide field there would be a market fair in the village. People of the steppes, with their felt tents, brought herds of sheep and droves of long-legged bay horses. From the mountains descended stern-looking vine-dressers with overgrown black beards to their eyes. Large daggers in ancient silver sheaths hung from their wide belts and over their shoulders – rifles with burnished barrels. In the fall, they brought casks of young sparkling wine, in the spring - wine from the last year, thick and sharp.

From the far-away town came curious self-propelled carriages – automobiles, loaded with fabrics, enamel plates, kerosene lamps, fragrant soaps and Chinese tea, without which nomads cannot live. Dresses and hats from magazines, sold from hawker's trays, invoked envy from the village's fashionable women.

Noise from the shouting, the neighing of horses and the

bleeping of sheep, beeping of the rare autos and blares of camels filled the air with the joy and excitement of commerce. After a week, the fair would close and once again only the wind from the plain would move the feather grass and only every Friday evening would there come a sustained male voice, singing from a large grey house – the village temple.

Maira was the youngest of seven daughters. Her father, eternally tired and prematurely aged from worry, would make barrels in their dusty courtyard – big and small, curved and flat, huge – for cellars, and tiny – for travel. Sometimes, his lanky figure would dive inside a massive flask and would be almost unnoticeable. He worked for days on end, in the evening sitting down on a stool in the kitchen and immediately falling asleep, before even having dinner.

Maira did not remember her mother. They said in the village that she was reputed to be a foremost beauty, even after breastfeeding so many children. The last births turned out to be the most difficult, the mother being way past twenty. She screamed for three days before Maira came into this world. Everyone thought that the mother would not be able to handle such pain and would die. But she got better, spending a lot of time looking at the newborn Maira with her large slightly slanted eyes, and then, met a dashing handsome horse-thief at the fair, quickly kissed her daughters goodbye and rode off with him to the steppes. No one has seen her since.

Maira's sisters were very happy village girls with curved hips and full breasts. Guys started eyeing them early - the daughters of the poor wretched Moses. Three of them, even without dowries, married at fifteen or sixteen.

But Maira was not like her sisters. She was thin and had

ash-grey hair and light skin with bluish veins. And her eyes were blue, not black like theirs. Poor Moses loved her more than the others, often talking to her, stroking his short beard.

Still in her childhood, Maira fell in love with old books, written with intricate swirls. In a singing voice, she would read ancient prayers and parables to her sisters and her tired father. The villagers would call her "strange" and "foreign." Maira did not have any female friends; young people avoided her and didn't invite her out. For stretches of time, she would sit in the courtyard with a book in her lap, watching how her father worked.

Much happened when a theatre troupe came to the spring fair. People of the steppes, mountain-men, not even the villagers themselves had ever seen a theatre. On a haphazardly constructed stage, twice a day, the actors would sing, suffer, laugh, love and kill each other. The cramped hall was always over filled.

Maira didn't have the money to go to the theatre, but she'd listen to each play through the thin tarpaulin wall. Usually she would stand near the exit where on the side of the walls sat a small orchestra of four musicians. Maira didn't see the musicians themselves, only heard the voices of their instruments. Nobody had really listened to music in the village before. For holidays or weddings, they would invite singers who played drums and tambourines.

So they wouldn't chase her away, Maira learned to hide between the folds of the tarpaulin. Replicas of the actors did not interest her since she couldn't see the performance anyway. From the music, she had a special liking for the high and clear voice of the small violin – she already knew what the small casket with four veins was called, and a stick that resembled a small hunting bow. Maira's soul would stand sweetly still and yearn; it seemed to her that she could listen to the violin forever.

The young violinist with blonde curly hair down to his shoulders soon noticed Maira. He felt pity for the young girl in plain clothes. She never before had heard real music, didn't know about Bach, Beethoven or Mozart. One time after the matinee, he called to Maira. She got scared like a wild chamois and ran off. But towards evening, she was overwhelmed by curiosity and she hid anew in her cozy corner near the orchestra.

That year the cherry-trees blossomed lushly on the slopes of the hills. Maira and the Violinist walked through cherry gardens as if swimming on white thinly scented clouds. The Violinist showed her how to properly hold a violin, how to press down the strings with the fingers of the left hand and how to move the bow with the right. Maira felt immediately why the sound changed with the position of the fingers on the neck and the movement of the bow. Innate musical affinity helped her to quickly learn to play simple melodies and uncomplicated dances.

One time, Maira's father saw them together. They were sitting on a bench in a garden and the Violinist was explaining what chords were. The father looked fixedly from afar, but didn't approach them so as not to meddle.

The fair was soon over and the theatre people had to leave for other lands where they were expected. Maira cried: she would never again hear such music nor see her Violinist. He stood, drooping and abashed, near the wagon with theatrical placards on the side, fiddling with his coat-button, removing and putting on his tattered top-hat. The horn-player gave the signal for departure.

Maira walked alongside the wagon as her fingers lightly

touched the Violinist's. For a second he disappeared inside and then jumped out on the road, holding his most precious possession – his violin. Maira froze, her eyes and mouth wide open. The Violinist placed the violin into her stiff hands, kissed her on the cheek and told her that he would return next spring – with the thatre or alone, but that he would definitely be back. The caravan started rolling down the slope, picking up speed, and the Violinist ran to catch up with his wagon.

Maira stood frozen, holding the violin to her heart, as she watched until the last dust-cloud settled and the wagons disappeared in the distant horizon. Violet shadows from the nearby mountains lay upon the plains. Maira went home. Her father didn't say a thing when he saw her with the violin, he just hugged her.

Maira got ready to wait for her Violinist. Each day, little by little, she practiced playing on the violin, so as not to forget the melodies that he taught her. Then she started playing more, adding more of her own to the music, as if talking to her beloved. Her father listened to the playing of her sad and gloomy music. Her sisters, at first, didn't pay any attention to Maira's new eccentricity – then they started whispering and laughing.

Once, when Maira was playing long and especially well, she became dizzy, she felt slightly nauseous and lost consciousness. She awoke in her own bed. Her fingers were still clasping the neck of the violin which Maira never let go of when she fell to the floor. Her dress was open and one of her sisters sat nearby - rubbing her stomach. With closed eyes, her father stood with the back of his head against the wall.

After that event, Maira began having black days. Adults would point their fingers at her and called her hurtful names.

Children taunted her and threw rocks and her sisters would not talk to her. Only her father tried to calm her, saying that the Violinist would definitely return and take her away from the village.

Maira stopped leaving her house. No one came to visit her, so she spent most of her time playing the violin. There was much sad and melancholy music, as she told the Violinist how bad and lonely it was for her. Often Maira and the violin imagined how the Violinist would return and embrace them both. There was also happy music when Maira recalled how they walked through blooming gardens and the Violinist told her funny stories about his travels with the thatre.

Word of Maira and her violin spread through the surrounding area – up the mountains and across the plains - the sound flew far. The curious started gathering on the street near her window. Travelers would take the long way just to stop by Moses' house and listen to the quiet melody of the violin. Caravans now passed through the outskirts of the town's inn and the tavern was empty. For the village people, especially the elders, this wasn't acceptable.

Summer passed, then autumn, Maira's stomach kept growing. One day she was sitting next to the window playing her violin and vacantly looking at the street. A company of armed cavalry came trotting by. On the head of one of them she recognized the faded top-hat. Maira's heart stopped, life around her froze, all sounds fell silent, only the grim-visaged bearded rider remained, slowly swimming across her line of sight, swaying in rhythm with the pace of his horse. How long did it take for the numbness to set in – a second or an eternity? Maira didn't know. She was brought back to life by a weak, but definite push from inside her stomach – there was someone there.

Rumor of the unusual violinist reached the local Baron – the owner and ruler of these lands. He lived in a remote estate on the plains, where he would order paintings from Italy, porcelain from England, wines from France. They would also bring him musicians, actors and circus-folk. The Baron's temper was wild, as often happens with people who have limitless authority and money. He ordered that Maira be brought to him at once.

Mustachioed footmen armed with sabers came to Moses' home. Without a word they put Maira in a carriage. They just whipped Moses across the back so he would not get in the way and then quickly took Maira to the Baron.

The Baron sat lazily in an ancient chair of red velvet. Under his feet was a Persian carpet and nearby on the table – fried hazel-hen, fruit, pastries, sweet wines in crystal decanters. An enormous stomach hung down to the knees – his face swelling from drunkenness and gluttony with traces of small pox and many vices. To the left and right of him sat about a dozen neighbors, while around them stood a wavering crowd of flatterers and parasites. The frightened Maira was placed in the middle of the carpet. The Baron examined her long and silently. Maira blushed; she was still dressed in what she was wearing at home – disheveled, barefooted in a single thin shirt that hung just below her knees through which her round stomach was visible. The servants and guests were whispering and snickering.

"Play," said the Baron finally.

"Play what?" Maira said barely audible.

"What you can. If you play badly, you will be whipped to death; if you play well, I will reward you richly."

Maira carefully tried the strings, tightening them a little, tuning, and then fell into thought. What to play for this beast and his herd? Happy songs? There were none left in Maira's soul. Sad ones? She was brought here to entertain the lords, not to depress them. No matter what she did, there was no way for her to get out of there alive. Poor father will die of grief. Dear Violinist, Maira will never see him again.

She tried the first chord, that very first one the Violinist taught her. Then came the melody of the traveling thatre, after that – the blossoming cherry garden in the moonlight. The violin sang the love of the young village girl and her musician, of the joy of their first meeting, of their happiness together and of their separation.

The music swam above the heads of the now quiet guests, over the high walls, into the plains and further across the mountains and rivers, across the forests and seas – to the one who Maira was waiting for. Everybody in the estate – guests, servants, stable-men, cooks, stood without breathing, listening to Maira and the violin. Tears glistened in the eyes of the grey-haired footmen while the women were crying into their aprons and handkerchiefs.

Maira finished playing and lowered the violin. She told them all she could – now she was prepared for the worst. In the silence, everyone was looking at the Baron, who sat with his hands covering his face. At last, he took one hand and reached out to Maira. He tried to stand up, but could not. His mouth helplessly gasping for air, he grabbed his chest and fell back against the back of his chair. His head dropped back – the Baron was dead.

They took Maira home before midnight. Misfortune galloped home ahead of the cavalry – a whole mob with torches gathered in front of her house. The powerless Maira was left in her room alone. In her stomach someone kept beating and kicking. Her father brought her water and covered her with a tattered quilt. The frightened sisters paced about in the foyer.

The village men and elders went to the temple. Prayers came from there throughout the night, interrupted by screams and arguing and followed by more prayers. By morning all was quiet. As dawn approached, most left the temple but a few were locked inside for some reason. In front, there came fierce, rigid old men with white kerchiefs on their heads. Behind them, lowering their heads and hiding their eyes, followed the rest.

"Moses, come out," they called the father.

The intimidated father was trying to button the collar of his shirt, but nothing he did came out right, so he came outside. No one in the house heard what the elders told him. The father screamed terribly and fell upon them with fists. Three muscle-men restrained him, tied him up with belts and threw him into a gutter next to the road. Several people went into the house, the sisters in terror pressed themselves against the walls.

"Maira, come with us," said one of the elders.

They took her under the arms and led her outside. From somewhere faraway within the village came a cry, then another, and before long all the women of the village were wailing like wounded she-wolves.

Maira was taken to a stone canyon whose white walls were corroded by cracks. Each of her steps came with effort, the crushed stone sliding beneath her feet, her large stomach made it hard to walk – all the time someone was moving inside, her head was splitting, red circles swam before her eyes.

They put her near a limestone wall where, nearby, a stream babbled peacefully flowing out through a crack. Some old man opened a case and placed a violin nearby. Maira bent down, took it in her hands and pressed it against her chest.

Three of the oldest grumbled a prayer with hoarse voices. Men covered their heads with kerchiefs and swayed from side to side, singing along with the elders. Then someone screeched and a rock hit the wall next to Maira's head. The second and third likewise missed, but the fourth grazed her shoulder, while the fifth painfully hit her in the rib. She tried to cover and protect the violin, but the stones flew more angrily. Then, with a sharp sting, her eyebrow was cut, blood dripped onto the white dust under her feet.

The chief elder yelled something and came close to Maira. In his hands he held a big jagged stone. The old man menacingly bared his teeth and lifted the rock high above his head. Out of fear, Maira dropped to her knees, still looking at the horrific stone. High above him shone the blue-blue sky.

There was a sharp whistle, a long whip wound around the old man's wrists, and an invisible force threw him backwards. Two riders – a man and a woman, dressed like nomads, pushed their way into the crowd, swinging their whips left and right. The villagers had never been brave and quickly dispersed here and there.

Maira came to her senses in the evening, as it was getting dark. She was in a canopy stretching between two horses. She was lying down, rocking back and forth, looking into the sky at the crescent moon– thin and elegant, like her Violinist.

A tall beautiful woman in soft leather pants rode nearby, pensively looking at Maira.

"You can't go back to the village, you have no life there."

"But my Violinist will return to take me away from there."

"We'll tell him where to find you. You won't be able to stay with us. We love riding, wind, freedom and danger. You're …

different. We'll send you across the ocean, contrabandists can get you on a ship. Beyond the ocean, our people will meet you and help you settle for the time being. Don't forget us, daughter."

*　*　*

In my friend's Park Avenue home, on the wall hangs an old violin. Inside it, with a heated needle is inscribed "Vincenzo," and nearby in a different handwriting: "Maira." My friend got the violin from his grandfather. According to family tradition, when the moon was full, his grandfather would come out on the roof of their multi-apartment building in Brooklyn and for long stretches would play strange unfamiliar music while gazing at the moon.

Monk Andrey

Two monks came out of the chambers of the Metropolitan and widely crossed themselves facing the domes of the Annunciation Cathedral – the main one in the Kremlin, bowed to the ground, and walked towards the Borovitsky gates.

Muscovites' houses huddled along the narrow streets, with their sturdy fences and chained angry dogs. The town was wooden: churches, store fronts, drinking establishments, bath houses, jails, even bridges – all were built out of pine or oak, chopped down in the surrounding forests. The rare stone buildings of the rich and especially important churches brought out the admiration and envy of passers by. The crooked streets by night were barricaded against outlaws with bolted toll-gates and guarded by marksmen with pole-axes and muskets.

The capital city of the great prince was beautiful on this September morning. The autumn sun brought out the gold of the church domes; the grey log walls seemed to have a fleshy color. Birches on the streets and clearings, apple trees in the gardens started to turn yellow, but the leaves were still holding on, not falling yet. The monks were walking along the smooth high road, rushing to make it back to the monastery in time for vespers – tomorrow was an important holiday – Birth of Virgin Mary, they could not be late.

One of the monks looked to be forty or forty-five years old, light-brown haired, with a beard that had started graying. The other seemed five years older, tall like a Russian knight if it was not for the cassock. Each one held a sturdy walking stick in his hands, over their shoulders – knapsacks. The younger one had something square in his bag, a Bible probably, what else would a monk have?

The travelers went outside the city walls, ahead of them –

fields, woods, streams. You could see far to the very horizon – where the vault of the sky meets the solid earth.

"Well, Brother Vitaly, shall we take the main road?" asked the light-haired one.

"No, Brother Andrey, that way is dangerous. You heard how Tatar raiders have been sighted right outside of Moscow the last three days. This would be a bad time to come across them, since you know what precious things we are carrying. We should take the other trail, even if it is longer, lest we run into them."

The monks veered off the main road and rushed down the secluded path over the fir-grove to the village on the hill. The rains had not started yet, so the ground was dry and a pleasure to walk on, their staves made a knocking sound as they made their way, admiring the nature around them - God's creation.

It is easy to talk on the road, if the fellow traveler is not gloomy, but rather sociable and smart.

"Brother Andrey, is it true what the other monks say, that you used to be a famous artist in the Prince's court, making lots of money? And that you took the oath recently, already in advanced age?"

"That is true, Brother Vitaly. Even as a child, I liked to draw with charcoal. Sometimes I would decorate the entire white stove, and my father - God rest his soul - beat me for behavior like that. Then he thought and thought and decided to send me to the icon-painters for training. I – keen-witted, quickly learned the craft. As an adolescent, I already painted better than the old men. They also beat me, when it happened that in the ancient outlined transfers, I added of my own, or changed something."

"Are you not allowed to change the old canon?"

"No, but how many times has it been drawn anew, how

many inaccuracies have piled up over the centuries! And the clumsiness and sloth of our icon-daubers! Divinity must be present in every face or bending of the head. Meanwhile, one draws angels with the hands of men who swing rakes all day, Lord, forgive me. I could not paint icons with such transfers."

Thus talking, the monks came to the village of eight households. A barefoot man was digging a well in the yard, and they asked him how to get across the swamp that lay beyond the village fence.

"Follow the path, it will be about 6 miles. Don't worry, we fixed up the log-path, a pedestrian can make it, a horseman – not on your life, or else the Prince's people or the Tatars would come our way."

The man whistled for a black shaggy dog and ordered it to escort the monks to the other side of the forest. The bitch turned out to be clever: never running too far ahead, always keeping in sight of the monks. At a turn in the road, it would stop and patiently wait for them to catch up, its pink tongue hanging out.

"A painfully smart bitch," grumbled Brother Vitaly. "Could it be a witch?"

"Come now, we are monks, God's people. What can happen to us?"

"Oh, I don't like her."

The forest was becoming more rotten, it seemed as if sounds were drowning in the thick moss. Ferns were stupefying with their smell, huge fly-ageric mushrooms reddened through the thorny bushes. Honey-agaric hanged in moldering clusters from the pine-trees, a spider-web draped like a shroud over the deadwood. This is an unkind forest, it would have been better to take the main road back to the monastery, but it is dangerous there, too. And what if Tatars or robbers stopped them? The monks had neither sword nor cudgel, only small knives to cut mushrooms and turnips with.

It was true, the monks were carrying in their knapsacks something precious. Brother Vitaly, a strong man who used to serve for a governor as captain of the guard, carried the bag of silver, which the Metropolitan paid Brother Andrey for the painting of the new stone chambers.

The master and his assistants worked for three months, decorating all the living rooms, waiting rooms, ceilings, and stoves with wondrous flowers, ornaments, birds of paradise, grapevines and berries. He also painted the house chapel: archangels, saints, God the Father, the Son and the Holy Spirit – like is suited to the Metropolitan.

His Eminence liked it and paid him accordingly, almost all of what they agreed upon. Only, Brother Andrey had no need for money, being a monk, thus the monastery will take everything. So Brother Vitaly was sent by the Abbot, to deliver the silver to the monastery's coffers. All Brother Andrey does is speak of the divine, only the lazy do not offend him, as for the money – there are plenty of tricksters on the road to relieve him of it. And so, Brother Vitaly picked the most desolate path.

Brother Andrey was carrying an icon in his sack, carefully wrapped in a soft cloth. He only recently finished it and took it to the Metropolitan for consecration. The icon was of the Holy Trinity, three angels sitting around a table with a cup, talking among themselves about angelic matters. The mountains of Jerusalem peek out from behind their wings. There is quiet and calm in the icon, as if the Holy Spirit came down and hung like a canopy over His paradise.

Brother Andrey had not painted anything finer than this small icon, even though he had been mixing paint and using the brush for over thirty years. He was even the Moscow Prince's favorite artist, painting his rooms and icons. And he went to other towns with his troop of students and helpers. He painted iconostases and walls in Moscow, Vladimir and Zvenigorod. There were few stone churches in Great Russia, and even fewer masters who can plaster them and decorate with frescoes. Even before he took up the cloth, Brother Andrew was considered the best. Theophanes the Greek and Daniel the Black were the only ones who compared with him.

Andrey had a comfortable worldly life: a house, a court, property, a wife and a small son. He worked hard, and his talent was rewarded in silver rubles by those who knew something about icons and painting – counts, boyars, church hierophants, merchants and the rich town-people.

Andrey's wife, the beautiful Natalia, was taken by the Tatars when Tokhtamysh sacked Moscow. Andrey tortured himself over his beloved wife a long time, even thought of doing away with himself. Only the Lord would not forgive the sin come Judgment Day. So Andrey had been going crazy since that time.

When his son grew up strong, he asked his father to let him go fight the Tatars in the Wild Fields, beyond the Oka River. He was hoping to find his mother, or at least word of her from those who escaped the captivity.

Andrey mourned, sold his house, his cow, dug up the jar of money from the yard – everything he saved up over the years of work. He bought his son a war-horse, a spear with red shaft, a broadsword that would cut through other swords, chain mail with a breastplate, a pointed helmet, a round shield with a sun in the middle and a powerful bow with arrows.

The son changed into his armor in his room; he came out and Andrey gasped deeply. Like a knight out of a fairy-tale – curly haired, strong, beautiful. They kissed each other three times in farewell, Andrey made a cross over his son, blessed him, and his Alexei rode away, like the legendary Alexei Popovich.

So, Andrey joined the monastery, which was twelve miles away, leaving the stressful worldly life and taking the catechism; he stayed silent for several years, thinking and praying.

The abbot allowed him to paint icons for the monastery: why should the prince's icon-dauber only read his Psalter and sing in the choir? And thus, Andrey continued doing what he always did. From fate, it seemed, there was no escape.

"Brother Andrey, why is it that in your icons Our Lord Jesus Christ seems so kind? Our people are supposed to fear God, who punishes them for their sins, or else they'll spoil themselves."

"Come to me, all you who are weary and burdened, and I will give you rest. Take my yoke upon you and learn from me, for I am gentle and humble in heart, and you will find rest for your souls, said the Lord in the Evangels of Matthew."

"But look at the times we are living in! The end of the world is around the corner: raids, wars, brother killing brother, Christians against Christians, the Orthodox slicing fellow Orthodox, usurers everywhere, pestilence and evil. The time has come to punish the people for their sins! Not your angels, but the angry Judge should hang in a red corner in every hut!"

"No, Brother Vitaly, Our Savior is not wrathful, does not take vengeance on His children. Nothing in the world is secret to Him. He is radiant and soft, even if firm and sorrowful. He brought us love, not the sword. It is easy to depict a fiery Gehenna, with devils and frying pans, to make it scary to both young and old. But how do you paint the Divine light, which comes only to the eyes of the worthy, or grace and the heavenly kingdom? And so that even the densest hunter could see the Holy Truth?"

"Wait, Brother Andrey, where did the little bitch go?"

So it was, during their argument, the monks lost track of the guide dog. It seemed she was just mingling under their legs and now it was as if she fell through the ground. They called for it, howled, even took out a loaf of bread to try to lure it back, but the dog was gone.

"I am telling you for sure now: it was a witch. It looked like a nun in the Metropolitan chambers," pressed Brother Vitaly.

The monks sat down to rest at the edge of the woods. The rotten forest ended, in front of them was a hollow with tussock and swamp reeds, beyond it – a bright birch grove, to the left flowed a small river, quiet and sunny.

"Look, Brother Vitaly, what a beauty!"

"It is not a beauty, Brother Andrey, but a swamp, black death."

Brother Vitaly wrapped his onoocha, tied the bast shoes tightly and stepped into the bluish puddle in front of his feet. He stepped and fell through up to his chest. His eyes became round and almost jumped out from under his brows. The puddle turned out to be a marsh, which was reflecting the sky and clouds.

The swamp grabbed on to the monk with sticky fingers, while vampiric hobgoblins latched on to his cassock. Brother Vitaly was sinking, but took the bag off his shoulder yelled: "Make sure it gets there if I die."

Andrey looked around, ripped off a long adler branch (where did he find such strength?), and stuck it in to Vitaly's hands.

The former captain grabbed on, Andrey is pulling him, there is only the sound of their sinews shaking.

Together they overcame the quagmire and Brother Vitaly was back on firm ground. The monks rested, prayed, washed themselves and had to go on. They equipped themselves with a pair of long staves, and made their way mound to mound, or elsewhere walking on branches, and got across the swamp. Verily, the black death had stared them in the eyes.

The sun was setting when the monks came out of the birch trees. They could see the monastery in the distance, if only they could make it before vespers. The travelers cheered up, only too soon. Misfortune does not come alone, rather visits man in pairs.

No sooner had they stepped on the unharvested field that the Tatars captured them. Brother Vitaly tried to run with nowhere to go. They threw a lasso and tied him up like a calf. In front – a young Tatar with a fiery steed, dressed richly: probably one of the younger nobles. With him, kunaks – friends as we say; behind – nukers, or low rank warriors, in hats with fox tails. Their eyes are all narrow and angry.

"What do you have in the bags?" asked the prince in Russian.

Death does not strike twice, and the one time you cannot escape it. Andrey untied the bags and took out what they were carrying: bread, an icon, a pair of onions, underwear – nothing interesting to Tatars. The purse was not there.

"Where is the money?" yelled the noble. "We know about everything, we have an informer in the Kremlin. Give us the silver!"

"That nun," gritted Brother Vitaly through gnashed teeth.

"Did you hide it? We are going to torture the old one now, give him a cruel death – while you watch him."

Nukers dragged Brother Vitaly to two birches on the edge of the forest. They bent the young trees down to the grass and tied a lasso around them so they would not bend back. Then they tied Brother Vitaly by the legs to the treetops. After that, holding the birches by the lasso, not letting them unbend, they waited for an order.

"I do not want your insignificant lives, what I need is the Metropolitan's silver. Where is the purse?" hissed the Tatar.

"We do not have anything," Brother Vitaly answered firmly for the both of them.

The noble slightly moved his finger, they let the lasso go a little, the birches unbent a quarter of the way. The monk moaned and hanged in the air above their head, his legs stretched out in a horizontal straight line.

"Well?" the noble repeated.

"Nothing," Vitaly said hoarsely.

The noble gestured with his finger again, they let go of the lasso a little more, the bones started creaking, coming out of their sockets. Vitaly ground his teeth and was covered in a red sweat.

"Well?" the noble lifted his finger.

"Stop, I know where the money is."

Andrey showed them where the agile Brother Vitaly managed to throw the silver right before their capture. One of the warriors picked up the purse from a puddle without getting down from his horse.

"Why did you not tell us right away? Instead, you just infuriated me!" the noble screamed and drew his curved saber from its sheath.

"My death is here," – Andrey had time to think as he said good-bye to life, kissed the 'Trinity'. "I cannot escape this cup," he remembered, looking at the cup he painted in between the angels.

The noble's steed was circling in place, while the Tatar searched for a way to chop down the monk and the icon in one strike; he lifted his saber and it came down in a glimmering arc onto the icon and Andrey's head.

The Damascus blade shattered to pieces, the Tatars screamed wildly among themselves. The noble's steed got up on its hind legs and sped away like an arrow, along with its rider. Kunaks and nukers rode after him.

*   *   *

When he came to, Andrey took Brother Vitaly down, set his bones as best he could, and lifted him up on his shoulder.

It was already getting dark when they made it to the monastery. All the brothers were on the walls, ready for a siege. In front of the locked gates, on his knees, stood the Tatar noble – barefoot, just in his shirt, a long whip tied around his neck. His eyes could see God's angels of the Heavenly host.

"Brothers, let me join you or kill me."

The Nymph of the Source

Vitruvius' head hurt, the ninth cup of Falerine was one too many, but Tranqueville insisted on the number of muses. Yesterday's dinner turned from a friendly gathering into a wild feast, like that of a freed, rich man.

Extravagant Fortuna suddenly smiled on honest Tranqueville; the Senate appointed him to the title of Curator Aquarum, overseeing all the plumbing in Rome. A golden spot, with it the rank of senator, but also an enormous responsibility. He said that he would exert the greatest of effort, so that the street pools will have running water day and night. Vitruvius, the chief architect of the Roman aqueducts, thus became the subordinate of his friend.

Yesterday Tranqueville looked happy, and ordered instead of the usual three courses, seven, and turned the dinner into a gastronomical marathon, into gluttony. Perpetually, they brought out silver platters: had to eat boar, rabbit, pheasant, ham, flounder, chicken, oysters, agaric mushrooms, pies with nightingale tongues, fruits and sweets. Everything was irrigated with heady wine. The wine scoop – oinohoia, went around the table without stopping. The slaves would take away the low tables, along with the utensils, and bring new ones, so as not to distract the guests, who were entertained by musicians, jesters, and acrobats. The host even paid for a few hetaerae, so as to shine before his friends. The triclinium was filled with noise and laughter; there was no opportunity for the typical Socratic symposium.

Vitruvius did not like feasts on account of their excessive eating, overflowing libations, and dissipation of morals. In the morning, the architect needed a clear mind, an accurate memory and a peaceful spirit. How could he do complicated mathematical equations, draw floor-plans or mark the ground for construction, when he spent the night drinking and partying, and in the morning suffered from a hangover?

When it came to his dinner, Vitruvius limited it to three hours, and, ideally, with the fewest possible guests. "No less than three, like the Graces, and no more than nine, like the Muses," – Vitruvius grinned at the country saying.

Yesterday was a stuffy evening. Warmed up by the food, wine and spectacle, the guests were sweating heavily in their lodges among the pillows and brightly colored fabrics. The servants covered them with blankets, syntheses, "...so the hot draft would not pierce to the bone."

That morning, Vitruvius went to the thermae, the best way to clean the body and bring his thoughts in order. He lived on the shore of the Tiber, near the Marcille Theater. The Forums of Caesar and Augustus were a stone's throw away, and behind them, the thermae.

The streets, temples, porticos and shop-stands, were overfull from morning on. "There are about a million people living in the city counting the visitors," Vitruvius reckoned, making his way through the multi-ethnic crowd. "Over a third of them, that is about 300,000, go outside daily and try, of course, to get to the center. Soon the streets will become too narrow. We will have to rebuild the city."

The Subura Street led out to the new luxurious thermae, finished two years ago. Vipsanius Agrippa, friend and associate to Emperor Augusts, gave them to the Romans free of charge. "He set a good example, the other rich people should build more places for public needs," Vitruvius thought to himself while undressing in the apodyterium.

He stood a while, acclimatizing to the bath house

atmosphere, in the warm tepidarium, and finally washed of yesterday's sweat in the hot water of the caldarium. Then he freshened up with the cold water from the frigidarium, and only after these ceremonies went on the heated mosaic floor into the laconicum filled with dry steam - the main space of all thermae. Vitruvius blissfully closed his eyes, stretching out on the marble bench. His headache passed. Now he could think peacefully.

There was much to think about: Emperor Augustus entrusted him, the most educated architect and military engineer, to make a unified work of architectural art. He must draw on all the achievements of Greek and Roman builders, write down and explain for future generations the chief principles of designing temples, fortresses, government buildings, and private residences, as well as those of city planning, water-delivery, lighting, defenses against malaria and many other things.

After the heat of the steam-room, Vitruvius took a dip in the pool with cold water, swam for a while, and went out into the sun-drenched courtyard – peristyle, where sport-lovers were exercising. Vitruvius stretched using his military gymnastics, played some ball. He decided not to fence or spar, the war wound in his left shoulder was bothering him – a souvenir of the Gallic War, when he served under the command of the divine Caesar.

During those campaigns, Vitruvius built catapults, ballistae, scorpios, walking towers, and many other machines designed for castle sieges, propelling stones, flaming sap, and arrows the size of a man. He needed perfect hearing to accurately tune the ropes on both shoulders of a catapult, otherwise the stone would not fly straight and go to the side. His developed musical ear would later help him build theaters, calculating their acoustics and installing resounding vessels. "And the knowledge of Pythagorean philosophy of numbers," - added Vitruvius out loud, settling in the laconicum with healing steam.

"The architect is the most educated person in society," Vitruvius was thinking about a chapter from his book. "Mathematics, astronomy, philosophy, history, drawing, sculpture, medicine, economics, mechanics – without these sciences, one cannot imagine an erudite architect."

Thoughts came easily in the thermae. It was rare good luck that there was nobody he knew around, the usual din of conversation did not distract him. Vitruvius had collected a lot of material for his undertaking: drawings and drafts for all the main buildings in the civilized world, plans and cross-sections, classifications of building designs orders, examples of wall decorations. He also added didactic stories, anecdotes from ancient authors and from his personal life, philosophical considerations and advices.

"What is missing?" thought Vitruvius to himself, laying down on the table for a massage. Resembling a Cyclops, the massive Abyssinian rubbed his body with an aromatic oil, and then took his time kneading the muscles with his iron fingers, setting the joints, slapping his wide palms on the back, returning flexibility to the backbone, pinching, smoothing, twisting and straightening.

After the torturously-blissful massage, Vitruvius returned to sit in the steam-room. "The scale and form of the building, the décor of the colonnade and entablement, sculpted friezes, the color and ornamentation of the walls, ceiling and floor – all create a harmonious unified system. There are beautiful buildings, and then there are the deformed, masculine and feminine, intelligent and thoughtless. But how do you mathematically explain their character and reveal their hidden meaning? Where is the measure of it all? What is the common denominator for any kind of building?"

Virtuvius swam around in the pool, dried himself and got dressed. He decided to go to the bottom floor and talk to the technician on duty, make sure that everything is in order. The book on architecture took up much of his time, but Vitruvius was still, above all, the chief engineer of the Roman aqueducts, the Senate did not release him of his direct responsibilities.

Vitruvius was rightfully proud of the holding he oversaw. The first aqueduct – Aqua Appia; then – Anio Vetus, named after the small river, built in honor of the spoils from the Pyrrhic War. Then there is the best one in terms of the taste and freshness of the water – Aqua Marcia, which praetor Quintus Marcius Rex commissioned after the victory in Carthage. Add to that the last plumbing project of the Republic – the Aqua Tepula and two new ones – Aqua Julia and Aqua Virgo.

A thousand stadiums from the city, the aqueducts gathered water from the mountain rivers and cool springs. The water ran through stone channels, covered from the sun, over the fields and forests, around mountains or through them in tunnels, bridging across rivers and ravines, to arrive in Rome clean and clear.

In the city, every aqueduct spread underground in many directions through ceramic tubes. The water from different sources was not supposed to mix, because in each stream or spring lives its own nymph. People worship them and make offerings.

Rome is full of richly decorated wells, fountains and pools; water always flows free from them. The splashing of fountains, the sound of the spring, is the general background to Roman life. The simple needs, as well as the splendor and luxury of the capital, gulped down an ocean of water daily. Hundreds of workers under Vitruvius' command looked after the aqueducts, fixing and cleaning them.

Vitruvius talked to the technician on duty, a former comerade-in-arms. The new thermae were working wonderfully. The customers above had no idea how many slaves were working beneath the mosaic floor. In general, they did not find it interesting, the slaves were created so as to service the Roman citizens.

Heading for the exit, Vitruvius heard from a secluded corner a giggling laugh and a woman's squealing. Somebody was singing happily:

"Baths, wine and love ruin the body's strength -
But then life's purpose is in baths, wine and love."

Freedom of morals always reigned in the thermae. There was no division of men and women in the baths; the voluptuous Romans would never have allowed such a thing.

After spending half the day in the thermae, Vitruvius got hungry. Quintus Horatius Flaccus, a famous poet, through the windows of his home, looked out on the roofs of the thermae. He always complained about the noise and screams below, which never let him sleep, still he did not wish to trade his home in the middle of the city. Vitruvius went to him right after the thermae. Horatius was getting ready to dine and was excited by the company of his old friend.

How much the modest meal of the poet differed from yesterday's feast! Fresh greens, cheap lettuce, cabbage, beans, brine from tuna fish, grilled goat, and for desert – grapes, dried melons, apples, a glass of Nomentum wine. What more could you wish for?

Across from the triclinium where the guests dined, Horatius installed a mosaic nymphaeum – a home sanctuary. From the bronze fountain in the wall burbled water and ran down the steps into a small round pool, covered by white lilies. The poet knew how to decorate his home with taste!

Arriving in Vitruvius' footsteps, came Dionysus, a learned Greek from Hellicarnasus, who recently came to fame through his book on rhetoric "On the joining of words." The three of them talked about the Stoic philosophy, Dionysus classically declaimed the "Illiad," Horatius read the loved-by-all "I created a monument, of firmly poured bronze…" which he dedicated to Melpomene, the muse of tragedy.

The dinner was praiseworthy. Vitruvius was thinking about leaving, but the host made a sign, and a musician with a reed flute entered the triclinium. His way of playing was enchantingly simple. The melody spun like the thread of Parcae, sometimes in a straight line, other times in intricate locks. "Probably the sacred music of the East," Vitruvius thought to himself.

The nymphaeum's surface covered by a sheet of white lilies shuddered, and from under it rose a beautiful woman's head with a thread of river gems in her hair. The nymph of the source! Dionysus and Vitruvius looked at the miracle wide-eyed.

The nymph stood up to her full height, the petals of the lilies sticking to her naked body. She graciously stepped into the center of the room and started her dance. Horatius was smiling broadly, enjoying the created effect.

Vitruvius traveled a lot in his life, with the army as well as by himself, studying the architecture of different countries. He had been to Greece, Gallia, Spain, Germania and to Africa, where he saw the dances of many cultures. His trained eye quickly recognized where a performer was from, or where they learned to dance. Horatius' dancer puzzled him, certain moves were Etruscan, others Greek or Libyan, some turns and bends were German, while the spins Egyptian.

Where does Horatius find slaves like this? Overall, Emperor

Augustus liked Horatius' poems, while Gaius Cilnius Maecenas, a rich noble and close friend of the Emperor, supported the poet.

The dancer moved lightly, almost weightlessly. It seemed like she enjoyed the dance, as if there was no one in the room except her and the music. The slave put three swords on the floor, point upwards. The tempo sped up, the dancer spun between the glittering edges, flying over them, doing cartwheels, bridges and other tricks.

Vitruvius looked at her ankles. He remembered seeing these slender legs. Narrow heels, a high arch, perfect calves, elegant knees, smooth hips…

On his way home, Vitruvius thought about the dancer. How skillfully Horatius set everything up! There is probably a secret hole through which the slave-girl snuck into the pool. But where had Vitruvius seen her before?

From the doors of the tabernas, through the windows of the multi-apartment insulae, one could hear singing and laughter. Rome never slept. The streets were filled with stumbling wanderers, questionable transactions, the sound of the night watchmen's thick-soled sandals and clanging weapons, and the lascivious invitations of cheap women.

Returning home, Vitruvius sat down at his worktable. He could not tolerate disorder in his mind or on his table. The papers were arranged in neat piles, his styluses and quills sharpened, the necessary books on a low ebony table. He opened his journals, they were filled with notes about his old travels, the names of dead friends, drafts of mechanic parts, drawings of fortresses and temples. On other pages – a record of his spending, faces, figures, costumes, fantastic animals and birds, but nothing about today's slave-woman.

Vitruvius opened his old army chest to get the books from the time of Caesar's campaigns – bearded Gaul faces, sketches of his first ballista. Upon praise from Caesar, Vitruvius wrote it down verbatim: "You will soon be in charge of all siege weapons, Vitruvius." The Roman Legions took eight hundred settlements, battling three million people, killing a million, and taking a million as prisoners. Caesar received many spoils of war, but was not greedy – he paid his troops generously, with whom he shared the hardships of military life.

There are the quick sketches of the feast in Lutetia after the peace treaty with the Gaul tribes. Wine cups like barrels, barbarian costumes of leather and fur, thick rings and bracelets on the notable women. An amusing chain wrapped around a woman's leg... Stop! He saw this leg tonight. The slave-dancer!

Vitruvius remembered the feast twenty years ago: the young woman, almost a child, danced for the guests. She was the daughter of one of the tribe's chieftains. Back then Vitruvius did not give her much attention, being in a hurry to draw the faces of the Gaul leaders for his report to Rome.

She had changed, of course. Her hips were wider, her pelvis rounder, her breasts were higher and fuller, her stomach was drawn in. She definitely did not have any children. But how was she enslaved and brought to Rome? Anything is possible in our tumultuous time.

The more Vitruvius thought about her, the more he needed to see her again. By morning, the feeling of necessity to see her again overgrew into a conviction. His inner voice whispered to him that he needed her as something more than a slave or a woman. Vitruvius stood at the threshold of a discovery.

When they decide to do something, Romans act fast. Before the first breakfast that morning, wrapped in a snow-white toga, Vitruvius went to Horatius. The poet liked to take solace in the kingdom of Hypnosis until noon, but was mercilessly pulled out of it.

"As an old friend, I ask a great favor of you," Vitruvius began, as the disoriented Horatius rubbed his sleepy eyes, "Give me your slave-girl."

"I don't want to sell her!"

Vitruvius continued trying to convince the poet until nightfall. Horatius tried to hide, run away, pretend to get sick, but the architect was stubborn. After sunset, Horatius gave up. He understood that, to Vitruvius, the dancer was not just some capricious whim.

Vitruvius put the girl in the room next to the study. He did not know yet how she would help with the writing of the book. It did not make sense to have her do household jobs – that was not the reason he paid Horatius enormous sums. Vitruvius hosted feasts with music rarely. In the meantime the girl was occupied with herself – swimming, putting on creams and perfumes, brushing her hair, painting her nails, plucking eyebrows and body hair. In short, she was doing nothing, lived like a queen, rather than a slave.

Vitruvius accepted her behavior calmly: he did not feel romantic interests in the slave-girl yet. He liked looking at her as she walked, dressed in a light, almost transparent tunic, putting flowers in vases or tastefully arranging the pillows and blankets on the benches and chairs.

The chapter on proportions was not coming out right. Vitruvius spent a long time struggling with it, analyzing facades of famous buildings; he was trying to find a certain numeral, a common denominator for formulating proportions. Certain parts of the theory seemed right. Thus, for example, the height of aqueduct arches or bridges was found in the proportion of the golden section to its width. The height of columns is divisible by the width, this proportion varied in different aesthetic styles. Width, height, multiplicity... What could be considered the universal coefficient for any building? Behind the window glimmered the night constellations.

The melodic clatter of thin bracelets came from the door. The slave-girl looked fixedly at Vitruvius. She was dressed only in jewelry, she held a candle in each hand, which cast a dim orange light. She danced slowly, without rapid movements or turns. The sound of the jewelry was the sole accompaniment.

Vitruvius studied the dancer pensively. A perfect body, intelligent eyes, the shape and size of her head were ideal for a sculpture. "That's strange," Vitruvius thought to himself, "I cannot say what it is that is beautiful in her. She is beautiful in her entirety, without divisibility into parts."

A leg with gold toe-rings made an arch over the worktable and smoothly went higher than the girl's head. A turn, then the other leg repeated the same movement. "The head and leg," sparked a murky enigma.

"Wait!"

The slave-girl, her brows raised in surprise, froze in the uncomfortable position: her left leg lifted above her head, her hands with the candles spread to the sides. One glance was enough for Vitruvius, the size of the foot's sole and the head were the same!

He placed the dancer on a low table, and carefully

measured her until morning: height, the length of her arms, legs, palms, fingers; shoulder-width, hips and pelvis. Then through the day he drew the naked slave-girl en face, in profile, placing the results of his measurements in the margins. He was seeing an order: the height was divisional to the size of the head; all the body parts are in a single system of proportions. He drew the figure into a circle, a square, checking his theory. Apollo himself must have sent the slave-girl to Vitruvius so that the latter could discover the symmetry of the divine harmony!

Vitruvius did not leave his house for several days, his thoughts demanded theoretical development. "Man is proportional, hence it follows that everything he creates around himself, strives towards the same harmony of the human body. Buildings are proportional to man!"

The insight overwhelmed Vitruvius. Emaciated from the work of the past days and nights, he tumbled exhausted onto a bench and forgot himself in a heavy sleep, similar to fainting.

He woke up for a second. His head was resting on the soft knees of the dancer, she was brushing his hair with a turtle-shell comb and sang softly. "Can a mortal encounter absolute beauty," came the thought, "or is that allotted for the gods? My nymph…"

When Vitruvius came to, the nymph (or the slave girl?) was not in the house. The porter said that she was in the garden trimming the roses. But he could not find her anywhere, not by the flowers, nor by the pool, nor in the fruit and vegetable gardens. He went down the narrow marble staircase to the river. The sun was setting, the waves of the Tiber glittered with gold. Nobody. On the last step next to the water lay the familiar tunic.

＊ ＊ ＊

Vitruvius finished his ten-volume work and dedicated it to Emperor Octavius Augustus. It is the only book on architecture to survive the millenniums. At the dawn of Christianity, the Emperor of the Franks and Lombards, Charlemagne, ordered the book to be transcribed and preserved in his palace-library Scriptorium. During the Middle Ages and the Renaissance architects learned from it as from an unsurpassed textbook. Leonardo da Vinci made an historic drawing "Vitruvian Man," draw in a circle and a square according to the proportions of the third volume. Skyscrapers and modern buildings are planned according to the principles outlined by the architect of Ancient Rome.

My wife studied at the Institute of Architecture, copying the designs of antique columns. "Dorian, Ionic, and Corinthian orders," she enlightened me. "Look at the designs of ancient cities and temples, read about how they were built," and she opened the book with the simple title Architecture. "Vitruvius formulated the concepts: sturdiness, comfort, and beauty. Everything in architecture has long since been discovered. What's left for us to do?"

Djavad

Djavad was lying on a cot in the corridor of the First City Hospital. The noise and hustle of the evening rounds long since ended. The nurse on duty was nowhere in sight – probably sleeping at her table, her head resting in her tired hands. But there is never a total silence in the hospital – you can always hear the creaking of the beds, groan and cries of accidental pain.

The rooms were crowded, so they put Djavad next to the door of the terminal patients ward. When the door opened, it would hit the metal bed-frame. After a whole day of this tapping, his head was splitting with pain, but he could not say anything, his tongue would not work – all that came out was a kind of moan.

After the evening rounds, the movements stopped. Squares of moonlight lay reflected on the floor. "Cerulean Blue" was the color that could capture this light, Djavad thought to himself. He could not sleep because of the pain in his muscles from all of the injections with dull needles.

The heart attack came suddenly, without sign or warning. Djavad collapsed in the middle of a crowded marketplace. At least, the hospital was nearby and the ambulance came fast. The doctors saved his life, but the left side of his body was paralyzed. He could move his right hand a little, and his eyes could still see, which meant he was still able to paint. However, he could not talk or move around on his own.

Djavad spent a long time following the moon, which slowly crawled from window to window. He loved the sun. In the East the sun is everything: life, death, birth, warmth, harvest, drought.

When he was born, his father showed him two coins – one gold, the other silver. The infant stretched out his hand towards the gold one with the winged lion. "My son can recognize gold," joyfully exclaimed his father, the owner of a small shop. "He will be rich!"

Djavad grew up indifferent towards gold. He never built up a fortune, as if money was always walking on the other side of the road. Yet as long as he could remember, he loved the sun, fire and painting.

When he was just a child, he painted a funny horse over the door of his parents' home with house paint. The powers that be have long since requisitioned the house and the shop. A year ago, Djavad walked down the street of his childhood – the horse still adorned the clay wall. All subsequent tenants carefully preserved her through all repairs and renovations.

The sun attracted Djavad since birth, he could look at it for a long time without blinking. In the Absheron Peninsula, the sun was gentle and kind, but could also be cruel and vicious. Djavad liked the contrast of yellow and orange with blue and violet – like the bright sunlight and dark shadows on the dried-up earth, or upon the molten mountains and in the blue depths of the Caspian Sea. "Color is the quintessence of my ethico-aesthetic understanding," he would write many years later in his Declaration.

His studies in the local art-school, plunged him into a liturgical dream, gave him nothing. He had no wish to paint the portraits of the local beys and other party officials.

In his hometown they pointed at him like, at a mad artist. One time, Djavad with his field-easel, instead of taking the easy road, climbed up the sharp side of a cliff overhanging the sea. The rays of the sun played merrily on the turquoise waters stretching to the horizon. Djavad picked up some small stones and painted them different colors. Then he threw fistfuls of them into the waves of light. The stones flew, flashing with fantastic hues, and hit the water in fountains of diamond sparks.

Djavad laughed happily, painted more stones, and with a wide swing of his arm threw them down from the mountain. When he happened to look behind him, he saw a bus filled with painters from the local artists' union who came for outdoor sketching. With bulging eyes, they looked on in puzzlement.

The ways of Asia were crude and simple. As a precaution, the authorities put the young artists behind bars, besides, it was wartime. In jail, the hardened criminals recognized Djavad's otherworldly genius and they took him under their protection. Djavad made remarkable flashes for tattoos – tigers, lions, dragons, mermaids, warriors, and the like. Generations of prison artists copied his designs, from the chest of one inmate to another, from arm to arm, from back to back, spreading to the far ends of the country.

It was in this prison that Djavad read Nietzsche's "Zarathustra."

Gobustan – the east end of the Absheron Peninsula that jutts sharply into the sea. The weather there was severe – broiling heat in the summer and piercing cold in the winter. From the desert across the sea, blows the raging wind Hazri, bending and crippling the trees, demolishing houses, filling water-wells with sand. The cliffs bare the drawings of Stone Age artists, bas-reliefs of animals and gods. At some point, the mountains were under the sea – you could easily find fossils of prehistoric fish, shells and plants.

It was here that Zarathustra composed inspired hymns for the sun a thousand and a half years ago. It was in these parts that the clairvoyant Mani was captured for advocating the initial unity of light and dark, good and evil. His enemies flayed him and nailed the skin of the philosopher to the gates of ancient Baku. Djavad could see the ruins of pagan temples, sanctuaries of fire-worshipers, and felt an umbilical chord connecting him to this land, soaked in blood, sweat and tears.

On this July midday, ringing from the intense heat, he stood on the stone where Zarathustra once prayed, and exposed his shaved head to the sun. He awoke from the heatstroke in the evening when it got dark and the temperature went down a little. The sun did not kill Djavad, but instead, turned him into a different man.

Art is a religion, and an artist – a prophet, Djavad understood. An artist carries within himself a Divine gift, which he must treasure and serve.

In the dusty faceless town square, Djavad screamed the praises of the Overman and condemned the souls for sale. People turned away from him, there were no friends; his passion for art filled everything around him.

In essence, man is small and weak. Djavad saw the limitation of his art in relation to the images before his eyes. A dim thought about the primordial connection of the artist to the earth, with its history and its people, demanded different methods of expression. It was impossible to solve this problem in the provinces, thus Djavad went to study at the Hermitage Museum.

He spent seven years in the cold and rainy St. Petersburg. He worked as a janitor, porter, and rigger in the famous museum, while copying the masterpieces of old and new masters. The art of the European avant-garde, African sculptures, masks from Oceania, the costumes of Siberian shamans, Azerbaijan miniatures, the heritage of Antiquity and the Renaissance passed through him and melted into an amalgam of the highest caliber.

Djavad spoke to almost no one, living like a hermit in the northern capital on the shores of the Neva River. By chance, at an exhibition "Scythian Gold" in the museum, he met a painter from the underground nicknamed Bream. They became friends in the same strange way as a meeting of ice and fire.

Bream grew up on the borderless steppes, but like Djavad, he loved the mountains of Caucasus, not only the sun-scorched cliffs, but the snow-capped slopes and ridges, reminiscent of bare bodies and soft feminine forms. Three-four months in the summer, Bream worked in construction or harvested crops. The rest of the year, he spent painting in a room that smelled of paint and thinners, in a communal apartment that he shared with his wife and small son.

His wife, a portly, blond housekeeper, fed the emaciated Djavad a rich borsch and sighed sadly, holding her head in her palm. The practical intellect of the wife always led Bream outside himself. He would yell at her for her "kitchen-sausage mentality" and throw her out of the room if she tried to get a word in between the painters when they talked about art. In the end, he left her for an ephemeral poetess. "You will be lost without me," the wife said in pity as she packed her husbands shirts into a suitcase. After that, Bream disappeared somewhere in the Himalayas.

Djavad had few women. Who needs an obsessed painter? He did not go to dances or restaurants, nor to the beach or the movies, either. He did not know how to court women gallantly. Money, to buy flowers or gifts, was another thing Djavad never had. In Caucasus, they would hide women from the eyes of strangers. Marriages were traditionally arranged by the parents, often the young betrothed met each other for the first time at the wedding. Djavad was never considered as a desirable husband, and he did not think about family life.

Djavad returned to Absheron and settled down in a remote place. On an abandoned farm, far away from other people, he made sculptures out of stone, cement, metal and wood; painted frescoes on the neighboring cliffs; laid out mosaics out of multi-colored stones on the sea shore; arranged decorative waterfalls in the nearby stream. The years spent in the village of Buzovni were the happiest and most productive time of his life.

"Mashala! So what was left of all this?" came a coarse voice.

Djavad turned his eyes to look – blocking the window, stood a dark massive figure with short horns on its head and with cleft hooves instead of feet. Shaitan. This was where he found the artist.

"Now, you lie sick and insignificant, while before you screamed about the fire of creation, saying you 'over-saturate the paint and image, overload space, placing mountain upon mountain, regenerate the spirit of titans ...' Be-e-eh. Where are the little pictures that you were thinking about?"

Djavad created many works in Gobustan. His sculptures stood along the roads, on the shores of the sea, atop mountains; his paintings, he hung near wells or from trees, where accidental passers-by could see them. He also kept a number of finished canvases in the shed.

One time, a girl from the neighboring dacha stopped by a painting on an old oak-tree near the painter's hut: a bull, tied-up and knocked-over, fiercely resisting some people with large knives. "Hills, Bull, People," the girl read the title of the painting out loud and looked at Djavad. Their eyes met. Words were superfluous, both could feel that this was fate, kismet, and that they could not hide from it.

In the morning, Djavad buried his creations in a big hole in the field behind his home, made some secret marking on a tree, drew a map so that he would not forget the location, and headed for the city to see the girl's parents so as to ask them for her hand in marriage.

A year later, he came back with his young wife to get the paintings. But by then, the villagers had ploughed the abandoned field to make a vineyard, and chopped down the tree. The map was of no help. The frantic work of ten years was lost to the earth. He had to start everything anew.

"And what did you accomplish? Constantly broke, ordeals around every corner, your beautiful wife scrubbing the floors in offices and rich homes. Nobody bought your paintings, no exhibitions accepted your work, the government labeled you as *socially and politically dangerous*. They would not even let you leave the city. Where is your world fame? Where are your museums and galleries? Zip – and you're gone and so are all your efforts!"

"You lie, shaitan! My art belongs to the world; I am prepared to give away all my paintings for free. People love them. Those who can, give lots of money for them, the poor, give what they can. They do not write about me in the newspapers and journals, but art is much higher than the articles of theoreticians. I paint because art is my life. Paintings are not the reflection of reality, they are reality. My body will die, but my soul will remain in hundreds of paintings. Each one has a piece of me and I will live in them forever. I don't fear death!"

"Ha-ha-ha! Now I will squeeze your heart a little and we'll see what kind of song you sing then ..."

A cool, soft palm touched his burning forehead. "Djavad, don't make a fuss, you shouldn't get worked up," said his wife, his savior. She was by him through all the hard years: his model and muse, goddess and cook, lover and nanny, secretary and diplomat. The silhouette in the night window, grumbling and dissipated.

Djavad got better, his organism, strong since childhood, saved him this time.

Critics consider the years after his heart attack the most important of his career. Paintings came like a stream, rather, like a caravan. Djavad tried to express everything that accumulated in his head and heart: wise men under the plane-tree, cavalry in caracole, processions of courtiers from the East, laden camels, beauties and monsters, giants and dwarves, shacks and palaces, tambourines and tandoori clay ovens – everything melted together in an epic cycle, "In the tints of sungazing."

The Iron Curtain was then lifted a little, and foreign collectors started coming to the country, while the connoisseurs of modern art at home became awakened. A film about Djavad came out, catalogs appeared and albums and articles about his art. Several successful exhibitions were held in the capital. From there, his fame spread to Europe, America and Japan. Towards the end of his years, came this belated recognition. Djavad opened art shows, went abroad, receiving medical care from local doctors.

In his native province, the government listed him as a pride of the nation. His lifetime enemy, a man of the same age, who was once the head of the secret police, and now the undisputed ruler of all the regions, sent him congratulations upon the opening of

the Djavad Museum, trying to bribe the former outcast who had
suddenly become an international celebrity.

* * *

Djavad and his wife were coming back from Denmark after
his exhibition in the Royal Museum. The express train rolled softly in
the cozy countryside through the kingdom of universal prosperity:
idyllic houses on clean lawns, proper cows with bells on their necks,
expensive cars on the roads. In Scandinavia, they readily bought
Djavad's sultry paintings; the Vikings wanted sun and warmth.

Somebody was sitting in the compartment opposite the
reclining Djavad. His wife went to the dinner-car to get some
mineral water.

"Did you forget? Zip, and you're gone and so are all your
efforts?" His heart squeezed.

"I was born and I died in my paintings a thousand times.
This is just another one."

Under the vault of the sky, one of his favorite paintings
gave off steam: a young Djavad holding the reigns of a black stallion;
next to it – a mysterious dwarfian woman with a tambourine. Out
of somewhere, ascended a multitude of paintings – nude beauties,
frameless canvasses of wise-men and prophets, fiery roosters, mighty
bulls, devas, ships on the Caspian and many, many other works. In
farewell, they spun slowly in a circular dance over Djavad's head.

Dark Eyes

Andrew worked as a programmer in the information technology department of one of the main banks in America. He was project manager responsible for switching the bank's system to a new platform, so that clients who used a mobile phone could perform financial transactions from any point on the planet.

The task turned out to be difficult, since he had to provide maximum assurance and safety for all operations. Andrew worked hard day and night, but didn't complain. When he was still in school he decided he wanted to be closer to money, as for computers – they, understandably, were the most promising development in business.

Andrew's family immigrated after World War I from Italy, where they still had distant relatives. The example set by Andrew's parents was not inspiring: his father worked as a flutist in the city orchestra, while his mother taught children piano lessons. He also had an aunt, his father's sister, who after high school left to conquer the theatre scene of New York, and from time to time would still appear in plays, but mainly dubbed voices for cartoons, performed in radio-productions and did other small shows.

Andrew didn't envy the artistic life, nor did he experience any romance for that reason. Seasonal contracts or occasional concerts did not appear to him as stable sources of income. He wanted to buy an apartment on Madison Avenue, a house in Florida, and to retire early.

His career in the bank went by its normal course. Andrew and his group developed new services, built protective firewalls to keep out hackers, and brainstormed other ways to increase the bank's revenue.

In the end of December, the American branches successfully

shifted to the programs created by Andrew's group. On this occasion, the board of directors held a celebratory banquet. Andrew's brigade expected to get distinguished prizes for their percussive work, but what they each received in reward was a baseball cap and a canvas bag with the bank's logo. Andrew accidentally overheard a conversation in the bathroom between two accountants: the higher-ups received astronomical bonuses, more modest bonuses went to the mid-level managers, while Andrew's immediate superior got a five percent salary increase.

His soul was bitter from the festive dinner and unfulfilled hopes. Clearly, those in charge always grab the biggest slice of the pie, even though all they know how to do is waste paper with their reports and instruction memos. Pity about the guys in the group, without whose heads none of this would have happened.

"Don't be sad," said Alex, a specialist in internal networking. "Let's go have a drink, there's a bar nearby that you might find unusual."

They walked down evening Broadway until they reached 52nd street. On the corner of 8th avenue glowed a red neon sign – a shot glass.

"Shot glass it is," elucidated Alex. "The Russian Vodka Room – a Russian bar."

Alex spoke English clearly, without an accent; he had a degree from Cornell with a major in "Computer Science." Andrew remembered someone telling him that Alex's parents brought him from Russia when he was still a child; here he went to middle school and later to the university. He's Russian, now it's clear why they're here.

They knew Alex at the bar and he familiarly greeted the maitre d' – the owner of the establishment, a waitress – a blonde with sumptuous hips and firm breasts, and the bartender – either an Arab or Columbian with a thin black mustache.

"Georgian," Alex replied to the tacit question.

Behind the bartender glimmered a battery of glass bottles filled with vodka and fruit, berries, garlic, cedar nuts, grasses and roots.

"They prepare their own infusions. Come on! Let's start with the cranberry one for an aperitif."

Andrew, following Alex's example, downed the shot in one gulp, three times bigger than a typical "shot" in other bars.

"Another right away," encouraged Alex.

Drink. They poured ruby-red vodka from a small decanter, sweet to the taste and without the smell of alcohol.

"To health," Alex made a short toast in Russian.

The chest got warmer, the soul – lighter.

The bar was filling with people: Slavic beauties with deep decollates smiled beckoningly, in ultra-short skirts and high heels; solid men in black leather jackets and short hair loudly discussed their dubious affairs; elderly Don Juans with thick gold chains around their necks from time to time took out wads of cash from their pockets and slowly counted their Ben Franklins.

Behind an old grand-piano, a female pianist in a concert gown played something from the classics. "Tchaikovsky, probably," Andrew reckoned. Men and women greeted Alex who introduced them to Andrew, but the complex Russian names were too much for him to remember. After a hard day and the disillusionment of the corporate banquet, they were both hungry.

"Let's go eat at the tavern over there," proposed Alex, "the Samovar."

Indeed, the second Russian restaurant was just across the

street. The shelves displayed shiny samovars, matreshkas and other such tourist trifles.

The friends were seated on a couch behind a table far away in the corner. Nearby hung a photograph of a bald senior citizen with tight lips.

"Brodsky," clarified Alex, "a famous poet in his small circle."

They were brought salted appetizers – fish, mushrooms, pickles, cabbage, some black and red caviar. They put the caviar on round pancakes, blintzes, which they rolled into tubes. They drank some more vodka, flavored with currant buds. Never in his life had Andrew heard of such novelties.

After the salted foods, they were served a hot red soup with small pieces of beets, then – pelmenie (similar to Chinese dumplings), followed by Arabic shish kabob (mutton roasted on a split). They kept bringing more and more vodka, Andrew was getting tipsy. Alex, however, seemed to get more concentrated and lucid.

In the crammed hall with a low ceiling, a folk ensemble was playing terribly loud – two guitars, a piano and a singer. The music – either heart-wrenching or insanely cheerful – several couples stomped out some wild dances unfamiliar to Andrew.

Across, behind a long table sparked a brief fight: men, heated by vodka, food and native music, started yelling and then swung to hit each other in their red faces. Bottles started rolling, glass shattered, women screamed.

The brawl was soon broken up by the two bouncers, professional boxers, and after a few minutes the instigators, having a drink to peace, were kissing and patting each other on the shoulders.

"They try not to invite the police in here," Alex was calmly observing the fight.

Andrew, bewildered, stared at the exotics. What kind of strange animals are these Russians? It's as if they're from another planet.

"That's how it is," Alex seemed to have read his mind, "each brought his own Zhmerinka.

"What's a 'zhmerinka'?"

"It's kind of like a hole in Ohio."

The singer began a soul-rending song. Andrew figured out that it was not in Russian.

"Sophie can't sing a real romance," swore Alex. "Let's go to 'Uncle Vanya', I heard Vasya the Gypsy is there tonight."

Andrew's head was spinning from all the vodka, loud music and the fatty food with it's mega-calories. Alex lifted him by the elbow and took him towards the exit.

"No-o, Sashka," their way was blocked by a heavily drunk man. "Still doing your electronic rubbish? Did you stop soiling paper by writing poems?"

"Get lost, Yuz," cursed Alex.

"Art comes from the heart, while you're trying to replace poetry with your little wires! You need to turn off your reason..."

Andrew and Alex squeezed themselves between the bar and the drunk and came out into the freezing air. Near the doors, smoking, was a whole crowd of the restaurant's patrons. The mayor of New York, Mark Bloomberg, performed his black deed banning smoking in all public places in the city.

"Nearby, two blocks from here on 54th is another Russian bar. We call it the Bermuda Triangle. It doesn't matter which place is third, in the end something weird always happens, and the going around in circles continues until dawn."

"Of course, if you drink that much vodka," thought Andrew to himself.

'Uncle Vanya' was the smallest of the three places, a former apartment remodeled into a family restaurant. Placards yellow with age, playbills and photographs of actors gave the interior a bohemian-theatrical look.

"Uncle Vanya is the protagonist in a play of the same name by our classic Anton Chekov."

It seems Alex knew more than just Linux and C++.

It was quiet in the room compared to Shot Glass and Samovar. At the round table sat two sultry brunettes with their satellites; a black richly incrusted guitar stood against the wall. A prematurely gray-haired man with rosy cheeks waved to Alex, who came up to greet him.

One of the women, with eastern eyes, looked twenty-five, the second may have been thirty, or forty, or fifty. Andrew had difficulty guessing her age.

"Sisters," whispered Alex. "The younger one used to perform with Vasily, when they were still at the gypsy theatre in Moscow, later they parted ways: she to France, while he came here. Yanka flew to visit her sister Lyuba, the older one. Today they ran into Vasily, something's going to happen! And the guitarist – a legend, there's no one like him."

At the round table they ate, joked, and clinked tall crystal glasses of cognac.

"The morning's foggy, the morning's gray..." Vasily started singing quietly.

"The fields are sad, covered with snow..." joined in Yanka.

The guitarist picked up the vintage instrument with the ornamented front and touched the silver strings. The restaurant went quiet.

Vasily had a beautiful dramatic tenor, while Yanka sang in a coloratura soprano. Andrew didn't understand the words of the Russian romance, he was hearing it for the first time, but he could see that the two used to be in love.

"Remember the many passionate words, the glances we greedily and gently would catch," Vasily's voice grew louder.

"First meetings, last meetings, the favorite sounds of the quiet voice," sadly continued Yanka.

Andrew figured out that to the gypsies song is a kind of mystery: you could feel the fatalism in each note. A gloomy passion hung tensely in the air of the crammed room.

Vasily stomped his foot, the guitarist virtuously strummed the strings.

"Ay da ne-ne-ne-ne-ne!" his voice flew upwards.

"Ay! Ay a-ya-ya-ya-yay!" Yanka answered him, the windows and the glasses on the table started to ring. And so she led with a flexible, pulsating chorus:

"Ay, da gai ya Li_ zka, gai ya Li_ zka ter_ ni, got_ va_ ri, ai, ne, ne, gai_ ya ne, ne, ne."

Vasily intercepted:

"Shel me ver_ sty, shel me ver_ sty, cha_ vo pro_ga_em, ni_ kai pa_ ra pec_ke na_lat_ chom."

"This is an old tabor song 'Shel me versty,'" Alex whispered in Andrew's ear, "I walked many miles."

The square rhythm sped up from the first stanza to the last, turning the song into a dance, into a pagan cult of an invisible deity.

They were competing against each other. The audience

didn't exist to them. Typically gypsies sing in restaurants when they're being paid, professional singers all the more so. Here, the two met after a long separation, meeting as rivals, man and woman. In addition to that, both were taken by curiosity, how well does the rival sing, what did they learn in the past years, are they deserving of their fame.

They were singing in Romani, figuring out their relations. The language is dark and incomprehensible, all interjections and exclamations. They were testing each other on some sort of old unfamiliar public of song. As if someone threw up a flowered shawl: in a sparkling torrent flowed nomadic, ceremonial and wedding songs, jokes, lamentations and farewells (as Alex explained later). Nobody in the restaurant had ever heard anything like that before, nor will they ever hear it again.

Unhurried, Vasily started the song "Give me freedom" in Russian, while Alex tried to translate the meaning for Andrew. The tempo sped up, revealing the dancing essence of the song, gradually the words dropped out until only exclamations and clapping were left. Andrew saw how Vasily, who was lightly rocking from side to side to the rhythm of the song, sprung, clicking his heels, into dance. Yanka, as if her saucy strength broke free, became a whirlwind, her bright skirt flying up into a colorful bouquet.

Alex went into squatting dance, crashing and slapping his palms on his hips, chest and heels. From the far table, tortured by a divorce, sprung up a Russian doctor who came for a conference from the University of Southern California – with him dancing was a spectacular blonde – a top model from Paris, who stopped by for a snack after a difficult photo-shoot. Another woman – a jewelry designer, who spent her day showing her portfolio to a prospective client, grabbed a silk kerchief and spun in self-forgetfulness, as if she was not in the center of Manhattan, but somewhere on the steppes. The guitarist with the imperturbable face did God-knows-what on the seven-string. The second gypsy – the older sister Lyuba, took a swig of cognac and started playing the tambourine. Andrew was lashed by the magical, enchanting events of the ancient gypsy camp. Behind the window, New York disappeared, along with the worrisome resentment of the bank and of tomorrow's meeting, along with past youth and the deserter wife. The frenzied ecstatic dance of the nomads from the borderless Eurasian plains shook the walls of "Uncle Vanya."

She spun round and round, until the gypsy skirts melted into a sheaf of fire, Lyuba deafeningly slapped the tambourine, and immediately the music stopped. Vasily and Yanka laughed and kissed each other. The spell was complete. The small restaurant roared with applause. The Americans who happened by, batted their eyes, unable to understand what they just witnessed.

The gypsies thanked the famous guitarist nicknamed Hlopchik, an English lord, who heard Gypsy music at a ripe age, fell in love with it, mastered the seven-string guitar, and became an unsurpassed performer on both sides of the Atlantic. "Another victim of the Bermuda Triangle," Andrew smiled to himself.

"Dark eyes, passionate eyes..." the older sister Lyuba entered in a thick strong voice.

Vasily and Yanka joined in, harmonizing with her lead part: now they were resting and singing simply for their own enjoyment.

Lyuba, apparently, used to be a superb beauty. The years put small wrinkles around the eyes, loosened the skin around the neck, made her to dye the gray of her hair, but her back was straight, her

legs – slender, her temper – fiery. She held her head up proudly, not afraid of strong makeup, massive rings - the kind preferred by many gypsies - adorned her fingers.

"How I love you, how I fear you, know that I saw you at the unkind hour," Lyuba led the romance.

Andrew had heard this song on the radio performed by Pavarotti, Domingo and Carreras. He didn't understand the words, but who needs them! A light chill passed over his skin: Lyuba was looking only at him. Her enormous black eyes devoured Andrew. A mighty power flowed from the gypsy's glance, pulling like a magnet. Andrew absorbed the music, it mixed with his blood, turning off his intellect.

"This is not possible, this is hypnosis or sorcery," he thought dismissively. "How she's tightening a noose around the heart. The Bermuda Triangle indeed."

"Gild my hand, darling," Lyuba was standing nearby and held Andrew's hand in hers.

He didn't like fortune-telling. First off – it's lies, secondly – also, third – how can you verify it with the future, and where will you find the gypsy if her prophesy isn't fulfilled? Andrew didn't say anything, he just swallowed and opened his left palm.

"Eh-eh, darling, I see that you don't see your own life," Lyuba was speaking with a strange accent. "Here, the line goes to the side. You need to change the path you're walking. Life – it's like a heart: it has to beat, not stand still. Listen," the gypsy placed Andrew's palm to her chest.

Andrew felt beneath the black silk blouse an ample soft breast, a hard nipple, and heard a strong heartbeat. He unintentionally tightened his grip. The gypsy, looking straight into his eyes, kissed him with a long open-mouth kiss.

* * *

Soon after that, Andrew went to Milan to install new computer systems in the Italian branches of his bank. By day he worked studiously, but in the evenings and on the weekends he took operatic vocal lessons with a teacher from La Scala Theatre. The cunning Italian, Andrew preferred to hide his secret hobby.

Upon his return to America, he started singing in amateur musicals, then – on the summer stages with seasonal troupes. He sang in a chorus and was an under-study, sometimes replacing the lead when he was sick.

After two seasons he acquired experience and confidence, his repertoire grew significantly. He was now singing in Italian, French, German, English and Russian. At the bank, only Alex knew about Andrew's thespian life.

In the third year, Andrew successfully entered the main cast of a theatre in Baden-Baden, Germany. Not the best theatre, but it was still the start of his solo career.

So, Andrew quit the bank and for his farewell invited Alex to "Uncle Vanya." They drank and ate.

"Gypsies love rings, but the rings aren't plain…" sang Andrew in Russian almost without an accent and took from his pocket a velvet box. Inside – a gold ring with a black diamond.

"Please give this to Lyuba. Tell her that her fortune-telling was right."

Butterfly

When his mother would play the piano, little Sergie would listen to her, sitting curled up in a ball on the deep leather couch. The sounds from her fingers came out in streams, overflowing into the sun in all the colors of the rainbow. Music seeming like magic.

Sergie couldn't understand how such beautiful music could come simply from the fingers pressing upon the keys. Several times he secretly tried to summon the music out of the piano, but for some reason it wouldn't come out. Quite the opposite, what came were ugly sounds, alone or in crowds when he would slam the keys with all his fingers, his palm or with a fist.

Once his mother caught Sergie hitting the keys, at first she got angry, but then she cheered up when he told her that he was trying to call out the music.

"Little one, you can't call out music. Music is performed by musicians and written by composers, who are very talented people. They think up melodies and then people sing and play them. I play the piano, but there are also violins, trumpets, flutes and many other instruments."

But Sergie couldn't understand how it was possible to think up music: there aren't that many keys, and on a violin there are only four strings. The mother tried to teach her son to play the piano, but she didn't have enough time, so Sergie started going to music school. He learned scales and chords, and with other children, he studied solfeggio and sang in the choir. Sergie worked hard in class and at home when he was doing his homework. Hence, he received good grades in school.

"He won't become a concert pianist," his teachers would say, "but he could become a music teacher."

But Sergie didn't want to teach music, he wanted to compose. He was the most diligent student in his composition class: learning harmony and counterpoint, theory and music history. Exercises in composition weren't a problem for him, but there was still no real music. Sergie got disheartened, sitting for long periods at the piano trying to compose. Nothing came out right.

Then one day in the courtyard he met a girl who would talk to him about fascinating things, about mathematics and physics, the cosmos and molecules, Pythagoras and Newton. The girl was pretty, with a long braid and checkered skirt. She gave Sergie "The History of Physics" and soon after, he stopped going to music school.

In those days the youth was more interested in the technical and exact sciences than literature and art. The work of an engineer or programmer was considered more important than that of a painter or actor. Sergie went to a university, defended his doctorial thesis and became a true physicist. For days he would sit in laboratories conducting experiments, analyzing data on computers, he wrote articles for thick science journals and went to special conferences.

After a few years he made a small discovery in his narrow field of physics and he was invited to work at a famous institute where the celebrated Albert Einstein spent the last years of his life. They showed Sergie, now Professor Sergei, the famous chair where the legendary physicist liked to daydream.

So, Sergie went to the institute, continued his experiments, wrote his articles, sat at the meetings of his department and of the Scientific Council, and taught classes. Everything was going well, former classmates have long since envied him. But sometimes Sergie would get bored and gloomy. He started getting depressed, especially after his son grew up and left home to travel around the world on foot.

Thinking about Sergie's melancholy, his wife – that selfsame girl, drove to the store and bought him a cabinet piano. The piano was modern, electric, with timbres and different instrumental voices. Sergie bought himself the notes to several pieces that he studied at some point in music school. Now, he would play a little after working in the lab, remembering the notes, while his wife was cooking dinner or watching TV.

On Tuesdays they held Scientific Council at the institute. However, there was little scientific discussion at these meetings: mostly they talked about the budget, future work plans, and the number of pages in the next compilation.

Sergie sat at the end of a huge table and barely paid attention, while some bearded man with a bald-spot talked about string theory of some sort. "Bass string?" Sergie thought listlessly, staring at a pinhole in the wall opposite him.

The tiny hole began to grow and turned into a circular window, looking out onto the meadow flooded with sunlight, all covered with grass and flowers. On the meadow there were many men and a few women. Most of them were dressed ordinary and bland, but a couple had outfits that seemed carnival-like. All of them had butterfly-nets in hand; they ran around, trying to catch the fluttering beauties. Hanging at their sides, each had a glass can containing their prisoners.

The young man wearing a short doublet turned out to be the most nimble. He happily exchanged smiles with the other catchers, while the butterflies seemed to fly right into his net. Another man with disheveled hair angrily swung his net and plucked out of the swarm the wondrous ones, unlike all the others. A tall big fellow in a powdered wig caught only graceful fliers of deep coloring. These

three had their cans completely filled. The rest of the crowd mostly
had two or three butterflies each.

One, who looked like a professor, with a broad thick beard
and in round glasses tried to catch a fat bumblebee, which flew from
one flower to another or circled around his head.

On the very edge of the field was a young boy in shorts, who
also tried to catch something. His can was still empty. Those more
skillful kept swinging their nets and catching the butterflies before
he could. The boy would get upset, but would patiently continue to
walk about the field. He carefully lifted his net and precisely lowered
it onto the grass. Inside his net was a tiny grayish blue butterfly,
resembling a moth.

Attentive scientist-Sergie observed that the number of
butterflies was dwindling, with no new ones arriving or being born.
This means that given enough time the people with the nets would
catch all the butterflies, the beautiful and the ugly, the big and the
small.

"Professor, are you following my train of thought?" the
presenter addressed him with a grin.

"Yes, of course, it's a very interesting and original thought"
recovered Sergie. Turns out, he was sleeping with his eyes open.

That night Sergie kept turning in his bed. He got up, drank
some water, turned on the television, turned it off, tried reading,
finally, he sat at the piano. He put on the headphones and turned off
the speakers: after all, it was an electric piano.

For several minutes he sat, picking at the keys and playing
familiar melodies. An interesting harmony came from under his
right hand. Sergie, trying to memorize, repeated it a few times and
then added several rhythmic bass notes with the left hand. It turned
out not bad. Sergie developed the theme in different keys, he sped up

and slowed down the tempo. He finished by returning to the simple harmony that he started with. He repeated everything from the beginning: a little simple, but not bad at all. An exact experimenter, Sergie wrote everything down (less than a page) into a sheet-music notebook and went to sleep.

The next morning, on the window of the guest bedroom Sergie noticed a grayish-blue butterfly with emerald spots on its wings caught in the transparent curtains. Where did it come from in November? Perhaps it was hibernating in a crack in the wall, woken by the warm air of the heater? Sergie placed the butterfly in a glass can left over from salted tomatoes and closed off the top with a piece of cheesecloth, so that the butterfly wouldn't suffocate.

At the institute, Sergie tried to find out from the biologists what kind of butterfly it was and what to feed it. The luminaries of the science scratched their tall foreheads, knit their eyebrows, but could not identify the butterfly.

In the evening some friends came over for dinner, Sergie played for them what he had written the night before. Everybody liked the melody and the arrangement.

Before going to sleep, Sergie again sat at the piano. The can with the butterfly stood on the right side atop the instrument. With pleasure, Sergie played his piece from memory, listening closely to each note. Through the corner of his eye, he saw that the fluttering butterfly, disarmed, folded its wings and settled to the bottom of the can.

From the computer came the sound of email and Sergie went to check it. The butterfly started moving its wings again: everything in order.

Sergie played Beethoven's "Fur Elise", getting ready to go to sleep. In the end, he couldn't help himself and repeated his own piece. The butterfly was lying down in the can as if dead, just barely moving its whisker-antennae. Sergie remembered his dream during the Scientific Council. Of course, "thoughts flutter through the air," that's a banal truth repeated through and through in science.

The butterflies – are melodies, chased after by composers! Now everything is clear: the skillful young man in the fancy sleeveless jacket – was Mozart. Sergie remembered Bach also, and Beethoven, and the professor type who tried to catch the bumblebee. That means that the young boy was Sergie himself, back when he used to go to music school!

But what will happen when all the butterflies-melodies are caught, placed in cans, or what's worse, pinned with needles and dried for herbariums or private collections? Frightening to imagine. But then, are Sergie's fatigue and flights of fancy befitting a modern man of science?

Sergie went upstairs to the bedroom, his wife was already asleep with her back facing him.

Again sleep wouldn't come. Sergie twisted and turned, trying to repel troublesome dreams about butterflies and composers, even counted sheep. "Very well" he decided, "let's conduct an experiment."

Sergie went downstairs to the guest bedroom, ripped out of the notebook the page with his composition, lit a match and burned it in the fireplace. Then he removed the cloth covering the glass can. The butterfly continued to lie on its side, wings folded. "We'll wait until morning."

When he was brushing his teeth in the morning, his wife told him that the dead butterfly flew away. "Nothing unusual," thought Sergie to himself. After breakfast his wife left for work, while he stayed at home since his schedule listed today as a research day.

He didn't want to write or read, intellectual thoughts wouldn't come either. Sergie spent some time outside his house, trimming the bushes, sweeping the driveway: dragging out the last stage of the experiment. After lunch he played a game of chess with himself and then sat at the piano.

He opened the sheet music of his favorite Rachmaninoff. Tried to see how the Elegy sounds – not bad. Then – the Punchinello. Pretty good also. Finally, the Prelude in B-minor.

"Opus 23, Number 5," announced Sergie aloud.

He performed the Prelude as he did some time ago at a competition of young pianists, where he received second place. Good.

"And now, Sergey's piece. Opus 1, Number 1," declared Sergie, imitating an emcee.

He went to fix the tails of his imaginary frock coat and artistically lifted his hands. No sound came, Sergie's hands froze above the keys. He couldn't remember a single note.

"It can't be," he said to himself, "there must be something still in my head."

He concentrated and tried again - empty - he couldn't even recall the first chord. Sergie sat for a long time, hoping, perhaps the fingers will remember – after all there is such a thing as muscular memory. The fingers didn't remember either.

For many days, the empty can remained on the edge of the piano.

Talisman

The Cossack fell in love with a Jewess. He did not know how it could have happened. Civil War was blazing around him, rivers of blood flowing, brother against brother, son rising up against father, while he, a Cossack yesaul, has only love on his mind. And for whom? For a beautiful Jewish Sulamif, the daughter of the village tailor.

After hard battles near Tsaritsyn, his regiment was sent to the home front, so they could have a couple of weeks to get healthy, sleep and recover. The regiment was stationed in a small place called Palihino, forty milestones from the nearest train station. All the cities and villages along the train track have already been razed and sacked. Whites, Reds, Greens, petliuravists – were all pillaging, killing and raping.

In the remote places, where the armored-trains' cannons could not reach, small detachments feared to venture and while the big ones had no business there, so life continued glimmering. The peasants ploughed and sowed, raised livestock, even had a few market days.

In such faraway villages, the troops were able to get medical attention and recover their strength for future battles. Though, it's true, they had to keep watch and send out mounted scouts, as the makhnovists could jump out from underground with their machine gun carts. Makhno was fighting against everybody – the Reds and the Whites.

The quartermaster led the Cossack Yesaul to an outlying hut – a cottage of daub and wattle, no better or worse than the others on the street. Without knocking, he opened the door to the well-lit room. A Jewish family rose up as they came in. The father – old, with a long crooked nose, smoothly shaved without peyos, in round black glasses; the mother – a grey haired woman with biblical eyes; and three children: the oldest daughter around twenty years old, with short hair and wearing a faded apron from the Sisters of Mercy; a son – a curly haired youth in a jacket from a non-classical secondary school; and another daughter – still almost a child, in a checkered dress.

"Jewish Ladies and Gentlemen," loudly declared the quartermaster, "the youngest Yesaul of our regiment will be boarding here, a hero and a great swordsman. You won't mess around with him!"

The quartermaster saluted the Yesaul, clicked his heels and went on with his work. The family remained in a quiet state of fear, the daughters pressing against their father.

The Yesaul put his backpack on a chest near the door, removed his saber, sat on a worn chair and looked around. There were several yellowed photographs on the walls, an old harmonium, a darned tablecloth, simple benches along the windows. In the red corner – a small icon of Archangel Michael. The Yesaul crossed himself.

"Are you Christened?"

"We took up Orthodoxy a year ago, on the day of Archangel Michael. Now he is our protector," the father explained in an unconfident voice.

"Were there pogroms?"

"Two. One in March – petliurovists. They took everything – money, clothes, food... They whipped me and my son Moysha with ramrods, as well as Rebecca, that is Katerina, who they beat before our eyes..."

"They raped her," the Yesaul thought to himself.

"...they did not touch the older Sophia – she was lying unconscious from typhus. But then a week later, the officer corpus conquered this place back. They whipped my son and me with ramrods again, and six of them together beat my wife and Rebecca. The poor child can't talk anymore, her tongue is paralyzed," tears streamed from under the old man's glasses. "They beat Sophia too, even though she was lying in a fever. They hoisted me up by the neck, demanding money. But where would we get money? The petliurovists took everything. That was when they pocked out my eyes and said that they will kill me, if we do not find ten thousand pre-war rubles. Ten thousand – an enormous sum! You could buy a fine cow with that. The wife begged the noble officers to let her go to the neighbors. The neighbors are Christians, kind people, we knew them for many years, they lent us the money. That was how we were saved."

An oppressive silence hung in the air.

The Yesaul got up from his chair:

"And the icon did not stop them... as long as I am here, there will be no more pogroms, but for aiding and abetting the Reds is punishable only with death by firing squad."

The Yesaul settled in the small room with a window overlooking the garden. Compared to the front, his life now was more like a resort: easy patrols, checking posts, and the rest of the time – eating, drinking, sleeping, walking around, breathing fresh air.

One time after his morning checkups, the Yesaul sat down with a book on a bench in the garden. It was getting hot so he was dressed like he was at home, in a shirt and riding breeches. The ground nicely cooled his bare feet. Apples were ripening over his head, their honeyed aroma almost made his head spin, which was tired from the thunder of artillery and endless nights. Bees buzzed peacefully, as if there was neither war nor revolution.

"What are you reading, Sir Yesaul?"

The Yesaul lifted his eyes: in the depths of the garden near the raspberry bushes stood Sophia with a bast-basket filled with ripe berries.

The Yesaul got a little embarrassed:

"A volume of poetry by Sir Nadson."

"How is it you came to know Nadson's poetry?"

"You see, my father is a simple Cossack, did everything in his power to give me an education, so at least one member of our family would make it into the 'proper' society. I had time to finish high school and was accepted to St. Petersburg University. From there, in 1914, during my second year, I left for the front as a volunteer. I've been fighting ever since, but the compositions of Sir Nadson have always been deeply sentimental to me."

"Oh, you lived in Petersburg? How interesting! Tell me, have you ever met Valery Bryusov or Vyacheslav Ivanov or Alexander Blok?"

"No, I haven't had the occasion."

"What about Andrey Bely or Igor Severyanin?"

"I heard Mr. Severyanin once in concert."

"How fortunate for you! Oh how I love his:

"When the steel dream descends upon the lake

I am beneath an apple-tree with a sick girl

And full of delicacy and tender yearning,

I kiss the fragrant leaves" finished the Yesaul. "I have his Cups of Thunder, I can lend it to you."

"Thanks," Sophia said with downcast eyes. "It's been so long since I've read poetry."

The Yesaul usually dined in his room, eating kasha and drinking tea. He came to eat at different times of the day – depending on his duties, but before it got dark, after his rounds, he always came home to the Rosenblooms – the family name of his hosts.

Spending the evening alone is boring, moreover, his hosts, though Jews are nonetheless Orthodox Christians. So it was, in the evening, everyone would gather around the samovar. Moysha would have been happier to sneak out, but he could not be seen outside on account of the curfew, though his father ordered him not to anger his guest either.

After an "Our Father" everyone crossed themselves under the watchful eye of the Yesaul and drank tea with snacks and sugar, with ring-shaped rolls or simply with bread, talking unhurriedly.

Old man Rosenbloom used to be a tailor, worked on his Singer sewing machine, making coats and jackets, breeches and pants, dresses and sarafans. He had a good clientele from ten miles around. Blind, he now relied on his wife and daughters. Sarah, his wife, toiled in the kitchen and garden and went with the other peasant women to the market trying to sell some of her homegrown vegetables. A long time ago she used to play the harpsichord, but over the hard years of war and revolution, she forgot all the notes.

The older daughter Sophia finished her coursework as a nurse in Kiev, and was now helping in the regiment's sick quarters. The younger Rebecca, which they continued to call her within the family, was stiff with fear at first upon seeing the Yesaul's epaulets and saber, but gradually, she stopped being afraid, and just looked around with her huge eyes, listening to the adults' conversation.

The Yesaul did not like Moyshe. He saw how the young Rosenbloom bit his lip when the Yesaul described the planned post-war organization of Russia. The Yesaul stood for the monarchy, as the most traditional and native form of government over the Russian people. It felt like Moyshe was ready to argue, but was held back by the presence of his father and fear for his family.

Talk of politics went past Sophia's ears: she just kept looking at the Yesaul. A tall blonde man, with grayish-blue eyes, medals and honors on his chest, his moustache carefully trimmed. His figure – thin, but strong. Sophia watched as the Yesaul showed how to slice a vine at full gallop: faster and better than anyone else in the regiment. "How fortunate that such an educated officer is living with us," Sophia thought to herself, "not like the other Cossacks – rude and already bored from doing nothing."

The sunset burned beyond the village fence, any minute now it would be dark. From the street came the sound of bare children's feet, ringing voices and a hoarse laughter.

"Who goes there?" yelled some drunken Cossack. "It is I – Pete Hramov, Tsar and God!"

"The Lieutenant," the Yesaul said, sipping tea from a saucer.

"And where are the Jews who live here?" bawled the Lieutenant. "I have an itch to look at them and pinch their sides!"

There came the whistle of a saber and the sound of a fallen branch.

"Here, uncle, here," came a child's laugh.

The Rosenblooms got quiet out of fear.

The Yesaul stood up from the table, brushed some bread crumbs into his hand and sprinkled them into the cat food bowl, went into his room, came back out, holding his sheathed saber in his hand, opened the door and went outside.

The Rosenblooms did not see what happened, but a minute

later, the Yesaul was leading the arrested Lieutenant with his hands tied behind his back.

"The Cup of Thunder," which the Yesaul gave to her, Sophia read, or rather swallowed it whole. It was as if she plunged into the pre-war life, faraway and irretrievable. The author of "The Cup," Igor Severyanin, was the idol of many young women and female students; Sophia was no exception. Some journals with literary novelties made their way to the village; Sophia had many pages of poetry memorized.

The Yesaul just had two books with him – Severyanin and Nadson. Talking about them, discussing poetry, reciting their favorite poems from memory, the Yesaul and Sophia met in the garden more and more often. What else does a young officer and a poetic girl need? Love, of course, sparked between them like gunpowder.

Sophia's younger sister gave her cunning looks, her mother kept a doleful silence, Moysha spit from indignation, the father tried to talk to her about it – but she refused to breach the subject.

The regiment was called back to the front. The Yesaul was sitting in the garden, polishing his saber. Sophia quietly stood in front of him:

"What will become of us?"

"I will come back for you when the war is over. We will get married."

"And if it never ends? Or drags on for ten or more years?"

"England and France are helping us: by winter we'll be in Moscow."

"And what if they kill you? I will surely end my life!"

"They won't kill me. Look here," the Yesaul showed her the hilt of his saber.

Sophia bent down to have a closer look. Embedded next to the sword knot was a golden Imperial: a coin of ancient craftsmanship – the profile of Emperor Alexander I, and on the perimeter – tiny diamonds. Such a beautiful thing!

"My great-grandfather received it from the hands of Emperor Alexander for distinction during the taking of Paris in 1814. Since then, all the men in my family are named Alexander, in honor of the Emperor-Protector, or Vladimir, Great Prince, Equal-to-the-Apostle and the baptizer of Russia. The Imperial is given from father to son in my family for over a century. As long as it's with me, nothing bad will happen. Besides, every man in my family died only after having a son. While I am not even married yet!"

Sophia rubbed the coin; the calm confidence of the Yesaul spread to her.

In August 1919, central command moved the regiment into the cavalry corpus of General Mamontov. With a wild attack, the corpus broke through the South front of the Red Army and went deep into enemy territory. The Yesaul, when he could, sent news to faraway Palihino: alive… fighting… victory soon.

The Mamontov's Cossack raid through the Russian provinces sent a wave of panic on the front. Bolshevik's government was getting ready to flee abroad. The corpus took Tambov. The Cossacks never saw spoils of war comparable to that of Tambov, in all of their history since the time of Zaporozhian Sich. They captured the city treasury - sixty million rubles; mountains of gold, silver, jewels, taken by the Bolsheviks from the nobles, merchants and churches, which the Reds did not have time to send to Moscow. A gigantic wagon train stretched for sixty miles. General Mamontov could not advance with such a load, so he turned back south. The opportunity to take Moscow was missed.

The Yesaul ordered a load of books to be sent back to his native Cossack village. His father, in turn, sent him in response a lash, that is, "I'll whip you out when I see you."

In October, the First Cavalry Army of Budyonniy took back Voronezh, and the military fortune of the Whites turned around. Through many battles, the Yesaul's regiment retreated from central Russia to the South. Morale was dropping because of all the misfortunes and defeats. Dejection and hopelessness could be read on many faces. Lieutenant Hramov led his squadron towards the Russians. From a regiment of a thousand and a half blades, barely four hundred remained.

In the cold February of 1920, they returned to the place where they spent the last summer. The only things left of the village were a couple of stone chimneys surrounded by ashes. There was not even anyone to ask about the Rosenblooms – all the inhabitants left or were hiding somewhere.

From a distant copse roared a three-incher. The shell exploded behind the burial mounds, then came the neighing of horses and the screams of the wounded.

"Fourth, fifth, seventh squadrons, sabers – drawn!" hoarsely ordered the old colonel. "Take no prisoners. Attack!"

The depleted squadron turned around in battle formation and rushed on the frozen, lightly snow-covered, ground towards the

Red cavalry. The Yesaul, along with his fellow country-men, stayed with the colonel. From the hill, they could see how two avalanches of riders smashed into each other: one – in lambskin Cossack papakha hats, the other – in sharp-pointed cloth helmets with red stars.

A saber battle! Lucky was he who came out of it alive, let alone with all his limbs intact. This time the regiment's enemy was not a bunch of Tambov men, who someone armed with a saber and dropped on a horse – these were Cossacks like them, who knew how to ride, shoot and wield sabers since childhood.

The Yesaul lifted the Zeiss binoculars to his eyes. Messengers kept riding up to a cavalryman in a black leather coat with a crimson sash on his chest. He gave orders, once dashed in attack, leading others after him and then returned to his post that was behind the fight, next to the trumpeter and standard-bearer with the red flag.

"Colonel, sir. Allow me to take the Commissar down?"

The colonel was looking through his binoculars in the same direction:

"Enter through the hollow behind him, there is almost no snow there. But be careful, Yesaul, I still need you alive."

"Yes, sir! Squad one, follow me!"

In a wide gallop, the Cossacks flew down the hill in a long curve and rode to outflank the Reds.

They came out of the narrow hollow like a bunch of devils, easily overpowering the nearby cavalry; they made their way into the thicket of the red stars. The enemy hurriedly turned around to change formation, but the Yesaul did not stop the swinging of his saber, going for the one in the black leather coat. Two Cossacks covered him on each flank, while he cleaved, wedged, and pushed forward.

The Commissar was close, the trumpeter and the flag-bearer next to him. The Commissar ineptly wiggled in his saddle, a Mauser in one hand, the reigns in the other.

Two of the Cossacks protecting the Yesaul were chopped down; the third was shot off his horse by a bullet.

"The red bastards," cursed the Yesaul, "now to get rid of the Commissar, and this will all be over!"

The trumpeter ran towards the Yesaul with a pike in his hand. The Yesaul deftly dodged it and chopped off his foolish head, which bounced and rolled on the uneven ground. The standard-bearer took a carbine off his back, but the Yesaul had already lifted his saber over the Commissar, who was cowering on his horse. Eyes filled with hate glowed from under beneath the cloth helmet.

"Moysha?" the Yesaul held back his saber for a moment.

The Commissar fired without aiming. The Yesaul's wrist burned as his shattered saber flew to the side. The bullet from the standard-bearer's carbine hit him in the chest and the Yesaul fell onto the snow, under the horses' hooves.

The fluffy snow fell slowly, covering the field in a white shroud. The violet twilight thickened. Sounds were barely audible, as if through cotton.

"Why didn't he chop you down? I saw how he held back his hand."

"He recognized me, comrade Hramov. And now he's paid with his contra-revolutionary life for the battle against the working class."

"Well, well…"

It took the Yesaul a long time to recover. He lay unconscious for several weeks, then mumbled, struggling with a fever. Sophia did what she could: changing bandages, soothing him, praying. There was no medicine, only the grasses she had collected in the summer.

She found the Yesaul the night after the battle and dragged him on a mat to the dugout, where she lived with her father and sister: having buried her mother in the end of autumn. The dugout was cramped, like a burrow, and dark. The homemade oven made a lot of smoke and every night threatened to poison everyone with charcoal fumes.

"This is nothing, daughter," her father would say, "God will help us and provide."

With his long gray beard and wild long since unwashed hair, he resembled an Old Testament prophet. He did not live till spring, following in his wife's footsteps. When the first snowdrops appeared in the steppes, the Yesaul opened his eyes and asked for some food. Sophia joyfully crossed herself: "He'll live!"

The wound in his chest closed slowly. The bullet went through the top of his lung and exited through his shoulder blade. The Yesaul was tenacious; otherwise there is no explanation for the miracle that healed him. Probably, generations of warriors created a unique breed of people, steadfast in hardship, and reliant only on their organism in healing wounds.

The Mauser bullet, which knocked out the saber, shattered the hilt and imprinted the Imperial into the Yesaul's palm. His wrist was healing, and Sophia hanged the coin around his neck.

Towards the end of June, the Yesaul started going out of the dugout. He sat on a hill, looking into the distance; the wind blew through his hair, which had grown to his shoulders, like a priest's. The younger sister Rebecca would sit next to him and play with her dolls, made out of multi-colored patches, moaning something to herself under her nose. Thus they sat days on end, the sick and the crippled. But Sophia was happy; at least they could watch after each other.

The Yesaul tried to pull himself out of his soul's paralysis and started remembering poems, which he once knew. He recited them in a quiet voice, looking at the horizon.

Sophia spent her days looking for food: gathering roots, and bringing seeds from the old garden to start a new one. Once, coming back from the remote farmstead, where she worked as a day laborer, she heard a child's voice, absurdly but touchingly saying:

"Her law whas ard for ard's sake,

Her commindmint, to surve beauty."

Sophia went down to the ground and cried from happiness.

In the fall, when the last Wrangel troops left Crimea, while the Yesaul almost completely recovered, a mounted patrol stopped by the dugout. A mop-haired boy, a pioneer and an informer, sat behind one of the Red Army soldiers.

"Comrade Rosenbloom, it has been brought to our attention that you are harboring a White officer."

* * *

They gave the Yesaul twenty-five years without parole, then another three years when he tried to escape. After his sentence, they chose where he lived and limited his civil rights.

They set him free on a frozen morning. The white snowy Kazakhstan steppe glimmered in the sun.

"Look, Yesaul, don't go against Soviet power again," the camp director addressed him in parting.

"Yes sir, comrade Director."

The gates in the camp wall opened.

"Come on, Yesaul, go on. It's ten miles to Akhtyrka, you won't freeze."

The Yesaul squinted his eyes from the blinding light. There were two figures standing in the sunlight – a male and a female. Angels? The young man was wearing a sheepskin jacket and fur boots, near him – a woman in a coat with a lambskin collar and soft felt boots. The woman removed her downy. The head was completely gray. The Yesaul looked in her eyes, which he thought he would never see again.

"Sophia, is that you?"

"Sasha…"

Behind the low windows of the Collective farmer's house – the village hotel, the sun had long since set. In the oven, made out of a steel barrel, burned saksaul. The son, tired from the shocks, joys and disordered conversations of the long day, was in the next room, sleeping the healthy sleep of a young man.

"Sasha, how did you handle everything?"

The Yesaul took from a secret pocket in his belt, a silk bag, from it – the Imperial. Then he took out a magnifying glass from a plywood suitcase and handed it to Sophia. He placed a candle next to the Imperial. The diamonds flashed like a fairy tale, the "Blessed" Emperor looked at them smiling. The Yesaul turned the talisman around.

"Every year, so I would not go mad, I would etch one or two important events here with a needle, so I could tell you about them later."

Sophia bent down low: a Jewish family is standing in a room, meeting the Yesaul; he is with her beneath the apple trees; the saber battle; the Revolutionary Tribunal trial; jail; Solovetsky monastery, turned into a concentration camp; the Vorkuta convoy of thousands who all froze to death along with the guards in the polar night; the Anadyr mines; a mutiny on the prison barge, which sank in an icy strait; a failed escape; solitary confinement; the tractor station; the Kazkhastan steppe.

"Sasha, we will always be together now. They need dentists even out here."

"We will be happy, but what about our son?"

"Volodya waited so many years for you. As an enemy of the people's son, they did not let him have a life: not in exile where he was born, nor later in the cities, where I studied and worked. They would not even take him into the army."

The coals flickered in the stove.

"Do you remember," the Yesaul began:

"When the steel dream descends upon the lake

I am beneath an apple-tree with a sick girl."

"And full of delicacy and tender yearning,

I kiss the fragrant leaves" Sophia finished quietly.

Scythian

In the spring, when the sun shone brightly, and the snow melted on the surrounding burial mounds, and the wind brought the aroma of far-away steppes, the Scythian wanted to die. The spring thunderstorms washed away the dust and dirt of the winter months. The earth stirred, the grasses straightened their stalks and let out pale-green shoots. The warm moist ground, the whispering of the growing grasses, brought his thoughts into disarray, confused his soul, and did not give him a chance to work or sleep. The subtle, barely noticeable aroma drove the Scythian mad. This was the sweet and torturous call of the steppes' feather grass, the silvery grass of his youth and adolescence.

The Scythian liked to gallop across the steppes on horseback without a saddle, with the fresh wind whipping him in the face. When he rode fast, the feather grass blurred into a dense, wavy carpet. The Scythian would laugh from the resilient wind, the open space, his youthful strength and the intoxication of limitless liberty. Freedom! The Scythian loved it more than life itself.

The Scythian no longer has a steed, nor freedom – there is only a metal collar around his throat and chains on his legs. He was sold into slavery as a youth of seventeen years.

The detachment from his tribe trotted in front of the main troops. The plan was that they would attack the Greeks, and then turn around to flee, luring the opponent out of his fortifications. On the steppes, the Greeks would be surrounded by the main force, while a third detachment would storm the fortress.

Everything was going according to plan. After a brief courageous storming, the Scythian's detachment picked up their wounded and retreated into the steppe. The gates opened, and out poured, at full speed Hippeus in flashing armor and helmets, and behind them, marched foot soldiers with spears and shields.

The Scythians rode to the previously designated burial mounds and took a defensive formation, the main force was supposed to be there any minute. The Greeks surrounded them from three sides and rained arrows and darts on them. The numbers were overwhelming, the Scythian and his fellow tribesmen waited for the reinforcements.

An unfamiliar horn blew a signal from beyond the mounds, and the Greeks responded to it. Horsemen, Scythians by the looks of it, were galloping in their direction. "Reinforcements!" someone yelled joyfully. The horsemen flew at full speed, in their hands, short-bows. Twenty steps away, they shot their arrows and cut into the defense of their fellow Scythians, swinging their swords left and right. Treachery! This was how Chigil, the king of the Scythians along the coast, decided to get rid of his relative, who could have become a dangerous adversary.

The Greek phalanx was advancing, cavalry from both sides, archers helter skelter. This was the Scythian's first battle, but he felt no fear. He stood back to back with his father, as they fought with their bows. His father was killed, run through by two spears. The Scythian was out of arrows, wounded in the hip by a dart, and as he was defending himself with his short sword, he was hit in the other leg, but he continued to fight while sitting on the ground. A Greek foot soldier smashed him on the head with a heavy shield, and the Scythian lost consciousness.

The remains of the detachment managed to break through the surrounding enemy, cross the Borysthenes and escape back to their native steppes.

The Greek, whose name was Stratonides, brought the Scythian on a wheelbarrow back to his house. Stratonides' family rejoiced at such a war trophy – a young healthy slave! So he's wounded a little, it'll heal. Normally slaves cost good money, and only the wealthy could afford to keep them.

The Scythian tried to run as soon as he regained consciousness. At night he climbed out of the house, but a block down he passed out again. They found him by following the trail of blood on the ground. Stratonides was not angry or cruel, but according to city law, he had to put a metal collar and chain the Scythian's legs, to prevent any future attempts of escape.

Once long ago, Hercules was passing across the steppes of Taurica on his chariot, and stopped to rest. While he was sleeping, his horses disappeared. When he woke up, Hercules went looking for them. Among the cliffs, he found a cave where Hylea, a lone snake-woman dwelled. Her upper body was like that of a woman, but beneath the fruit, there was a long snake tail.

"I have your horses," she said, "and I will return them if you copulate with me."

Hercules wanted to get his horses back so he entered the snake-woman. She demanded that he repeat the act many times. Satisfied, she was impregnated by Hercules with three children and returned the horses. When the children grew up into men, the snake-woman named the Agathyrus, Gelonus and, the youngest, Scythian.

The Agathyrus people settled up along the River Istros; the Gelonians went to the east, crossed the river Tanais and blended into the blue-eyed and red-haired tribe Budini, the forest-dweller; the Scythians ended up living in the Steppes between Istros and Tanais along the shores of Pontos Euxeinos.

The Scythians were a nomadic people, they did not build houses, nor did they till the land. The felt wagon on wheels served as a mobile home for a family. The only thing they would mark, were the burial mounds, where the Scythians passed. All the tribes worshipped their ancestors and remembered fallen warriors. After death, they would dress up the deceased for life beyond the grave, put his weapons with his body, rations, clothes, killed his horses and wives, so they could serve him there also. Renowned warlords were accompanied into the other world by dozens of bodyguards.

On the right shore of the River Hypanis, not far from the sea, since time immemorial the Scythians met with Hellenes merchants. They traded skins, furs, and grain they got from the other tribes, for goods like wine, weapons, fabrics, and jewelry from distant Greece. The place in Scythian was named Olbiapolis – the land of heroes.

Greeks from Miletos built ship-docks there, as well as shop stands and warehouses, an Apollo Temple and an agora, and raised fortified walls and towers. The town started to grow through trade and craft. The Scythians would buy grain from their neighbors and sell it to the Greeks at a profit. Those in turn sent the grain by ship to Attica.

There were skirmishes and small wars all the time: they would capture slaves, rob, commit arson, kill, and then make peace. The city was re-built. The Scythians brought horses and sheep from the steppes and pitched tents next to the fortress walls. The marketplace came to life as the trading continued.

It was to this city, Olvia, that Stratonides brought the wounded slave; he did not tell him his name. As soon as the Scythian healed, they put him to work taking care of the domestic animals and the two horses belonging to the household. And who could have done it better? Everyone in the Oecumene knows that Scythians were the first people to tame horses and ride on their backs. The Scythian fed the animals and birds, cleaned the stalls, and changed the blankets.

The neighbors, all craftsmen painted fabrics, fired clay pots, and made furniture. During peacetime, the Scythian's owner worked in sculpture, making statues of gods and heroes for the city's temples, bas-reliefs, funeral stelae. Things were not going well – from Athens came beautiful statues, readymade columns, capitals and decorative elements, copied from famous examples in the studios of old sculptor families.

Stratonides was looking for an additional source of income and started making mosaics - if nothing else, they were not yet sending them from over the sea. Out of multicolored stones, he would make ornamented floors, pools and fountains, decorating the walls of temples and rich homes.

Stratonides showed the slave how to cut marble into small cubes the size of a fingernail. From morning to night, the Scythian swung the sharp hammer, breaking the stone over a metal tooth stuck into a wide block. Then, he would sort the stones by color and tone: it turned out that the same piece of marble could be snow-white, grey, and reddish in different parts. The Scythian prepared green, brown and even black marble for his master Stratonides.

They fed the Scythian pretty well – the owners prized the slave. Stratonides had a large family: wife, five children, his old mother, and his widowed sister with two children of her own. The man was stooped under all the responsibilities, and at forty already looked like an old man.

So he would not have to hire expensive Greek helpers, Stratonides started taking the Scythian to the walls more and more often. The Scythian mixed the lime mortar, and later learned to make ornaments out of mosaic, before long making images of animals and birds, dolphins and horses. The Scythian had a fine eye, and was able to repeat a picture from a vase or an amphora after seeing it only once, all the while adding something of himself.

Stratonides did not make mosaics in the winter; the cold made the mortar freeze. He sat at home, bored, endlessly complaining to his pregnant wife and drank wine. There was less work for the Scythian as well.

Since the old days, nomads decorated everything they could. "Though I have few possessions, they are all the most beautiful and precious," – a tent will not hold many goods and chattels. Gold was a metal long favored by the Scythians, which they bought from other people. Every tribe had a camp blacksmith. The men liked to have gold on their weapons and their horse harnesses. Women adorned themselves with bracelets, earrings, chains, and diadems. His father taught the Scythian to carve figures of people and animals from wood and bone, and to make beautiful buttons and clasps.

When a cold wind came in from the sea and wandered across the barren winter of Olvia, the Scythian carved a comb from the root of a rock-hard box-tree. He did this in the stables, where no one would bother him. Instead of a handle, he made three Scythian warriors with swords and shields; on the sides – foot soldiers and in the middle – a rider. Between them lay a dead horse with its hooves up in the air. The comb's teeth looked like the straight swords of the yellow-faced Huns from the Great Steppe.

Stratonides gasped when he saw such an artifact on the

Scythian's belt. At first, he thought the comb was stolen, but then he realized how much money he could make with the Scythian.

The next day, Stratonides had a furnace for melting metal installed and bought Scythian the necessary instruments. They made a clay cast from the box-tree comb and made several wax copies of it. Then they attached the combs together on one stem, a "tree." The "tree" was covered in a plaster cast, leaving a hole on top and bottom. The hardened cast was heated, until the molten wax poured out of it.

Stratonides gathered some gold coins, asked his wife for some of her jewelry, and went to his friends to borrow some gold dust.

Towards the evening, they started melting the gold. In the furnace of the dark workshop, small pieces turned into a glowing liquid. The Scythian could feel the magic when he held the ceramic cup filled with molten sunlight.

They carefully poured the gold into the cast, waited for the metal to cool, and lowered the cast into a bucket of water. The water dissolved the cast and freed the golden combs. Stratonides loudly exclaimed thanks to Apollo, - all the combs came out successfully. Early in the morning, he went to visit some rich citizens. He came back satisfied; all the combs were bought without haggling.

All winter, the Scythian made combs, earrings and bracelets. He made gold ornaments on Greek swords and armor, adding his favorite horses, fellow-tribesman warriors, mythical animals and birds of paradise. Hellenes readily purchased such wondrous trinkets. Stratonides rubbed his hands as he counted the profits. Soon, other jewelers in Olvia started to imitate the Scythian, mixing Attic themes with barbarian exotica.

Painful dejection, a restless soul, and an indifference towards everything overcame the Scythian in the early spring. He was lying on the straw in the stables, not eating or drinking for days on end. Stratonides knew that it was better to leave the slave alone: it would be easier to kill him than to make him work. The Scythian longed for the steppe, for freedom, for horse milk, from which women made a frothy drink.

A man from the Noor people, who came to sell salt, said that the Scythian's tribe moved on to the northwest after many men died in that battle. Chigil did not chase them, fearing an ambush in the distant steppes. He conquered all the coastal trade with his greedy hands. Chigil's tribe started calling itself the "Royal Scythians."

On the first day of his slavery, after the unsuccessful escape, the Scythian wanted to kill himself, but who would bury him and how? They would probably just throw his body over the wall, where the carrion crows would eat his corps. Not being buried after death was not a fate the Scythian wanted for himself.

He had been a slave for over three years, learned the Greek language, poured and cast gold in the winter, made mosaics in the summer, but thoughts about freedom and escape never left his mind. The chains were long since removed, there was no way to escape on foot – riders and dogs would have caught up to him quickly. But Scythians can patiently wait for the right moment: they were born of the Snake-Woman.

After one particular market fair, he found an abandoned colt by the city walls. The small one was really sick, covered with lichens, its wool hanging in clumps from bare sides, its hooves cracked. Stratonides did not allow him to bring the mangy horse into his stables. The Scythian set up a place for it in the corner of the courtyard, constructing a cover from the rain and sun, and spent a long time nursing the poor animal with concoctions of medicine grasses and incantations.

Nobody believed that the small horse would live, but it recovered. In his wild language, the Scythian told it about his family, his homeland, and about the hardships of servitude. The small horse listened, moved its ears, and understandingly laid its head on the Scythian's shoulder. Stratonides decided not to touch the horse – the Scythian was more useful and precious to him.

The small horse grew into a restive black steed. It did not let anyone except the Scythian near it, stomping its hooves and baring its teeth angrily. Every day, one melting into the next, they passed like the wind along the fortress wall to the assuring yells of the watchmen.

The Scythians worshiped horses, never attaching them to carts, or forcing them into heavy labor. Men ride horseback, women only in carriages attached to oxen. The Scythian and the black steed became like brothers, one could not live without the other. Everyone around understood that the gods united them in a shared fate.

In the beginning of the summer, Stratonides' wife died. He mourned, wept and took a boat to Pantikápaion - a house without a woman's touch will not stand. Two weeks later, he returned with a young childless widow. Her name was Olvia, like the town.

The Scythian saw Olvia and knew that he could only escape with her. Olvia was nineteen-twenty years old, with dark hair wrapped in a scarlet bow, slender legs in high-laced sandals, and a golden dolphin on a chain around her neck. They almost never talked, when directing the housework, Olvia gave orders quietly, embarrassed and blushing.

Stratonides and the Scythian spent that summer decorating

the agora – the central square with temples and porticos, the meeting place for the citizens to do business and exchange news. Among the intricate decorations on the walls of the main temple, between the faces of Hellene gods and goddesses, the Scythian weaved in a portrait of Olvia as a nymph. In the confusion of the construction, no one noticed whose face it was; otherwise there would be no escape from misfortune for the Scythian.

A Greek historian of the people from the shores of Pontos Euxeinos came on a trade ship from Athens. He frequently talked to the Scythian, asking about his native tribe, customs, gods, and dress. From him, the Scythian heard the alarming news – Sarmatians, the enemies of all the coastal tribes, were gathering their army on the shore of River Tanais.

The Sarmatian women wore men's clothing and fought alongside the men, distinguishing themselves by their cruelty. The Greeks called Sarmatian women Amazons, while the Scythians – Oiorpata, killers of men.

At the end of the summer, the Greeks loudly celebrated the Delia in honor of Apollo, god of light, healer, patron of new colonies, seafarers, artists, musicians and poets. The celebration lasted for several days; war was put on hold. Feasts, dances and theatrical shows filled the minds and souls of Olvia's citizens.

The Scythian did not recognize Chigil, who was festively dressed in Apollo's temple. The old enemy did look unusual without his soft boots and leather pants, instead, in a tunic with a golden wreath on his head. The traitor Chigil loved opulence, expensive clothes, wine from the Peloponnese, refined and lascivious delights of dancers. He was growing tired of the nomadic life and secretly bought a house in Olvia, and lived there a few days at a time, enjoying the life of a sybarite.

The ceremonies and sacrifices in the temple went well into the night. In the city and beyond the fortress walls, the celebration was turning into a bacchanal. A singing procession in laurel wreaths came out of the main temple. Chigil was dancing among young beauties with torches - the traitor of fellow-Scythians and the defiler of the ancestral faith! The Scythian grabbed the sword from a drunken guard and threw it over the heads of the priests into Chigil's chest. Blood spattered in all directions onto the festival costumes. Women started screaming, the men ran to catch the Scythian.

From the eastern gates came a terrible roar and whistling: the first wave of Sarmatian cavalry overran the peacefully drinking guards. They did not have time to close the gates; the Sarmatians broke through, crushing everyone in their way. Screams, crying, and moaning filled the city.

The Scythian ran towards Stratonides' house. In the artisans' quarters, the Amazons went wild; the blood ran down the roadway. Olvia hid under the overhanging with the black stallion. Three Amazons with short-swords tried to get to her, but the steed beat them with its hooves, protecting Olvia. The Scythian took a charred log from the burning roof and came down on the Amazons, who retreated toward the house. The Scythian jumped up on the steed, grabbed Olvia, and took flight.

In the clumps of smoke on the street, the Greeks were chopping at the Sarmatians. On horseback, the Scythian weaved through the overflowing streets, dodging swords, spears and arrows. There was no exit.

The steed knew what to do on its own. With a running

start, it jumped up on the roof of a nearby house, from there – on to the next, and so on, from roof to roof; it got closer to the notched wall. Sparks flew as it hit the roof tiles and soared up into the night sky, surrounded by the flames of the fire. The Scythian held the frightened Olvia close to him. Far beneath them, swam the fortress towers, houses, temples, and porticos, the line of horsemen flowing into the city.

They fell down onto the burial mounds overgrown with brambles and rolled down the hill. Their clothes ripped completely and fell from their shoulders. The steed was the first to jump up on its feet and snort joyfully, moving its round eye. The Scythian and Olvia started laughing, and together they made for the faraway steppe, where wandered the native tribe of the Scythian.

Roxel and the Princess-Frog

Roxel worked in a brigade that rebuilt old houses in a modern manner. Two carpenters, two stucco men, a mason and an apprentice – Roxel.

During the Great Depression, these houses were built out of cheap concrete for low income families in a swampy corner of New Jersey. High subsoil water, constant moisture and the summer heat soaked the cement walls, ceilings and floors. The buildings were becoming covered with mould, green moss and poison ivy. The local residents suffered from constant diseases, fevers, and tried to leave the place. For many years the village did not attract any attention, nobody was buying the houses.

After 9/11, some people as a precaution started moving out of New York to the neighboring states. Thus the village in a swamp became a strategically important region – halfway between New York and Philadelphia, near a turnpike and Route 1. The old houses were bought up by nondescript firms (major construction companies did not bother with such small fry). The homes were cleaned, disinfected, gained second floors, air-conditioning, Jacuzzis, and were resold for three times the price.

The contractor, who the brigade worked for, was a hairsplitter. He paid less than others, would delay salary, and wrote rubber checks. The amicable guys grit their teeth, cursed, but continued to work hard. Some of them were in debt to the contractor, for others it was a temporary thing while they looked for another job, then there were those who came to the country illegally and didn't want any problems.

Roxel came from the island of St. Vincent, which was near Barbados. His father had long ago divorced his mother, and was on his third wife, but did not forget about his oldest son.

On his native island, Roxel grew up like many youth of his age. At fifteen, he finished school, where he barely learned to read and count. Got some striking tattoos on his arms and chest, grew a stook of dreadlocks like Bob Marley. Drank watered-down beer in third-rate bars, squeezed party girls in the bushes, got into fights on the beach with guys just like him. He was jealous of foreign tourists, who came in on white yachts or lived in expensive hotels.

After yet another fight, Roxel and his friends were taken to the police station, where they were beaten with rubber batons and warned, that another fight would mean jail for at least ten years. The government and the businesses did not want to lose dollars, euros or yens, brought in by the tourists, on account of snot-nosed kids like this.

Nursing his wounds at home after the beating, Roxel understood that there was nothing on St. Vincent for him. He did not have the education to get a good job, nor money for college. All he knows is simple manual labor. On the island, he could mix cement twenty four hours a day, and he would still die a pauper. Roxel wrote a weepy letter to his father, who was silent for a while, but, finally, got the necessary documents to invite his son to the States and found him a job.

This was how Roxel came into the brigade, under the direction of an enormous Slovak named Martin. The other carpenter was Polish; the stucco guys – an old man from Granada and a three-fingered Chilean, who barely spoke any English; the mason – a Russian with glasses and long hair, pulled into a pony-tail by a rubber band.

The work went at its own pace ten hours a day. The carpenters knocked with hammers, or plugged in the wailing electric saw, installed studs for additional walls. They put in a new roof, expanding the cramped house up and outwards. They sheathed the wooden carcass with plywood, on top of which they hammered decorative plastic siding to make the house look more attractive. The old man from Granada and the Chilean made textured ceilings, put floor tiles in the bathrooms and the kitchen, while the Russian worked on the home's façade – decorating it with natural stone or laying out paths around the house.

They brought some beautiful stones this time – a field sandstone of yellowish-orange tones. The Russian worked artistically: first laying out a dozen stones on the ground, he would arrange them according to color and shape, then he applied a thin layer of mortar to the wall, a thicker one to the stone, and – allyoop – the stone is on the wall. He would then hammer it lightly with a rubber hammer, so it would sit deeper, he would fix the joints, and then, backing up a few steps, evaluate his work. At the end, the Russian would go over the joints again with a bristle brush: "So it would look rustic," he explained.

Roxel helped the Russian – mixed the mortar, carried the stones, evened their edges, washed the tools after work. The walls were getting done fast, the neighbors would stop by to look at the once wretched house.

One time, during a short lunch break, rather, a snack break, the mason noticed Roxel drawing on a piece of cardboard.

"What are you drawing?"

"A warrior?"

"Can I see?"

Roxel gave him the cardboard. The warrior's head did not make an impression on the Russian. He nodded politely and handed back the drawing. It was clear that the Russian knew something about art, but didn't want to say it to Roxel.

"What do you think, is this a good drawing?"

"It's not bad."

"I always draw, whenever I have time. I like to draw people, their faces, but I never learned how to."

"You need to go to college."

"I don't have the money. But even without college I can make many good drawings like this one and become a famous portrait painter."

"Unlikely..."

"Why?"

It was true, Roxel drew a lot. After work, he would come home to his father and his new family. In the corner of the living room, near his fold-out bed, he would settle in with a notepad and a pencil, and draw until he fell asleep from fatigue. Drawing became an escape, where he dreamed about another fantastic and beautiful life.

Roxel would portray himself as a tall athlete, making his flat short nose straight, like in the marble statues at the hotel "Diplomat." Next to him, he would draw a long-legged beauty with full African lips, and the slanted eyes of comic book heroines.

Roxel liked his drawings, his stepsisters also praised them, while his father approvingly nodded his head and smoked his pipe. Finished drawings, Roxel would rip out of the lined notebook and hide in an office folder, so they wouldn't crumple.

"Unlikely..." was what the Russian said about his dream to be a painter. This was hurtful. "What does a mason know?"

"Give me your pencil."

Roxel stretched out a pencil stub, which the carpenters used. The graphite in it was shaped flat, so it would not break on rough surfaces like stucco or plywood. The Russian sharpened the pencil into a cone, making the graphite long and elegant.

"You, Roxel, are trying to draw beautiful proportional faces, this is called 'Classical drawing.' And look what you got here, - the Russian drew a thin vertical line through the face in the portrait. – The left and the right side of the face were different in width. The eyes, - two parallel lines went through the corners of the eyes and eyebrows, - on different levels and under different angles. The ear had jumped to the crown, the nose moved into the skull, the mouth slanted to the side, the chin sloped inward like a psychotic.

The pencil flew across the cardboard, fixing this here, and that there.   "Where is the back of your warrior's head? It's as if he's cut off. The cheekbones and the corners of the jaw are on parallel levels. It's important to show the tear ducts and the roundness of the eyeball. The top eyelids are always longer than the bottom, the lower come from under the top. The pupils are the darkest points on the face; the highlights in the eye, the brightest. Always divide the light, shadow and half tones. Show the shadow falling from under the chin onto the neck, from the nose to the upper-lip, from the eyelids onto the eyes.

With sweeping movements, the Russian softly shaded the face of the warrior, laid down some shadows under the eyebrows and the upper-lip, then pulled out an eraser out of somewhere and enhanced the light contrast on the forehead and cheek, with two touches, he brightened the pupils, and then accented the folds near the mouth. From the cardboard, as if living, stared the warrior Alexander of Macedonia. Roxel was speechless with surprise and could not believe what became of his helpless drawing.

"Break over, time to work," came Martin's loud voice.

Roxel brought over a bucket of water, a bag of cement

and three bags of sand, poured the cement and sand on a sheet of plywood, and mixed it carefully. In the little hill, he made a cavity, like a crater, with his shovel and then poured water into it. Little by little, he then proceeded to fill in the crater from the edges – thus all the water was used inside like in a bag. He mixed it all with measured movements. The mixture turned out well – neither too thin or too thick. Then he started carrying stones over to where the Russian was working.

A pile of stones lay near the far corner of the house, it has been two weeks since the truck dropped them off. After yesterday's rain, the stones were cold and moist. There was a smell of stale water and rotten wood - after all, the village was on a former swamp. There came an incomprehensible vibrating sound from below.

"Jabba's croaking!" yelled Martin, and dropping his hammer, came stomping on the stones with his huge work boots made out of pork hide.

The croaking continued. Martin was turning over the stones in excitement. Under a wide flat boulder sat a grayish nondescript frog.

"Jabba!" Martin rejoiced and lifted his foot to squash it.

"Wait, Martin!" - came the Russian's voice from behind. "That's the Princess Frog. Whoever kills her will end up unhappy, but whoever falls in love with her, she will bring him a fortune in gratitude."

"Eh, you and your fairy tales," Martin swore, but the frog did not hop away.

Roxel did not believe in voodoo or other such scary stories. He was not a very educated youth, but the movies and the internet taught him a reasonable skepticism. The Russian's words for some reason sounded alarming. Who knows with them, these polar bears

from the northern forests, where there grows nothing but Christmas trees?

When the workday was over and everyone else went home, Roxel quietly turned over the stones and found the frog. She sat calmly and looked at him with her round eyes. Roxel slowly stretched out his hand and the frog jumped into his palm.

At home, Roxel put her in a shoebox, gave her some fresh greens, put in a plastic bowl with water, so the frog could swim about. He asked all his relatives not to touch the new guest. From the internet he learned what fresh-water frogs like, and caught some mosquitoes and flies for her.

Soon, they were all accustomed to the frog. Sometimes she would go for a walk around the apartment, but always returned to her box.

Roxel did not have friends in the States, no girlfriend either. He spent most of his time at work, and on Sundays he would sleep until lunchtime, then go to a movie or surf the net. The box with the frog stood nearby on the table. The frog often sat on the lid and looked at Roxel without blinking. He would tell her his dreams and hopes for a better life. Roxel wanted to meet a beautiful girl, marry her, have a family, house, bank account and go on vacation to his native island.

The Russian mason helped Roxel a few other times with drawing. He patiently explained how to draw the skeleton and muscles, talked about composition and proportionality. The Russian refused to give lessons, telling Roxel that he could not afford it, but that they could talk about art during their breaks. Roxel hung the

Russian's drawings above his bed and diligently copied them in the evenings and on the weekends.

The drawings came out better and better. Roxel bought good paper and expensive pencils, and learned to work with sanguine and pastels.

At the end of the summer he got a scholarship to go to the community college – the last couple of drawings helped out. Overjoyed, he came the next morning to tell the Russian about his good fortune.

Around the house where they were working, everything looked neatly cleaned, the stones of the new path recently washed. The Russian was nowhere.

"He said the mallows are blooming in Provence," Martin blurted out from the roof, laughing.

* * *

The first Monday of September, Roxel got ready for college. He wanted to say good-bye to the frog, but she had run out of her box somewhere. She was catching flies under the couch, probably.

The college was nearby – just three miles from home. Roxel drove his beat up Chevrolet Cavalier, bought with the money he earned over the summer.

A joyful hubbub resounded in the corridors, the semester had just begun. On the wall, next to the dean's office, hung the works of new students. Roxel stopped by his drawings in red sanguine - muscular men and beautiful women.

"Hi, Roxel," he heard a chest, barely audible voice. A cute Mulatto girl was smiling at him. "My name is Princess, I think we're in the same class."

To Sasha

The Old Man and the Girl

The Artist was really old, while the Girl – very young, maybe eleven years old. She saw the Old Man in the field surrounded by daisies, vetch, and cornflowers. It was a July noon – everything around was burning with bright colors.

The Girl noticed the wide-brimmed straw hat about forty yards away from her house. The tall grass and thistle concealed the man. The hat did not move, attentively suspended in place. The Girl was overcome by curiosity and she made her way through the tangled grass to get closer.

The Old Man was sitting on a foldable tarpaulin chair. In front of him stood a three-legged field easel with a painting in progress. The Artist was looking at the sea of yellow flowers in front of him, mixing the colors on his palate, and with brief precise strokes put them on the canvas. There you could already see the field, the line of trees along the canal, the university cathedral on the horizon.

The Girl politely greeted him and asked if she could watch how the Artist works, that is, if it's not a bother. She was well mannered and went to a small private school for girls, where she learned etiquette and other sciences, Ancient Greek and Latin.

The Artist looked in wonder at the amusing little lady. The Girl looked like a porcelain Dresden doll, with big blue eyes, puffy lips, flaxen hair in thin curls and a pink dress. He told the Girl that she would not be a bother to him at all.

The small canvas filled up with paint; the Artist painted quickly. The painting was almost finished, when he took out of his vest pocket an antique pocket-watch, looked at it, muttered something under his breath and started packing.

The Girl noticed that the Old Man's left hand was not as skillful as his right. And the left leg had a strange way of dragging, when, with his easel hanging from his shoulder, carefully holding the canvas with wet paint, he started towards the road.

The Girl went with him – her house was that way, anyway. The Artist barely got to the small bus in time, which had just arrived. Inside sat several old men and women, with many bags, boxes and bundles from different stores. The Girl asked if the Artist would come tomorrow.

"I don't know. I will come if there is no rain," he promised.

The next morning, the Girl saw the bus stop, and the painter came out in the same straw hat. He, limping, walked to the far corner of the field beneath the branchy elm trees.

The Girl asked her mother if she could go see what the painter was making. Her mother thought about it and permitted it. She could see everything like in the palm of her hand, and the guards were always watching from the governor's house. The area where the Girl lived was considered the most prestigious and respectable in the town.

The Artist painted in oil paints, the field, the trees and the ruins of a marble portico beneath them: the remains of a staircase and a few preserved columns; the tiled roofs of the university, where at some point worked the famous Einstein; the tall belfry, which can be seen from everywhere. Happy clouds ran across the sky.

The Girl was filled with joy. She gathered the field flowers, braided it into a wreath, and put it on her head. Then she made another one and offered it to the Artist. He smiled and put it right on top of his hat.

The Artist almost never talked, concentrating on the

painting. Quietly, so as not to bother him, the Girl sang a song, and then slowed down, and started reciting poetry. She did not say them from memory – the poems came of their own, flowing effortlessly out of her. She just needed to be in a good mood, for the poems to be good also, and if she was sad or bored, the poems came out likewise.

The Old Man was amazed when he heard her recite like she was waltzing.

Of course, at first, knowing little about poetry, he thought she must have a great memory. But when the Girl read a poem about him, his palette, his painting and his hat, the Artist figured out that she was composing them as she went.

He put down his brushes and listened to the Girl, until she got tired.

"How do you do that?" – he asked.

"I don't know, they flow of their own."

"When did it start?"

"Over a year ago now."

For someone her age, a year was a very long time.

"Do you write them down?"

The Girl told him that she had a thick notebook, where she saves the poems that she remembers. There are many poems in the notebook and even more in her head. Only they don't like her at school because of the poems, sometimes making fun of her or calling her names. She tried to stop composing poetry altogether, but couldn't do it, they simply found ways to escape out of her. Even her best friends often gestured with the index finger next to the temple, when they saw her freeze, and looking up at the sky begin to recite. Wanting to be like the other girls, she hung up a poster of a famous boy-actor, whom everyone in school was in love with. Several times she went to the huge mall with her friends, going from store to store, eating ice cream like everyone else, trying to talk about boys and fashion. She found it excruciatingly boring.

The Old Man thought for a while and then looked at the Girl in a different way.

"Bring your notebook with you tomorrow, maybe we will figure something out together."

On the third day of their acquaintance, the Girl noticed that the Artist walked more heavily somehow, and had to stop twice to rest. She brought the notebook, and he read it for a long time, settled in his folding-chair. The easel with the aluminum legs, which has been repaired many times, lay nearby on the grass, like a loyal dog.

The Girl so liked the metaphor, that she immediately composed a poem about the friend-easel-dog. The Artist cheerfully clapped his hands after hearing it. He took out a pad of watercolor paper from his canvas bag, ripped out a sheet and folded it in half. He then quickly watered some paints and in one half drew the shaggy dog that was laying under the easel, with its pink tongue hanging out.

After he finished, he asked the girl to write the poem in the other half of the sheet. The Girl carefully wrote down the poem with a pencil, so it would be easier to fix mistakes. It looked pale. The Old Man looked around and picked up a couple of feathers, which came from the Canadian geese along the canal. He showed the Girl how to sharpen them, and how to write, dipping the feather in ink.

They made three more other picture-poems that day. Two – the Girl copied from her notebook, and the Artist made the

illustrations, and the other one – the Artist painted the sea, on it
– a distant white sail, palms along the beach, and by the edge of the
water, there is a woman looking towards the horizon.

When they were later sitting together on the side of the
road, the Girl asked him what that bus was that came to drop off and
pick up the Artist, and why he didn't drive a car.

"The bus brings me here from a house for lonely old men.
Why the others are having fun in the center, buying random things
in the stores or just wandering, I make my paintings. As for the car, I
cannot drive any more, my left hand and leg don't work very well."

The next morning, there was a light rain, but it stopped
after breakfast. The Girl looked through the window, covered with
raindrops, and thought that the Artist would not come. But he came
out of the bus in a raincoat, waived to her from afar and started
stumbling towards the marble portico. The Girl ran after him.

This time they wrote a poem about the rain, the wet flowers
and grass, about how boring it is when the sky is grey, then one
about a bike and its glimmering wheel-spikes, and the last one about
an amusing crow, which was sitting on a branch, ruffling up her
feathers.

While waiting for the bus, the Artist painted a watercolor of
the heavy clouds, wet greenery of the trees, the mirror-like road and
a small running horse. He asked the girl's full name and signed it for
her as a memento.

Her mother was really surprised to find the picture in the
Girls possession, and deciphered the signature. She went to the
gallery and ordered it framed, and in the evening, immediately
becoming important, the picture was hanging in the guest-room
above the fireplace.

The day after tomorrow was the Girl's birthday. Early the

next morning, she signed in her round handwriting an invitation for the old Artist and ran to meet him at the bus.

The driver helped the Artist, asking him insistently about something, and then the bus left.

The Artist thanked her for the invitation, petted the Girl on the head and said that he would definitely come.

They sat down on the shore of the canal. At one point river barges went down it, delivering shipments to and from the ocean. All that was left now were drawbridges and water locks, as if from the paintings of the impressionists. Along its shores, parents strolled with their children, couples together, and athletes ran past.

The Old Man spoke slowly.

"A small blood vessel popped in my brain last night and, forgive me; I find it hard to move my tongue."

He could barely lift his left hand. The Girl helped him rip out a sheet of paper and fold it in half. They already had quite a few of these sheets from the days that they knew each other.

"I will sew them together and make a beautiful cover. This book will be my present to you on your birthday."

They drew and composed less that day, and talked more. The Artist – slowly, the Girl – rapidly. He told her about his children, who had long since grown up and moved away and are now here and there. She talked about her childish problems and joys.

When the bus came, the driver lowered a special wide step with a chair. He put the Old Man there and raised him inside. Seeing this made the Girl very sad.

The Girl's birthday fell on a Saturday – the best day to have guests over. Since early morning, she received visits from grandmothers, cousins, uncles and aunts. They all brought many presents in different colored boxes and bags, there was a whole pile of them.

In the garden, they set up tables with food for the kids and adults. They had a six-piece orchestra play music, a magician performed various tricks, the juggler – juggled apples and oranges, and a pony gave kids rides on its back or in a small carriage. They were all heartily enjoying themselves, but the Girl was waiting for someone else. She sneaked off to the road and waited there, until they noticed her absence.

In the evening, garlands of multicolored lanterns lit up. Her father ordered actual fireworks in the field outside, bringing astonished faces to the windows of the Governor's house.

When the guests left, the Girl started crying. Her mother and grandmothers were consoling her, but she only cried louder: "He promised to come and bring me the book, which we made together. He wasn't here, something must be wrong! We have to find him!" the Girl begged.

The mother put her fingers to her head and closed her eyes. The father was on the phone, talking to someone for a long time. Around midnight the father started their black car, and took the girl to the town, that same one with the belfry and the tile roofs. They arrived at the hospital, it was large and modern.

Again, the father spent a long time patiently explaining something to the doctor on duty. Finally, they led the Girl to a distant room, where the Artist was lying down on a high bed. Tubes and wires were wrapped all around him, different color lamps blinked on the multiple machines.

The Old Man opened his eyes and looked at the Girl.

"How pretty you're dressed," he said. The pipe which was

supplying his oxygen wheezed quietly. "I could not come to your birthday party. You can see what happened to me. Forgive an old man."

The Girl started crying again. She felt bad for the Painter, for herself, their barely started friendship.

"Don't cry. I have a present for you under my pillow – take it. I can't move at all, at least I can still talk."

The Girl stretched out her hand and retrieved the book in Moroccan binding, their book. The sheets of watercolor paper were solidly stitched together. On the first page in elaborate gold letters were the names of the Girl and the Artist.

The Girl hugged the Old Man and pressed her tear-drenched face again his cheek.

"You are my only friend in this town," the words came to the Old Man with more difficulty. "I am dying, but I will be dying for a long time. I will stop talking, become like a helpless plant. I feared this kind of end the most. I don't want to die in a hospital, it would have been better to die there – in the field with my easel. When I was young I thought it would be good to die in battle, on horseback, or to fall off of a mountain, or from a knife in the back. But the way it is now – torturous and shameful. We worked well together. The book will stay with you, take care of it." The Girl had to bend down to the Old Man's mouth to make out his words. "They will cremate me, don't be afraid of that word. I don't have any relatives or friends left apart from you. All my friends – dead, relatives – far away. Please take my ashes, when you can, and scatter them in the field where we met. On that spot, there will grow a tree. I will live in it, and you should come to talk to me and read your fabulous poems. You promise?" The Girl nodded.

"I can't move – everything is paralyzed. Do you see that

valve? Close it slowly and hold it, until you are sure that I'm asleep forever, then open it like before. Don't worry, I won't feel pain. Are you ready?"

The girl, streaming tears, nodded again.

"We will laugh again yet. Everything will turn out well for you. Thanks. Farewell."

*   *   *

Many years passed. The field was still a field with its flowers and grass, after all the Governor's house looked out on it. A tall elm grew in the middle of it. Under the crown of the tree, a woman often sat on a folding chair. Usually, she was reading, writing or thinking to herself. Her little daughter would run up, and the mother would tell her something.

Tango

Sandro appeared on our horizon in the middle of November, when winter had not yet started in Moscow, and autumn turned from golden to dank and rainy. We were introduced at one of the "apartment" exhibitions. He was looking for a private drawing and painting instructor, while I was looking for any sort of work – it was very hard for an independent artist to feed himself in Brezhnev's time.

Any art student could teach a foreigner the basics, realistic art being the foundation of Soviet education. I turned out to be the only one who could freely speak English. My going to a specialty school, which taught the language since the second grade, along with English and American literature, gave me a priceless advantage over the rest of my clan.

We soon started meeting twice a week: first for drawing, second for painting. Sandro paid honestly in dollars and I sold to black market moneychangers, which was quite dangerous. If I got caught, I could get up to ten years in jail. But for me, the amount of money was enormous, so I took the risk. Thanks to the lessons, I could support my family for two years.

Sandro was Argentinean. He came to Moscow with his English wife, who worked as an attaché to the British Embassy. She worked day and night, while the young, handsome Sandro had nothing to do. He often went to official and semi-official exhibitions, and out of boredom remembered his childhood interest in painting and decided to try to insert himself into the art world.

Not so simple! As long as he brought whiskey, gin, tonic and other exotic things from the duty-free store, everybody loved him. However, when he showed them his paintings, at best they would smile politely, and if they had time to down a glass, would laugh openly. Sandro would get terribly upset, disappear for ten days or so, but then return with yet another creation.

Somebody told him that without the elementary knowledge of color, composition, drawing and anatomy, he would not be able to do anything worthwhile. Sandro could not go to an art school or a university, nor did he want to waste years in Soviet routine. So that was how we met.

Sandro would come to my two hundred square foot apartment, and we drew plaster heads, still lifes, portraits of each other or of my wife, if she was available. Also, I would teach him how to stretch canvases, prepare prime ground, tone paper with tea or coffee, cleaning and wrapping the paint brushes so they dry better.

Towards the evening of the lesson, my wife would come home. On the way, she would pick up our son from kindergarten and stop by the bakery next to our house to get warm poppy-seed bagels, Danishes, treacle cookies and aromatic pumpernickel bread.

The four of us then drank tea with cherry preserves and watched the sunset and the thickening violet twilight. To the right – the Moscow River and Park of Culture, to the left – the grey box of the Central Exhibition Hall, further to the left – Ostozhenka Street and the domes of Immaculate Conception Monastery, right above them – the stars of the Kremlin, and on the far left, the Stalinist Ministry of Foreign Affairs on Smolensky Square right beneath our windows – Garden Circle and Zubov Square, with one of the most dangerous traffic patterns in the city – cars crashed there almost every day. We had to run to cross this extremely wide square, with its two traffic lights.

Typically, after the lesson, Sandro would take out something foreign – a bottle of Porto wine, Italian liquor or Scotch whiskey.

He'd give my son American gum or something else sweet.

Occasionally, we'd get wound up and visit the studios of my friends – unrecognized geniuses. It happened that we'd have to deliver the unconscious Sandro to the check point of his diplomatic home for vodka and other Russian drinks. Sandro would get too weak, got drunk quickly, blurted out some nonsense and would fall asleep. We then tried to give the visitor from beyond the sea, something lighter.

Gloria, Sandro's wife, would get very angry over our excursions, several times having serious talks with me, and I tried to protect my precious student from the excesses of the bohemian lifestyle.

In the House of Culture, named after Gorbunov, we were able to get an exhibition of the avante-garde artists. This was a unique event under the conditions of the totalitarian regime. Painters from many different cities, hearing about such an opportunity, brought their works. I begged the bulls of non-conformity to hang Sandro's small picture instead of one of mine – Ah! The sacrifices that one makes for their students.

The administration had a foyer for the exhibition in front of the concert hall. It had high windows, tall ceilings, the walls wrapped in brown cushions. We, the painters prosecuted by the government, never had such a place. The director of the Palace of Culture took a big risk upon himself, dealing with art outlaws like us.

When we were hanging the paintings, there was a practice session in the ballroom dance studio in the foyer. The dancers were preparing for a Pan-Soviet Union competition.

There was languorours music, pairs in measured movement, sometimes freezing briefly before the next step. The metronome dryly counted thirty beats a minute.

"Slow - slow - quick - quick - slow," came the sharp voice of the studio's instructor, a stern woman with a strong chin. "Step - freeze. Step - freeze."

The dancers with very straight backs kept their distance from each other, lightly touching the hands of their partners with the tips of their fingers.

"They don't know how to dance the tango," said Sandro, following the couples with his eyes.

"And how do you know?"

"I'm Porteño, a native of Buenos Aires. Tango was born in my quarter of La Boca. We dance the tango since childhood."

"Well then, go and show them how it's done."

Sandro dragged me to the dance instructor, and I had to translate what was the problem. A real living Argentinean in Moscow's outskirts of Fili – a rare event indeed. Out of curiosity, they let him show them a tango that wasn't sick, a truly authentic one from the shores of La Plata. Dancers and intrigued painters crowded around.

Sandro invited a young girl, almost a teenager, with thin legs like a foal's, and a barely protruding chest. Why he picked her and not the experienced soloist – I do not know.

They stood in the middle of the circle of curious viewers. She was in a short dress which seemed to have been sewn by her mother or grandmother and in old shoes with high heels. Sandro – in a thick sweater, wide corduroy pants and warm winter boots. Not tall, almost the same height as the girl, he looked funny. Both were still, waiting for the music.

Clumps of snow slowly spun behind the window.

There was a click from the tape player, and a passionate melody started flowing from the speakers. For a second, the two in the middle of the circle did not move, what kind of magic was happening behind them? Sandro looked the girl in the eyes, and they stepped – softly and confidently.

Tango is a dance of passion, man leads. The woman must follow in step with her partner. The macho man displays his character, his relationship to the woman, to his competitors and the world in general.

Sandro held the woman not in a sickly way, but firmly – chest to chest. The girl followed Sandro, intuitively divining unfamiliar movements and turns, and added something of herself, as if this "something" was something organic inside her. The dance was heart-felt and outspoken.

Before our eyes, the bumpkin Sandro, who painted out of boredom, turned into a great dancer, a maestro.

The music stopped. Sandro gallantly bowed to the girl, who stood red to the roots of her hair. The dance instructor was swallowing air, speechless.

"This dance… is so indecent… It is completely strange and unfamiliar to my students… They will never let us advance. Thank you, Argentinean comrade, for the courtesy, but we will continue the preparation for the ballroom dance competition, and not pornography," the lady was a stoic Parteigenossin.

"This style is called "Tango Milonguero," Sandro explained when we were on the subway train going home. "It is danced very close, developed in the cramped restaurants and clubs of Buenos Aires in the very beginning of the 20th century. And what about this competition that nag was talking about?"

Chandrika was a fiery woman. Her genes were a mix of her Indian father and Jewish mother. We were same year students at

the university, but in different departments - she in philology, I in philosophy, until I delved headfirst into painting and the underground. We met in the smokers' hangout in the foyer of the Humanities building, where those who were cutting their lectures and seminars smoked, sitting on the radiators.

Chandrika asked for a cigarette and Armen and I each took out a pack of Java (neither of us smoked, but both kept a pack around just for girls). The scorching beauty smiled sweetly, took two cigarettes from each pack and went back to her friends. We just batted our eyes.

Kozik came out of the elevator, saw Chandrika, casually walked over, greeted her, kissed her on the cheek and then walked over to us.

"Kozik," we started yelling "introduce us!"

"Guys, she was in my high school class, married since eighteen, you don't have a chance."

I saw Chandrika throughout my years at the university, but we'd only say hi.

Life went on in its own rhythm, at the end of my fifth year I got married, soon after we had our son. We met Chandrika again when our kids where in the same group at kindergarten. My wife became close friends with her and they would spend hours on the phone together. Chandrika worked near the subway stop "Park of Culture," and would drop by our place to talk, complain about problems at work or about yet another husband.

Chandrika had a passionate nature. She always lived as if today was her last day alive. She studied ballroom dancing since childhood, which gave her an outlet to her overflowing feelings. She loved the tango especially – the erotic music, movements filled with hidden meaning, the intrigue of man and woman.

Her job as a simultaneous interpreter took her to different countries with many delegations. When abroad, Chandrika always sought out a tango studio and spent her free time there, away from translation. Upon returning to Moscow, she would always stop by our place, and drinking tea with St. John's Wart, tell us how they dance in Europe, America and Japan. After her story, I had the impression that the world is covered with Tango studios like in a huge net.

In the spring, when the snow began to thaw and dirty streams ran down the sidewalks, the Old Man, Bream, Sandro and me were standing and smoking next to the entrance to the Seleznevsky bath-house. Tuesday was our bath day. At noon, we put out our cigarettes and went inside. The steam has begun.

"Breathe with your nose and mouth, angels," Mikhail Andreyich roared, the first bass in the 'Vivat' choir, "complete the inhalation." And he splashed an infusion of medicinal herbs on the heated rocks of the stove.

In the steam room, on the top shelf beneath the measured swings of a switch of oak twigs, Sandro admitted that in a month he was going to participate in the All-Union Tango competition. We, naked angels in felt hats, stared at him, dumbfounded.

It turned out that sneaky Sandro made arrangements to practice in the dance studio of Gorbunov's House of Culture, trying to flirt with the young girl. Gloria, Sandro's wife, suspected something wasn't right from the beginning. To prevent Sandro from straying, who was eight years younger than her, she started going with him to the studio.

In her youth, Gloria studied choreography in the Royal Academy of Art in London, danced for two years with the corps de ballet on Broadway, and met Sandro at a tango festival in Buenos Aires. They continued going to Gorbunov's for several months, and Gloria was grasped by a passion. She started making diplomatic channels, and they accepted them into the Pan-Soviet Union competition as a non-competing pair, meaning that their dances would be on a par with the others, but they cannot win any prizes like the foreigners.

The big prize of the Pan-Soviet Union competition was a trip to Paris for the European competition, and for the finals, a trip to Buenos Aires, the birthplace of the tango.

In the evening, Chandrika came by our place to introduce us to her new suitor.

"This is serious," she had time to whisper to my wife.

In our bohemian communal apartment, Victor, as her beloved was called, felt himself obviously not in his milieu. We drank some cognac to mark our meeting, and then Chandrika asked my wife to read their fortune. She tried to decline, but Chandrika and Victor convinced her.

Natasha, my wife, sometimes reads cards with her close friends. She does not do this readily, because it makes others pester her all the more, since they place great faith in the predictions. My wife swiped away the crumbs from our only table and shuffled a worn deck. For a long time, she moved around the cards, flipping them up, down, I cannot tell you everyhing, because I don't know anything about divination.

"Here's the Queen of Clubs, a passionate love, weapons and a distant journey..."

My wife also saw blood and death in the cards, but did not say anything.

"That's true," Chandrika said, "Queen of Clubs, that's me. Long journey – Victor and I will win the competition and go to France, as for the weapons – Victor is in the army."

Victor was an officer of the General Headquarters. At one time, he served in the Soviet Army Chorus and Dance Ensemble and later, he finished the Military Academy and was now making a career at headquarters. They met half a year ago. Victor had just gotten divorced and was spinning his head looking around , and in his search for new meetings, he found himself in the tango studio on Volhonka Street. Chandrika and he felt a spark, and they were now getting ready for the Pan-Soviet Union competition.

Sandro got us tickets to the Palace of Youth. Everything Soviet, as you know, is the best. Thus the powers organized the competition as a demonstration of the triumph of Soviet cultural politics. Television, radio, journalists of all kinds, workers' representatives – all in all, everything as usual.

I had to borrow a black suit and tie, otherwise, they would not let me into the building. My wife sewed a dark-violet dress with sparkles, no worse than those worn by the competitors. I had time to spend two days in the library, liquidating the knowledge gap about tango, its history, music and choreography ... so I could have some idea what the deal was.

Participants came together from all over the country, even from distant autonomous republics. Burats and Yakuts looked funny dressed in tuxedos and frock coats, dancing a South American dance.

The pairs spun on the gleaming hardwood floor of the enormous, stadium-sized, hall. The men had white napkins with numbers on their backs. I soon got bored, and wanted to drink some scarce Czech beer at the buffet, but my wife made me sit next to her. It was as if she was memorizing the outfits, hairstyles and jewelry. Many of the dresses were truly beautiful and interesting – with flowers, ribbons, scarves and various other things. Conservative, but pleasant, the competition in Moscow was broadcast throughout the Soviet Union and socialist countries.

Chandrika and Victor danced in the middle of the day – the best time – sound and lighting are still tuned and working properly; the staff isn't tired yet and the cameramen are taking the best pictures.

Chandrika – in a black-red dress with a large rose in her hair was a genuine Carmen. Victor – in parade uniform – wearing golden epaulettes and aglets. The camera-lenses were glued to this dazzling couple. Their dancing was simply amazing, and it drew applause even from the jealous competitors.

Almost at the very end, after five hours of my thirst and boredom, they announced the pair that did not enter the competition – Sandro and Gloria. Her co-workers from the embassy came to support Gloria, and on the tribune of honorable guests, they unfurled two Union Jacks. There were no other couples in the circle of light; they gave the foreigners two and a half minutes of their own time.

The hall fell silent. Gloria wore a dress like one would see at a carnival in Buenos Aires: a light tunic on thin straps, an open back and a low cut on the chest, a diamond diadem, a pearl necklace, platinum bracelets and rings with emeralds that glowed throughout the entire Palace. Sandro was striking with his gelled hair, an impeccable frock coat, made somewhere on Bond Street, with cufflinks and a tiepin, also with diamonds.

In our grey and hungry Moscow, with its empty store shelves, they looked like the heroes of Hollywood movies – fantastic and foreign. The light from the projectors showed through the fabric of Gloria's dress, her jewelry dazzling like in a fairy tale. Everyone held their breath. Music, and both of them stepped with the left foot. The apologists of classical ballroom dances gasped, this move was unacceptable to their principles. Gloria and Sandro kept very close, pressing the upper body against the partner's. When he would bend back, she would fall forward.

They moved in line of the dance (La Ronda) that is counter-clockwise, sometimes changing direction or moving the opposite way. Our dance instructors were grinding their teeth from such liberties. Everything in Gloria's and Sandro's dance was contrary to the Soviet system. There were no staccato-steps; they were gliding romantically. The movement came from the body, and the legs followed the body's impulse. They stepped with the heel or the entire sole, cat-like, freezing momentarily in the crown steps of Argentinean tango.

Oh, what happened in the dance hall when they performed several moves unknown to us! Gancho! What is one name worth? Gloria hooked her leg dressed in a black net, stalking it around Sandro's leg. The audience gulped from such "shamelessness." Sandro made a Parada – his leg deep between Gloria's legs, then Arrastre and Sacada – gently kicking the leg of the partner out of his way.

They had never seen such outspoken dances in our snowy capital. It was beautiful and depraved! When the music stopped, and the pair fell still in a bow, there was a complete silence for several seconds, which then exploded into wild applause, screams of joy, and whistling.

The jury deliberated deep into the night, everyone was

pining in impatience and fatigue. Finally, the jury representative, a member of the City Communist Party Committee, announced the winners. First place and the trip to the European competition in Paris – Chandrika and Victor! Special prize from the jury and the audience – Gloria and Sandro! Me and my wife were bursting with pride for our friends, as if we ourselves had won the competition twice over.

A month later, Chandrika and Victor went to Paris as part of the Soviet tango delegation – they would not let them go without KGB supervision.

The creative Gloria pressed the right buttons to get a letter of recommendation from the USSR Ministry of Culture to include Sandro and her in the European competition. After the oil crisis, Europe largely relied on Soviet oil delivery, thus they ended up among the competitors as an amusing international couple. So, a precedent had been set.

We followed the European competition on television, which they briefly featured on the evening news. Soviet TV broadcasted only Chandrika's and Victor's triumphs, how they moved from 32nd to the semi-finals. My wife and I clapped our hands and danced around in our little room.

Chandrika called us from a Paris hotel, and told us the news, which was not on television. From her, we found out that Gloria and Sandro also made it to the semi-finals and were going to Argentina. We never expected such a crazy development. Both couples, our friends, would be in the finals! The Tango Committee was paying for the trip, lodging and some spending money – it was serious business.

But… as often happens in the very character of tango, you can't get by without a tragedy. Immediately after the award ceremony of the European tour, the Faulkland Crisis took place, and war broke out between England and Argentina over some microscopic islands in the Atlantic Ocean.

Victor was hastily summoned back to Moscow, Gloria likewise, sped back to her embassy. Chandrika decided to stay for a while; her visa was for two months (a gift from generous France to all participants in the competition). She also had some cash – the prize for her win in the semi-finals. The Soviet delegation tried to take Chandrika back forcibly, but she secretly snuck out of the hotel. KGB agents ran around Paris here and there and then returned back to Lubyanka Street to receive the scolding for "errors in work-conduct."

Sandro also remained in Europe to wait-out the dubious times.

Soon the steel lady of Downing Street sent the British fleet a hundred thousand miles into the Atlantic. The atomic submarine "Conqueror," using intercepted information from a soviet spy satellite, located the main Argentinean cruiser "General Belgrano" and sunk it with torpedoes echoing the time of World War II. Brave Scottish paratroopers fought off the Falklands from the occupying troops and freed the subjects of the British Empire.

From here on, I tell the story as gathered from the words of the key participants, newspapers, magazines, and programs of Voice of America, the BBC, and Radio Freedom.

When the war finished and the Argentinean dictator Leopold Galtieri resigned, and the political turmoil quieted a little, the new government decided to conduct the postponed final round of the World tango competition.

England, obviously, refused to participate. Gloria sat in Moscow and cried. Russia took the predictable position.

Headquarters told Victor to not even think about dancing.

Chandrika and Sandro, two winners from the semi-finalist couples, decided to compete as an international pair. The situation was becoming complex, but there was already a precedent (Gloria and Sandro), so they accepted them into the finals.

It's easy to say: "Change your partner." But in practice, this is almost impossible. It's like being married and then waking up with a stranger in bed next to you. Different culture, habits, dirty laundry...

A few years later, in New York, Chandrika told us that sparks flew instantly with her and Sandro, the moment she did the gancho during their first practice – hooking her leg around Sandro's. What and how they practiced afterwards – I cannot say.

The finalists from different countries came to Buenos Aires ten days or so before the competition, to get used to the climate and the time difference. The city was festively decorated, multi-colored posters could be seen everywhere with the logo of the competition – a pair of funny creatures doing the tango.

According to the rules of the finals, the competitors were required to show sixty-seven different tangos. The whole program lasted five days, each segment to be held in a different neighborhood, "barrio," so as to show the locations which were connected to the history of the tango.

The new Argentinean government was trying with all its might to fix the unattractive political façade, passed down by the military dictatorship. A Tango competition – the first worldwide event, a demonstration of the positive changes in the country.

Daily television broadcasts went to almost every country in the world. We followed every stage of the competition on TV. The first night was in Sandro's native barrio La Boca. His townspeople met him with quite a commotion. They carried him into the building and covered him with flowers. A son of these poverty-stricken streets, he, and accordingly Chandrika, were the targets of more cameras than the other competitors.

We watched on the screen of our old black-and-white TV set how, as soon as they touched each other; their faces changed, eyes misty, dreamy smiles appearing on their lips. A real passion was boiling between them. If me and my wife were able to divine this passion, what does that say about Gloria and Victor!

Gloria promptly took time off for "family reasons" and flew to London, from there to New York, and then a direct flight to Buenos Aires.

Victor convinced his general to send him on some needed assignment to GDR, to East Berlin. From there he snuck across the wall to West Berlin and took a train to Holland, then from Amsterdam – a plane to Argentina. Where he got the money and the fake documents - he didn't tell anyone.

Both Gloria and Victor appeared in Buenos Aires on the

eve of the last performance. Gloria arrived at the international Aeropuerto Ezeiza, while Victor managed to take local lines to the Aeroparque Jorge Newbery.

The security outfit for the competition did not allow meetings with the finalists, did not pass on notes or forward telephone calls. The competitors could contact the outside world, but were forbidden to leave the hotel without accompaniment as a safety precaution: who knows what fans and provocateurs are capable of? Sandro and Chandrika knew nothing about the arrival of Gloria and Victor, and, all in all, made love and never left their bed.

Gloria knew Buenos Aires well because of her work. She got a room at an expensive hotel and purchased from scalpers an insanely expensive ticket to the last night of the Competition at Teatro Colón.

This theatre is known as the best on in Latin America. It was built in the beginning of the twentieth century in the style of the Renaissance, richly decorated with Carrarian and Veronian marble, carved plaster moldings, gold-leaf, velvet, frescoes, and busts of famous musicians.

First-rate stars performed on the stage of Teatro Colón: composers Richard Strauss, Igor Stravinsky, Camille Saint-Saëns; the conductors Arturo Toscanini, Herbert von Karajan, Zubin Mehta; soloists Arthur Rubenstein, Mstislav Rostropovich, Andres Segovia; vocalists Enrico Caruso, Maria Callas, Kiri Te Kanawa, three tenors - Carreres-Domingo-Pavarotti; all the great ballet personalities – Anna Pavlova, Vaclav Nijinsky, Rudolf Nureyev with Margo Fontaine, Michail Barishnikov.

Victor joined the last excursion around the theatre, which they ran from 10 a.m. till 5 in the evening. Once inside, he said he was sick, and headed towards the exit, but then skillfully hid behind a curtain past the guard. From there he got to the gallery, and then snuck up to the attic.

The theatre filled up with people long before the concert. After decades of military dictatorship, the loss of democratic freedoms and, especially - the freedom of assembly - everyone was filled with happiness and enthusiasm.

Zealous connoisseurs of tango came from all the continents to root for their favorites. The theatre could only accommodate three thousand people, that is why ticket prices reached impossible heights.

They removed the chairs from the orchestra section to make room for the dancers. The oak hardwood floor, polished to mirror-like shine, glowed in the rays of the projectors and camera flashes. Film, television, radio and the papers were everywhere. Countless security and bodyguards added to the confusion and the importance of the event.

Experts predicted that the main battle would be between the Argentinean couple and the dancers from Uruguay's capital Montevideo, a town that has always contested the primogeniture of the tango. The Americans were considered the best at ballroom interpretation of the tango, for several years they soloed in Broadway musicals, and each of their performances played to a full house. The Chinese surpassed everyone in acrobatic tango. This was no shock, since both the soloists were trained in traditional Peking Opera and were both Olympic gymnastics champions. No one took the Israeli couple seriously, what kind of tango can you have in the Middle East? Chandrika and Sandro caused the greatest suspicion and puzzlement. Nobody knew what to expect from this strange pair.

The jury was composed of many authorities: tango choreographer Carlos Alberto Estevez, creator of many steps, turns and poses that are used throughout the world; composer Eduardo Arolas, who affirmed bandoneon as the chief instrument in tango music; actor and director Robert Duvall, American, who glorified tango in modern cinema; poet Saavedra Lamas, a passionate admirer of the tango, who was once president of the League of Nations.

Among honorable guests – Dr. Bernardo Hussay, Porteño, Nobel prize laureate in medicine, the literary celebrities Jorge Borges and Julio Cortazar, and the love of all Argentina – soccer player Diego Maradona.

Right before the beginning of the concert, into the theatre arrived the president of the country, along with his cabinet of ministers and senators. The new government showed itself in all the flash of the super-class.

On the stage, Astor Piazzola with an Orguesta tipica (bandoneon, guitar, violin, counter-bass, piano). Behind them – the complete symphonic orchestra of Teatro Colón – one hundred twenty musicians.

There is no point in relaying the competition in detail. You can now buy the DVD and see it with your own eyes. The numbers of competing pairs alternated with the demonstrations of different schools of tango, children's ensembles, and musical performances.

On the scoreboards, the jury's scores lit up, rating each pair. After the mandatory five-day program, the following picture was coming together: Argentina and Uruguay were nose to nose, rather, heel to heel; behind them – Americans, then Chandrika and Sandro, then Chinese, and last – Israelis.

The main difficulty for the participants was that in each performance they had to use a different style of tango. So they had to constantly rebuild themselves, change their moods and the emotional overtones of the dance.

Tango Canyengue was danced in the 1920-30s, when women wore narrow long dresses, which limited movement. The step was short, on semi-bent legs, the tempo – two fourths. Chandrika did not like this style very much; her sole strove for other, more passionate forms of expression. In the Canyengue style, the Chinese turned out the best, each step was controlled and exact to the millimeter, they moved so smoothly that you could put a full glass of water on each of their heads, and they would not lose a drop.

Tango Liso developed in close quarters and cramped restaurants in the poor neighborhoods, when the male population of Buenos Aires was a hundred thousand greater than the female. Liso is danced pressing closely against each other, with many turns, but there is no room for the most effective poses. This dance was closer to Chandrika's and Sandro's mood, additionally it gave them a rest before the more technically demanding styles. Probably it was the calm-concentrated mood of the two that made the performance – the jury chose our friends as the best in the style.

Tango Orillero, inversely, stands out by its wide sweeping moves, the interchanging of quick and slow steps, a mass of striking ganchos, sentados and voleos. The Argentineans and the Uruguayans got the same scores.

Ballroom tango is often considered to have the opposite character of traditional Argentinean tango. It is preferred in Europe because of its reduced physicality and sexuality, considered more appropriate in polite society and expensive restaurants and clubs of the upper crust. For the hot-headed Latin-Americans, ballroom tango is too vapid. Here, victory went to the Israelis.

The penultimate, 66th dance that week, - Tango Phantasia. It, of course, is the most theatrical and spectacular, includes many improvisations, solo movements and acrobatics. Tango Phantasia is more appropriate for a single couple performing on a stage, it is impossible to dance in a small space, in a room or at a restaurant between tables. Here, Americans displayed unparalleled imagination. They said that the best Broadway choreographer Bob Fosse prepared this number as a major hit of his next season's program, and the competition in Argentina was used as an international commercial for his upcoming musical. The success of the Americans was indubitable, recognized even by the Argentinean patriots.

As a result, before the final dance, all five couples were tied even, like horses at the start of Hippodrome Argentino de Palermo. Just three more minutes, and everything will be decided!

The couples went to change, while a dozen of six-seven year old kids in traditional outfits poured out onto the dance floor. Boys dressed like gauchos, in wide straw hats, in sharp-nosed boots with silver spurs. The girls wore dresses with aprons sewed with Indian ornaments. They danced seriously, imitating the grownups.

There was a deafening sound of the gong, all the spotlights and footlights were extinguished, only a single projector focused on the main musician of the evening – maestro Piazzola. He announced the closing dance and invited the other musicians to the stage. No one in the theatre or watching it on television in other countries could predict anything like this. How did he manage to bring together such stars?! What kind of money did it take?

Guitars – Jimmy Page and Carlos Santana, saxophone – Charlie Parker, trumpet – Louis Armstrong, cello – Yo-Yo Ma, piano – the old Vladimir Horowitz, and behind an enormous drum set – John Bohnam. Last to come on the stage was completely white-haired, but the ever elegant and graceful Carlos Gardel – the absolute number one star in tango, a legend, an idol to several generations, beloved by all Argentinean women and the bandoneon teacher to Astor Piazzola himself.

The theatre screamed with excitement, and this roar ran across Latin America, through the States, swept over Europe, covered Asia and the Far East and, finally, fell silent in Africa. Carlos Gardel smiled a wide smile, known to millions from his movies, postcards and photographs, blew a kiss into the dark hall and pointed to the dancers, ready for the final competition.

The couples stood to the left and right of the stage. Now, every little detail meant a lot.

The Argentineans dressed in the style of clubs a la Gardel: the man in a straw hat with black ribbon, a silk neck-scarf, black jacket, white striped pants. A true Porteño! Only thing missing is a folding-knife behind the belt. His partner - in a dress from the 30s, with a décolleté deep like a canyon.

The Uruguayans were in costumes with the colors of their national flag – blue-white stripes and a sun sewn in gold on the lapel of the jacket and the bodice of the dress. Yankees – he was in an Uncle Sam frock coat with a cylinder hat, she was in a tunic with the diadem of the Statue of Liberty. The Chinese – wearing intricate national costumes of heavy silk, decorated with dragons and quotes from Mao Dze Dun. Israelis – the most modern outfit by Versace – she was almost naked except for a tiny bit of silk; he – in a tight-fitting black tricot.

Chandrika put on a serious outfit of a businesswoman, a minimum of makeup and no jewelry. Sandro was in a grey tux, only his half-boots with the sloped heels suggested that he was Porteño from the ancient barrio La Boca, the heart of tango.

"Libertango," announced Piazzola in a voice quivering with excitement, and played the first note on the bandoneon.

Such a performance by such an orchestra no one will ever hear again! Of course everything was recorded on tape, but can a magnetic strip communicate the lightest nuances of sound from the grand piano of Vladimir Horowitz, or the fantastic duet of two guitars, or the sorcery-rivalry of the horn and saxophone? Or the voice of Carlos Gardel? The record that came out after the competition - merely a pale copy of that music, which cannot be preserved.

The couples froze for a second, catching the rhythm, and then simultaneously stepped in the line of La Ronda, counterclockwise. Tango Milonguero – the closing point of the five-day marathon. Whatever happens, it was imperative to dance the number to the last note, to the final step. Three thousand people in the Teatro Colón and millions at television screens were watching the dancers' every move.

The most important thing in tango is the step. There exist a great number of steps and their variations, any Argentinean can easily show you two-three dozens. What is important is to find your own unique step, distinct from everybody else's, which people will recognize instantly and remember forever. Each couple secretly worked on its step, hiding it until the last dance. Today, these different styles of step are in the schoolbooks, and are studied throughout the world, bearing the names of their couples-inventors.

Chandrika and Sandro danced close together, "heart-to-heart." They looked into each other's eyes throughout, feeling the other's heartbeat through the dress. The theatre, the audience did not exist for them, they were together alone in the Universe.

The first bullet passed right by Sandro's ear, when they were doing the support parada, which is also called "sandwich." The bullet diagonally cut down a rosebud in his lapel and sunk into the hardwood floor near Chandrika's heel. Splintered wood flew at the nearby spectators. The second bullet made a hole in the collar of Chandrika's jacket. She was saved by the sweeping move in gancho – she hooked her leg around Sandro's hip and stretched almost into a split.

The Israelis responded instantly to the gunfire. Both of them went down to the floor and rolled out of the spotlight in opposite direction towards the chairs in the audience.

The American raised his brows in surprise, not knowing what's going on. The third bullet went through the top of the Argentinean's hat. That's when the Yankee got it, and throwing his partner over his shoulder, took three leaps and was safe in the darkness.

The security also realized that the scene was developing according to its own laws. The bodyguards gathered around the president and quickly led him out of his box. Radios started beeping and security rushed to the upper level and under the roof.

In an authentic tango, the man, macho, always goes first. He can move sideways, turn and change direction, but to glide backwards – never. The second law – never to bump into or make contact with other couples, otherwise – immediate disqualification and shame till the end of days.

Another bullet went through the sun on the hem of the girl from Montevideo. The woman took out a pin from her tall hair, which was a thin stiletto, shook her head, and her hair in a black wave covered her exposed back.

Somewhere from the darkness of the theatre, someone threw a knife, facon, – the typical gaucho sidearm. Spinning, the knife slid across the floor toward the Argentineans. The compadre in the white neck-scarf performed a corkscrew enrosque with virtuosity as he picked up the knife.

Carlos Gardel on second bandoneon was improvising the main theme of the Libertango together with his former student Astor Piazzola. Santana strummed a twelve-string Spanish guitar. Page pressed down on the distortion pedal and took the high riffs. Armstrong and Parker were overflowing with excitement on the brass, old man Horowitz was beating away on the bass keys, Yo-Yo Ma, it seemed, bent the cello into an arc, which fluctuated with the music. Bonham was impeccably exact – the thundering of his drums kept everyone in rhythm.

The Argentineans and the Uruguayans would come together and apart through the dance, trying to reach the opponents with a knife or stiletto. You could not bump into the others, but you were allowed to kill them. Madness broke out in the theatre; some ran for the exits, others beat their way towards the dancers.

The Chinese distinguished themselves in their own way. In the midst of chaos, they were singing revolutionary hymns and waved a red flag with an image of Mao.

Chandrika and Sandro moved as if they could see everything that was happening around them. Their hearts were beating as one, their souls together became indivisible.

On Chandrika's head and Sandro's back, quivered the red points of laser-sights, but the bullets would pass by. Each time Chandrika dodged, or turned, or did something else, pulling Sandro with her – somehow unexplainable, the bullets would miss them.

Sandro looked into the Chandrika's brown eyes that understood something not right was happening around them, but her eyes said: "Be with me," and Sandro simply followed her.

Finally the musicians played the last note. The four couples stood still in their farewell poses. The floor was pierced in places by bullet holes, the Argentinean dripped rubies from his cheek, the Uruguayan streamed blood from the ripped sleeve. The Chinese were holding their red flag and portrait of the Great Pilot. Chandrika bowed in a beautiful way, Sandro was holding her by the fingertips. From the closest exit a shadow darted towards him. In that instant, when the music had stopped, but the applause had not yet started, in the silence there popped a quiet gunshot.

The grey yard bird from the Gorbunov's House of Culture fell on Sandro's chest, and with weak hands, he held on to him by the neck. On her back, spread a bloody stain.

*   *   *

On a grey, rainy, cold day we were smoking by the entrance to the Seleznevsky baths. Exactly at noon, across the whole endless country there was a din of factories, cars, trains, and ships, – the entirety of our progressive humanity was burying our Communist Party's General Secretary.

"Twelve o'clock – our steam," said the Old Man, and we went inside.

After the steam with St. John's Wart and mint, Sandro gained some color, looking more like a human being, and did not dodge from every look or question.

Two hours later, soft and kind, we were standing in a smoky fast-food place around a high table with glasses of beer mixed half with vodka. Sandro told us that, for obvious reasons, no one at the competition received any prizes. The fanatic-sniper from among the Argentinean admirers was shooting at the two Uruguayans. The other sniper was hired by the Uruguayans, to eliminate their main competitors, the Argentineans.

Gloria used her connections in the British secret service to kill Chandrika. At her own risk, she hired an agent without a name, a past or fingerprints on file. Victor was shooting at Sandro from a rifle, which was brought into the theatre by Argentinean leftists, who used to be supported by Moscow.

How the young girl from Gorbunov's House of Culture appeared in Teatro Colón, nobody knows. They had quickly taken her body away and put it somewhere.

Sandro and the other dancers were questioned for a long time, but then released. He then divorced Gloria, but had to leave Chandrika as well. Between them forever would be that reed-thin girl, even though she and Sandro had just one dance together.

Poseidon and the Glasses

My wife and I purchased the new eyeglasses together. An important matter – since not only do I have to like them – but more importantly, my better half must approve. Not to mention that it's my birthday, which means it's a present.

We were deciding for a while. There are hundreds of fashionable frames on display, but almost no good ones. After about two hours we finally found a pair of web-frames that satisfied us both. The lenses blocked ultraviolet rays, didn't glare and shone with a greenish tint, like the lens of an expensive camera. My head spun a little; I could see so well. These weightless glasses didn't press down anywhere, as if they didn't exist. The wife ordered some chameleon-lenses, so as to not go to the optician for nothing. We paid a mountain of money and after dinner, the three of us, including my son, drove off to Florida.

From here to Miami, it's about 1200 miles, but we three drivers, constantly switching at the wheel, got there in about eighteen hours. It's not the first time our friends have invited us to Florida; they have an apartment in a building right next to the ocean. We got there late in the evening, drank a bottle of cognac with our host Henri, to mark our arrival and dead tired, went to bed.

We woke up early. The sun had just risen and it's rays played cheerfully on the glittering path from the horizon to the beach below. My son was still asleep – nowadays youth does not open its eyes until after noon.

Together with my wife, we went down to the beach. The building is well-planned, the lobby leads to a terrace with a pool and from there – a few more steps – you're in the ocean.

I love the morning hours, when even on the most popular

and populated resorts you still can't see anyone. A few sparse swimmers and a pair of nudists – that's all. The waves were quiet and gentle. My wife put on sun-screen with great concentration, so as to not get sunburn the first day in the south. I stepped into the water and softly dove into the larimar waves. The water was a little chilly, but after the long hours in the car and yesterday's Salignac, it pleasantly refreshed and washed off all the pre-vacation anxiety.

Having swum my fill, I came out onto the beach, dried myself with the double towel and reached for my glasses, which, by habit, I leave in my straw hat. The glasses weren't there. I checked in my shorts – no, not in the beach bag – either.

"Dear, have you seen my glasses?"

"No."

"Wherever did I hide them?"

We started looking together. Nowhere.

"Did you swim in them?"

I remembered how, entering the water, I admired faraway sails on the sharp line of the horizon. It seems my glasses were swept from my nose the very first time I dove in. That's sad, spent a load of money and a ton of time. Of course, I have a backup pair, but they didn't compare to those, which now lay on the sandy sea floor.

"Oh well, we'll buy another pair."

"On no," my wife replied, boiling, "show me where you went in the water. We're going to look for them."

A hopeless venture – to find such a trifle in the ocean. The sea-floor is even, but the glasses are of a colorless plastic with a frame a hair thick. No way to identify them through these heavenly waves. We zigzagged combing the ocean bottom, square by square, feeling the sand with our feet.

"Dear, let's not waste time. I have another pair in the

suitcase."

My wife's face became thoughtfully dismissive.

"Check what's under my foot."

I took a small breath and dove in. Between the toes of her right foot there was a golden hoop. Carefully taking the glasses, I swam up and showed them to the wife.

"Idiot, moron, imbecile!" she happily exclaimed to the whole beach and started beating my chest with her fists. "Who did I marry to suffer all these years with? My mom was right when she wouldn't let me go to see you!"

The respectable public looked on in astonishment.

Soon after we came back, at breakfast, we told our incredible story about our lost and found in the ocean. We all laughed together at the jokes of Poseidon.

On that day, like normal vacationers, we sunbathed, swam, and in the evening ate in a Spanish restaurant, La Barraca, where the chef came out to greet the guests and ask about their opinion of the cuisine. A virtuoso-guitarist played in the hall, as two majas dressed in black and red skirts, sang and danced flamenco with castanets.

The next day was the Fourth of July, Independence Day. Tired, after all the adventures, the wife slept soundly. So, my son and I went out to the sea. A light breeze pulled from the east.

"Son, are you going in the water?"

"I'll sunbathe a little first…"

I always prefer to quickly dive in, to immediately feel like I'm in a different reality. Swimming before breakfast; a pleasure that charges me up the whole day.

The glasses weren't in the hat.

"Son, I drowned the glasses again, like yesterday."

"Mom won't be happy when she hears that."

"Start looking while I go get the masks. Maybe we can find them that way, the waves are picking up."

I went up to the apartment, quietly snuck into the room and got the bag with the diving equipment. Two masks, two snorkels – no need to bring the fins since we're looking near the shore.

Went back down, my son was walking towards me with a puzzling smile: "Here they are! Found them with my foot, like mom. They were almost covered in sand. Another minute or so and we would have never found them."

I had to tell the wife what happened. She got upset: "You know, this is the chiaroscuro for the family vacation!"

"They're very light, I can't feel them on my nose."

"That's not even funny, losing your glasses twice. You're beginning to spoil the whole vacation."

She took the Jeep and drove off to Miami Beach to window-shop and calm down. The best psychotherapy for women is to buy something they don't need.

My son set himself up on the beach chair on the balcony, put his laptop on his stomach, connected to the internet and started chatting with friends from all over the world.

I loafed around the apartment, didn't feel like reading. Don't watch TV even when at home. Henri was working in the office, tracking the fluctuations of stock on the Tokyo exchange. His wife Ella was researching the statistics of Russian crime in New York over the last twenty years for an article. Not to be in anyone's way, I went back down to the beach.

Across the sky, a plane was dragging an enormous banner – four beauties in mini-swimsuits advertised some investment bank. Carefully, I placed the glasses in the hat and put the hat in my bag, zipping it closed. I slowly went into the water and swam without immersing my face, just in case. Once I got away from the floundering kids and surfing teenagers, I lay on my back, spread arms and legs wide and stopped moving. A position of absolute calm. Relax, look at the sky with its curly-headed clouds, listen to the sea and think about something pleasant.

Water – around 80 degrees Fahrenheit, almost body temperature. You lie there and can't even feel it, definitely steaming in weightlessness. It's good in the south, should move here … palm trees, the warm sea, women in bikinis year round. What a joke. Poseidon threw them out though, who to tell – no one would believe it. Why would he need my glasses? No waves, a light wind, should try not to burn – need to return before lunch … I snapped back after a loud splash. A pelican flopped nearby, grabbed a large fish and, flapping its wet wings, flew up into the air. I flipped from the surprise, swallowed some salt water and immediately woke up.

Dozed off in a daydream, there, cradled by waves. Probably missed lunch. The wife, of course, would likely come back and will be yelling again. "Turn towards the beach," I ordered myself.

This is a sticky situation! Where did it drag me off to? Looks like a current caught me up and, like an inflatable mattress; it pulled me out into the ocean. Where were the acclaimed lifeguards looking? Okay, most importantly, don't panic and don't make any sudden moves. The sun is entering its last quarter in the southwest. A little to the right and then swim, economizing the batteries. The current must have been pretty strong, can't even see the skyscrapers of Ft. Lauderdale.

They'll remember me towards evening, sound the alarm and start searching. That's only if they don't go to a movie first, figuring that I was upset and planned to wander around the beach until someone calls me for dinner.

Of course, I got thirsty immediately. I tried to swim west, but what can a mere man in nothing but red trunks do against the ocean?

"They'll look for you," I assured myself.

It's a pity that they don't make waterproof cell phones. Just attach it to your forearm and no problems: "Dear, I'm sinking four miles from the shore!"

"Don't mess with my head! You're drunk again? Who is she? If you drown, don't come home!"

"Bubble-bubble-bubble ..."

Jokes are all fun and good, but what's to be done? What kind of advice does world literature have?

Old man Santiago would know where to go and had even a boat with a sail. The sharks devoured his record-sized marlin though. Brr ... that's what we don't need right now. Two times this week sharks attacked teenagers who were boogie-boarding. From below, the bottom of the board and the person's legs look like the silhouette of a manatee. That's why the sharks attacked them. I, however, am laying quietly, spread out like a starfish. What if they think I'm seaweed. How's that, they're not so stupid!

There was some movement below me and I guessed. I turned over to look without a mask or glasses (I'm nearsighted) – looks murky – two grayish bodies with narrow noses. Sharks!? Oh, God, save and protect me, a sinner! What did I do in my life that was so bad? There were, of course, some stupidities, but why send me to such a death?

I started working at full capacity to swim away as far as possible. But can a man compete with a sea-dweller? Soon, I was out of strength.

Through the course of the day, the sun baked my head, red

circles started to glimmer before the eyes. Will they devour me? Oh well, otherwise I'd just drown anyway ... Poseidon, I'm a tiny insect, a shrimp, a drop compared to the Ocean. Why do you need my death? What's its use? I promise you – What can I promise the God of the seas, naked ... in the middle of I don't know where. Twice, my glasses have been washed off. Apparently you like them. I'll make them a gift to you, just please get rid of these horrible sharks....

I spun around, fearing an attack. One of the shadows moved upward towards me. This is it, the end. Spraying me with a fountain of water, a dolphin jumped out within five feet from me and, standing on its tail, danced across the sea's glassy surface. The second, cheerfully clicking, turned summersaults, nearby. My heart was torn with gladness. Not sharks, I'm saved!

Soon the dolphins left about their business, I was alone again. If there are dolphins here, then that means there aren't any sharks. Still, how am I going to reach the shore?

I lay on my back and try to think it through logically. It's still light, another hour, an hour and a half, before sunset. It's most likely that they'll start worrying about me around midnight. By the time they contact rescuers and the coast guard, who will start combing the sea bottom and sending up helicopters (if they do), it'll be too late. They won't find me at night. Realistically, that would all start tomorrow. By then, the current will pull me even further away. And the thirst – God forbid I should get heatstroke – lose consciousness and drown. Misery...

It got dark.

"Poseidon, you saved me today, turned the sharks into dolphins and didn't allow the sun to melt my brains. Help me, you're omnipotent in the sea, for you it's so easy to save the life of a man. I am an artist, what can I do, how can I thank and praise you? The

Ancient Greeks, they lived close to the gods. For us, it's all different. We remember the deities of the sea, of the forest, of rivers and deserts only when we're in a bind like the one I'm in now. Poseidon, I understand your power and your grandeur. Save me, return me to my beloved wife and son…" Thus I prayed, rocking on the waves and gazing at the starry sky.

I don't know how it happened, but something changed suddenly. Instead of light waves I felt a resilient current. To try to get out of it was pointless. I thought to approach the event philosophically – "I'm in no shape to overpower the current, best I can do is keep myself afloat."

"Become a part of the Ocean," I told myself, "unite with him. He can be angry and dangerous or, inversely, kind and gentle. All of mankind is not strong enough to defeat the Ocean. Love him and bow to him …" The ancient seafarers probably whispered something similar during their treacherous voyages.

A little star blinked on the black horizon, after it another. Then bloomed tiny bouquets of multicolored sparks. That's – fireworks! Today's the Fourth of July, Independence Day! There are firework displays all along the shore, with bonfires and barbeques.

Like an insane river wheel steamer I started slapping the water, darting in the direction of the beach. Soon, of course, I was exhausted. The current, wide and smooth, carried me towards the faraway lights.

The waves spilled me onto the shore not far from my bag and straw mat. All around me people were celebrating – detonating cartridges, grilling sausages, drinking, eating and dancing. No one noticed when I crawled out of the water. Staggering like a drunk, I limped to my bag with the hat and in one gulp, quaffed a bottle of water. I recovered my breath and laid down on firm, solid sand. After a while I gathered my things and headed back to the house.

It was strange and surreal going up to the forty-fourth floor in the speeding elevator staring at mirrors on the walls. I opened the door to the apartment and entered. Inside, an orange lamp glowed cozily. The wife and Henri and Ella were sitting at a coffee table, sipping liquor and admiring the fireworks through the window. My son was talking on the phone.

"We were thinking of going to look for you."

"Everything's okay. Swam for too long and then dozed off on the beach."

I decided not to talk about my adventure. What's important is that I'm alive.

Nonetheless, one must do what is promised to the gods. On the following day, I called my son to go diving. Aboard the boat "Ibis," we went out to sea with four other scuba divers. I didn't feel comfortable – a little seasick. We got to the reef, which for some reason they call "German." Maybe they sunk a submarine there? Twenty-five, thirty feet to the reef. That's good, after yesterday, I don't even want to think about depth.

We went down in twos, each pair with its own buoy, a red flag with a diagonal white line. One in each pair pulls it along by a thin cord wrapped around a reel. The buoy afloat shows the boat where the divers are.

My son clipped the reel to his belt and we started swimming. The corals were beautiful, but far from those of Paradise Island! However, this time my goal is completely different.

A huge sea turtle went up from a wide, white rock that looked like a piece of a broken column. There it is! I let my son go in front and reached into my vest pocket to take out the case with the glasses. I opened it and placed it atop the rock. The glasses sparkled, rainbow tinted from the ultraviolet filter. I admired the rock-column in parting. Pure white marble, for some reason seaweed and coral didn't grow on it. Could it be there specifically for sacrificial offerings?

A year later, I won a contest for making a mosaic for the boardwalk of a new seaside hotel. A massive cement wall of the building's garage towered over the freshly-poured beach, dwarfing everything around. My project with Poseidon, god of the seas, appealed to architects, investors and municipalities. Having decided on an estimate, I received the advance and bought smalti in Venice. A little more, six months, seven, and I will keep the rest of my promise.

Sax Solo

That's it! Finally Anna was rich! Gone were the dark times when she had to refuse herself everything just to pay for her apartment. The years of penny-pinching and lengthy servitude to credit card companies were gone forever. No more will she have the shameful fear of not having enough money to pay for her groceries at the register. The heart pains from poverty and constant struggle for a piece of bread subsided.

Now – it was no longer a problem to eat out in any restaurant, to fly to Europe for the weekend or to call a masseuse for a house visit. She did not have to wake up with the awful alarm clock to rush to work. Most importantly – she did not have to work! She had enough means to last the rest of her life, with a little left over. Her soul stopped moaning that the years were passing, while she had neither stake nor claim.

Anna's new house – a Colonial style eight-bedroom mansion – its interior – dark oak and expensive leather. The house was built on the slope of a hill, overgrown by a thick forest, a clear stream ran over the rocks. It was a large property of over a hundred acres, which could not be seen from the highway below, to which it was connected by a winding cobblestone path.

The feeling of calm, confidence in tomorrow and other attunements did not come right away. Anna often shook at night, afraid she would wake up in the old bedroom, looking out upon garages and garbage cans. But gradually, she got used to the thought that everything was grounded and would not disappear overnight like a dream.

At night on the bed next to her slept her husband Edward in warm pajamas. Usually he slept on his side, facing Anna. His hand, overgrown with thick white hair, hung over the edge of the bed almost to the floor. In his sleep, he would sometimes knit his brows or smack his lips. A weak nightlight illuminated his tall forehead and big nose. The wrinkles in the corner of his mouth seemed to Anna symbols of character and strength of will.

In the morning, Edward made coffee and toasts, which he brought on a silver platter up to Anna still in bed. In earnest, she would have preferred to have time to freshen up and to have breakfast in the kitchen, but, not to offend her husband, she sat with her back propped on the pillows, drinking the aromatic coffee carefully, so as not to drip on the fine linen sheets.

After breakfast, they would have sex, and then Edward would go to the office. He had more than enough money, but he did not like to sit around doing nothing. So, more for personal entertainment, he ran an advertising/marketing firm.

While Edward was out doing business, Anna distracted herself: went to the nearby town antiquing and spoiled herself at the Korean spa, where they washed, steamed, and provided her with a manicure and pedicure. She stopped by the bistro to grab a croissant and an herbal tea. Around four thirty – five, she came home and made dinner if they were staying in that night.

Life went swimmingly, without sudden changes or events. Anna was glad and did not want anything to disrupt the harmony, even if it would be for the better.

Things went wrong in the autumn, when leaves started to fall, and in the mornings the puddles were covered by a thin ice. Anna was going grocery shopping at the supermarket, she drove out of the warm garage and carefully went down the hill: the Mercedes' new tires were slipping on the turns. Before the ramp for the turnpike, she stopped, and looked both ways.

Nobody to the left, to the right – a car about a hundred yards away, it was not going fast, but Anna decided to let it through anyway. As the car was passing Anna, a deer with curled horns jumped out on the road. The driver slammed on the brakes, the deer jumped into the bushes, while the car started spinning on the ice, out into the other lane, slamming Anna's door with its bumper. The airbag worked, but Anna lost consciousness out of fear.

The ambulance, which a passing trucker called, came quickly. The collar-bone, along with the left shoulder-blade was broken. Edward dashed to the hospital, roused up all the doctors and nurses, called an old friend of his – a department chair of orthopedics, and they took Anna by helicopter to the celebrated medical center adjoined to the university.

Two hours later, after additional examinations and analyses, they locked her damaged hand into an ingenious contraption – you could not simply call it a cast. They put Anna in her own room, with a view of the well-groomed park and the Old English buildings of the university, one of the first in the country.

On the beige wall hung a remote controlled television. On a stand nearby – a vase of flowers, a glass of juice, a bottle of water, and several books, which Edward bought in the university store that was open day and night.

Edward went home to deal with the insurance company, the other driver's lawyer, and the repair of the car. He promised to come back tomorrow and to stay in a hotel nearby until Anna gets better and leaves the hospital.

From the window of her room, Anna could see the main entrance and the ER. She reclined comfortably in her bed, which could change its configuration at the press of a button, going from flat to angled, folding into a chair or rocking like a cradle.

It was getting dark. Sometimes ambulances would pull up to the ER, and they would bring out stretchers with bodies strapped to them, so they would not fall out. One of the patients was struggling, trying to stand up, with his free hand he was pressing to his chest an oblong case from a musical instrument.

Cars of different brands stopped by the main entrance, out of them came old people, adults, and children – probably visiting their friends and relatives.

Gradually, the stream of cars dwindled, night came. Anna did not sleep, but dreamt a little. Around midnight, next to the entrance to the hospital stopped a big expensive car, from which came a man, a woman, and a crying girl.

"Who are they and why here at this hour?" Anna wondered lazily. But then, every hospital always has its share of tragedies and untold history.

In the corridor, she could here nervous hubbub, muffled voices, quick footsteps, and walkie-talkies. From somewhere above, as if from the sky, came music.

"Saxophone," through her dream, Anna could recognize the timbre of the instrument.

The window to her room was open – she liked the fresh air. The saxophone sang softly, the tender melody lulled, calling from an idyllic world. Anna relaxed. From somewhere within the delicate harmony came alarming notes, which sounded louder and soon grew into an intense theme. Anna did not expect the music to effect her so much. The rhythm sped up and now pulsated by her temple like a headache. A little more, and the melody pierced her brain like a molten needle, the music turning into a soul-wrenching scream!

There was a rumbling in the sky – a police helicopter

appeared and hanged over the hospital. Lights went on in windows, the curious poured out into the street. The searchlight of the helicopter circled the backyard, around the bushes and suddenly lit up the figure on the roof of the building to the left.

A naked man, thin as a skeleton, stood on the edge of the parapet. Torn bandages fluttered in the cold wind. Pieces of plastic tubes and some sort of wires stuck out of his arms, legs, veins, neck, chest and stomach, as if he was just escaped from a reanimation. The long hair, tangled in locks, unfurled in the mad wind caused by the blades of the helicopter, and whipped him across the cheeks, chest, and back. The sound of the engine almost overpowered the saxophone, but Anna had already understood everything. She got out of bed, went to the window, with difficulty lifted the heavy frame of the window, and peeked outside.

"Son of a bitch, you want to ruin my life again?" she yelled into the chopped night air.

Anna was sitting on a bus going across the hot, dusty city. She cut across the downtown with its banks, offices, municipal buildings and courts; then passed through the "sleepy" neighborhoods, then went across the outskirts – endless storehouses, fences, oil refineries; behind them – angled mineshafts with waste banks, trucks, and railroads. A grey dust covered everything around. Boredom, anguish and poverty.

People would get off and get on when the bus stopped. The air-conditioner was not working: it was hard to breathe even though all the windows were open. Anna sat in the second to last seat in the back, and kept going and going.

"It's good that today is a Wednesday, and not Sunday," She thought to herself.

On Sundays, the chemical refinery opened up its filters and let out the gases that accumulated over the week. An unimaginable stench would hang over the entire town. It was useless to complain or protest. The refinery provided three quarters of the town with work, paid for the hospitals, schools, churches, stadium, the town bureaucracy and even the symphonic orchestra.

Anna worked for the refinery in the Department of Landscaping and Urban Planning. They paid badly, but had good medical insurance and two weeks paid vacation.

The bus left the industrial zone and drove across the prairie. It was easier to breathe now. Soon they were at a standard apartment projects – a satellite of the refinery. The five-story twin buildings of grey brick stood so close to each other that you could see the steam from the teakettle in the kitchen of the other house.

Anna got out at the final stop. The bus went around a circle, picked up some new passengers, and rolled back in the other direction. Next to the bus stop was a worn storefront that read "Products," a bar with a neon sign, and a gas station.

To save herself from the midday sun, Anna put on her straw hat down to her eye brows, took out her sunglasses, and walked down the cement path deep into the complex. To her lover.

Anna was a natural platinum blonde, a little under six feet tall, with legs starting at her arm-pits, firm breasts and a seductive low back.

"Don't be timid, Annie," her mother used to tell her when she was young, fixing up in front of the mirror, "you need a bigger butt, men like that!"

Truly, Anna had a great butt. Men, especially the small and black-haired, went pale and lost the gift of speech, when she would walk by, swinging her hips.

    She and Oscar used to work in
the same department. Anna put miniature
trees and bushes on architectural
maquettes, while Oscar the accountant,
composed an expense estimate for them.
They would go out to the street together
for cigarette breaks; nothing brings
people together like smoking.

    One time they had to stay late, with the quarter deadline
almost there. Without noticing – behind all the joking, coffee,
and cigarettes – they fell right on the office table. Afterwards, they
laughed about strange things that happen when one works over
time, and went to their separate homes.

    Anna has been married for ten years, Oscar is remarried
with a small child, his kids from the first marriage already finished
college. There was no talk about continuing their romance.

    After a couple of months, Oscar inhaled some crap at the
refinery, started having nose-bleeds every day, and soon lost his
sight. The refinery's managers summarily gave him his severance
package and put him on his pension. The young wife quickly got
tired of the invalid, and left, taking the kid and a large divorce sum.

    The compassionate Anna called to support the former
colleague. Oscar was happy at her phone call, invited her for a cup of
coffee, and so Anna ended up giving him some more. This time – out
of pity – but then, out of the goodness of her soul, started visiting
him every other week.

    There was no mighty love or fiery passion between them,
but Anna understood, that for Oscar, her visits were a ray of sunlight
in the oncoming darkness, while for her these meetings were

manifestations of her feminine charity. Besides, she liked the feel of his wide palms and strong black fingers on her hips and buttocks.

Oscar only had four percent of his vision left, but he deftly maneuvered around the crammed kitchen: made a heady tea, prepared sandwiches, took out jam and cookies, beautifully laying out the plates and saucers on the checkered tablecloth. They drank tea, talking about this and that; they then put the dishes in the sink and went to the tiny bedroom. Barely crammed in there stood a one-and-a-half bed, a night stand and a wardrobe with mirror-doors.

Oscar liked to unbutton her dress, unhook her bra, and take off her underwear. Now, his fingers replaced his eyes. His sense of touch had developed; he rubbed, feeling all of Anna, without skipping an inch.

He lay on his back; Anna turned her back on him and sat on his hot member. She liked this position, it went in deep, she did not have to look in Oscar's face, and his blind eyes.

She steadily went up and down, swaying from side to side, sharply moving her hips back and forth.

"Oh baby," Oscar whispered hoarsely.

Anna sat facing the wardrobe, in the slightly opened door was the reflection of the window with flowery curtains in the house across. The netted halves moved slightly, something was happening behind them. Between the curtains, came a thin woman's hand, long painted nails sinking into the windowsill. On her pinky, glowed a large green stone, from the ring ran a thin golden chain that was attached to the nail. Never before had Anna seen such a piece of jewelry. Out of curiosity, for a second she even forgot what she was doing.

"O, baby, help me out," sharply whispered Oscar.

These things happened: the poisoning at the refinery and

the nervous stress caused certain dysfunctions in the organism of the former marine. Anna got off the sweaty Oscar, went down on her knees on the floor, and helped him finish with her hands and lips.

In her character – a conservative, Anna was more than satisfied with two-three basic positions, and did not strive for creativity or variety. But she was a kind woman, and so often accepted "unseemly," in her eyes, requests. "All men are disgusting," she had long since decided.

Normally, after sex, Anna did not stay long, quickly gathering her things, as not to experience the growing feeling of pity towards Oscar and guilt because of her husband.

She went out into the sultry, dusty street with its wilting trees, and walked to the bus stop. She could still feel the taste of herring on her tongue, even though she had rinsed with Listerene. Anna decided to stop at the bar by the circle and drink a shot of liquor, to cover the saltish aftertaste.

After the glaring sunlight, she did not at first notice the solitary female figure in the dark bar, sitting on a tall stool next to the oak bar. A Martini glass was standing in front of the woman. Anna ordered an Amaretto and sat down nearby.

"I think we've seen each other before," the pale miniature woman with the dark-reddish hair addressed her.

Her hips were covered by a leather mini-skirt, on her feet – cowboy boots, on the pinky of her right hand – a ring with a chain.

The last thing Anna wanted was to be recognized in this neighborhood, let alone to enter any conversations. But the woman inspired trust and carried on their talk with surprising tact. After the third round of Amarettos and Martinis, they felt like old friends, though they did not say their names. They made fun of men and what lustful goats they were, how easy it was to manipulate them.

The reddish one was the mother of three from different fathers, lived in the neighborhood with a regular working Joe. She had moved the kids to her mom's farm – closer to nature, clean air and fresh milk.

Her life was fun and uncomplicated. While the working Joe was at the construction site, she met her lovers – always hot between the legs. In evenings, her Joe came home, ate pasta and cutlets, drank beer, watched football on the television, had sex with her, and tired, fell asleep. Then, the redhead would get dressed, put on her makeup, go to the bar, and pick up somebody, better yet two or three, and had fun with them in the bathroom or a car. The working Joe often beat her for her cheating, but then she would give him magical sex, and the world was restored.

"My dream is to spend a night in a men's jail," the reddish one concluded.

Anna told her about the musician, who spent a long time playing at the local restaurant "Havana," but it has been a year since he lost his job, the jazz band was replaced by a disco. There was no more work for a saxophone player in the town. He tried to join other orchestras, mailed his demos to other cities, but no luck. The couple of private music lessons he gave were not enough to feed them. Anna's paycheck was barely enough for the apartment and the electricity. Good thing they did not have kids.

The musician took any work: washed dishes in restaurants, painted walls, cut grass, pumped gas, but did not stay anywhere long. His intelligent face and glasses irritated other workers, while the bearing of a free artist annoyed the employers.

Anna chastised him, yelling, – he would retreat into himself, refusing food, all the while writing something in his college-ruled notebook. She once peeked into it – incomprehensible formulas, notes, abbreviations and ciphers instead of words.

"What are you writing?" she asked in desperation, returning from the store with just a box of pasta.

"A retrospective analysis of a theory of musical improvisation."

"We have nothing to eat, and you're doing stupid things! Go sell your panpipe!"

"You can sell it after I die. You will even get my insurance."

Their intimate life eventually fell apart. Anna was never in the mood, and he could sense her bad feelings. There was a time when they loved each other, but that love went somewhere, dissolved in the murky stream of endless problems.

The redhead took a deep swing of her Martini:

"Leave him!" the ring with chain rang against the glass melodiously.

"Where? There is no one decent in our countryside."

The redhead told her about how her neighbor, a librarian, placed an ad on the Internet from her work computer, saying that she wants to get married, adorned it with two photographs of herself. By the third week, she had found someone who she wanted, more or less, and quickly made arrangements to get out of here.

"The probability – hundred percent!" encouraged the redhead.

Anna left the bar late, when it was already full of people, and the redhead caught her first victim. Anna did not want any adventures, so she got on the bus and went home. The bus went slow and long, with endless stops and delays – Anna was tortured.

The light was on at home, the husband was sleeping on the couch. On the coffee table was an envelope and a pretty box. In the envelope – a birthday greeting, and in the box – a ring with a large aquamarine stone and a chain, that links to the nail.

Replies to the Internet ad came fast and in good number. Unsurprisingly – Anna placed her photo, which she ordered from an expensive professional: effective, but tastefully displaying all her assets. She met several candidates, had dinner with them, went to concerts and the theater, but not as far as the bedroom. Patiently awaiting the right opportunity.

Towards the end of the fourth month she stopped waiting: he was wealthy, not young, divorced, his children had grown up, his alimony paid off, looking for a tall blonde with no bad habits.

On the second date, Edward brought her an enormous bouquet of roses the price of Anna's monthly salary (she checked the next day at the store), he took her to a restaurant where they simply did not put the price on the menu, and, saying goodbye, gave her a necklace of black pearls, each the size of a walnut.

Anna melted. Edward behaved properly, no mistakes, always serious and purposeful. After a month of 'dry' meetings, Edward brought Anna to her lawyer, in his presence he proposed and asked her to sign the marriage contract. Anna's head started spinning when she saw the monthly allowance for free spending. Never in her life did she have so much money. She signed her name with a quivering hand.

To the formal question of whether she was currently married, she answered in the negative. A long time ago, a little after high school, she married a musician in an old forgotten church. Except for the newlyweds and the priest, there was nobody at the church. The priest had promised to mail the certificate of marriage, but never did. The church itself burned down – they passed its ruins a few years ago. Anna admitted that she was living with the musician, but legally speaking they were not married, so there should not be any problems. Anna also decided to quit smoking.

Their wedding celebration was modest by Edward's standards. They invited fifty guests to a secluded hotel-mansion in Aruba. Everyone that came was highly respectable, no Bohemians. After all the nuptial ceremonies, congratulations, gifts, banquets and dances, around midnight the couple got to the bedroom.

Walking in front of Anna with a glass of collector's whisky, Edward explained, that in the twilight of his years, he wanted to calm himself in the embrace of a young beautiful woman, whom he selected long and hard. His personal astrologer made charts for each candidate, and Anna was a favorable pick. Her soft character and simplicity in interaction appealed to Edward, while her queenly butt sealed the deal.

Of course, you have to pay for everything in life. The old epicure Edward made it clear, that of all the kinds of sex, he preferred the "French," that is anal, and asked Anna to forgive him if this offends her, but he is an old man, and cannot change his preferences. If his passions are too much for her, they can get divorced, but the contract is set up skillfully so that she would not get a dime.

Anna breathed deeply, pretended to smile, lifted her fluffy white dresses and bent over. After all, some pay with their front end, others with their back.

She tried not to think about the musician: out of sight, out of mind. Rumors reached her that he lamented, starved himself, unsuccessfully tried to commit suicide, but Anna firmly decided that a grown man could find a way to provide for himself.

Still, sometimes, in the quiet forest she thought she could

hear a tenor-saxophone melody and the ringing of distant bells. She repelled such painful phantasms and would go buy some trifle, to let loose, or just go to a movie. Gradually she forgot her old life, and became a respectable lady in a Mercedes: fate loosened its grip around her throat.

And here, into her life again charges this horror of the past!

*   *   *

"I hate you and your wretched horn!" she yelled into the freezing air.

The man seemed to not hear or see her. He stood on the very edge of the parapet, the soles of his feet half standing on air. The tubes and wires sticking out of him curled like a ball of snakes.

He was playing with his eyes to the sky. From the horn of the saxophone came drops of blood that sparkled in the beams of the police searchlights. The musician was blowing out the last sparks of his life, love, suffering and unfulfilled hopes.

A crowd of people gathered below, the windows of the hospital were being filled by awestruck faces. Visual images were being born out of the music: in the turbulent air hanged concert halls, studio recordings, smoky jazz-clubs, summer dance-areas, wild spectators, flowers, applause. Millions of notational flourishes weaved together into an intricate arabesque weaving lace out of melodies, wrapping the musician in a glimmering cloak.

People saw how the specter of love flew out of the saxophone – a young girl appeared, and then dissolved in the darkness. Out of its touching harmony, the melody broke into a wheeze – the light-haired naked woman was giving herself to the blind man. The horrors cawed like crows, paranoia moaned, the psychotics ground their teeth. The people below were grabbing their heads, closing their ears, shutting their eyes.

In the sky, through the ray of the searchlight, appeared the girl in the wedding dress, and reached her hands to the musician. He came to and took a step off the parapet. Together, they walked on the beam of light until they disappeared in the heights.

Thorne-Apple Flower

Gomka sat on the balcony in a beat-up armchair and smoked nervously. A spliff – marijuana mixed with tobacco. Cats were scratching at his soul, his stomach hurt, and a stone has been tossing and turning in his left kidney for two days now. His head ached from lack of sleep. The weed relieved the pain for small stretches of time, so he had to keep smoking, nonstop.

The spliff finished burning; Gomka flicked the roach off the balcony with a snap of his fingers. It traced a glowing arc and disappeared somewhere far below. Gomka took out another stoagie from his pack and tapped, pushing the tobacco onto a newspaper, and then took out a pinch or two of weed from a polyethylene bag. For a while, he stared at the cigarette guts, then he wiped them off the table and filled the empty rolling paper with pot. He lit it with a cheap lighter, and closed his eyes in relief.

The stomach ulcer no longer tortured him, the kidney stone stopped moving, and a blissful languor flowed through his body. The dome of night inspired calm. Gomka started dreaming.

He saw a log cabin sunken into the ground, overgrown with weeds and ivy, next to it, an abandoned garden of branchy apple trees and old cherry trees. Under the antonovka apple tree – there were three beehives in the depths of the garden – a tiny stream-puddle with goldfish, and near the fence – a doghouse with the German shephard Linda, his best friend from childhood.

Smoke came from the summer oven; grandmother was calling him to take the foam off the preserves. Gooseberries with cherry leaves! He set aside the worn volume of "Captain Breakneck," got out of his cot, which stood in the shadow of the apple tree, and went through the bushes towards the house.

Clusters of black currants hung from the pliant branches. Gooseberries sparkled in the sunrays, through their amber skin shone the outline of seeds.

Burdock stuck to his shorts, the thorns painfully scratched his naked legs, impeding his walking. Gomka understood that he could not get to the tub with preserves and decided to go back and around the bushes from the other side. But there was no way back! The burdock surrounded him in a thick wall, it went above his head, its stalks winding and stretching towards the scared boy. Someone giggled nastily, in the middle of the violet thorne-apple flower sat a tiny naked man with a big bumpy head, wrinkled face and lips smeared with preserves. He looked like Gomka, only forty years older.

Gomka shuddered – two fighter-jets flew low over the houses and disappeared behind the hills. Soon afterwards there came a glow, followed by the thundering of a rocket salvo. And again the world was quiet.

The extinguished spliff lay on the stone floor. Gomka picked it up, lit it and took a long pull. The sky was turning gray, the night stars were going out. He did not like these hours, filled with inescapable boredom. Useless ideas about the emptiness of life and an existence without meaning crawled into his head. The appropriate time for suicide: everyone else is sleeping, no one would interfere if one was to tie a belt around the neck in the bathroom of some Angleterre Hotel.

In the morning gloaming, the silhouettes of the village huts could be made out on the adjacent hill. Flocks of sheep were squeezed in the pen. On the stone road, neither man, nor machine.

The silence heralding the dawn was cut by the bellowing of a donkey, it was joined by another, then the dogs chimed in, roosters, goats, and in the crescendo – the camels.

"Cursed place," Gomka swore.

Just as suddenly, the concert stopped. A rosy line appeared to the East, and the surroundings were filled by the muezzin's prayer, repeatedly amplified by powerful speakers. The mountains answered with an echo: "Allah-il-Alla-a-a!"

"That's it, now there will be no rest."

Gomka hid the roach for another time, opened the balcony door and went to the bedroom. On the wide bed under a thin sheet slept a woman with round hips. Gomka lay next to her and hid his head under the pillow.

Gomka was born in East Berlin. His mother was German, his father – an officer in the Soviet army. Since an early age, Gomka spent eight to nine months a year in Germany, and in the summer traveled to Russia. His mother had an apartment on Unter den Linden not far from Shtaats Opera, and his father had one in South-West Moscow. The two grandmothers tore their only grandson to pieces, trying to pull him close. One lived in a house beneath red clay roof-tiles in the mountains of South Saxony, the other – in a wood hut on the Oka River. Gomka spoke freely in German and Russian, and had a decent grasp of English, thanks to West Berlin television.

After high school, he went to the University of Arts in Berlin, studied under Gottfried Bammes, author of the famous anatomy textbook for artists. Under his influence, Gomka started painting nude figures leaning towards a warm palette, reminiscent of the old masters.

Following the destruction of the infamous Wall and the pulling of Soviet troops out of Germany, his father had to return to

Russia. But his mother refused to make such a move.

Germans did not like Russian, even when they were building Socialism. The son of the Soviet officer was constantly reminded of the historical affronts to Russia by Germany. His friends and acquaintances also changed for the worse.

Gomka moved to Moscow, at least there they did not consider him an occupier. And it was far more fun in the land of the golden domes! Gorbachev announced the Perestroika, independent galleries opened up, opening days spun, the artistic life boiled and bubbled. Gomka signed his paintings with his mother's last name, to appear foreign.

An enormous amount of beer, Porto wine and vodka was drunk. Long and loud arguments went on about the ways of modern art and the position of the artist in society. Gomka recalled those years nostalgically. Everyone was young, poor, talented, and felt themselves to be in the avant-garde of world art.

From living at the limit, eating this and that, meeting emancipated women, alcohol, and later – due to the cheap hashish from Afghan and Chechnya, all made Gomka really thin, only his eyes kept burning when he lifted his glass in a toast: "Art – eternal!"

Conceptualism raged in Mutterland, they did not accept Gomka's art there. He filled his canvases with Renaissance athletic torsos, entangled bodies, whole mountains of muscle. Critics speculated on the theme of a homosexual basis in his work. That was when his friends shortened his last name Gomulka to the funny nickname Gomka.

He was not gay, quite the opposite, he took great pleasure in the women around him. But his paintings were readily purchased by Soviet and foreign pederasts, and Gomka held his tongue about his hetero leanings.

The American Gay and Lesbian Association decided to hold an exhibition of his work in New York. Gomka decided: "Why not drink when it's offered?" – and quickly packed to cross the ocean. The show was a success; Gomka turned out to be the first from the Soviet Union with such subject matter. Almost all the paintings were sold – it figures – the prices were 2-3 times lower than for similar works in other SoHo galleries.

The owner of the gallery "Morningstar," Lola Morgenstern, ooed and aahed about what a fabulous artist Gomka was, insisting that, with his talent, he would soon be riding around in a Mercedes-Benz. Due to his kind soul, he slept with her at one Bohemian drinking party. He gave her so much pleasure, that she temporarily switched her lesbian orientation and got Gomka H-1 visa for four years, saying that the artist was working for the gallery.

Unfortunately, her business soon failed, and the creditors got a court order to take all her possessions, including the paintings by Gomka and other artists. In the steps of this misfortune, came the recession, and the people grabbed their pockets and stopped wasting money on trifles, like art.

So, Gomka had to run around like a dog with its tongue hanging out. He painted the walls of bars, made t-shirt designs, submitted articles about art to newspapers, even translated between Russian Mafia and American businessmen. He survived. Later, he got his Green card, and after another five years, his citizenship ripened.

He continued making paintings of naked body-builders. When he could not afford a model, he would draw in the Society of Illustrators or in the life-drawing class at the Arts Students' League.

In the art store, Pearl Paint, he ran into his friend Jenka Spur. Jenka, it turned out, had long since moved to Israel, grew out his peyos, cut off half his member, turned into an Orthodox Jew, and most importantly, worked as the curator at the Museum of Modern Art in Jerusalem.

They had a strong drink to mark their meeting, looked at paintings, drank some more, finally, over shish kabobs on a roof in Tribeca, Jenka, rather now – Zeev, broke and offered Gomka an exhibition.

A year went into the paperwork, but they signed the contract. His first show in a big museum! Inspired, Gomka nailed together boxes, glued frames, packed the paintings, wrote out checks for the insurance, handling, etc. The museum rats moaned that the Ministry does not give them money, so the artist can figure it out himself. The exhibitor must also pay for the catalog, advertising, and champagne, but the money needs to first be transferred to the museum account.

Gomka gathered every copper, borrowed from whom he could, but paid. An exhibition in a museum means that he is a recognized genius!

Burning with impatience, Gomka flew to Israel to pick up the containers with his paintings. What followed was total darkness and misfortune. Arab suicide bombers had detonated another series of explosives. Among the crew of the ship that carried the paintings was a relative of one of the terrorists. They impounded the cargo, the crew too, everyone in the least way involved, everyone who the Mossad could reach, were interrogated.

Meanwhile, in the cafeteria, Gomka's wallet with his passport, money and credit cards was stolen. He was in it deep up to his ears. No money, no documents, paintings – impounded. There was no point talking about an exhibition; at the museum they freaked out and cancelled. In the American embassy, on the matter of the passport, they just shrugged and said: "Wait."

Where to go for a Teutonic-Slav?

It's a small world, and Israel, itself the size of New Jersey, is even smaller. At a concert in Tel-Aviv, Gomka ran into an old girlfriend of his, Nadya Zaharova. In another life, she worked as the costume designer in the Viktiuk Theater in South-West Moscow. Now she sat with helpless old people, went by Nehama, and was a deep-rooted Zionist, though she did not have a single cell of Jewish blood.

Nadya lived in the village, Moshava, about half an hour away from Jerusalem. Her Jewish husband could not handle the austerities of religious life and returned to Russia, meanwhile, her son served in the Israeli army. Gomka agreed to temporarily rent a corner in their guest-room. He only had enough money for the first month, so he went from renting to cohabitation. Sometimes, he got hackwork for cash – painting walls or replacing the toilet bowl. The Arabs would beat any price, making it impossible to compete with them.

Without money, a driver's license, or a car for that matter, Gomka sat in the village like in a trap. Moshava resembles a fortress – with army guards, checkpoints, barbed wire and other fun things. Gomka rarely left the cordon and always came back before dark in order to avoid random document checks. The local police department provided him with a temporary ausweis, but Gomka was tired of explaining himself to guards on duty about his circumstances and why he was there. The vigilant young guards always intently examined Gomka, made phone calls, searched him, and detained him until they were satisfied. He disliked the Promised Land, to the point of grinding his teeth.

Gomka awoke to a knock on the door – in came Ilya, his

friend from the second story. Ilya sometimes published poetry in limited edition anthologies, full of symbols and misty allegory, while supporting his extended family by programming for a mainframe computer.

"Poets are absurd creatures, flighty, unable to compose without inspiration," Ilya took out a bottle of vodka from his string bag.

Nadya was working till morning. There was a leftover fried sausage in the pan, some pasta, in the fridge – dull hummus. Ilya poured two glasses of arak – the cheapest locally-brewed alcohol.

"You should at least filter it through charcoal," Gomka grimaced, downing the first shot.

"Its proof would go down," the former physicist joked, taking a bite of matzah.

They drank on the balcony, admiring the sunset. Below them – an arab village, in the distance on the Mount of Olives – the steeple of a tall bell-tower.

"How's the imperishable, how are the muses doing?" asked Ilya.

"I smothered the damned trollops. Their corpses are lying in the corner, under the rags."

They fell silent. Nobody bought art in Israel. Artists, musicians, actors and other brethren came here by the legion.

"Tomorrow," Ilya began, "friends of my friends are coming here from Chicago. They can't speak a word of Russian, want to see Old City, the Via Dolorosa, etc. I will drive them there and back, while you should accompany them around town. There is no reason for me to go into Christian and Arab neighborhoods wearing a kippa. They pay in dollars."

Gomka led a couple of mini-excursions   down Via

Dolorosa. They went by: Pilate's palace, Herod's palace where he fell the first, second and third time, the Gates of Judgment, Golgotha, and the Church of the Holy Sepulcher. From there, they went past the Tower of David and through the Jaffa Gates down to the subterranean garage. Fifty dollars in his pocket for two hours of work.

The old couple from Chicago knew the Evangelical history much better than Gomka. He relaxed and enjoyed the cool May afternoon. The heat, with its mind-numbing hamsin had not yet started.

They went down the Way of Cross. The old people often stopped to pray. Gomka was bored and tactfully stayed to the side.

Everything was going smoothly, only the St. Alexander Nevsky Church, with the Threshold of the Judgment Gate, was closed. Because of its disastrous condition, the municipal government ordered it closed, but – for a few dollars – one could get in.

Gomka knocked loudly. The steel door opened a crack – They could see a mother and her daughter. They knew Gomka; this was not the first time he brought tourists. He greeted them politely and showed three fingers: "Three of us," and then two fingers for two dollars each. The mother shook her head negatively and showed five fingers: five dollars each. Gomka then offered three, and she nodded in agreement.

The women smiled invitingly and started telling the tourists the history of the Imperial Orthodox Palestine Society, the St. Alexander Nevsky Church and the Russian Excavations. They also told about the discovery there at the end of the nineteenth century where they found the pavement and a part of the city wall with the remains of the gates through which the Romans escorted those sentenced to death. Jesus Christ, likewise, went through these gates and stepped on the threshold stone that bares the grooves where pivots of both wings of the Gate were turned. They also showed them an arch – part of the antique temple, built by the Roman Emperor Hadrian and in the Palestine Society museum – a piece of the wall from the monastery refectory of the Knights of the Holy Sepulcher, who guarded the site of Christ's Tomb during the Crusades. The women often ostensively closed their eyes and crossed themselves repeatedly.

"Thieves," mumbled Gomka to himself.

On a flea market in Haifa, he had seen a catalog of this once rich museum. The only things left in the collection now were rusty ascetic's chains.

The women spoke pretty good English, laughing about how the Great Count Sergey Alexandrovich outwitted the Ottoman Empire and the Patriarch of Jerusalem, and managed to build the Russian church above the Judgment Gates. During the story about the count's wife, St. Elizabeth Fedorovna, martyred by the Bolsheviks, Gomka quietly snuck out to the stairwell; he had heard these many times before.

He descended the wide stairs, went through Hadrian's Arch, ahead – the sacred stone under glass. To the left of the Threshold was a hole in the wall called the "Eye of the Needle." In the old days, they would let travelers in through it when the main gate was closed. There was no way for a laden camel, a horseman, or an armed and armored knight to go through the Eye of the Needle. One lightly-armed warrior could guard such a portal.

In the depths of the Eye of the Needle, a shadow shifted, and an enormous spider came out into the light. Its hairy front legs were rubbing each other, round yellow eyes saccading on its sides, predator jaws clicking, on its head, the bristle went up and down, folding in the form of a miter.

The spider climbed onto the fence around the Threshold, and scurried about left and right, up and down, spreading his web. He did not see Gomka. The Threshold was quickly getting covered in a web as thick as a thumb, the spider wrapping in like a cocoon.

From the crack in the floor came out another spider, tow-haired and thin-legged. He was smaller and seemed younger. The tow-haired one rubbed his legs, and the corner of the Threshold disappeared under a pale-orange shroud.

The black one angrily snapped its jaws, jumped onto the young spider's back, and sunk its teeth deep in the other's head. The tow-haired one started squealing, fought back, and they started rolling towards Gomka's feet. He kicked them like a soccer ball. They flattened upon hitting the wall, fell separately to the stones of the ancient pavement, quickly got up and minced towards Gomka.

Mein Gott! Standing up on their legs, they were waist high to Gomka! He grabbed a dusty candle-holder from the corner and swung it at the black one's head. The chitin cracked, and a bright-green sludge poured out of the wound. The other spider fled cowardly through a fizzure in the floor-tiles.

"You offend the Bishopoppy!" – the two kikimoras hanged on Gomka's shoulders. He slammed them against the wall of Herod the Great and dashed for the exit.

In the Temple of the Holy Sepulcher, there was a reverential silence. The gigantic building was divided into a multitude of chapels and prayer booths, each confessional had its own little corner. Gomka led the old couple to Golgotha, showed them the hole made by the Cross, then the well where Queen Helena found the crosses of the executed.

In the middle of the Temple, there was a small church. Inside was the Holy Sepulcher itself. The couple prayed inside it, lit some candles, and said that they would like to go around the Church one more time, and left Gomka to wait for them.

There were almost no people in the Temple that day. The recent explosions in buses and on the streets of Jerusalem had reduced the influx of pilgrims and tourists nearly to zero. Gomka saw an Ethiopian, or maybe an Abyssinian, go inside with a bundle of candles and a stack of small papers – probably lists of names and prayers for the deceased. The Ethiopian did not come out for a long time, and when he did, he was quiet and pensive.

On Easter night, they lock the Patriarch of Jerusalem inside the small Church, wearing nothing but his shirt. At midnight, they say, a blue light appears on the cover of the Sepulcher, at which time the Patriarch lights two candles, comes out, and from his candles the flame spreads to others. The first couple of minutes, the Holy fire does not burn you, people run the flame across their faces, beards, and hair, without harm.

This piqued Gomka's curiosity. He was a grown man with a skeptical mindset, he led excursions and relayed Evangelical tradition and historical facts, he never considered himself a believer, and the throngs of pilgrims irritated him.

Gomka hesitated at the entrance: "Looks like a porthole, an opening. Well yes – this is the cave of the Resurrection." Bending down low, he went in. It was a tiny low-ceiling room, to the right stood a marble sarcophagus. Nothing special. Gomka studied the decorations on the stone: "Did Jesus Christ really lay here?"

He thought back to Easter in the village church of Horoshovo on the shore of the Oka River. The parishioners were just a few old ladies. The priest with a long grey beard swings his censer. It smells of myrrh and frankincense. Grandma Nelly stands next to her grandson. He is looking at an old darkened icon. The eyes of the Savior are wide open. Christ looks stern, but then his gaze softens and he smiles gently at the boy with the homemade beeswax candle.

Gomka's legs buckled, he fell on his knees and pressed his forehead against the cool marble of the Holy Sepulcher.

*   *   *

The old American couple watched as Gomka, barely shuffling his feet, exited the Temple, lowered himself on the nearest bench and started crying quietly.

Alexandrian Imperial

The avalanche of cavalry rode toward the artillery flèches. There was no sound of yelling, nor horse neighing – only the dull stomping of hooves.

The officer on duty rubbed his eyes with his fist – should the cavalry go uphill or towards the fortified battery? Should they send sabers and pikes against grenades and grape-shot? The short horses were determinedly getting closer, as if gripping onto the slope of the hill. Through the clumps of morning fog appeared the bearded faces under shaggy hats. Cossacks!

The officer kicked the trumpeter, who was sleeping in the trench. He jumped up, not sure what was going on, and lifted the horn to his lips at attention. There was a resounding alarm call.

From behind the Cossacks, a cloud of arrows flew over the morning fog.

"Arrows at Montmartre? In 1814?" the officer was wonderstruck. "This can't be!"

The arrows went into the sky in a sharp arc, hung momentarily in the air, as if seeking out their targets, and flew down at the soldiers of the Young Guard.

"To arms!" The officer on duty had just enough time to yell and fire a shot from his pistol, before an arrow with a heavy head pierced him from top to bottom.

The soldiers started waking up, grabbing their rifles, aiming their cannons, but the first line of Cossacks already passed the redoubts and with wild cries and whistling stormed the hilltop towards the tent with the tri-colored flag – the headquarters of the Neapolitan King Joseph, blood brother of the Emperor Napoleon.

On the vanguard, rode a young Cossack with a Turkish

saber in his hand. He was slicing left and right, deftly dodging bullets and bayonets, diving under the horse's stomach, jumping down in full gallop, and then pushing himself off the ground back into the saddle. The Cossacks were rushing towards the banner. Two stern bearded men helped him from the sides, behind them, two more with pikes covered the three-man shock squad.

Atop the steep Mount Chaumont, from the opposite side of the town, the Russian Emperor Alexander I and the Prussian King Wilhelm monitored with spyglasses the battle for Montmartre, the last stronghold of the French Army in Paris. They both saw how the thin wedge of Cossacks cleaved through the thick defense of the Young Guard, how the aides-de-camps covered the wounded Marshall Mortier and took him off the battlefield, how the French and Russians chopped at each other in front of the standard-bearing tent, and how it shook and toppled. From under the pile of human and horse bodies came the young Cossack on his hairy steed, standing full height on his saddle, and waving the procured flag, rode towards the advancing Russian infantry.

"Wild," said Emperor Alexander, pleased. "Which divisions attacked the enemy?"

"The Orenburg Cossacks, Kalmyk archers, Akhtyr hussars, and the infantry of General Langeron," reported Barclay de Tolly, the commander-in-chief of the Russian army.

"The one who captured the flag, send him to me," ordered the Emperor. "So," he addressed the Prussian monarch, "the enemy is retreating, maybe it is time we had breakfast."

The sky heralded a warm spring day. Soon, the capitulation was signed, and Talleyrand, the leading French politician, delivered to the victors the key to the city of Paris.

The next morning, Russian, Austrian, and Prussian troops triumphantly marched through the city. The Parisians were afraid that the Russian would take revenge for the burning of Moscow in 1812, but the Emperor forbid any abuse; his words were repeated everywhere: "We bring peace, not war." Crowds of curious residents poured out into the streets and boulevards to see the allied troops.

The Russian soldiers managed overnight to bring their uniforms, tattered from the last difficult battles, into exemplary order. In parade formation, to the sound of drums, and with banners unfurled, they came down the boulevards.

"How beautiful these northern barbarians are," the Parisians exclaimed, "not like the Prussians!"

Flowers flew through the air, women tried to touch the marching soldiers, boys ran alongside each division. Russian officers replied to the greetings and general amazement by trading jokes in French.

The troops went down Boulevard d'Italien and Boulevard de la Madeleine, then neared Place Louis XV, where the celebration in honor of Emperor Alexander and King Wilhelm was being prepared. In the square, stood the cordons of Akhtyr Hussars and the Orenburg Cossack regiments. They were controlling the giant crowds, which fluctuated and stirred like the sea. The Akhtyr colonel Denis Davydov, a renowned partisan, poet and swordsman, commanded three regiments in the battle the day before, after the commanders of the other two died in the attack on Montmartre.

It had been four hundred years since a foreign army entered Paris. Thousands of people went into the streets. The joy from the peace treaty reached a frenzy when the allied monarchs appeared; the Parisians were pushing each other trying to get close, kissing harnesses and feet of the sovereigns.

The convoy kept back the dressed-up crowds. Denis Davydov gave short commands. Next to him was the hero of yesterday's battle, the Cossack Matthew, promoted by Emperor Alexander to corporal.

"Monsieur General," came a ringing female voice.

Next to him stood two beautiful women, the first in an expensive dress – the other – in a much more humble one.

"Colonel, Madame," politely answered Davydov.

"We would like to see the Russian Emperor, but the view from the walkway is bad. Lift me up to sit with you."

"But of course, Madame."

Davydov gallantly lifted the one in the pretty dress behind him.

"Matthew, let the other sit with you."

The woman, girl really, looked up with her pleading blue eyes towards the Cossack. Matthew with one hand, skillfully placed her onto his horse. Both women laughed joyfully – now they could see the whole square.

"I am Countess de Périgord," the first woman introduced herself.

Talleyrand's cousin, as Davydov recalled.

"…and this is Nelly, my lady's maid and confidante."

Emperor Alexander's retinue appeared: white plumes, multicolored chevrons, gold epaulettes, medals and aiguillettes, flashing in the sun. Surrounded by his retinue, rode the Emperor, smiling amicably. The crown cheered joyfully, the countess and the maid clapped their hands as the procession went by.

"Monsieur Colonel, please come to my place this evening for dinner. My house is the third on the right from the Arc de Triumph in the Champs-Élysées."

"It would be my honor, Madame. I just need to quarter my men."

That evening, Denis Davydov and Matthew, in parade uniform, went to the countess. Davydov – an ancestral nobleman, once an Imperial Guard officer, renowned through hussar poetry, which brought him into disgrace, flirted with the countess, speaking in a friendly manner about literature, theater, and about his partisan exploits.

Matthew – the young Cossack from the eastern steppes, picked up a little French over the course of the campaigns of 1812-14. The light-haired Nelly, was the niece of a writer L'Abbé Prévost, listened in amazement, when on Davydov's insistence, Matthew recounted yesterdays storming of Montmartre and the capture of the flag.

"But I would not have been able to do anything alone," Matthew explained. "My two uncles were covering my flanks, my brother and my brother-in-law were supporting the back with pikes, while I chopped through the front."

"Oh, don't be so humble," Davydov smirked, "you Cossacks are always putting family first, tell them what His Majesty said."

"His Majesty congratulated me, said I was brave, patted me on shoulder and, here, bestowed the Alexandrian Imperial."

Matthew took out the Imperial from inside his coat, carefully wrapped in a white cloth – the memorable gold coin with the portrait of the Emperor on one side, and the Russian two-headed eagle on the other. Along the edges on both sides were rows of tiny diamonds.

"Take care of the Imperial," Davydov warned firmly. "In addition to the fame and honor, it carries a great price."

Dessert was served. Out of curiosity, Nelly touched Matthew's green-hilted saber.

"I got this in a duel with a basi-bozuk," explained Matthew, "when we were fighting with Turks in Bessarabia."

Nelly scrutinized the not tall but well-proportioned Cossack. Someone like him probably does not fear long journeys, sleeping in the snow or in the desert. It was easy to imagine him spinning like a devil on his horse during battle. While his eyes – intelligent and slightly sad.

"Colonel, I would like to show you my collection of amorous drawings and engravings," the Countess said languorously.

"With pleasure, Madame," Davydov clicked his heels.

The Countess led him by the hand through the suite of rooms.

Left alone, Nelly and Matthew fell into a shy silence. The young girl liked the Cossack right away, as she did back at Place Louis XV. There was an inner strength in him, which Nelly could feel through the broadcloth of his uniform. And you cannot lie to a woman's heart – it knows what it longs for.

When Matthew lifted Nelly onto his horse, he blushed the color of poppies. It was good that she could not see his face as she was trying to see the Emperor. Matthew's love flared up fast: soldiers have hard souls, but when they fall in love, it is fast and forever. Those minutes in the square seemed like an instant to him. "Oh, to ride with her across the steppe," – thought Matthew, but as soon as they are finally alone – all the words disappeared.

"Where in Russia do you live? St. Petersburg?"

"No, my village is over a thousand milestones from the capital."

"What is it called?

"It does not even have a name, just a number, 4."

"Why is that?"

"For us Cossacks, a village only gets a name when its native squadron distinguishes itself in battle. Our neighbors in village 1 were granted the name Kasell, 2 and 3 got Ostroleka and Fère-Champenoise, while earlier, in the Italian campaign of Generalissimos Suvorov, village 8 won the name Trebbia. They say we will get Paris..."

From the depths of the suit echoed the countess' laugh and Davydov's muffled deep voice, then the soft shutting of a door. Nelly lowered her eyes, while Matthew coughed into his fist.

"I'll make some tea," Nelly gathered herself.

They had tea for a long time, Nelly laughed at how Matthew drank tea from the saucer and snacked on sugar, while refusing éclairs and marzipans. They agreed to go for a walk the following day.

Matthew's squadron was stationed in the park near the Champs-Élysées. The Cossacks pitched faded tents, hung their travel pots from tripods, and made horse-posts by nailing iron rings into the poplars along the boulevard.

People were constantly mingling around the camp, feeding the Cossacks various delicacies, asking questions: the Parisians were glad that the frightening tales about the Cossacks had not come true, about how they lash all the citizens with their whips, or drag them for fun with their lassos. There were cheers of: "Viva Tsar Alexander! Viva Bourbons!"

Matthew and Nelly met every day, they would walk along the River Seine or the Tuileries Garden, sometimes going to a tavern, which is now called a "bistro" as a backhanded reference to the Russian officers who wanted everything 'quickly' – pronounced "bee-stro" in Russian.

Many things interested the young Cossack: the history and costumes of Paris, the rare plants and flowers in the conservatories, the paintings in the Louvre, the multi-storied buildings and the secrets of French cuisine. Oh, how Nelly tried to slake his curiosities, talking to him, leading him around Paris.

Social life boiled in the home of Countess de Périgord: dinner parties were replaced by balls and by spiritual séances or concerts by famous musicians. At many of these was the Countess' uncle by marriage, the powerful politician and intriguer, Charles-Maurice de Talleyrand. The glowing warriors of the allied forces, glossy diplomats, aristocrats, those returning to France after many years of exile, swindlers, in short, a whirlpool of people occupied the reception halls.

As the companion and distant relative of the Countess, Nelly met the guests, talked to them, smiled, danced, but in her heart, she was always with Matthew and stole away every minute she could to be with him.

That was how the summer went by. On the first Sunday of September, after the liturgy in the regiment chapel, Matthew came to Nelly in parade uniform with all his medals, his hair meticulously cut and brushed. Nelly understood that something important was going on.

They slowly walked down Champs-Élysées. Matthew shared the news, his squad would soon set out back to Russia.

"Was that it? Will I never see you again?" Nelly was afraid.

Matthew gathered his breath and tired of tumbling over the French grammar, pronounced that light does not shine for him without Nelly, and that they should get married on the following Sunday.

The Countess laughed when Nelly told her about the match with Matthew.

"Why not marry him! According to the Colonel Davydóff, your Cossack's family has thousands of acres of ploughed fields, herds of horses, cows and sheep. You will be a Queen of the Steppes. You can even get mail and fashion magazines over there."

Her love for Matthew turned out to be stronger than that for Paris. Three days later, she was baptized into Russian Orthodoxy, the betrothal set for Sunday.

On Thursday, after his daily rounds, Matthew visited Nelly. They walked down the boulevard and then had a seat in the shade of the poplars. Matthew took out a morocco box – in it laid the thin wedding ring and the Tzar's Imperial! Nelly was breathless. A skillful jeweler cut the Imperial across the middle, so that there were now two, one with the portrait of Emperor Alexander, the other – with the two-headed eagle. On their backs, Matthew and Nelly's names were engraved along with the date of their wedding. Both halves hung from golden chains.

"Now, we are kind of like these two halves," Matthew explained, carefully putting the half with the two-headed eagle around Nelly's neck.

"Beloved," Nelly said softly in broken Russian as she pressed herself to his shoulder.

A shadow fell on her face – a tall man was standing in front of them, blocking the sun.

"Nelly!"

"Gérard?!"

The man did not seem to notice Matthew, who had stood

up – but was only up to Gérard's shoulder in height.

"Where did you come from?"

"A Russian prison. I walked all the way from Smolensk to Paris, and the first thing I see is you with a Russian! Whore!" the Frenchman swung back his hand, as Nelly covered her face in fear.

The Frenchman's palm did not have time to reach Nelly's cheek: Matthew hit him on the head with his sheathed saber. The Frenchman toppled.

"Who is he?"

"Captain Gérard, he courted me before the war…"

"Do you love him?"

"No! I love you!"

Several Cossacks were already rushing over from the horse-post, a few onlookers stopped along the boulevard.

The Frenchman sat, rubbing the bump on his head.

"Russian pig," he grunted, "taking advantage of the fact that I'm unarmed."

"Uncle Egor, give him your saber!"

"And what else…"

"Seriously, give it to him, I tell you! I can't chop him down just like this!"

"Chop, chop…"

From somewhere, over the heads of the gapers, flew a long broadsword, which fell at the Frenchman's feet. He took the blade, and without letting go of it, cast off his well-worn frock-coat, standing in just his shirt. Matthew also removed his tunic.

Duels were forbidden in the occupied Paris, the new Russian governor Saken harshly punished violators of his decree. And here – a fight with sabers right on the Champs-Élysées! A crowd soon gathered around Matthew and Gérard, hungry for spectacle.

Nelly stood barely alive, white as a sheet.

"Matthew, Gérard," she begged, tears running down her face.

Gérard attacked first. The broadsword, gleaming in the autumn sun, traced deathly arches. It was evident that the Frenchman was a skilled fencer. Matthew defended himself with sparing motions: the curved Turkish saber being shorter than the straight broadsword.

A might match, Gérard looked much stronger than Matthew, and he got lucky with the broadsword – the familiar weapon for the former cuirassier, but he could not hit the short Cossack. Matthew put his left hand behind his back, and only side-stepped, dodging from the opponent. The Frenchman got angrier, advanced – Matthew would turn slightly, coolly parrying his lunges.

Gérard started to tire – heavy cavalry attacks in an onslaught, overwhelming the enemy, while not being able to go side to side – the weight is not right for that. Matthew felt the change immediately and went on the offensive. Now it was the Frenchman who had to defend himself, his forehead covered with beads of sweat, as he retreated towards the horse-posts. His height made it difficult to dodge the saber, his large frame became an easy target. Gérard's back was against the poplar – there was nowhere to retreat to.

Matthew sped up the tempo, Gérard furiously defended himself. Matthew bit his lip, made a fake move, pretending he was slipping, and the Frenchman darted forward. Matthew avoided his blade in a spiral motion and marked the wrist of his opponent with the tip of his saber – the broadsword went flying to the side, the bloody hand was hanging like a whip. Gérard stumbled back and drew a dagger from his boot with his left hand.

This was nothing for Matthew. From half a step he disarmed

the dagger and his saber flew up over the head of the Frenchman.

"Matthew!" Nelly screamed pleadingly.

There was no way to stop the strike, Matthew could only lift his elbow a little – the Damascus blade missed Gérard's head by a finger's breadth and cut through one of the thick iron rings, which the Cossacks used to tie their horses.

The Frenchman rolled to the side and disappeared in the crowd.

Their wedding was modest, only fellow Cossacks. Denis Davydov was the substitute father. Countess de Périgord giggled at the offer, but agreed to be the stand-in mother. Nelly's father could not make it – he was lying sick and semi-paralyzed in his house, a former mill in a village on the Loire River. She did not have any other family.

In the morning, they announced to the highest order for the return to Russia. Nelly asked to go visit her father, but his duty prevented Matthew from accompanying her.

Three days later, a rider brought a note from Nelly's father. Through the rheumatic squiggles, Matthew was able to decipher the terrible news that Nelly had drowned trying to cross a river over a weak bridge.

At breakneck speed, Matthew galloped to the small village. The old father mumbled with his toothless mouth, crying all the while, and could not really explain anything. The neighbors said that they found Nelly's muslin shawl, which Matthew gave her, in the reeds downstream, and saw the broken boards from the old bridge. Nelly had gone across the river to visit a childhood friend and, evidently, fell in the water, and could not swim out.

Mad with grief, Matthew walked along the shore of the

river until morning. Davydov sent two Cossacks after him. Carefully, almost like they were handling a child, they put Matthew on a horse and took him back to Paris. The next day, the Russian troops set off – back home, to Russia.

* * *

It was quiet in the exhibition hall with my art, a few people were going from painting to painting, more puzzled than interested.

Noise came from behind the plywood walls of the room, the festival of the town-namesake "All of Paris" was in full swing. Paris, Arkansas; Paris, Argentina; Bolivia, Peru, even India and Cameroon – unbelievable how many big and little Parises there are scattered across the world. Hundreds of tents, marquees, and temporary pavilions were strewn across the big field in front of the capital's hippodrome. Each one told the story of how the local Paris got its name, about the celebrities that came out of it, and of what was happening today.

In the pavilion of our Paris, in the Nagaybak Region of the Russian Federation, there are information stands about the thoroughbred horse-farm, photographs of stallions – winners of various races and all sorts of prizes, trophies and diplomas. The horse-farm is the only industry in our little Paris.

My art is from a slightly different dimension, which does not fall under the reigning mood of joy and brotherhood. Fighting stallions, bared teeth, ruffled manes... Too strong emotions. I felt that my paintings were inappropriate for such an occasion, but the festival's organizers on the Russian side convinced me to support my village and its famous horse-farm with my culture. And here I am – alone in a room of my paintings, while all the people are crowding outside, looking at stallions and chatting with jockeys.

I was dying of boredom. The only person in the exhibition hall was a light-haired woman with a loose cloak a *SoHo Woman.*

"Parlez-vous français?" she addressed me.

" In our Paris, they teach us French since second grade," I answered in French.

"How fascinating! So you live in your village and paint?"

"I left while I was still a child, went to a boarding school for gifted children in the Surikov Art Institute in Moscow. I graduated and became a painter, and now live in the States."

"Why so far?"

"Because life there is freer, and my paintings with their wild horses sell better in America than in Russia."

The woman listened intently to the history of our exotic Paris, in the steppes near the Ural Mountains, and our people – the Nagaybak Cossacks, who were baptized under Ivan the Terrible and served as a reliable shield on the south-east boarders of Russia.

"Do you ride?" she asked.

"My father put me in the saddle when I was three…"

"Come, if you want, to the Vincennes Forest tomorrow, and we'll ride together. I have four horses in the stables there."

Covered with goose bumps from the morning cold, we rode at a trot, then at a walk, through the autumn park on the outskirts of Paris. It somehow happened on its own, that at the end of a long alley we kissed. From the Vincennes Forest, we darted to her apartment near the Arc de Triumph, where we wrestled in her bed for a long time.

"I am invited to a big event this evening at our City Hall - the Hôtel de Ville. Would you like to accompany me?"

"With pleasure. I have a tux, meanwhile the guards can watch the exhibition."

I reached the Hôtel de Ville by metro – because of the evening traffic, taking a taxi was pointless. I walked up and down the puddles along the carriage-way near the entrance, searching for my lady friend. Mercedes and limousines pulled up to the ancient building, out of which came lavish women in furs and diamonds, accompanied by respectable-looking men. She came in a sporty BMW, I walked toward her.

How much a woman transforms, when she dons a beautiful dress for a rendezvous! I do not like social receptions, but I was prepared to endure it for her. Arm in arm, we walked into the City Hall, which was filled with the cream and strawberries of the crop in Parisian society. Waiters in white gloves brought champagne; there were some sort of speeches, ringing of applause. I do not know what the evening was celebrating; I was looking only at her. I had a strange feeling about her since the day before at the exhibition.

"Where did you get your tie-pin?"

"My great-great grandfather received it from the hands of Emperor Alexander I in 1814, for heroism during the taking of Paris."

I wheedled the Imperial from my grandfather right before the trip to Paris. For a while, he resisted relinquishing the family heirloom, but I convinced him, that the descendant of the famed Cossack clan should arrive with some such thing in the town once taken by the squadron from his native village: "So they remember how our horses drank from the Seine!" A jeweler-friend attached a pin, not to damage the Imperial.

"And what's on the other side?" she asked, uneasy.

I took off the pin and turned it over: "Matthew."

With shaking hands, she took a beautiful old medallion with the portrait of a light-haired woman from around her neck and clicked it open. Inside laid the golden half with the two-headed eagle, small diamonds running along the edges. Remote, looking into my eyes, she turned the coin over.

"Nelly" – I read on the back.

"My great-great grandmother and your great-great grandfather got married in Paris in 1814."

My heart started beating wildly, my head spinning.

We were sitting in a small Café "Le Musset" across from the Louvre Museum.

"What happened to Nelly? Where did she disappear?"

"She was kidnapped from her sick father's home. When Gérard found out that she married Matthew, he threw her in the river. Nelly did not drown, but washed up much further than the places where they looked for her. Some farmers found her unconscious, and she lay sick in their house for several weeks. Nelly was pregnant, I'm her great-great granddaughter."

Night came down on The City of Lights. I felt an eternal love for the woman across me:

"When will we get married?"

"Tomorrow."

The Woman and Death

All morning and through the first half of the day, the Woman was very busy. By seven thirty, she prepared her husband breakfast–eggs and bacon–and saw him off to work. Then she drove to the supermarket to buy groceries for the week ahead. Afterwards, she did laundry and cleaned the house. Following that, she went to the mechanic to change the oil in the car. When she returned home, she cooked the evening's dinner. She took a shower, did her hair and nails. Finally, after all the running around, she turned on the television and lay down on the couch. Hazily, she flipped through the channels, not particularly interested in anything.

The Woman was past forty, two kids – a son and a daughter were already grown up. The daughter married young while still in college; she now lived far away, rarely calling on the phone. A year ago, the son went off to school and lived in a dormitory. He lived nearby, just a hundred miles from home, visiting his parents once or twice a month with a big bag of dirty clothes. He would catch up on eating and sleeping, take some money for living expenses and leave.

The husband, after many years of honest work, night jobs and chronic sleep deprivation, earned a good salary. The Woman left her regular job, since the family budget could now handle that.

Their home was small, but cozy. The Woman tried to decorate it as much as she could. On the husband's holiday bonus they finally carried out their long planned renovations, added a terrace, and laid a stone path from the door to the mailbox. When the husband lit the fireplace in the evenings, the flames played in the reflections of the crystal glasses in the cupboard and on the golden spines of books, standing on the dark oak bookshelves. Both of them – the Woman and her husband, preferred for everything to be strong and durable.

The television, as always, was showing many commercials, snippets of soap operas, cartoons, old black-and-white comedies and discussions between egg-headed intellectuals about who-knows-what. On the educational channel, there was a program about the art of the Middle Ages, or the Renaissance, the Woman was not exactly sure which. Skulls grinned from the old engravings, skeletons were dancing, embracing the peasants, clerics and courtesans. "What a gloomy topic for an educational program," the Woman said to herself. Through the cold forest of trees without leaves, a pensive knight rode on horseback. Nearby, on a thin old horse followed a bearded old man with snakes around his neck and head, in his hands – an hourglass. Behind, a creature with a boar snout and a crooked horn. "A devil, perhaps?" the Woman thought to herself. A half-breed mutt was running under between the legs of the war-horse. "The Knight, Death and the Devil" – they displayed the name of the engraving.

"No," the Woman decided, "Death can not look like an emaciated old man with a tangled beard. Death – she is feminine. Nature – Woman gives life; and Death, also woman, takes it away. Birth and Anti-Birth, or maybe, Birth with the minus sign."

Sometime in the past, the Woman finished a technical college, and loved to apply the knowledge she gained there toward everyday questions.

Now they were showing paintings – images of skeletons, gallows, bonfires and mountains of skulls. The Woman was tired of all these horrors, so she reached for the remote that had fallen on the carpet. Their television was the latest word in technology. Plasma, or whatever you call it, took up the better part of the wall, sound came from all around, creating a complete illusion of presence.

To harpsichord music on the television, evolved something in a loose fitting gown with a traditional scythe in its hands. "Come on, that's enough,"– the Woman decided and pressed the button for the next channel. The screen flashed, the gown fluttered and its edge dropped to the hardwood floor of her room. The figure straightened itself, its hood was almost six-feet up. The blade of the scythe reflected the glittering of the television screen.

"What good special effects the Japanese do nowadays," the Woman was astounded, "how do you come up with something like that?" She clicked the remote again. The channel switched to the news, the gown with the scythe stayed in the room, blocking the family photographs on the wall. The Woman felt alarm and turned off the television altogether. The gown remained, standing without moving.

"I probably just overexerted myself today," the Woman tried to calm herself, "I should not do so many things, after all, I'm not young anymore." She got off the couch and walked towards the kitchen.

"I came for you," there resounded a deep, slightly raspy, female voice.

"Who's there?" The Woman was seriously scared now.

"I – your Death".

"What a stupid joke! And what a sloppy costume, it's not Halloween. Who are you?"

The figure in the cloak lightly swung the scythe in a semicircle. Two flowers in clay pots–an azalea and a cyclamen, wilted instantly. The fish in the tank floated belly-up and the bright green parrot fell off his perch to the cage floor.

The Woman became truly afraid, but the rational mind of the family's mother refused to accept this carnival costume. Maybe the fish, bird and flowers were just a skillful trick by some friends or relatives. She took the bird in her arms – the small corpse was already growing cold.

A reddish spaniel ran into the room – the love of the whole family. From the wide sleeve of the cloak stretched a long knotted finger. The dog felt the ill will, tucked its tail between its legs, and whining, fled and hid under the armchair.

"Why?" The Woman could not understand. She was still relatively young, she did not have any dangerous or fatal diseases, and this was not even a car accident! She was just at home watching television and then suddenly – Death? It didn't make sense, no explanation.

"Questions – useless," Death interrupted, "Time."

"But this is unjust! There, the neighbor across the street has been lying paralyzed for six years. Why not him? Or my husband's uncle – he's past ninety, now, and still messing around with women. Or my friend Violetta – she has a genetic heart condition and has had two heart attacks. Why not her?"

"How boring! You people are all the same. First, why me? Then – take someone else. In the end you start haggling – I'll do this, promise that. I don't need anything from you. My job is to bring you from here to there. No emotion, nothing personal."

The Woman's heart tightened, it was clear that this was serious and permanent. But she hadn't even started living! She was always busy: school, marriage, children, family, work. Finally, it got a little easier and – there you go! They only appointed her husband as chief assistant to the vice-president of the company yesterday. We didn't even have time to celebrate his promotion. The children were finally grown up–she could start living for herself. She never even really loved! Her husband was good and kind, they were in the same class in college. All her friends were getting married, so it was time for her also to join that category. But what about love?

"You had a student before your husband, even two," Death interjected.

"That happened completely childishly and not serious."

"What about the military man in Cancun?"

"That was because my husband refused to come with me to the sanatorium. I just got a little carried away – south, sea, rest, aimless laying about."

"And then for a year you cried into your pillow about how you could have run away with the officer, but didn't."

"You're cruel, Death."

"No other way. Get ready."

"Do I need to take something with me?"

"No, it was just a figure of speech. Sit down, think a bit, and then – click, ready."

The doorbell rang.

"Who's there?" the Woman asked startled.

"You know who. Your lover."

The Woman blushed, even her ears turned red, like a schoolgirls.

The door opened softly and a middle-aged man entered. From his shoulder, on a canvas belt, hung a shabby flat plywood box, under his arm he had a white stretched canvas.

"Here he is," croaked Death, "to paint your portrait, so he said, but all he did is lift up your skirts. If he at least traced a line or two, but instead, he just drags around an empty canvas."

The man looked with wonder at the Woman and the

grotesque figure with a scythe.

"Normally, others can't see me," said Death. "However, it looks like you did not just merge physically. He's looking at me through your eyes."

The Woman embraced the man, pressing hard against him, she whispered something hotly into his ear. His face changed several times, from amazement to horror. He put his box of paints on the floor, leaned the canvas against the wall, gently kissed the Woman, fixed his corduroy shirt, ran his hand through his hair and addressed Death.

"Madam, this was completely my fault. She did not do anything. I ask you take me instead of her."

"You, lovers, are all alike – so quick to offer your petty lives. I came for her, there is no room for haggling. Your turn will come, don't rush. I know in your family, few of the men reached old age: some killed in wars, some in fights, others in different ways.

"Of course, you're right. I used the pretense of the portrait to come here. But now it seems, I will never be able to paint the portrait of my beloved. You are taking her away. Pardon my manners, as I work up the courage to ask You to pose for a while, if it is not too great an inconvenience? To paint from nature, the portrait of Death – this is a unique opportunity in the life of any artist.

"No time for me, though I'm tired from the road, all day I swung my scythe in Zimbabwe."

"You have my sincere condolences, but imagine, madam: in the world history of art there is not a single accurate image of Death! Trivial skulls and skeletons – mere attributes of the decaying human body. The artists fantasized, trying to convey your characteristics, or painted you from memory, if they happened to briefly meet you. A portrait will not take much of your time – I paint quickly, and can finish later in the studio without a model, if you will allow me.

The artist spoke with a silver tongue, and there really was no rush for Death, She had eternity.

"Oh, what the hell?" Death agreed and removed Her hood.

A bald skull, with a terrible grin of the bottom jaw, eyes rolling out without lids or brows. Death struck a pose in the style Quattrocento – leaning on one leg, turning in two incomplete turns, the arm stretched out with the scythe. A classical pose for the Academy of Arts.

"Madam, may I be so brave as to ask You to remove Your scythe? It is too direct a symbol. It will oversimplify your image."

Death thought for a moment and then leaned the scythe against the wall in the corner. In Her craft, she used many different tools for taking life. Death crossed Her hands across Her chest and looked straight at the Artist.

"Madam, You, of course, noticed that the bald faces of men and women can look very similar. Sometimes it's difficult to tell who is standing in front of you – male or female? Your robe, excuse me, your cloak, is too roomy. It seems, it is comfortable for Your line of work, but it almost completely obscures the outlines of Your body.

Death dropped the cloak off one shoulder and coquettishly stretched out her bare leg.

"That's a little better, Madam, completely natural. May I ask You to unveil the other shoulder as well?"

Death showed her other shoulder, holding the cloak to her chest with both hands, so that it would not slip to the floor. Bony shoulders and a protruding collar bone held together the freakish neck with the hideous skull. Her breasts full like wineskins.

"Madam, please show me more of Your leg, so that the line of the hip is more expressive."

Death liked this unusual distraction – posing for a painting. She swung the sides of the cloak out and stomped her foot down, like a countrywoman, with sparks.

The Artist saw an enormous heavily laden stomach. Death was pregnant!

"Madam, I think in the current pose, we do not have sufficient levity and freedom. Relax, walk around a little bit."

Death, limping, walked around the room. The Woman was long since lying unconscious.

"This is spectacular!" exclaimed the Artist. "We found the one true setting! Please, drop you cloak – it is not helping. Death, the way she is, without any wrappers or frills!"

Death became shy of her nudity and her belly, but the Artist convinced Her that this sincerity would overcome everything that has been done in the history of art on the subject of Death. Death took down an old flute she saw hanging on the wall, and started playing it to distract Herself, "Danse Macabre" by all the famous composers.

The Artist painted fast. The basis of the composition – contrast of the large black spot with the rose-violet. Death – rear view with a lean to the left and a slight turn. The hands with the flute created a movement to the right. The protruding vertebrae of her spine made Death look like a lizard, her crooked legs spread wide.

Death got caught up in the music, beating the rhythm with her left foot. It seemed like she forgot about the painter and her surroundings. Just a little more and She'll start dancing, from which will come greed, envy, war and destruction.

"Where is your lover?" Death suddenly remembered the aim of her visit.

The Woman was gone. When she came to herself, she crawled off the couch and snuck off while Death was playing the flute.

The Artist put down his brushes, at a loss. He, of course, was trying to save the Woman from the beginning, but then got so deep into the painting that he did not even notice when she left. Before him stood terrible naked Death. Her stomach was kicking.

"What are you pregnant with?" he quietly asked her.

"War, you idiot."

Death put on her cloak, donned her hood, from under which glowed Her wrathful eyes. In her hand – the scythe. She looked at the canvas, the painting was almost done. "Sneaky bastard!"– Death thought.

"Take me instead of my beloved."

"There is no order for you. I will come back for her, while you think what lie you will tell your wife. Go, sign the painting."

The painter bent down and in the bottom corner of the canvas signed it with the other end of his brush, the year and date. When he lifted his head, Death (or her vision?) was gone.

In the doorway stood the Woman's husband with a dropped jaw staring at the wilted flowers, dead fish, immobile parrot and the strange, paint-covered man with the terribly unexplainable painting on the chair.

Gurzuf, Poste Restante

We got to the Kursky Train Station two hours before departure. It was a clear and sunny morning, the end of June in Moscow.

We unloaded next to the nearby buildings, instead of the glass box entrance to the station: there would be no room for us to turn. The Baron went to talk to a brigade of baggage-carriers, meted out three-rubles to each of them as an advance, so that we would have our stuff ready thirty minutes before the train. They, hungry for money, loaded the boxes onto their carts, but the Baron had not yet given the command, still looking at his watch. At last he said: "Time!"

The column of baggage-carriers with carts cut through the summer crowd of passengers, we were trotting at the sides. Without losing speed we dove through a subterranean tunnel, from which we hopped out onto the platform to our train, where we heard the announcement for the Moscow-Sympheropol Express. There was a reason why the Baron gave two rubles to the information desk. While the stampede of passengers were grabbing their suitcases and spinning their heads, where to run, we were already undoing the belts on our carts.

The conductor was flabbergasted upon seeing our mountain of boxes and suitcases.

"Everything's all right, papa," the Baron handed him the tickets, "three compartments for the equipment and three for us, the musicians."

Between the tickets, he inserted a red fifty-ruble note. The conductor stood blinking his eyes, while we and the baggage-carriers were stacking the boxes in the car. Nine minutes and they were all inside. The other passengers were still streaming in, while we already shelved everything and were having our first bottle. The Baron poured the Port wine into glasses:

"To the success of a hopeless venture," he made his traditional toast.

We clinked our glasses, the train took off, vacation and the summer tour had begun.

Our band was going to the south coast of Crimea, Gurzuf. The Baron did not like terms like "Vocal-instrumental ensemble" or "Orchestra," or even "Rock Group."

"A band is a band," he would say. "One for all and all for one."

The nickname stuck to the Baron last summer, when we were working in a student camp in Pitsunda in Caucasus. Most of the responsibility rested on him during the concerts, before and after. He would argue with the authorities concerning our repertoire and volume, got musicians out of various scrapes, resolved conflicts (sometimes with his fists) with the aborigines, and at night soloed during the concert.

The Baron was a natural born front man. Usually, he stood on the edge of the stage near the ramp, sang, played the most difficult parts, while with the corner of his eye looking after each of the band members, heeding every mistake or wrong note. After the concert, he would scold those responsible for poor playing: "No hackwork, even before the deaf."

He quickly lost his temper in arguments, especially if he was convinced he was right. "Why don't you wiggle your brain folds and you'll understand! I cannot waste time on useless fights!"

"Baron, whatever you say" once quipped Mishka-Hendrix, and so the moniker was born.

In the end of April, the Baron stuffed a backpack with a pair of new white jeans, two shirts and a sleeping bag, as he set off hitchhiking from Moscow to Crimea to look for a place to play in the summer.

He first got off in Alushta, but the city park was already booked by Time Machine. From Alushta, he took a tour-boat to Frunze Village; but that was home to the Apothecary, the wildest disco from South-West Moscow. On a different motorboat, the Baron went around Mount Ayu-Dag and docked in Gurzuf.

"I knew right away, this was it!" he recalled upon his return.

The Baron made arrangements with the director of a local Culture club for two months of our concerts. We had to work every night, without weekends, except for rainy days. We received 50 kopecks on the ruble, the rest went into the director's pockets, his bosses, and a little for the club. The Soviet officials governed the region, but everyone in the south made ends meet and during the summer months made enough money for the rest of the year.

All in all, it was a dull time. The Soviet troops had recently invaded Afghanistan, Brezhnev was on the throne of the Communist Party, dissidents were put down throughout the country, Jewish emigration and such things were blocked, and the party censors raged in the art world. It was forbidden to sing in English, and officially rock music did not exist. Like the joke: "You have an ass, but no word for it."

Many rockers despaired at their prospects for breaking through to the stage and only recorded underground tapes. But the Baron could not live without live performances and contact with the audience. He would submit fake set-lists to the Department of Culture with songs by members of the USSR Composers

Union, thereby getting the necessary stamps and permissions for performance in public places. With these notorious indulgences we would rock out in bars, student dorms, and anywhere else that would have us. Party inspectors sometimes checked our "cultural work," but then they would get a bribe from the business administrators, so we could still continue to play.

In Sympheropol, a bus came to pick us up at the train station. The Baron tipped everybody, no penny-pinching, even though the coffers were not that full. Out of the dusty humid town, the bus climbed over the ridge. An enormous glowing sea lay below.

"Hurrah!" we exclaimed.

"I am going towards the sea…" sang Jenka.

Our spot was on the beach, only a rhododendron alley with flower beds separated it from the sea. At the end of the alley was a public toilet and a beer vending machine. The spot was surrounded by a metal fence, the stage made out of concrete, covered by a roof. Next to the main entrance were a one room stone house and a ticket-booth. In the opposite corner, was a small wicket-gate.

We unloaded the boxes and went swimming. Ingenious! The sea was a stone's throw away, we are living where we work, separating ourselves from the others and sunbathing.

While we were unloading, the Baron was approached by two overzealous Komsomol functionaries who asked many questions about who we were, from where and what for.

"Damn clingy bastards! They came here to vacation, but they spotted us and decided to show off their ideological vigilance! Pederasts!"

Our band was small, but powerful. The Baron on lead

guitar. It was obvious that he was the leader. Kozik on bass; Alex, a conservatory student, and the Baron's younger brother, on keyboards; and me on the drums. Everyone also sang.

Jenka and Vadik - the Dynamic Duo, on sax and clarinet. We did not especially need horns, but the Baron invited them into the "dead souls," and they played two-three songs with us, while the pay was split up among the main members. That is, there was no stress for them, they could swim all day, relax, and in the evening they had to be not too drunk so they could stand on their feet.

From the beginning, the Baron insisted that we buy the best, most expensive instruments. That was how we performed: a month's work – a bass guitar with a marble fret-board for Kozik; another month – a twelve-string guitar for the Baron, custom made by a gypsy master; two months – an electric Gibson guitar, once again for the Baron; three months – and Alex had a synthesizer, an authentic Moog!

But the main investments were into me. From the black market dealers, the Baron bought a poster of Led Zeppelin; Jon Bonham was on the stage with his drums.

"You can play no worse than him," the Baron told me. "We will work and buy you a kit just like that."

So we worked, playing dances, weddings, funerals – as long as they paid. After a year, the quality of our instruments was staggering!

The music we played back then was two fold. On the one side – what we needed was to be fed and get work; on the other – we would turn our noses up at the vomit all around. "Can't Buy Me Love!" We can get by without concert halls and stadiums. If they cut off our air, we will play in apartments and dachas. Long live Rock and Roll! The Baron wrote most of the music, he was the one to define the style of our band. The others also composed, each having three or four truly good songs.

We came to Gurzuf back then to perform on the open-air dance floor. Two hours of mandatory performance and our thirty minutes for requests. If you want to dance, you have to pay. Simple and understandable.

The vacationing public pined away for two days in anticipation, while we climbed up the posts, attaching lights, speakers, projectors, and such.

We hung posters throughout Gurzuf with "M-42 (Moscow)." So they would register us in the Department of Culture, we humbly named ourselves "Marathon." The Baron thought long and hard what we could make out of "Marathon." The hip name of the B-52's was solidly lodged in his mind. His thoughts followed the abbreviations and analogies: GAZ-24 – funny; AK-47 – fraught with problems; M-16 – an American rifle. In the end, he gave birth to M-42 – short, trenchant, easily memorable. It was simple to explain to bureaucrats - the distance of a marathon is 42 kilometers.

Every band, even the smallest, is more than just the musicians on stage. The sound-guy can be more important than most performers on stage: on him depends the quality of the entire performance.

Our Mishka, nicknamed Jackson, was a genius in that department. At his defense factory, he put together speakers one and a half kilowatts each. We could blow all of the Gurzuf dancers into the sea with sound, and only refrained from doing so out of innate humanity.

"The sound and light come from all directions. Every audience member should be able to see and hear everything equally well," was the principle formulated by the Baron for our performances. He probably read that in articles about Pink Floyd.

The Baron was always overcome by ideas about the visual effect of the performances:

"Our genius music plus awesome sound and theatrical lighting: in the end – we are the only real band in the Soviet Union!"

The Baron loaded Mishka-Jackson with the task of creating a master-remote for controlling the lighting: ramps for lighting the musicians, spot lights and projectors on the perimeter of the hall or dance floor, slide- and movie-projectors, a smoke machine, black-lights and others.

In the West, they were just starting to use strobe lights with weak lamps from flash photography. While we were in the USSR, still all our stuff was the better and bigger! The Baron bought at the aerodrome sixteen lamps for a TU-144 passenger jet. When during my drum solo they turned on all these strobe lights, while Mishka-Jackson sent them in different orders – in a circle, in pairs, to the beat, or on a diagonal – the people were falling over in shock!

We bought the laser from some physicists in Chernogolovka Center of scientific research and we were the first to use one for a concert. You could get anything in the Soviet Union, pretty cheaply at that – you just had to have friends in the different departments of science, industry and agriculture.

The other Mishka, who went by Hendrix, was not a guitarist, but worked as a photographer. He documented every day of our life for posterity. The Baron was convinced that we would soon break through to the world arena.

It was also impossible to get by without your own security service. The expensive instruments and technical equipment require attention, while during the performance, you have to maintain order on the dance floor, first and foremost – with your own strength. Peskov studied with the Baron at the boarding school, they sat at the same desk for eight years. They kicked Peskov out of the army over some scandal, it did not help that he played for the Army water polo team. The Baron took him with us: Peskov provided order at our concerts, and, all in all, was skillful and sociable. During his free time from the band, he worked at a clock factory, and made us different contraptions for stage effects.

On the first night, we knocked out all of Gurzuf. In the beginning, Mishka-Jackson played background music, boring the public with anticipation. We, the musicians, in the house next to the gates behind a closed door poured glasses of port wine "13 Cypresses."

"To success," said the Baron.

We drank, and he was the first to run onto the stage, into the projector rays and started playing rock and roll on the guitar. Then came Kozik on the bass, then Alex on the synthesizer, and when I finally burst in on the drums – the crowd started screaming and ran to dance.

Mishka-Jackson set the lights to semi-automatic, and our 300,000 watts made such a magic sight, that on the next day, some campers came down from Mount of Ayu-Dag to ask what that was.

We played great, fast and loud. There was partying at other spots in Gurzuf. At the international camp "Sputnik" performed some mustachioed guys from Minsk, at the "Korova" (nick name for the resort named after the artist Constantine Korovin) – a homebrewed disco, while at the restaurant on the mountain – typical barroom jazz.

Our beautiful and mighty sound made its way through the coarse chords of the other groups. Soon, the people from the other dance spots came our way towards the beach. Within an hour of the first night, we had over a thousand people dancing, instead of the expected three hundred. Financial success was assured; the director of the Gurzuf Culture club rubbed his hands from excitement. Our nervous feelings about the first performance also disappeared. After all, it's a pleasure when hundreds of people are dancing to your music.

By the second week we developed a routine for all our work. We swiped some beach-chairs, on which we put out sleeping bags. The Baron slept separately in the ticket booth (a Baron after all!) – where there was room for only one trestle-bed. It was always important to him to have a good night's sleep, or he played badly.

Alex, Peskov and I lodged in the house by the gates. Kozik and both Mishkas slept on the stage, which at night was covered by a tarp. Jenka and Vadik set up under the acacia by the fence. In terms of a Soviet resort, we lived lavishly – our own lot with gates: we let in whoever we want, and who we don't, we keep out.

The beer-dispenser at the end of the alley served as a magnet for those parched beneath the midday sun. The beer from the dispensers was the only cold one, but the Baron forbid anyone who was singing to drink it. Instead of beer, for prophylactic purposes, at three o'clock he would have teatime. At first we resisted, but then we got used to it and enjoyed sweating in the shadow around the teapot.

After swimming, lunch and tea, we were relaxing under the acacia. During these pauses the Baron composed something new, or worked on general enlightenment. Pedagogy was his second calling.

At the Gurzuf public library, he took out books on the history of the region, the technology of wine-making, and anthologies of the legends and myths of Ancient Crimea. We lay in a dreamy siesta, Mishka-Jackson soldered something, while the Baron read smart books out loud. Life was good!

The Baron was often bothered by external problems: first Jenka and Vadik were caught by a vine-yard's guards, then Peskov made work of some poor fool over a girl, then the young Alex outplayed some preference-enthusiasts, and they come to clarify their relations.

The Baron readily declared that he was the president, that all responsibilities and questions should be addressed to him. And as always he figured things out: went to the town council, paid the fines; bought cognac for the cops; explained to the beach-sharks that Alex played fairly, and that he had more brains than all of them put together.

Gurzuf was the most hippest place on the Black Sea. The people were mostly from Moscow and St. Petersburg. "We speak with ours in our language" (Baron). Around the resort of the Union of Artists, swarmed crowds of rowdy bohemians from Stroganov Art College, Surikov Art Academy and Moscow Architectural Institute. "Savages" with backpacks settled in the mountains above the highway, so the police wouldn't bother them. "Sputnik" foreigners from the brotherly socialist countries brought in western accents, while the young officers from the Navy sanatorium profitably contrasted the rosy crowd. Bandits and profiteers squandered money at the bars; smalltime plough-shares from various party committees proudly puffed up their cheeks; tanned womanizers spread their bright feathers, like the female fans of extreme southern relaxation; the hard-working who put in their hours for a whole year, deservingly stretched to their full heights; young creations, having escaped the watchful eye of their parents partied happily with the poor, yet carefree students, and so on.

Word of our performances quickly spread across the Southern coastline, people came by land and sea from as far as Kerch and from Sevastopol. All kinds of people and picaresque figures appeared on the dance floor. It was fun, and everything hinged on the Baron.

From Astrakhan, one of his friends came down hitchhiking; he appeared barefoot, with a woven knapsack over his shoulder and a reed flute. The Baron talked to him about philosophy, fed him at the diner, bought wine. "Severe" Max had just finished his first monumental mosaic and was spending his money freely and easily. Volodya-Sun came from Moscow – the first "registered" Soviet hippie. Though he was already old, at least ten years our senior…with a garland of drug-addled girls, Vaska Baturin flew down, and was the "substance" cook. The Baron got him out of Gurzuf immediately, the last thing we needed was problems with narcotics!

Johnny Malinin was the most active dancer – he got started from half a turn, and got those around him dancing. Too bad he already crossed to the other side. The dreamy boozer Fred, a student of the Talmud, – a hundred-percent Russian from Oryol, taught himself Hebrew and Yiddish – the Baron often argued with him about Judaism.

Valera Gusev, master of the Buddha Palm, came in the mornings when it was cool to practice on the lot. A year later, the Moscow government would make him an example by putting him in jail for five years for the "illegal" teaching of Kung Fu.

On a black chrome motorcycle, decorated with devils and mirrors, came Bob Sinichkin – leader of the Crimean Hell's Angels.

The old sea wolf – a writer, creator of the amusing Captain Vrungel, would come down from his bachelor house by the docks to talk with us – youth from the capital.

The summer went by like a fairy-tale: the sun, sea, Massandra port wine. There were no hangovers in Gurzuf, because of the healthy climate. Whoever doubts it – should go there first – then we'll talk.

In the south, love affairs are simple and quick. We were overgrown with women within an hour, only the Baron kept himself isolated: thoughts, you see, were brooding in his head. At night, Jenka and Vadik were shaking their trestle-beds under the acacia, while the Baron, in the moonlight, pensively fingered the strings, searching for something.

Now, that many years have passed, I understand what Baron saw clearly - that which never occurred to us. First he felt it, then he rationalized it, that on the big score, we were all in a dead-end. Our Soviet rock lived by the principle of self-fertilization. Of course, we listened to records from the West, but that was not enough for evolution in music.

Most importantly – there were no original musical ideas. The groups from the proletariat tried to imitate Deep Purple, the romantics – more like the Beatles, the intellectuals from the conservatories – more like Yes, while half-foreign Estonians spun their jazz-rock. One can imitate forever, getting cheap applause from an unsophisticated audience and make good money – but there will be no independent music. People often object saying that the important thing in Russian rock is the words. Dudes! The most important thing in music is music!

The principal breakthrough in the Baron's creativity came when the Barelegged One appeared. We played the wild rock "Blue

Suede Shoes;" Mishka-Jackson turned on the black light; the Baron, Kozik and Alex were glowing like aliens. The party was on fire! That was when onto the stage came a curly haired beauty in white shorts and dark-blue suede shoes on tall heels and gave quite a show. "Everything but a striptease!" – the ticket lady later recalled.

I don't understand how these things happen to this day. He never met her before, nor even seen her, and suddenly, he's playing and singing only for her. True – the legs, the breasts, face and everything else, but still, why does he get stuck on her? Moreover, the Baron is the president and the authority...

That evening the usual "one glass – before, another – during, and three – after" did not take place. Nakedlegs was waiting while the Baron was putting the guitars in their cases, and they went swimming. The moon hung high in the starry sky. I saw from the stage how they undressed and went into the water. The Baron was everywhere first and best, but was a weak swimmer, not like Peskov, the master of the sport, who swam with his Olympic girlfriend behind the horizon.

The Baron and Nakedlegs soon returned and locked themselves in his "penthouse." Moans, screams, and sobs could be heard under the acacias, the thin wooden walls were shaking.

"How much more?" Jenka and Vadik asked themselves, smoking and pouring another glass.

"They're in the ninth round," Kozik reckoned.

We were asleep by morning, but the ticket-booth kept shaking.

Nakedlegs came with her parents to the Navy resort. Her father was an admiral, her mother, accordingly, a female admiral. They brought their daughter so she could gather her strength after entrance exams into the Moscow Architectural Institute. The south, fruits, vitamins, sea microelements... A fat-faced Komsomol functionary tried to look after her, but nothing came of that. Nakedlegs liked to dance, she came to our spot, and that was where her love for the Baron sparked – at first sight.

I still have the photograph taken by Mishka-Hendrix. We are standing by the docks – young, longhaired and bearded, in short shorts that look silly today. In the middle – the Baron with his arm around Nakedlegs – I am to the left of them, Alex on the right, the tall Kozik behind, Jenka and Vadik are sitting in front, their legs folded Indian-style. The Baron dragged us that time on an excursion to the Nikitsky Botanical Garden.

We played throughout July, then came August – the most profitable time. If you work August, there'll be enough money for the entire winter. Our life on tour went by measured and smoothly. Only one time, some misfortune crashed down on the Baron, he went around all day not being himself, barely getting through the concert, and spent the night on a bench, with his head in Nakedlegs' lap, staring at the stars.

The Baron often got lost in thought, as if, the affair with Nakedlegs catalyzed that which had been building up in his head and his soul.

One time during our siesta, when the sun was scorching heartlessly, and it was better to hide in the shadows, the Baron played some new melodies for Nakedlegs. He always improvised them effortlessly. Nakedlegs lay on the chaise-lounge in her mini-swimsuit, and the Baron sat next to her in his trunks with a guitar.

Jenka and I sat nearby, cutting cigarette holders out of sequoia: "Like the millionaires got." The wily Jenka noticed a sequoia tree at the Nikitsky Botanical Garden, and secretly broke off a branch. The main cigarette holder was named "Zmey Gorynych." Jenka would put three cigarette butts in it at a time and smoked through the three tubes.

The Baron picked the strings, then fell silent for a long time and disappeared in his thoughts, without even answering Nakedlegs' questions. He went to the stage, took the third string from Kozik's bass, put it on his guitar and completely retuned it. Instead of the traditional E-A-D-C-B-E he tuned it C-C-D-G-A-D, and played us a few familiar songs. The guitar sounded completely different, even looked newer, such dramatic and unfamiliar harmonies. Nobody in the West played like that, much less in the East, beyond the Berlin Wall.

The new music by the Baron did not suit fast dances very well: it was too refined, but was appropriate for slow dances or solos, while the other musicians rested. That day, in our naiveté and proximity to the Baron, we did not understand the genius of the discovery that happened before our very eyes.

There was still a ways to go to the New Age, but that very night, the Baron tried out his new style on the public. After his improvised solo, the people stood around astounded, and could not understand what strange new thing was discovered in Gurzuf. There were stunted claps, which soon grew into unanimous applause.

We did not record our little dances. What was the point? Half of what we played were covers of famous hits. We postponed the recording on the Baron's new guitar until our return to Moscow. A pity. The only thing left of Gurzuf is photographs by Mishka-Hendrix and his half-minute film.

Everything toppled on the Day of the Navy Fleet, when there was a parade in Sevastopol and sailors were walking everywhere. The vacationers relaxed to the degree of their ability and imaginations.

As usual, after our morning swim and breakfast, we went into town. Our spot was below, next to the sea, while the marketplace, bus stop, stores, post office and bank were uphill. Gurzuf is a mountainous place, always walking up and down. Alex, the youngest one, was dragging empty bottles to recycle for a refund at the store. Kozik bought two watermelons in the marketplace and carried them down.

I went with the Baron to the post office to check the mail. My grandmother had sent me some smoked sausages and cookies. The Baron received a plain grey envelope poste restante. He frowned, but did not open it in front of me. We went down to our spot, and I went swimming, forgetting all about the envelope.

In the evening, we played as usual; only the Baron did not sing and refused the glass of Massandra port before the concert which he always drank for a better tone. The music thundered, the projectors glowed, the strobes blinked and the rotators and disco-balls spun, all creating different effects.

After the power hour, each member played a solo for one and a half to two minutes, to give time for the others to rest and have a cigarette by the gates. Kozik played on the bass a crowning version of "Smoke on the Water," and the crowd went nuts. After him, with my drums and cymbals, I raised the temperature a few degrees higher. Alex with his Moog, smoothly transitioned the crowd out of their aggressive mood. The Baron was left alone on the stage with a simple guitar.

I understand now, that he made a point to wait until we left, to make sure we were safe.

From the new tuning of the guitar, I did not recognize the song from the first chords.

"Imagine… there's no heaven…"

Oh, pell-mell, in the middle of the navy holiday he was singing John Lennon's "Imagine" in English!

"No hell below us… above us only sky…"

Couples danced slowly, pressing their flushed bodies tightly against each other.

Crud, the Russian troops are in Afghanistan, a military psychosis is spreading throughout the country, they are sending young guys off to die half a world away, and the Baron is singing an anti-war song loud enough for a stadium!

"No need for greed or hunger… a brotherhood of man…"

But maybe no one will understand what he's talking about. The song is quiet, the melody pleasant, and the guitar sounds so strange…

"Living life in peace…"

I saw how the young fat-faced Komsomol functionary ran out of the crowd down along the beach. My heart got cold.

"You may say I'm a dreamer…"

From down along the beach, blinking its headlights and sirens, through the alley towards us came a police car.

"…some day you'll join us…"

The police car pulled up right to the stage; out of it poured four cops and the Komsomol guy. The Baron was standing in the middle of the stage; his white shirt and jeans glowed in the black light. Across from him, down on the dance floor next to the ramp stood Nakedlegs.

The cops came up to the Baron from both sides and simultaneously hit him with clubs on the head and the ribs. He tried to remove his guitar, while protecting himself from the raining blows, but they knocked him off his feet and continued to beat him before everyone's eyes.

The crowd was dumbstruck and didn't know what was going on. Screams of indignation flowed into the trills of the police whistles; the requested backup was rushing to the dance floor. The crowd dissipated into the darkness.

We ran after the police car, into which they threw the bloodied Baron. There was a guard on duty in front of the steel door to the Police Station; he had an automatic rifle instead of a pistol. The cops got everything quick.

To our yells and questions the cop barked:

"Spreading Anti-Sovietism!?"

For a while it was quiet, then we started recognizing barely audible punches and the laughter of several people. They were beating the Baron in the basement, the window there was opened a crack so that fresh air could get in. The Baron was saying something at first, but then he stopped. We got scared. Mishka-Hendrix disappeared somewhere, Nakedlegs was crying.

"Run to your daddy-admiral," Peskov ordered Nakedlegs, "otherwise they will beat the Baron to death. We will raise a ruckus in Gurzuf meanwhile."

Nakedlegs ran to the sanatorium, while we dispersed split up in opposite directions, running and screaming:

"People, help! Murder! Murder at the Police Station! Help!"

The patrol officers tried to chase us, but who could catch us on windy streets at night?

Nakedlegs brought her admiral in his service cap with a golden crab and navy jacket filled with an iconostasis of military honor slats. From under his jacket, one could see striped pajamas, and flip-flops on his bare feet.

The guard tried to keep the admiral out of the police department, but the admiral only knotted his brows – and it was as if the cop was blown away by the wind.

After a few minutes, the admiral came outside and went back down to the sanatorium, we ran after him. Once we got to the shadows, he motioned us over.

"He was beaten badly. Those mean, miserable coppers. They will bring him back now. You all have to leave here as soon as possible. I took care of the cops for tonight, but tomorrow morning the KGB will come, and they will want to interrogate you all. Abandon everything – your things, instruments, equipment. Take the money and run. It's unlikely that they will go chasing musicians: you're small fry, but who knows what will get their goat."

The police car did indeed arrive shortly. The same cops, who beat the Baron on the stage two hours earlier, threw him out of the car, unconscious, next to the ticket-window. The Baron's shirt was all bloody, the face bruised, nose broken, two swelling black-eyes.

Out of nowhere reappeared Mishka-Hendrix and started photographing everything.

"Where were you?"

"I'll tell you later…"

Peskov was in charge now, and everyone obeyed. He ripped off the Baron's shirt. His body was one big bruise. Nakedlegs stood nearby, white as a sheet.

"Four ribs are broken and the kidneys are bruised," Peskov declared after a cursory examination. "And there is a concussion. We need an ambulance."

Alex ran to the shore to call from the phone booth. He came back shortly:

"They are saying that they will not come, they already got a call from the police."

"He will die..."

"My grandmother might be able to help," – Ravil came out of the shadows, the student friend from the Moscow Architectural Institute.

"She cures many people around here with herbs and incantations."

"Get her quick!"

"She's old – already past ninety."

"Jenka and Vadik, you're big guys, come bring her here, while we take care of the Baron."

Peskov washed the blood from the Baron's body with water from a three-liter can. I was holding the bloody shirt. From the breast pocket fell a grey piece of paper, folded into four parts: the news from Afghanistan, that the Baron's twin brother had died, honoring the international aid to the Afghan people.

The Dynamic Duo came running, brought on criss-crossed hands the old Tatar medicine-woman. She slowly moved her palm over the Baron, who still had not regained consciousness, then talked in Tatar to her grandchild, who tried to heatedly explain something to her.

"Between the Adalary, the twin-cliffs across from Artek, from the bottom flows a spring of Life Water," Ravil translated. "You have to take your friend there, and dip him in three times, keeping him in for two minutes each time. If he doesn't drown – he will be healthy, and all his wounds will heal."

"But, it's time for you to run," Old-woman Izergil concluded, and relying on her grandson, started hobbling back home.

"We'd still have to reach to the Adalary... Where would we

get a boat?"

"Vrungel has a motorboat," recalled Alex.

"That it! We'll put the Baron on a beach-chair like on stretchers, and carry him to the docks."

Peskov sent me and Nakedlegs to talk to Vrungel. He, once seeing us, did not ask any questions: news traveled fast in Gurzuf. Vrungel draped an old pea-coat over his sailor's vest, grabbed a flashlight, and we rushed towards the docks.

Vrungel's motorboat was small, with a tiny cabin to protect from the rain and other bad weather. Nakedlegs, Alex, and Peskov sat on the one side, holding the Baron, who lay across their knees. Mishka-Hendrix and I sat across. Peskov ordered the others to coordinate the evacuation.

The Baron awoke, silently looking up at the stars.

We stopped between the Adalary – those stone twin-brothers. Vrungel dropped the anchor. The sea undulated lightly; a few lights could be seen in the summer camp on the shore. Now came the important part.

Peskov repeated the prescription of the old Tatar shaman-woman. The Baron understood and signaled with his eyes.

"We have to dive three times. The depth here is about ten meters. I will tie you to myself. Don't lose consciousness, or you will drown. Underwater, let out the air little by little, don't try to hold it. We have a flashlight. I will keep an eye on you, and will bring a cellophane bag full of air just in case. Well, Godspeed!"

The former center of the Army water polo team took off his clothes, tied himself and the Baron together with a rope, showed him how to breathe in properly before a dive, stuck the flashlight in his belt, grabbed the Baron with one hand, counting off: "One-two-three!" and they slipped into the night water.

They descended along an anchor rope. We saw how the spot of light got smaller in the darkness and turned into a faint dot. Everyone was counting the seconds. Peskov, clock master in the outside world, had the best internal chronometer, but who knows?

They came back up 2 minutes 45 seconds after the dive. Rested for five minutes, and then went back under. Vrungel was smoking a pipe:

"God forbid the border patrol should stop us, then they'll definitely arrest us all."

The light on the sea-bottom went out, we started stirring, but after 2 minutes 36 seconds two heads appeared on the surface.

"Looks like the batteries died," Peskov explained. "Brace yourself, Baron, only one dive left."

Mishka-Hendrix was taking pictures on night-film. The Baron sank into unconsciousness; they beat him pretty bad after all. Peskov slapped the Baron on the cheeks; it was as if he woke up again.

"Don't zone out. Hang on. Don't close your eyes. If it gets difficult – give me a sign. One-Two-Three, let's go!"

They disappeared under the water. One minute, two, three, three thirty, three forty, three forty-five, four... What happened? Nakedlegs sank her nails into the boat's covering board.

"A-a-ahh," – they came out with a loud splatter.

The Baron was holding onto Peskov's shoulder. We pulled them into the boat.

"The rope got stuck on the carcass of some vessel, had trouble untying it in the darkness. Barely made it back up."

The Baron was lying on the bench, out of strength, but it was clear that life was returning to him.

Vrungel let out Alex, Kozik, Hendrix and me on the shore

of Artek. The kids, the best Pioneers in the country, slept peacefully.

Vrungel took the Baron, Nakedlegs, and Peskov to Alushta. There they got on the first morning trolley to Sympheropol. From there – a train to Moscow because they do not check the passport when buying a train ticket.

We agreed, if it was possible, to meet in the park next to the train station, if not, we'd see each other in Moscow.

Mishka-Hendrix wanted to photograph our spot for history's sake. Being careful, we first snuck into Max's room. He lived in the "Korova" and his window looked out on the spot. The other three were already there. They said that they got the money, and some clothes, and stopped by Max's, to collect themselves.

The dawn was breaking when we were drinking instant coffee. Through the crack in the curtains we could see a bus of soldiers that had pulled up. Mishka-Hendrix photographed them – as they used field shovels to destroy the musical instruments and the wonders of sound and light-technology.

After them, came the workers, who threw the broken pieces of culture into the garbage trucks. At eight in the morning, when the first swimmers were coming out to the beach, the spot was completely clean, as if we had never played there.

We waited a day and a night in Max's room, and then left Gurzuf in pairs. Jenka and Vadik got back to Moscow hitchhiking. Jackson and Hendrix got on the "Rocket" in Sevastopol and went to Odessa by water, from there flying to Moscow. Alex and I got out of Crimea through the Kerchensky Strait, then by train to Taganrog-Moscow.

Peskov drove Nakedlegs and the Baron to Moscow, fooling the KGB and the cops, who were looking for them at the train station and the airport. He cut the Baron's hair short and shaved his beard, while bleaching his own hair from brunette to blonde, and gluing a mustache on from the hair he cut off the Baron.

Mishka-Hendrix managed to photograph the beating of the Baron, through the cracked basement window at the police station. These photographs and others, he sent over to the West. They were printed in the New York Times, Washington Post, Paris Match, Globe and many other newspapers and magazines. DJ Seva Novgorodtsev ran our single tape over and over on the BBC. Once again, there was a commotion about human rights in the Soviet Union.

The Baron was soon kicked out of the country as a dissident – the only rock musician. Otherwise, they threatened to put him away under article 58 "propaganda and agitation against the Soviet Union." The pregnant Nakedlegs left with him. The Admiral retired. We scattered here and there. There was no more Baron and his charisma, there was no more band M-42.

* * *

I talked to the Baron on the phone a few years ago. He's living in the States with Nakedlegs and his son. The cops broke his fingers on both hands, he can't play anymore. He was working odd jobs – construction, owned a gallery for a while, taught at a college, even patented some invention.

He said that at first they were helped by a musician Michael Hedges. The Baron showed him a new guitar tuning. Michael became a star, though not for very long – he died in a car crash in California.

The Baron did not want to return to the Soviet Union, that is Russia. "Many other countries are waiting for me," he said. He remembered Gurzuf without any pain, even joked about it, sent his regards to everybody and invited them to visit. In farewell, he said:

"Tell Mishka-Jackson, the only band with better lighting than us is Pink Floyd."

I put down the receiver, it was way past midnight – the time difference – eight hours. From the wall, from a yellowing photograph taken at the docks of Nikitsky Botanical Garden, we are looking back – young, happy, and confident. Our whole life ahead of us, fame and world acclaim. The Baron – twenty-four years old.

NOTES

1. BEAST was written January 12, 2005, East Windsor, NJ, USA.

2. NANETTE was written December 28, 2004, East Windsor, NJ, USA.

3. LEONARDO AND THE HORSE was written December 7, 2004, East Windsor, NJ, USA.

4. PARADISE ISLAND was written July 25, 2003, Puerta Plata, Dominican Republic.

Society for Traveling Art Exhibitions was a group of Russian realist artists with democratic ideals, who formed in 1870 an artists' cooperative as a protest of academic official art.

Quattrocento was an artistic and cultural movement of the 15th century (from 1400 -"millequattrocento" in Italian).

The Barbizon school (1830-1870) - was a group of landscape and outdoor artists named after the village of Barbizon, France. They expressed realism in art and preceded Impressionism.

Ars Longa Vita Brevis is a Latin translation of an aphorism by Ancient Greek physician Hippocrates: Art is long, Life is short.

5. PAGANINI, OR THE MYSTERY OF THE BOW was written March 12, 2005, Hightstown, NJ.

Niccolò Paganini (1782-1840) was a celebrated Italian violin virtuoso, violist, guitarist, and composer.

Bartolomeo Giuseppe Guarneri (del Gesù) (1698-1744) was one of the greatest Italian violinmakers of all time. His grandfather Andrea Guarneri (1626-1698), the first of the Guarneri family of violinmakers, was an apprentice of Nicolò Amati from 1641 to 1646.

Antonio Stradivari (1644-1737) is generally considered the most significant Italian crafter of violins, cellos, guitars and harps. "Stradivarius" was the Latinized form of his surname. In 1658 - 1664 he worked as a pupil in the workshop of Nicolò Amati.

Niccolò Amati (1596-1684) was the most famous luthier of the Amati family. His model "Grand Amati" became the most sought-after violin, and is credited for the basic design of the modern violin.

Maria Anna Elisa Bonaparte Baciocchi, Princesse Française, Duchess of Lucca and Princess of Piombino, Grand Duchess of Tuscany, Comtesse de Compignano (1777-1820) was the fourth surviving child of Napoleon's parents - Carlo Buonaparte and Letizia Ramolino.

Felice Pasquale Bacciocchi (1762-1841) was a noble from poor Corsican family. He served as an officer in the French army and married Elisa Maria Bonaparte in 1797. They had 3 surviving children.

Charles Philippe Lafont (1781-1839) was a French violinist and composer of the classical technique. During the French Revolution he fled to Russia and he was chamber violinist to Czar Alexander I. In 1815 he returned to France to become the first violinist of Louis XVIII. He had a contest with Paganini in La Scala in 1816.

Arlecchino, Colombina, Scaramouche, Pantalone are the characters of Italian Commedia dell'Arte, improvisational theater popular since 15th century.

Louis Hector Berlioz (1803-1869) was a French composer known for his Romantic symphonies and operas, and conducting his own works.

6. THE DOUBLE was written January 29, 2005, Hightstown, NJ, USA.

7. LET'S DIE, OLD FRIEND was written January 22, 2005, Princeton, NJ, USA.

Adalary - twin-cliffs near Gurzuf (Crimea, Ukraine) in the Black Sea.

Karelia - an area in Northern Europe, which is currently divided between Russia and Finland.

"We all come in here living, but no one gets out alive..." - from a poem of Alexei Aitouganov.

8. LITTLE VIOLIN was written December 16, 2004, East Windsor, NJ, USA.

Steppe – a dry grassy plain in the south-east of Europe, Russia and in Asia.

9. MONK ANDREY was written January 5, 2005, East Windsor, NJ, USA.

Andrey Rublev (1360s-1427 or 1430) was the greatest painter of the Russian Orthodox icons and frescoes.

Theophanes the Greek (1340-1410) was one of the greatest icon painters. Born in Constantinople (capital of the Byzantine Empire), he moved in 1370 to Russia and was a teacher of Andrey Rublev.

Daniel the Black (Russian: Daniil Chyorny (1360-1430) was a Russian iconographer, worked with Andrey Rublev on several projects.

Tokhtamysh (d. 1405), Khan of White, Blue and Golden Hordes, was a descendant of Genghis Khan.

Alexei Popovich i.e Alexei the Priest's Son, was a popular character of Russian fairy tales and legends.

Bast shoes (bast sandals) were the main type of common peoples' footwear in Russia. Bast shoes were woven from the bast stripes of linden or birch trees. They were fastened to the legs with a bast lace in the manner of the Greek sandals.

Onoocha - a cloth to wrap feet in bast shoes.

10. THE NYMPH OF THE SOURCE was written April 3, 2005, Hightstown, NJ, USA.

Marcus Vitruvius Pollio (80-70 BC - 15 BC) was a Roman architect, engineer and writer.

Triclinium was a formal dining room.

Thermae - bathhouse.

Apodyterium was the entry in the baths, a changing room.

Tepidarium was the warm room heated by under floor heating system.

Caldarium - various hot bathrooms.

Frigidarium - cold bath room.

The Pyrrhic War (280-275 BC) was a series of battles between Rome and the states of ancient Greece.

The Punic Wars (264-146 BC) - three wars between the expanding Roman Republic and the Carthaginian Empire. Latin word Punicus meaning "Carthaginian" referred to the Carthaginians' Phoenician ancestry.

Quintus Horatius Flaccus (65-8 BC) was the leading Roman lyric poet during the reign of Augustus. In the English-speaking world he is better known as Horace.

Halicarnassus - was an ancient Greek city on the southwest coast of Caria, Asia Minor. It was the site of the battle between Alexander the Great and the Persian Empire. The ruins of the famous Mausoleum are tourist attraction till present days.

11. DJAVAD was written March 27, 2005, Hightstown, NJ.

Djavad - (Arab) generous.

Absheron Peninsula - is a region in Azerbaijan; it extends 37 miles into the Caspian Sea and reaches a width of 19 miles.

Bey - (Turkish) is a title for "chieftain," the equivalent of duke in Europe.

Friedrich Wilhelm Nietzsche (1844-1900) was a German philosopher and classical philologist. "Thus Spoke Zarathustra" - is a philosophical novel deals with ideas of the "eternal recurrence of the same," the "death of God," and the Overman.

Zarathushtra or Zoroaster (11th/10th century BC) was an ancient Iranian prophet and religious poet.

Mani (210-276 AD) was the founder of Manichaeism, an ancient gnostic religion.

Baku is the capital of Azerbaijan, is one of the oldest and biggest cities in East.

Devas - anthropomorphic or zoomorphic monsters in the folklore of Caucasus.

12. DARK EYES was written July 5, 2005, Hallandale Beach, FL, USA.

Tabor was a convoy or a camp formed by horse-drawn wagons.

13. BUTTERFLY was written January 12, 2005, East Windsor, NJ,

USA.

14. TALISMAN was written February 16-17, 2006, East Windsor, NJ, USA.

The Russian Civil War (1917–1923) was a war within the former Russian Empire after the Bolshevik Revolution of 1917. The principal struggle was between the Bolshevik Red Army and the anti-Bolshevik White Army. Many foreign volunteers, nationalist, various political groups and warlords also participated in the war on both sides. Bolsheviks won the war, during which about 20 million people had lost their lives.

Yesaul - a Cossack equivalent to Major in Russian and foreign armies.

Tsaritsyn (1589–1925) is a city on the western bank of the Volga River in Russia; now it is called Volgograd and Stalingrad before that (1925–1961).

Green Armies were groups of armed peasants who fought to protect themselves from requisitions or reprisals by Red or White armies.

Symon Petliura (1879-1926) was a Ukrainian journalist, politician and statesman, Head of the Ukrainian State (1918 – 1920); was assassinated in Paris (1926).

Nestor Makhno (1888-1934) - Ukrainian guerrilla leader with an independent Anarchist Black Army during the Russian Civil War (1917-1920), who tried to organize the Free Territory of Ukraine. He was also an inventor of tachanka - a horse-drawn carriage with a heavy machine gun installed on it.

Red corner is a traditional place for the icons in the Christian Orthodox homes usually across the entrance door.

Semyon Nadson (1862–1887) - Russian poet. With only one

book of poems published (he died of tuberculosis). Nadson achieved a significant success.

Valery Bryusov (1873-1924) - Russian Symbolist poet, writer, critic, translator, and historian.

Vyacheslav Ivanov (1866-1949) - Russian poet and playwright, philosopher, translator, and literary critic, one of the principle members of Russian Symbolism movement.

Alexander Blok (1880-1921) - celebrated Russian lyrical poet.

Andrei Bely (real name Boris Bugaev (1880-1934) - Russian Symbolist poet, philosopher, writer and literary critic.

Igor Severyanin (real name Igor Lotaryov (1887-1941) - Russian poet, a leader of a group of Ego-Futurists.

Sarafan - a traditional Russian long, shapeless dress with shoulder straps worn by women and girls.

Kiev - capital of Ukraine, located on the Dnieper River; it is one of the oldest (founded in the 5th c. BC) and largest cities in Eastern Europe.

Konstantin Mamontov (1869–1920) – one of the most successful and popular White Cossack commanders during the Civil War in Russia.

Tambov - city in Russia about 300 miles southeast of Moscow.

Zaporozhian Sich - the fortified military and administrative center of the Zaporozhian Cossacks, from the 16th century to the 18th century. It was located on Khortytsia Island in the middle of the Dnieper River (now Ukraine). The term has also been used as a synonym for the whole Zaporizhian Cossack Host.

Semyon Budyonniy (1883-1973) - a Soviet military commander and Field Marshal. Budyonniy was a war hero during

WWI; after the revolution in 1918, he organized a Red Cavalry in his native Don region. His First Cavalry Army helped to win the Civil War for the Bolsheviks. Budyonny was a devoted ally to Joseph Stalin.

Voronezh - an important industrial city in southwestern Russia.

Baron Peter von Wrangel (1878-1928) was a commander of the White Army in Southern Russia to the end of the Russian Civil War.

Pioneer – mass Soviet youth organization for children 10-15 years old.

Vorkuta - a coal-mining town north of the Arctic Circle. It was the centre of Stalinists Gulag labor camps in European Russia.

Anadyr - town in Chukotka, the extreme north-eastern part of Russia.

15. SCYTHIAN was written April 8, 2005, Hightstown, NJ.

Hippeus was the social class who owned horses, like the Medieval knights.

Borysthenes - Dnieper River.

The Tauric Chersonese - Crimea.

Istros – Danube River.

Tanais – Don River.

Pontos Euxeinos – Black Sea.

River Hypanis – Southern Bug River.

Hellenes - natives to Greece, Cyprus, neighboring regions and diaspora communities.

Miletus was an ancient Greek city on the western coast of Anatolia (is now Turkey).

Oecumene – for ancient Greeks and Romans, it was the

known part of the earth.

Pantikápaion - an important Greek city and port in Tauric Chersonese, founded by Milesians in the 7th century BC; today's Kerch.

The Delia were festivities and games celebrated for the worship of Apollo, who was believed to have been born on the Island of Delos.

The Peloponnese is a large peninsula region in southern Greece.

16. ROXEL AND THE PRINCESS-FROG was written July 3, 2005, Hallandale Beach, FL , USA.

17. THE OLD MAN AND THE GIRL was written February 2, 2005, East Windsor, NJ, USA.

18. TANGO was written September 23 – October 4, 2005, East Windsor, NJ, USA.

Nikolai Gorbunov (1892-1938) was a secretary of the Council of People's Commissars of the USSR, CEO of the Russian Academy of Sciences. He was sentenced to death and executed in 1938.

The German Democratic Republic (East Germany) was a socialist state that originated from the Soviet Zone of occupied Germany. GDR existed from 1949 until 1990.

19. POSEIDON AND THE GLASSES was written July 4-5, Hallandale Beach, FL, USA.

Larimar is a rare blue variety of pectolite mineral found only in the Dominican Republic, in the Caribbean; used for jewelry.

Salignac is a brand of cognac.

20. SAX SOLO was written September 19, 2005, East Windsor, NJ, USA.

21. THORN-APPLE FLOWER was written September 1, 2005, East Windsor, NJ, USA.

22. ALEXANDRIAN IMPERIAL was written September 27, 2005 – December 31, 2006, New York (NY) – Princeton (NJ), USA.

Flèche – a small fortification built from earthworks whose faces make an angle towards enemy.

The Battle of Montmartre was fought on March 30, 1814, between Coalition forces of Austria, Prussia and Russia and the troops of Napoleon. The Coalition won the battle, entered Paris, and Napoleon was forced to abdicate.

Young Guard - elite soldiers of Napoleon Army, his bodyguards and tactical reserve. Based on the experience the Guard was divided into the Old Guard, Middle Guard and Young Guard.

23. THE WOMAN AND DEATH was written February 16, 2005, Hightstown, NJ, USA.

24. GURZUF, POSTE RESTANTE was written October 5-9, 2005, East Windsor, NJ, USA.

Crimea is a peninsula located on the northern coast of the Black Sea.

Gurzuf is a former Crimean Tatar village, now is a fashionable resort.

Alushta is a resort town in Crimea, founded in the 6th

century AD.

Mount Ayu-Dag (Bear Mountain) is a peak on the southern coast of Crimea. It is Nature reserve now.

Sympheropol is the capital of Autonomous Republic of Crimea, located in the center of the Crimean peninsula.

Komsomol (est. 1918) - The Communist Union of Youth (an abbreviation from the Russian Kommunisticheskiy Soyuz Molodyozhi), was the youth wing of the Communist Party of the Soviet Union. The age of its members was from 14 to 28, while Komsomol functionaries could be older.

GAZ-24 - The Volga GAZ-24 is a car manufactured by the Gorkovsky Avtomobilny Zavod (Gorky Automobile Plant) for the Communist party, Soviet government, ambulance and taxi.

Korova – (Russian) cow.

Kerch is a city on the Kerch Peninsula of eastern Crimea.

Sevastopol is a port city in the Crimea peninsula. The former home of the Soviet Black Sea Fleet, is now a naval base mutually used by the Ukrainian Navy and Russian Navy.

Astrakhan is a city in southern European Russia on the Volga River.

Oryol is a city in Russia, located on the Oka River, approximately 225 miles south-south-west of Moscow.

Nikitsky Botanical Garden was founded in 1812 and was named after the settlement Nikita by the shore of the Black Sea.

Zmey Gorynych - a Slavonic dragon has three heads and spits fire.

Artek was an international Young Pioneer Camp (est. 1925) near town of Gurzuf. There were 150 buildings, a school, film studio, swimming pools, sports stadium (over 7,000 seats), playgrounds etc. Artek was a year-round camp, it was considered to be an honorable award for Soviet children as well as children from seventy foreign countries.

Old-woman Izergil is a popular character from a short story of Maxim Gorky, a Russian/Soviet author, a founder of the method of socialist realism in literature.